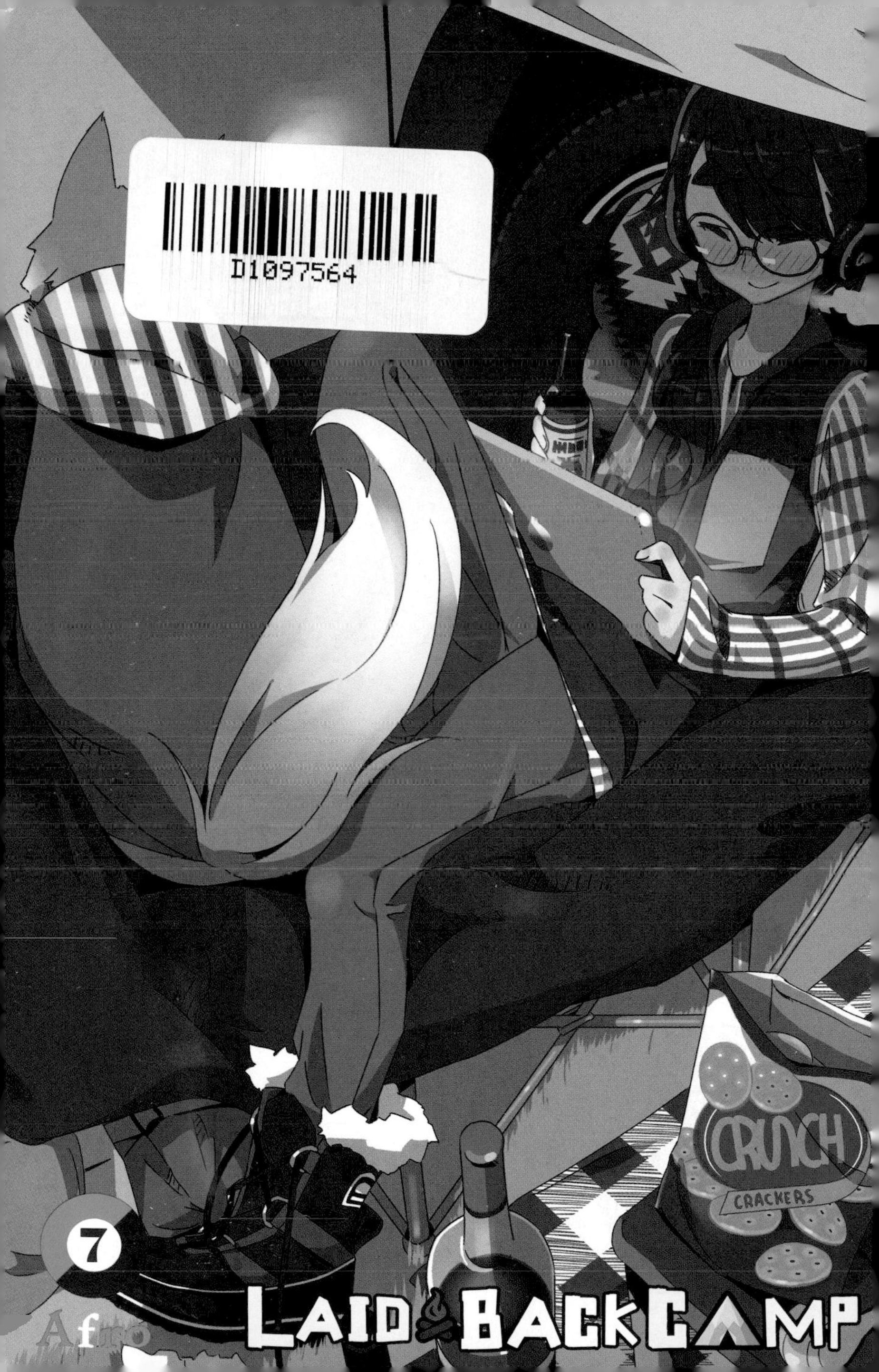
CRUNCH
CRACKERS

7

LAID BACK CAMP

Afro

7

LAID-BACK CAMP

contents

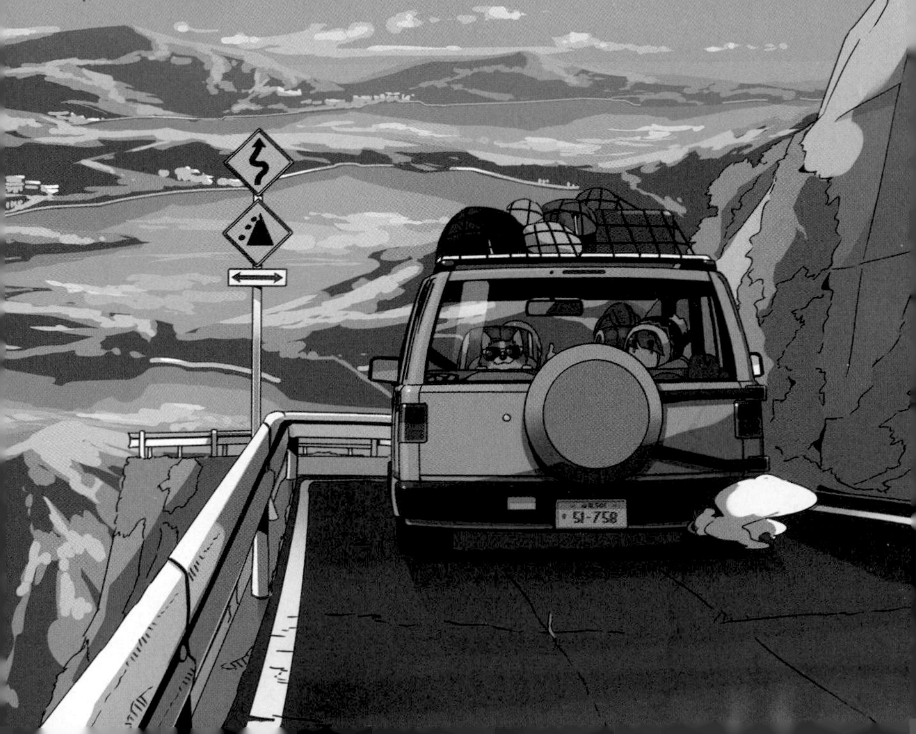

51-758

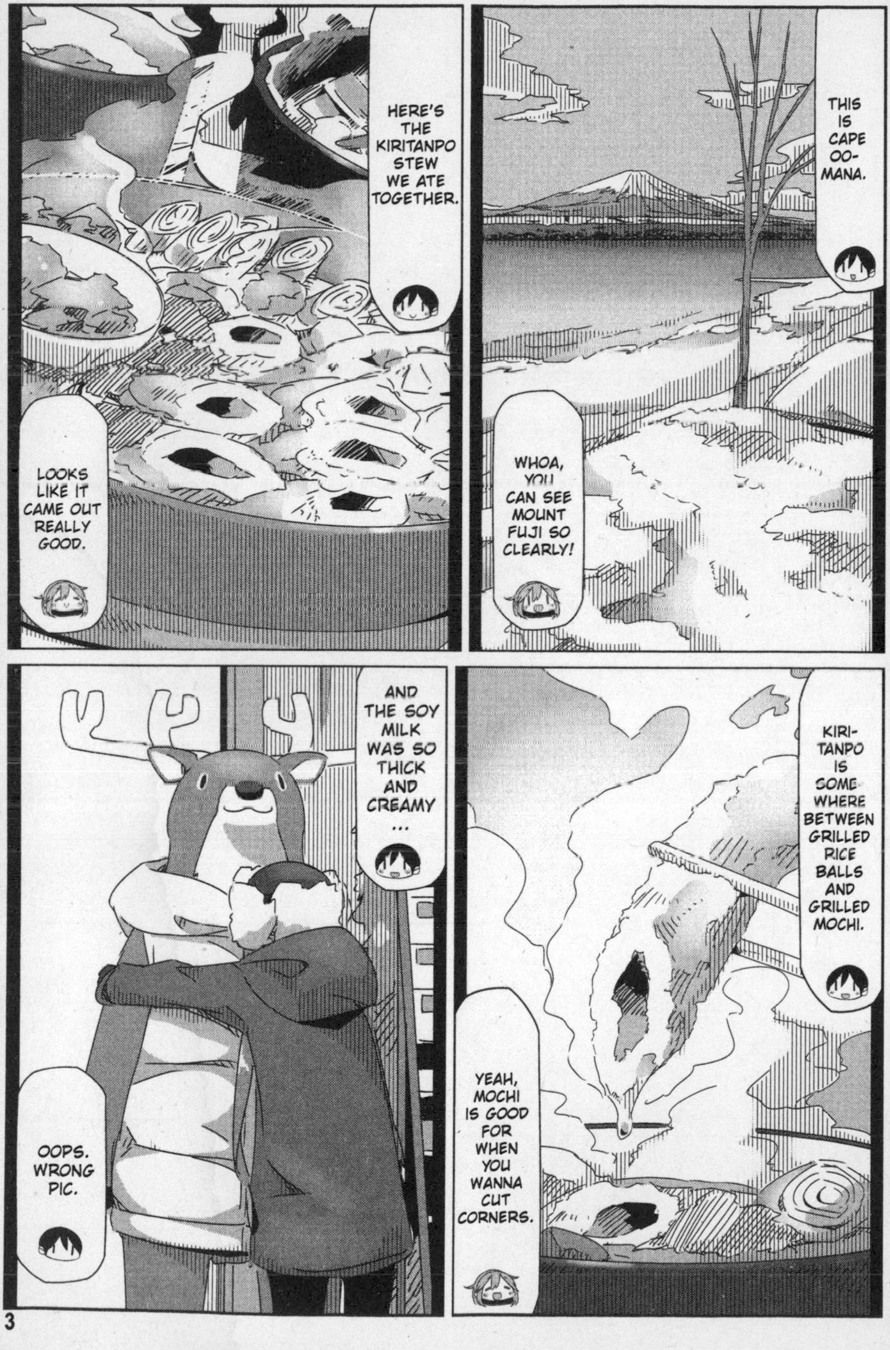
THIS IS CAPE OO-MANA.
WHOA, YOU CAN SEE MOUNT FUJI SO CLEARLY!
HERE'S THE KIRITANPO STEW WE ATE TOGETHER.
LOOKS LIKE IT CAME OUT REALLY GOOD.
KIRI-TANPO IS SOMEWHERE BETWEEN GRILLED RICE BALLS AND GRILLED MOCHI.
YEAH, MOCHI IS GOOD FOR WHEN YOU WANNA CUT CORNERS.
AND THE SOY MILK WAS SO THICK AND CREAMY...
OOPS. WRONG PIC.

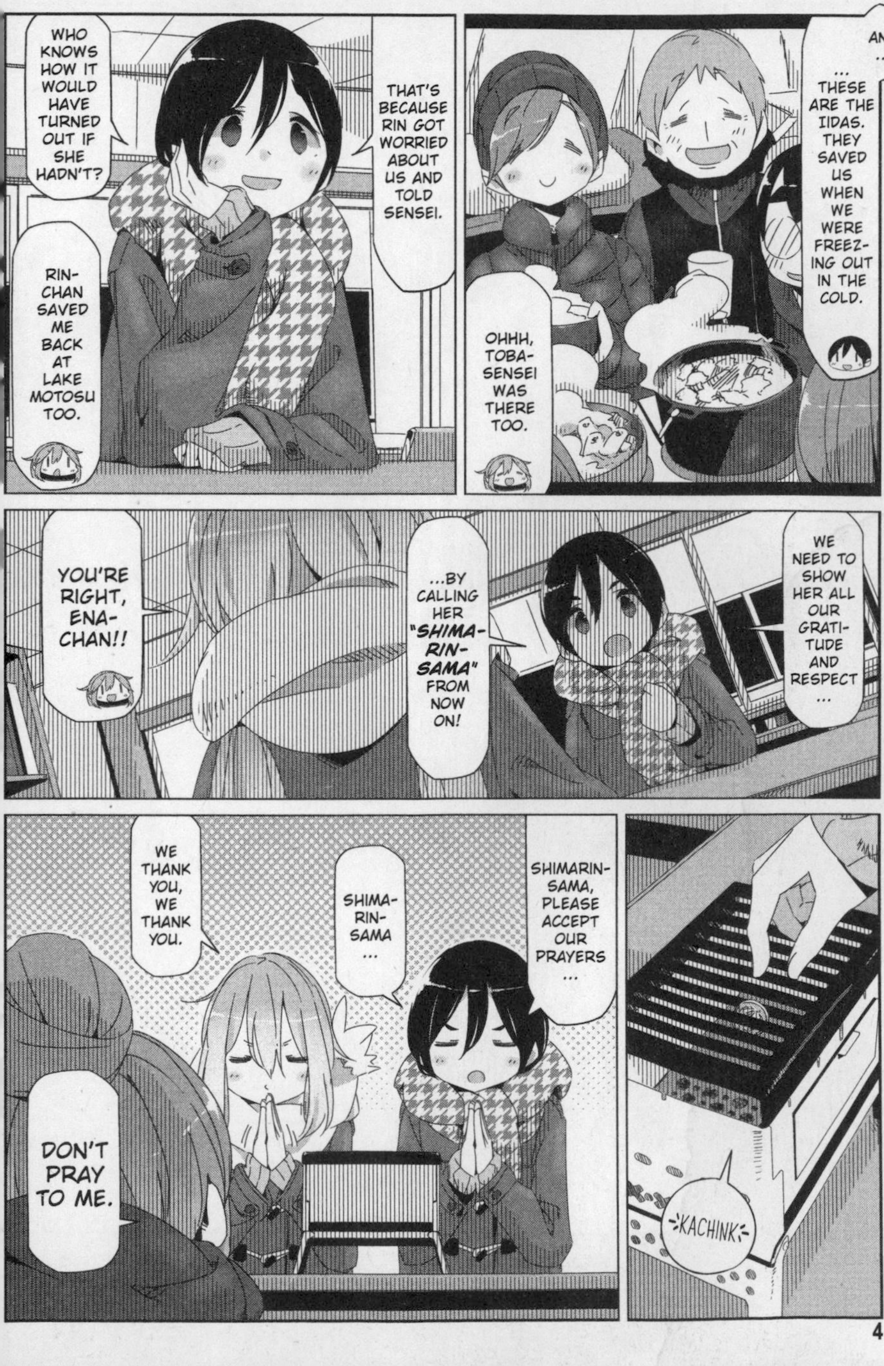
AND ...
... THESE ARE THE IIDAS. THEY SAVED US WHEN WE WERE FREEZING OUT IN THE COLD.
OHHH, TOBA-SENSEI WAS THERE TOO.
THAT'S BECAUSE RIN GOT WORRIED ABOUT US AND TOLD SENSEI.
WHO KNOWS HOW IT WOULD HAVE TURNED OUT IF SHE HADN'T?
RIN-CHAN SAVED ME BACK AT LAKE MOTOSU TOO.
WE NEED TO SHOW HER ALL OUR GRATITUDE AND RESPECT ...
...BY CALLING HER "SHIMA-RIN-SAMA" FROM NOW ON!
YOU'RE RIGHT, ENA-CHAN!!
KACHINK
SHIMARIN-SAMA, PLEASE ACCEPT OUR PRAYERS ...
SHIMA-RIN-SAMA ...
WE THANK YOU, WE THANK YOU.
DON'T PRAY TO ME.

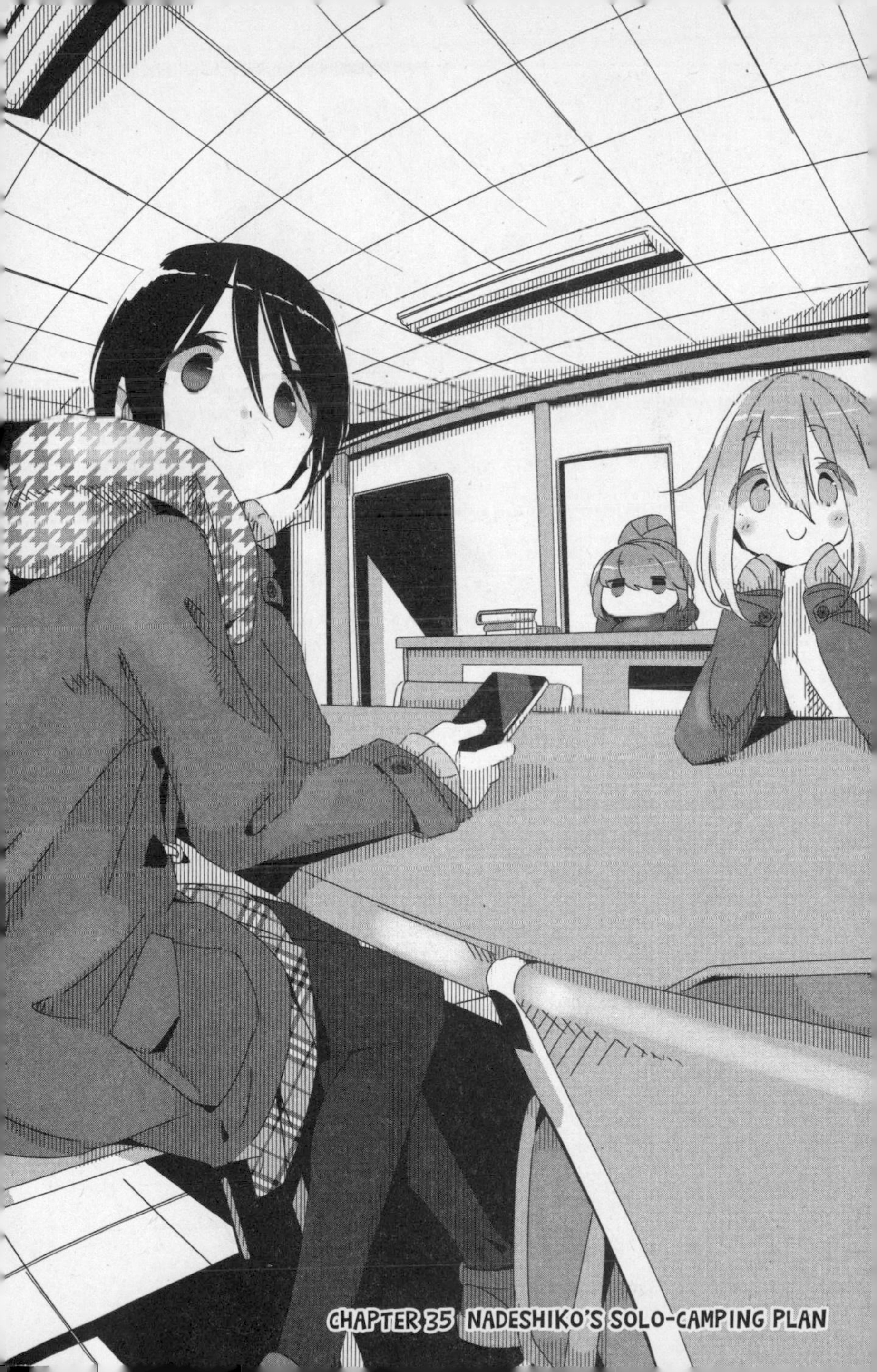

CHAPTER 35 NADESHIKO'S SOLO-CAMPING PLAN

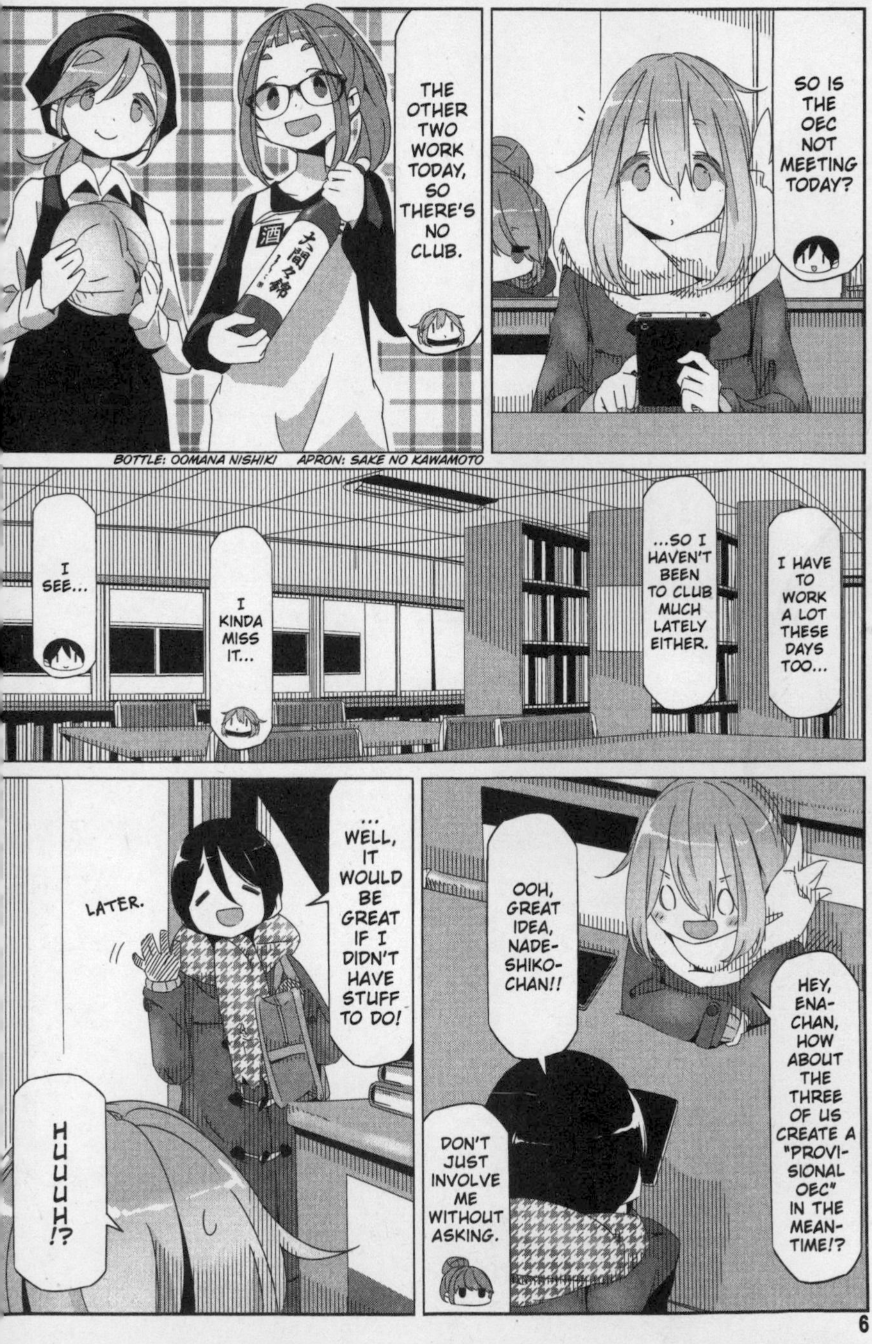
SO IS THE OEC NOT MEETING TODAY?
THE OTHER TWO WORK TODAY, SO THERE'S NO CLUB.
I HAVE TO WORK A LOT THESE DAYS TOO...
...SO I HAVEN'T BEEN TO CLUB MUCH LATELY EITHER.
I KINDA MISS IT...
I SEE...
HEY, ENA-CHAN, HOW ABOUT THE THREE OF US CREATE A "PROVISIONAL OEC" IN THE MEANTIME!?
OOH, GREAT IDEA, NADESHIKO-CHAN!!
DON'T JUST INVOLVE ME WITHOUT ASKING.
...WELL, IT WOULD BE GREAT IF I DIDN'T HAVE STUFF TO DO!
LATER.
HUUUH!?
BOTTLE: OOMANA NISHIKI APRON: SAKE NO KAWAMOTO

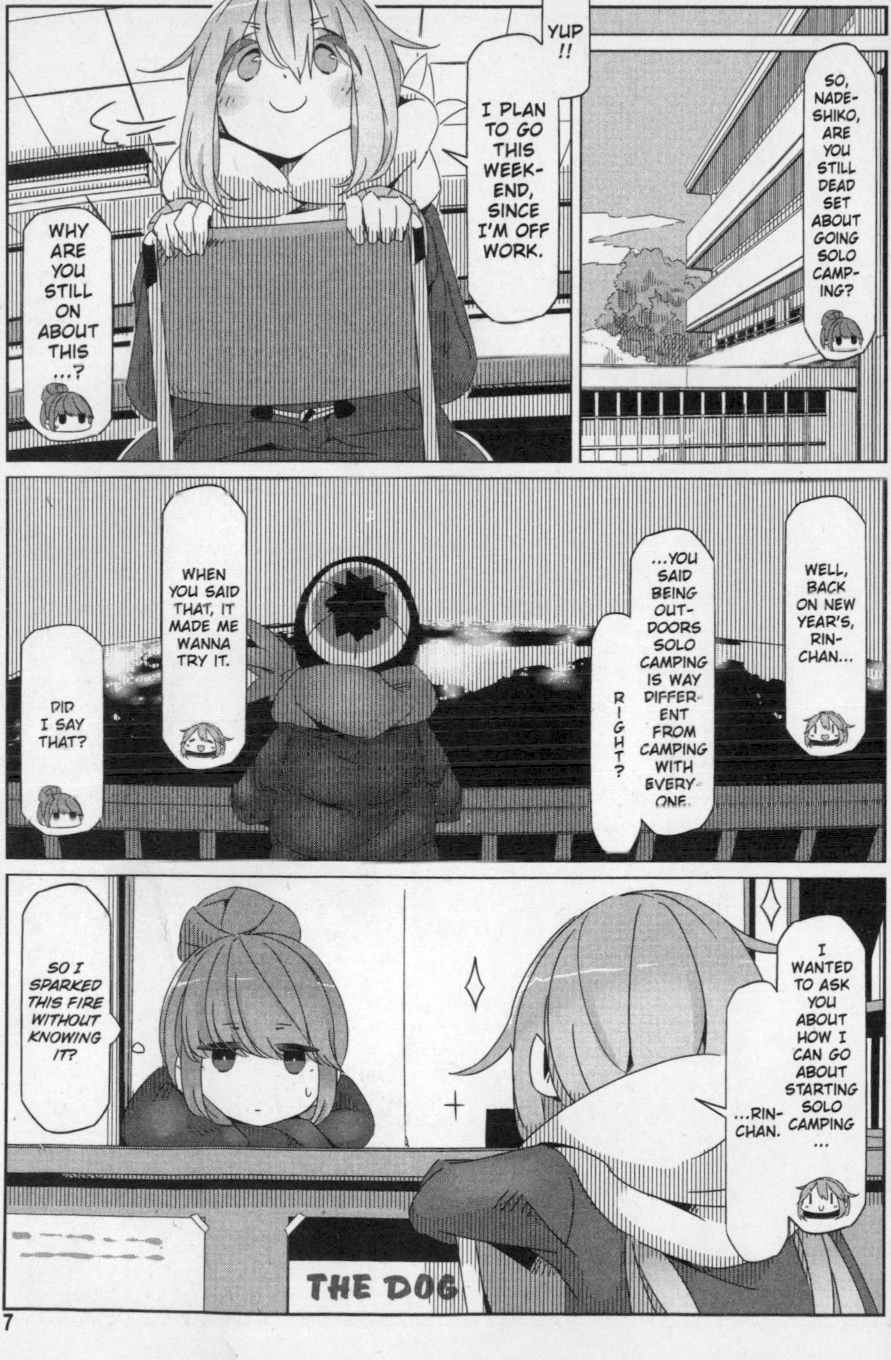
SO, NADE-SHIKO, ARE YOU STILL DEAD SET ABOUT GOING SOLO CAMPING?
YUP!!
I PLAN TO GO THIS WEEK-END, SINCE I'M OFF WORK.
WHY ARE YOU STILL ON ABOUT THIS...?
WELL, BACK ON NEW YEAR'S, RIN-CHAN...
...YOU SAID BEING OUT-DOORS SOLO CAMPING IS WAY DIFFERENT FROM CAMPING WITH EVERY-ONE,
RIGHT?
WHEN YOU SAID THAT, IT MADE ME WANNA TRY IT.
DID I SAY THAT?
I WANTED TO ASK YOU ABOUT HOW I CAN GO ABOUT STARTING SOLO CAMPING...
...RIN-CHAN.
SO I SPARKED THIS FIRE WITHOUT KNOWING IT?
THE DOG

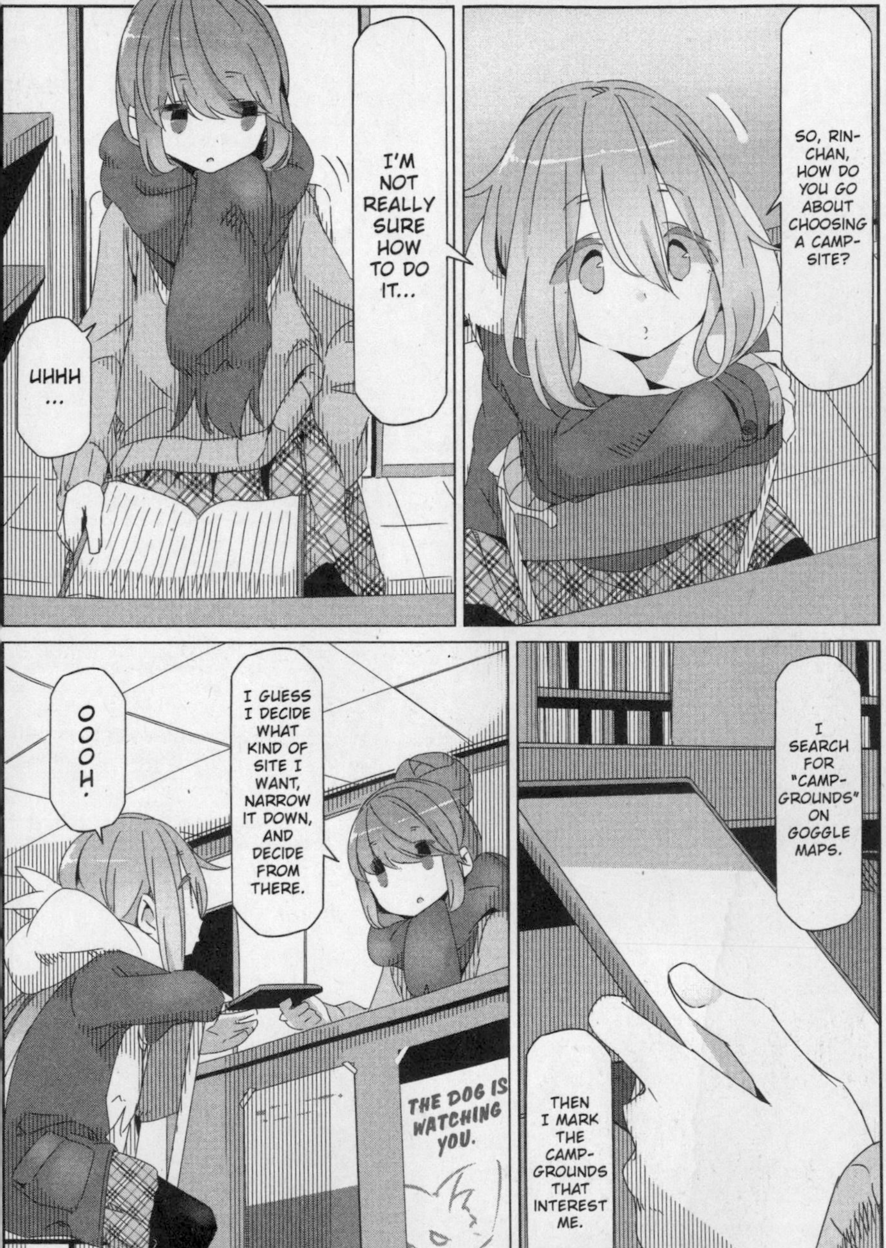
SO, RIN-CHAN, HOW DO YOU GO ABOUT CHOOSING A CAMPSITE?
I'M NOT REALLY SURE HOW TO DO IT...
UHHH...
I SEARCH FOR "CAMPGROUNDS" ON GOGGLE MAPS.
THEN I MARK THE CAMPGROUNDS THAT INTEREST ME.
I GUESS I DECIDE WHAT KIND OF SITE I WANT, NARROW IT DOWN, AND DECIDE FROM THERE.
OOOH.
THE DOG IS WATCHING YOU.

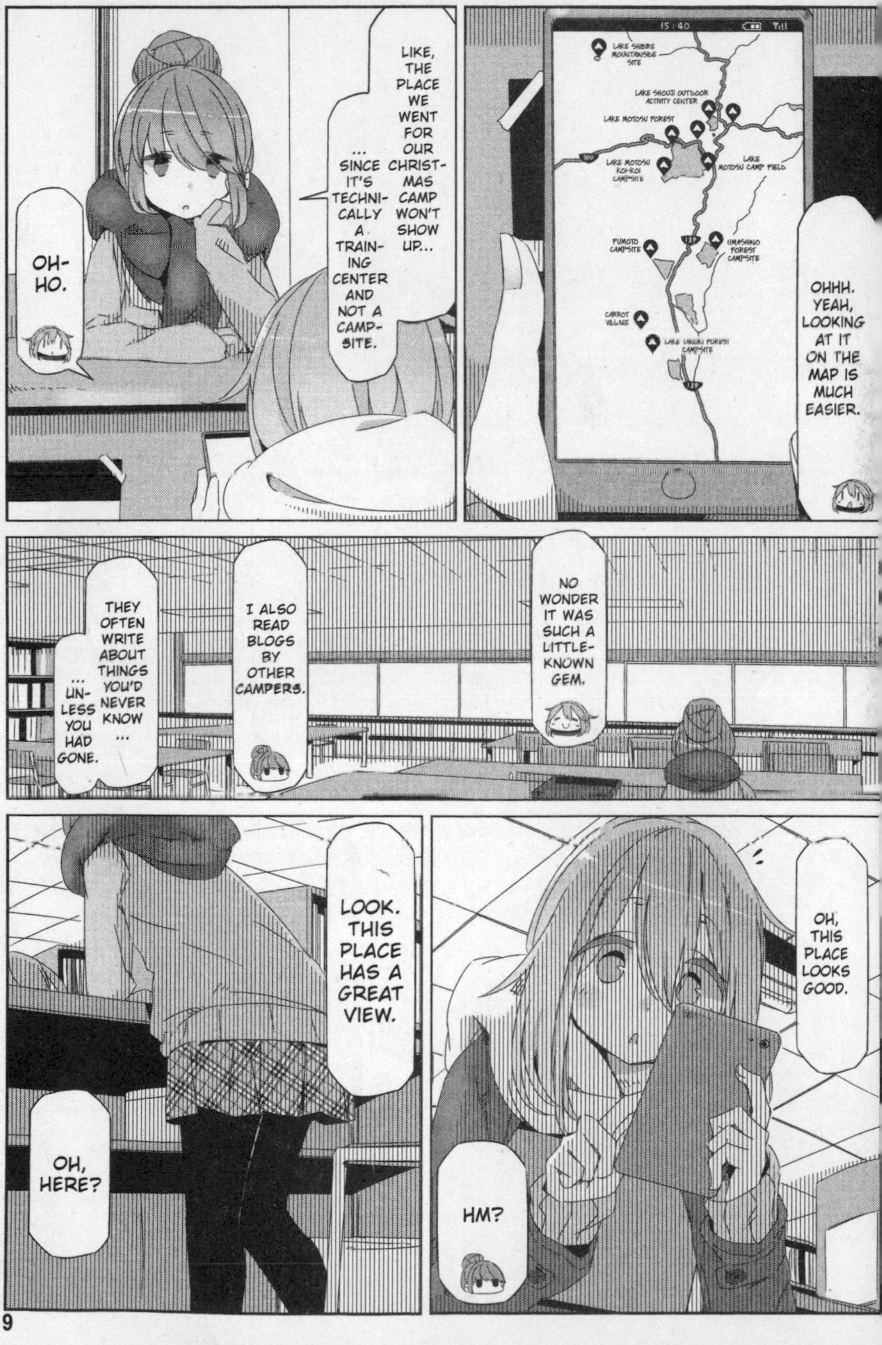
15:40
LAKE SHIBIRE MOUNTAINSIDE SITE
LAKE SHOUJI OUTDOOR ACTIVITY CENTER
LAKE MOTOSU FOREST
LAKE MOTOSU CAMP FIELD
LAKE MOTOSU KOI-KOI CAMPSITE
300
UMASHINO FOREST CAMPSITE
FUMOTO CAMPSITE
139
CARROT VILLAGE
OHHH. YEAH, LOOKING AT IT ON THE MAP IS MUCH EASIER.
LIKE, THE PLACE WE WENT FOR OUR CHRISTMAS CAMP WON'T SHOW UP...
...SINCE IT'S TECHNICALLY A TRAINING CENTER AND NOT A CAMPSITE.
OH-HO.
NO WONDER IT WAS SUCH A LITTLE-KNOWN GEM.
I ALSO READ BLOGS BY OTHER CAMPERS.
THEY OFTEN WRITE ABOUT THINGS YOU'D NEVER KNOW...
...UNLESS YOU HAD GONE.
OH, THIS PLACE LOOKS GOOD.
HM?
LOOK. THIS PLACE HAS A GREAT VIEW.
OH, HERE?

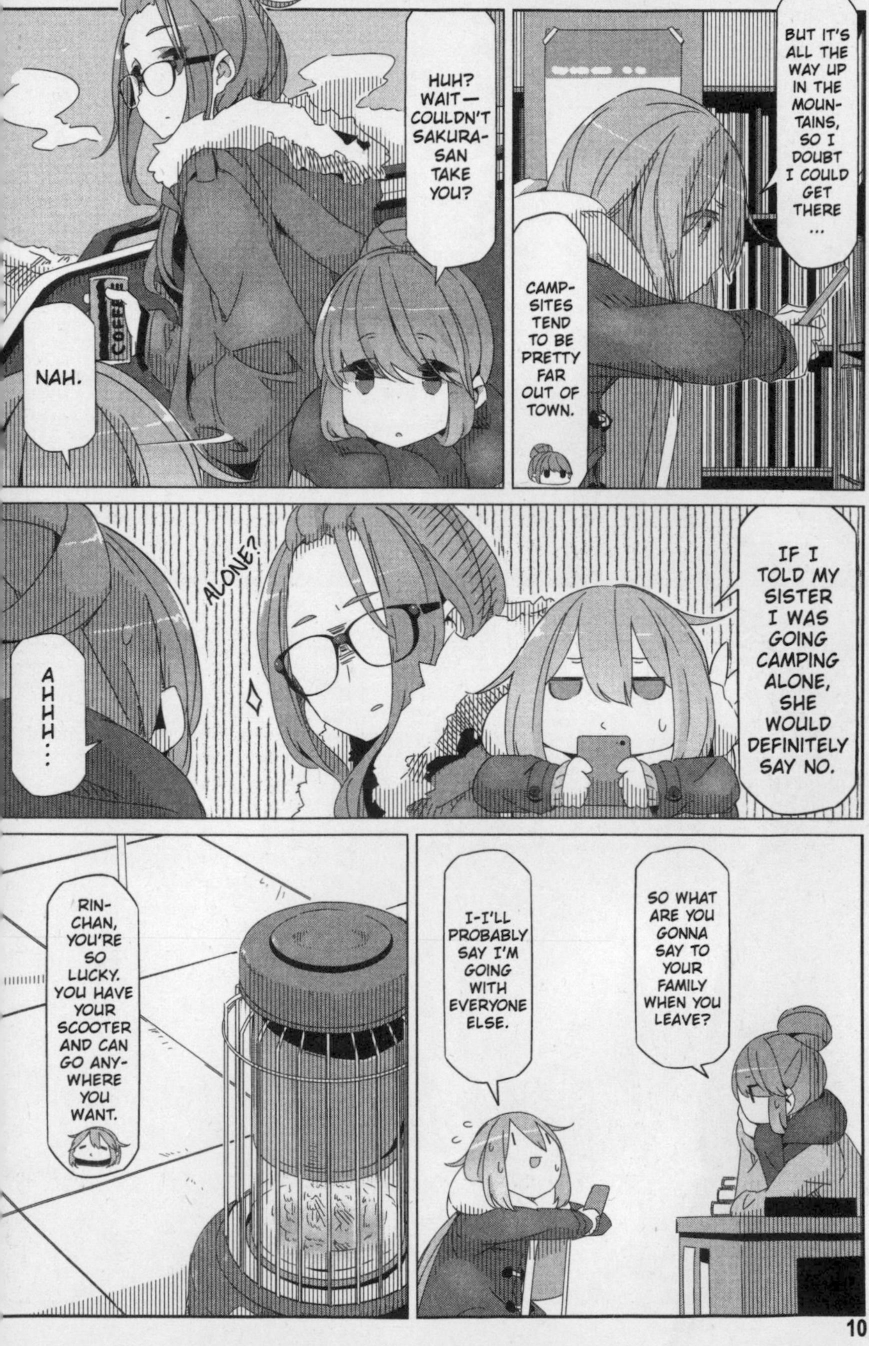
BUT IT'S ALL THE WAY UP IN THE MOUN-TAINS, SO I DOUBT I COULD GET THERE ...
CAMP-SITES TEND TO BE PRETTY FAR OUT OF TOWN.
HUH? WAIT—COULDN'T SAKURA-SAN TAKE YOU?
NAH.
IF I TOLD MY SISTER I WAS GOING CAMPING ALONE, SHE WOULD DEFINITELY SAY NO.
ALONE?
AHHH...
SO WHAT ARE YOU GONNA SAY TO YOUR FAMILY WHEN YOU LEAVE?
I-I'LL PROBABLY SAY I'M GOING WITH EVERYONE ELSE.
RIN-CHAN, YOU'RE SO LUCKY. YOU HAVE YOUR SCOOTER AND CAN GO ANY-WHERE YOU WANT.

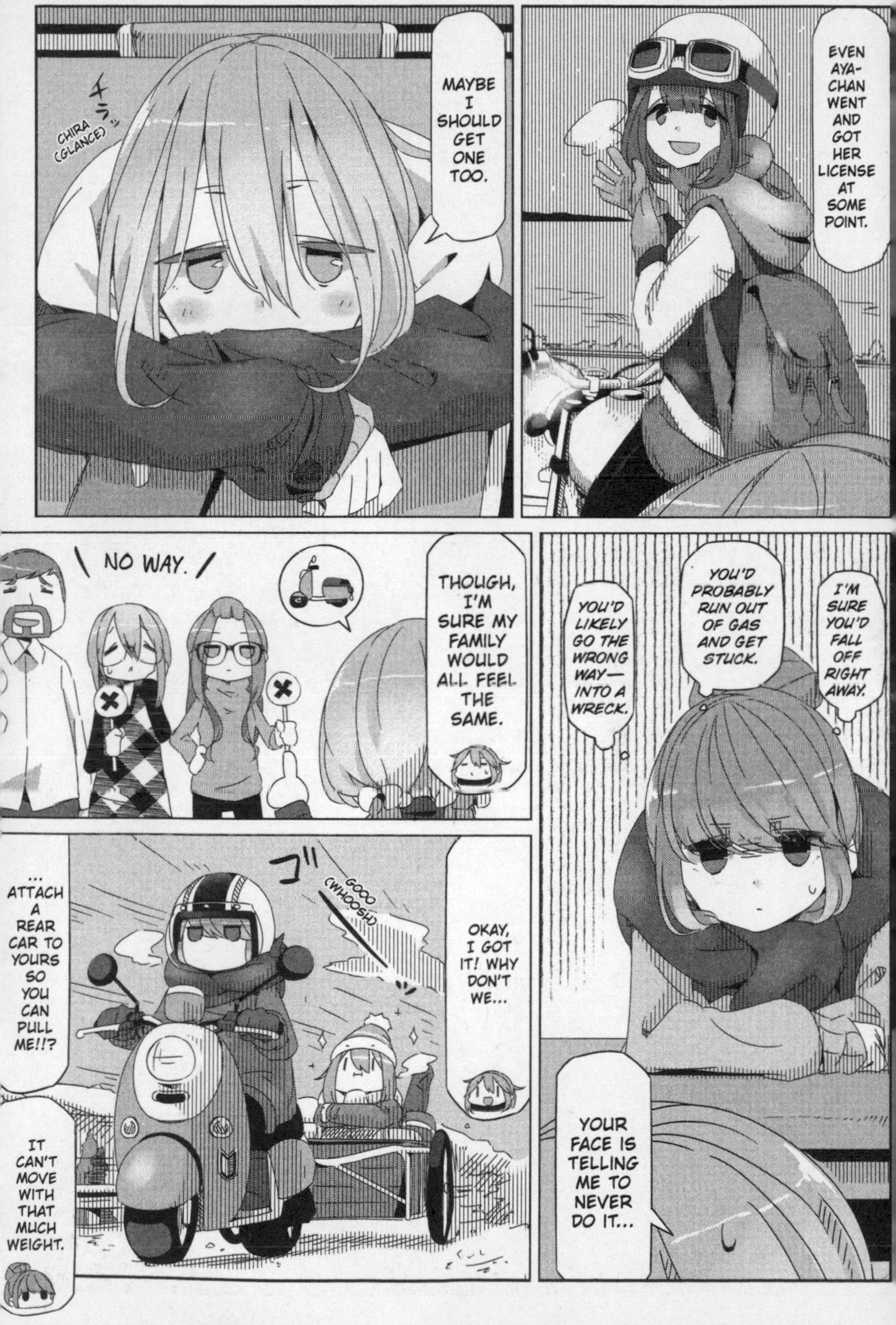
EVEN AYA-CHAN WENT AND GOT HER LICENSE AT SOME POINT.
MAYBE I SHOULD GET ONE TOO.
CHIRA (GLANCE)
I'M SURE YOU'D FALL OFF RIGHT AWAY.
YOU'D PROBABLY RUN OUT OF GAS AND GET STUCK.
YOU'D LIKELY GO THE WRONG WAY—INTO A WRECK.
YOUR FACE IS TELLING ME TO NEVER DO IT...
THOUGH, I'M SURE MY FAMILY WOULD ALL FEEL THE SAME.
NO WAY.
OKAY, I GOT IT! WHY DON'T WE...
GOOO (WHOOSH)
...ATTACH A REAR CAR TO YOURS SO YOU CAN PULL ME!!?
IT CAN'T MOVE WITH THAT MUCH WEIGHT.

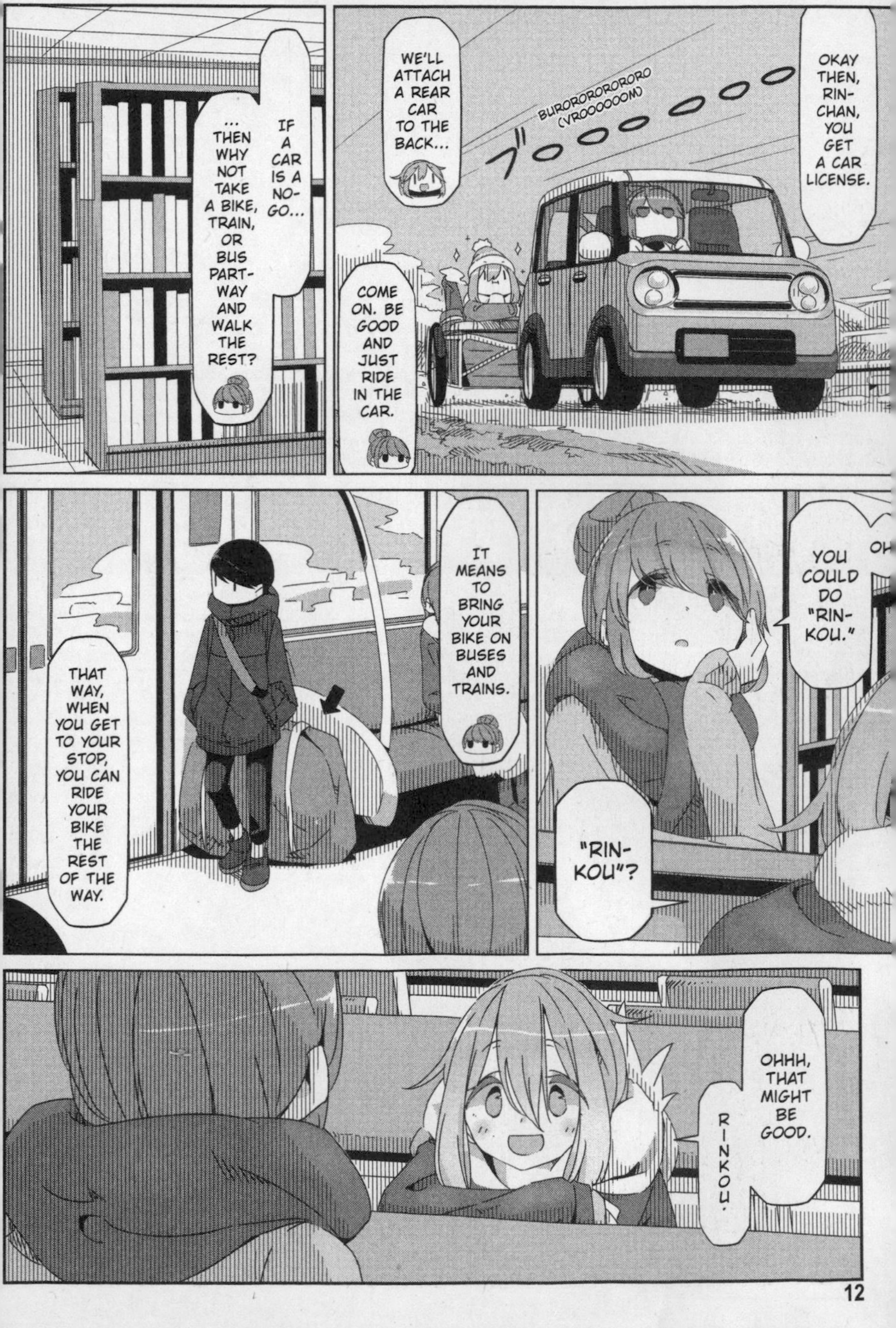
OKAY THEN, RIN-CHAN, YOU GET A CAR LICENSE.
BURORORORORO (VROOOOOOM)
WE'LL ATTACH A REAR CAR TO THE BACK...
COME ON. BE GOOD AND JUST RIDE IN THE CAR.
IF A CAR IS A NO-GO...
...THEN WHY NOT TAKE A BIKE, TRAIN, OR BUS PART-WAY AND WALK THE REST?
OH
YOU COULD DO "RIN-KOU."
"RIN-KOU"?
IT MEANS TO BRING YOUR BIKE ON BUSES AND TRAINS.
THAT WAY, WHEN YOU GET TO YOUR STOP, YOU CAN RIDE YOUR BIKE THE REST OF THE WAY.
OHHH, THAT MIGHT BE GOOD.
RINKOU.

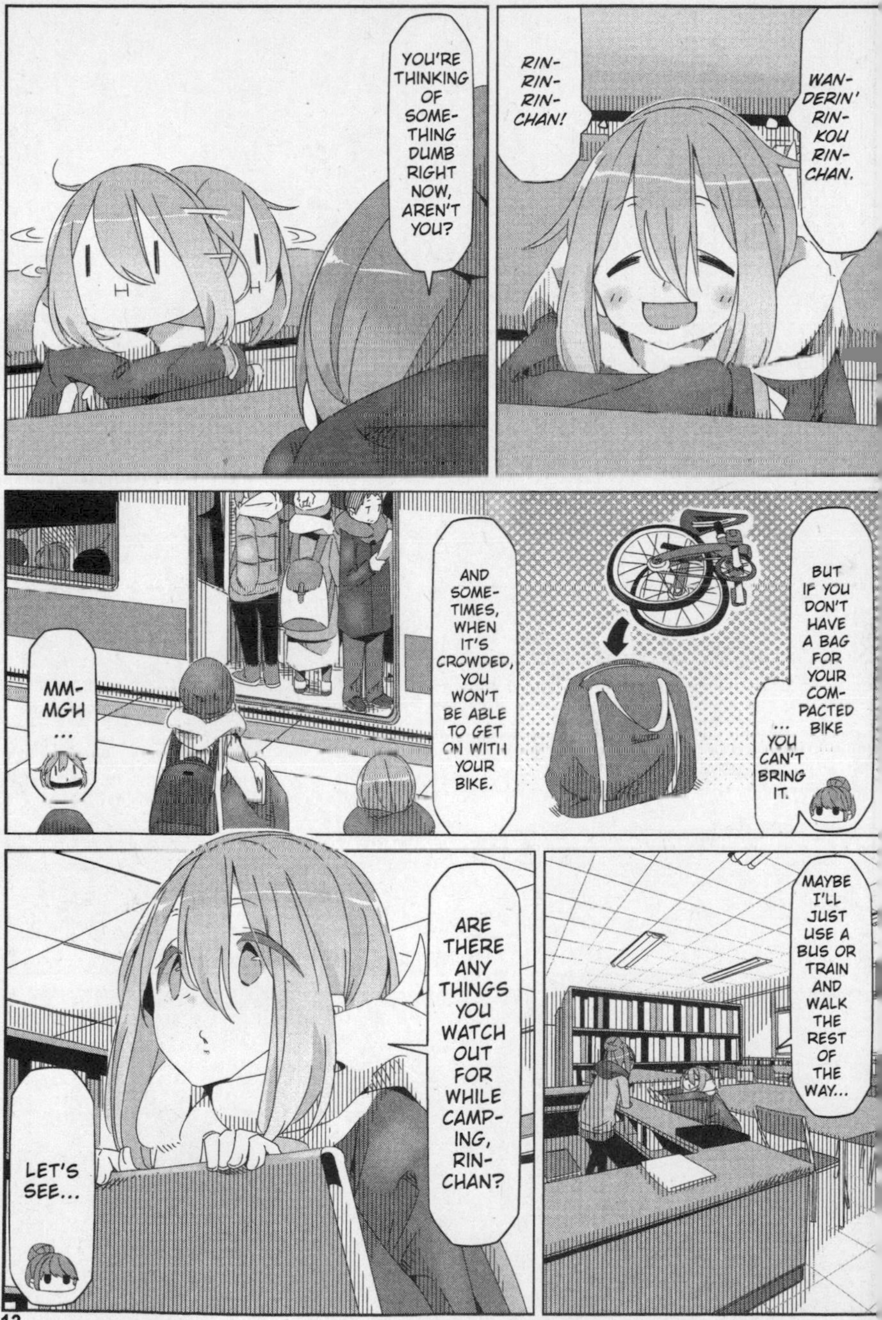
WANDERIN' RINKOU RIN-CHAN.
RIN-RIN-RIN-CHAN!
YOU'RE THINKING OF SOMETHING DUMB RIGHT NOW, AREN'T YOU?
BUT IF YOU DON'T HAVE A BAG FOR YOUR COMPACTED BIKE
...YOU CAN'T BRING IT.
AND SOMETIMES, WHEN IT'S CROWDED, YOU WON'T BE ABLE TO GET ON WITH YOUR BIKE.
MM-MGH...
MAYBE I'LL JUST USE A BUS OR TRAIN AND WALK THE REST OF THE WAY...
ARE THERE ANY THINGS YOU WATCH OUT FOR WHILE CAMPING, RIN-CHAN?
LET'S SEE...

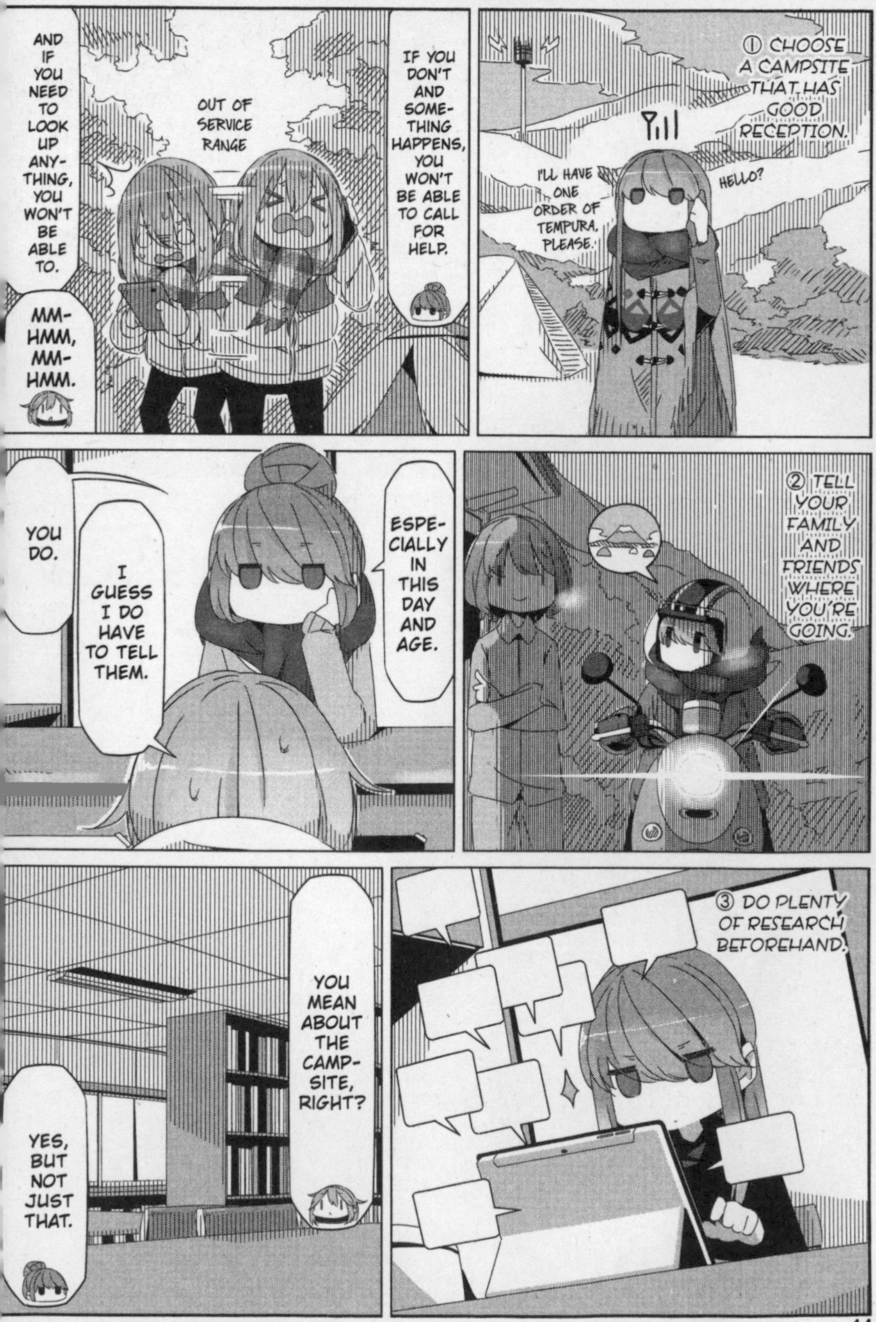
① CHOOSE A CAMPSITE THAT HAS GOOD RECEPTION.
HELLO?
I'LL HAVE ONE ORDER OF TEMPURA, PLEASE.
IF YOU DON'T AND SOMETHING HAPPENS, YOU WON'T BE ABLE TO CALL FOR HELP.
OUT OF SERVICE RANGE
AND IF YOU NEED TO LOOK UP ANYTHING, YOU WON'T BE ABLE TO.
MM-HMM, MM-HMM.
② TELL YOUR FAMILY AND FRIENDS WHERE YOU'RE GOING.
ESPECIALLY IN THIS DAY AND AGE.
I GUESS I DO HAVE TO TELL THEM.
YOU DO.
③ DO PLENTY OF RESEARCH BEFOREHAND.
YOU MEAN ABOUT THE CAMPSITE, RIGHT?
YES, BUT NOT JUST THAT.

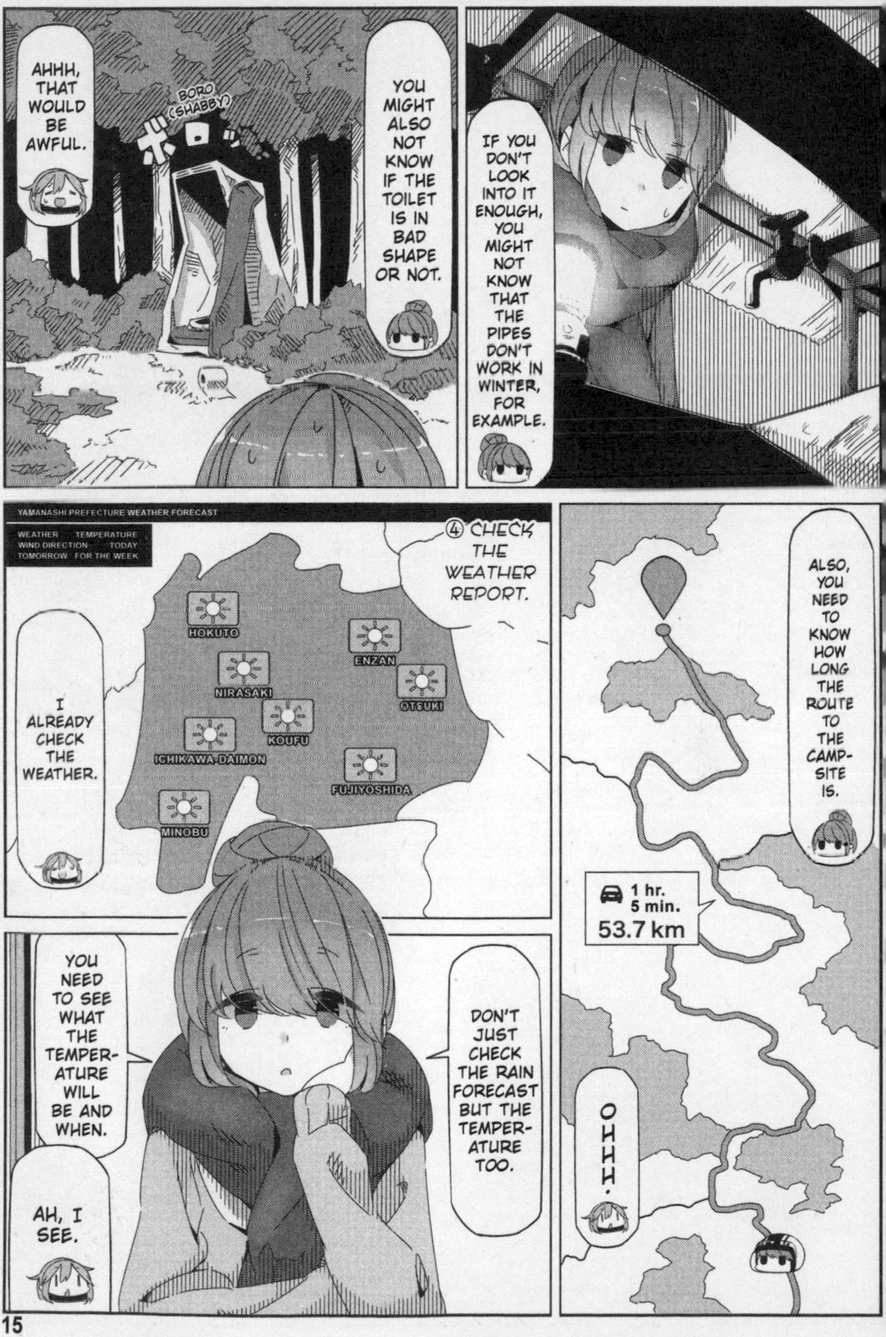
IF YOU DON'T LOOK INTO IT ENOUGH, YOU MIGHT NOT KNOW THAT THE PIPES DON'T WORK IN WINTER, FOR EXAMPLE.
YOU MIGHT ALSO NOT KNOW IF THE TOILET IS IN BAD SHAPE OR NOT.
BORO (SHABBY)
AHHH, THAT WOULD BE AWFUL.
ALSO, YOU NEED TO KNOW HOW LONG THE ROUTE TO THE CAMP-SITE IS.
1 hr. 5 min.
53.7 km
OHHH.
YAMANASHI PREFECTURE WEATHER FORECAST
WEATHER TEMPERATURE
WIND DIRECTION TODAY
TOMORROW FOR THE WEEK
④ CHECK THE WEATHER REPORT.
HOKUTO
ENZAN
NIRASAKI
OTSUKI
KOUFU
ICHIKAWA-DAIMON
FUJIYOSHIDA
MINOBU
I ALREADY CHECK THE WEATHER.
DON'T JUST CHECK THE RAIN FORECAST BUT THE TEMPER-ATURE TOO.
YOU NEED TO SEE WHAT THE TEMPER-ATURE WILL BE AND WHEN.
AH, I SEE.

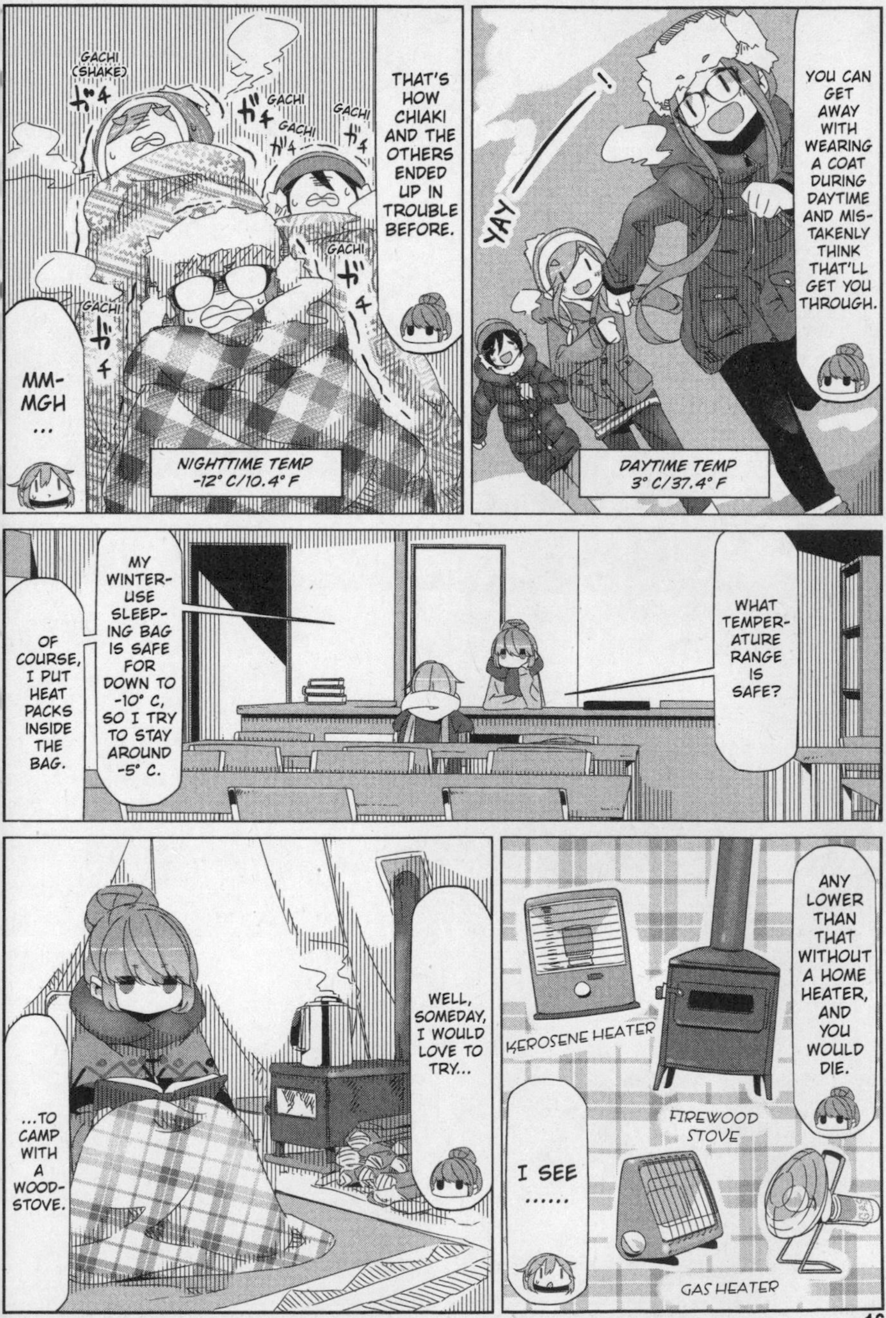

YOU CAN GET AWAY WITH WEARING A COAT DURING DAYTIME AND MISTAKENLY THINK THAT'LL GET YOU THROUGH.
YAY—!
DAYTIME TEMP 3° C/37.4° F
THAT'S HOW CHIAKI AND THE OTHERS ENDED UP IN TROUBLE BEFORE.
GACHI (SHAKE)
GACHI
GACHI
GACHI
GACHI
GACHI
MM-MGH...
NIGHTTIME TEMP -12° C/10.4° F
WHAT TEMPERATURE RANGE IS SAFE?
MY WINTER-USE SLEEPING BAG IS SAFE FOR DOWN TO -10° C, SO I TRY TO STAY AROUND -5° C.
OF COURSE, I PUT HEAT PACKS INSIDE THE BAG.
ANY LOWER THAN THAT WITHOUT A HOME HEATER, AND YOU WOULD DIE.
KEROSENE HEATER
FIREWOOD STOVE
GAS HEATER
I SEE......
WELL, SOMEDAY, I WOULD LOVE TO TRY...
...TO CAMP WITH A WOOD-STOVE.

※ COMFORTABLE TEMPERATURE

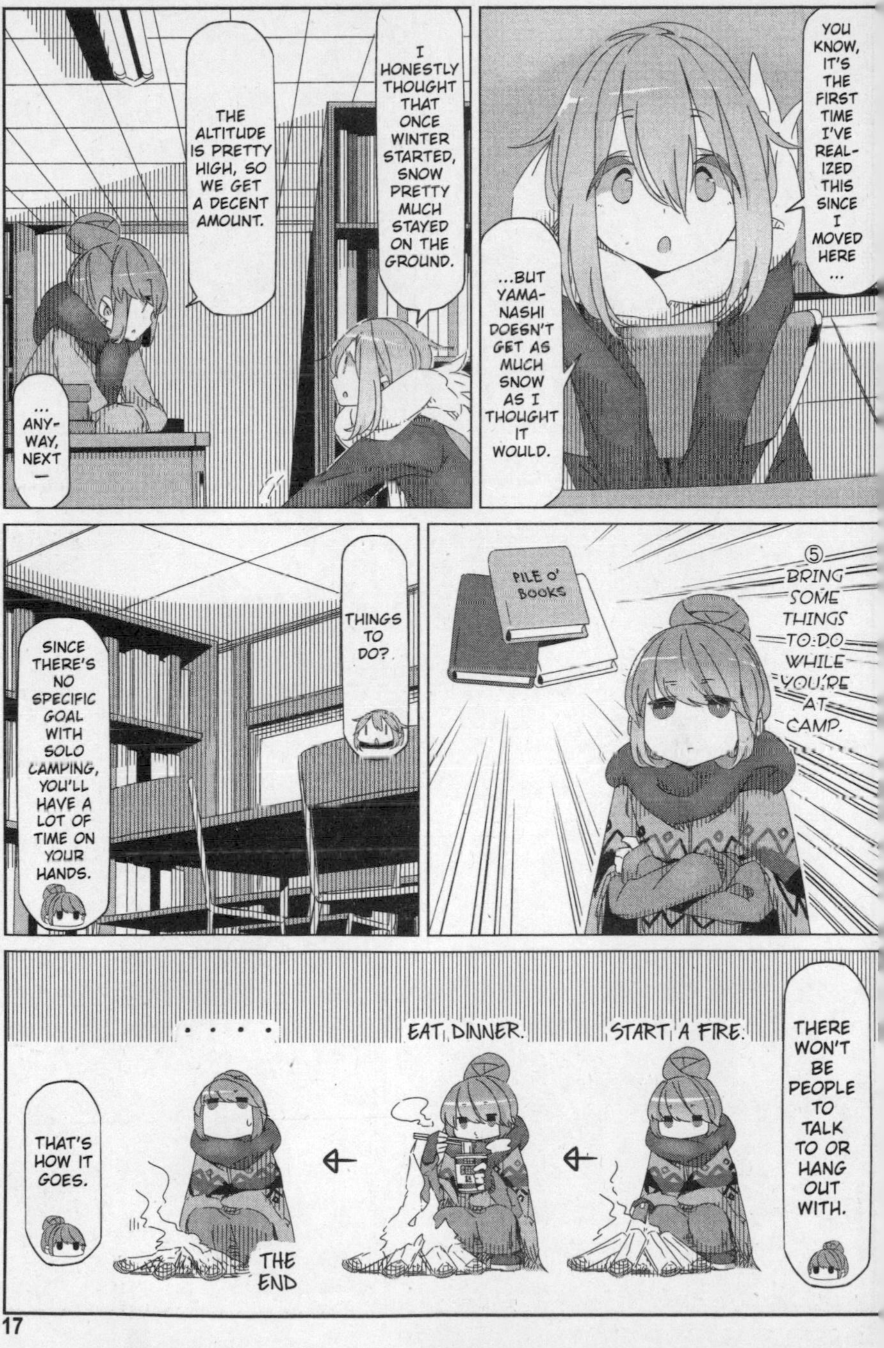
YOU KNOW, IT'S THE FIRST TIME I'VE REAL-IZED THIS SINCE I MOVED HERE ...
...BUT YAMA-NASHI DOESN'T GET AS MUCH SNOW AS I THOUGHT IT WOULD.
I HONESTLY THOUGHT THAT ONCE WINTER STARTED, SNOW PRETTY MUCH STAYED ON THE GROUND.
THE ALTITUDE IS PRETTY HIGH, SO WE GET A DECENT AMOUNT.
... ANY-WAY, NEXT —
PILE O' BOOKS
⑤ BRING SOME THINGS TO DO WHILE YOU'RE AT CAMP.
THINGS TO DO?
SINCE THERE'S NO SPECIFIC GOAL WITH SOLO CAMPING, YOU'LL HAVE A LOT OF TIME ON YOUR HANDS.
THERE WON'T BE PEOPLE TO TALK TO OR HANG OUT WITH.
START A FIRE.
EAT DINNER.
. . . .
THAT'S HOW IT GOES.
THE END

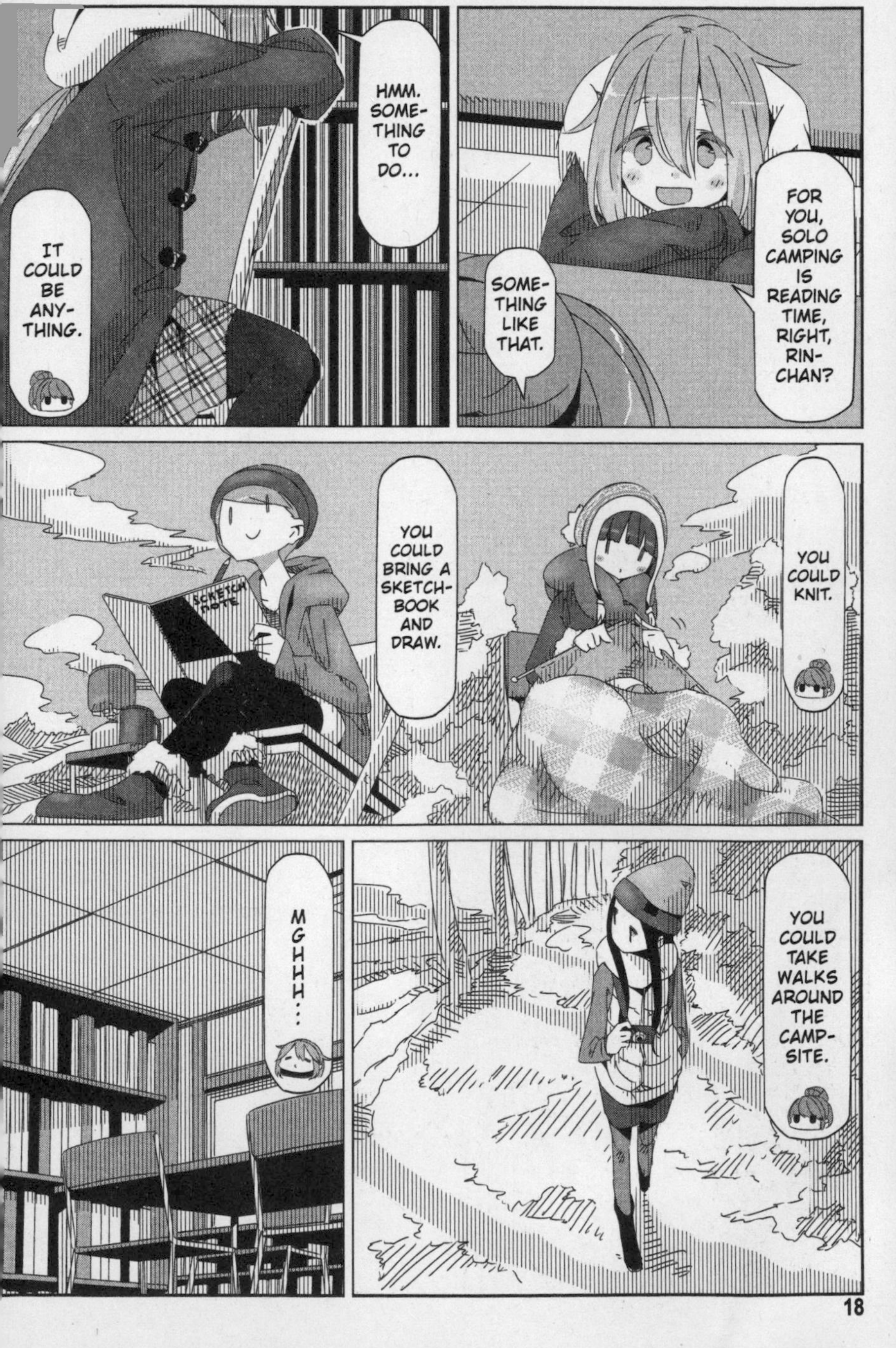
FOR YOU, SOLO CAMPING IS READING TIME, RIGHT, RIN-CHAN?
SOME-THING LIKE THAT.
HMM. SOME-THING TO DO...
IT COULD BE ANY-THING.
YOU COULD KNIT.
YOU COULD BRING A SKETCH-BOOK AND DRAW.
SKETCH NOTE
YOU COULD TAKE WALKS AROUND THE CAMP-SITE.
MGHHH...

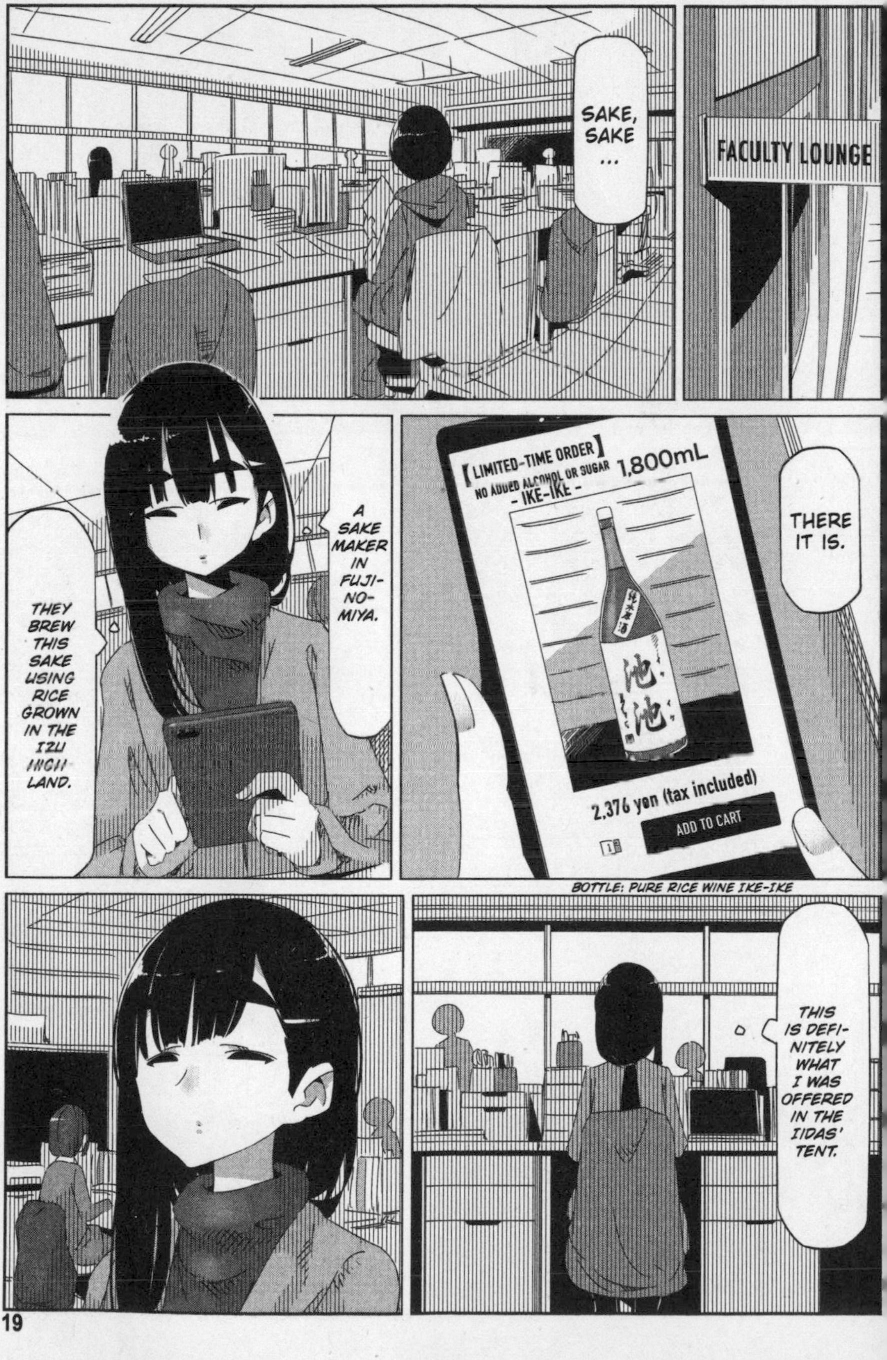
FACULTY LOUNGE
SAKE, SAKE ...
THERE IT IS.
【LIMITED-TIME ORDER】
NO ADDED ALCOHOL OR SUGAR
- IKE-IKE -
1,800mL
2,376 yen (tax included)
ADD TO CART
BOTTLE: PURE RICE WINE IKE-IKE
A SAKE MAKER IN FUJI-NO-MIYA.
THEY BREW THIS SAKE USING RICE GROWN IN THE IZU HIGH LAND.
THIS IS DEFI-NITELY WHAT I WAS OFFERED IN THE IIDAS' TENT.

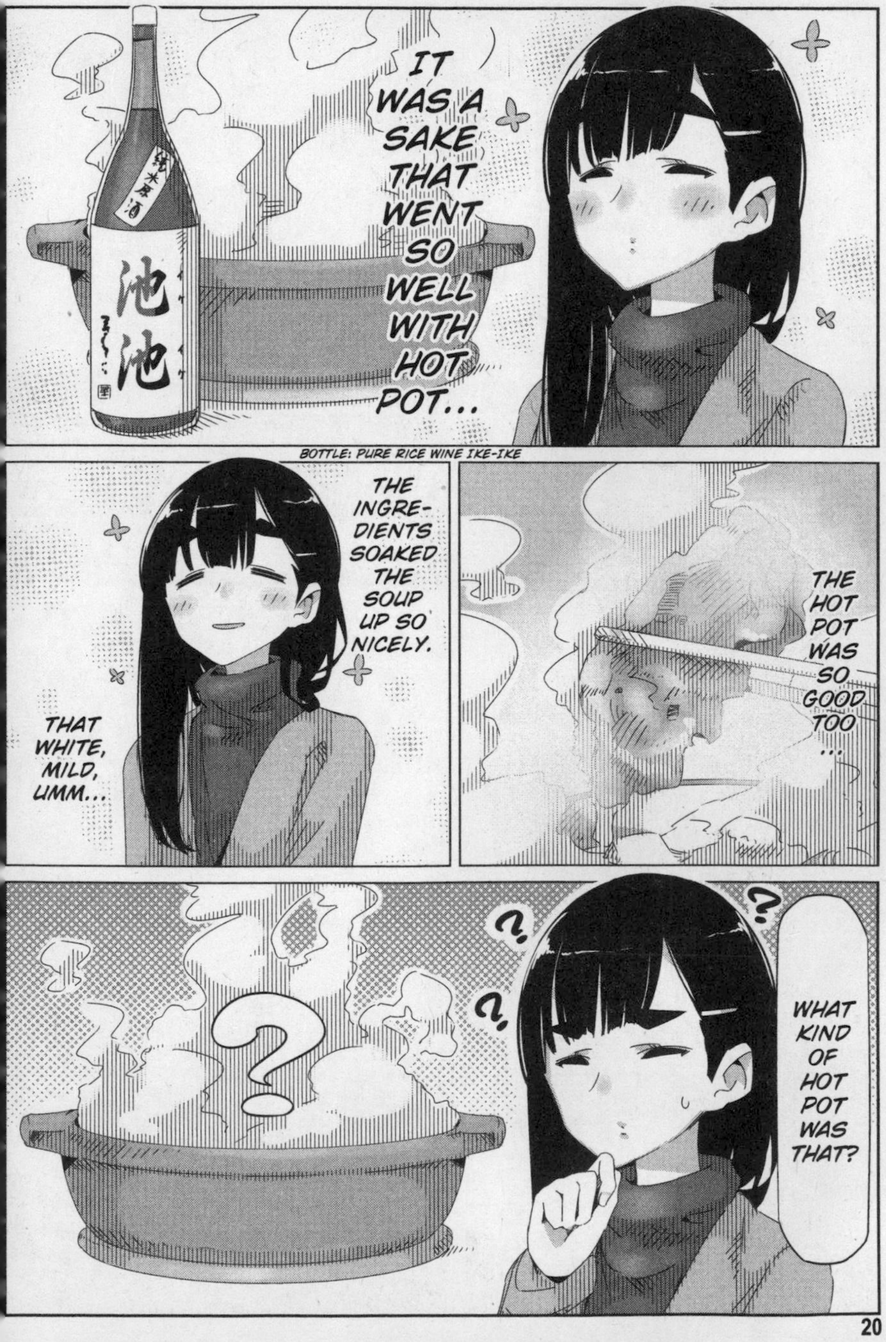
IT WAS A SAKE THAT WENT SO WELL WITH HOT POT...
純米原酒
池池
BOTTLE: PURE RICE WINE IKE-IKE
THE HOT POT WAS SO GOOD TOO ...
THE INGREDIENTS SOAKED THE SOUP UP SO NICELY.
THAT WHITE, MILD, UMM...
WHAT KIND OF HOT POT WAS THAT?

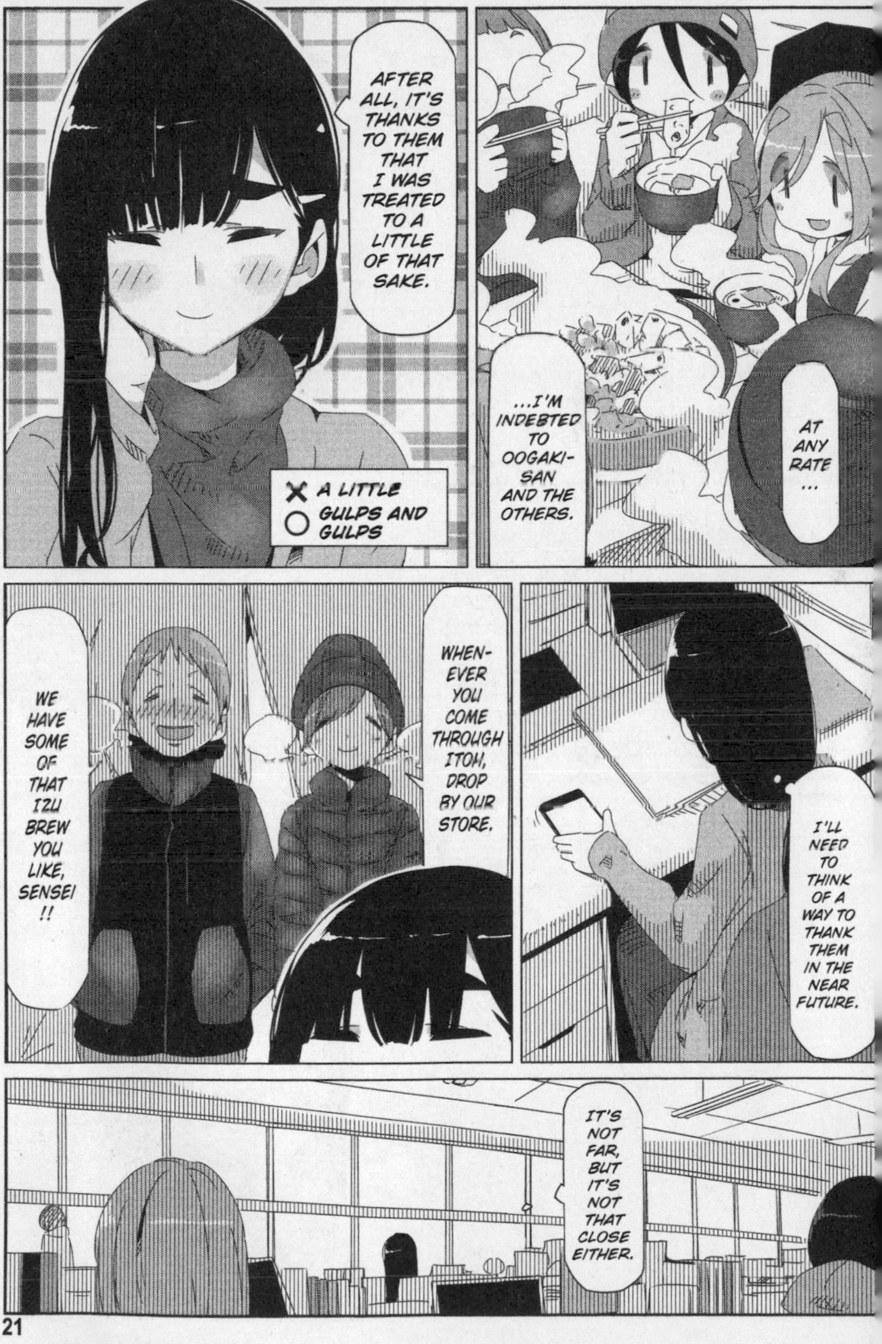
AT ANY RATE ...
...I'M INDEBTED TO OOGAKI-SAN AND THE OTHERS.
AFTER ALL, IT'S THANKS TO THEM THAT I WAS TREATED TO A LITTLE OF THAT SAKE.
✕ A LITTLE
○ GULPS AND GULPS
I'LL NEED TO THINK OF A WAY TO THANK THEM IN THE NEAR FUTURE.
WHENEVER YOU COME THROUGH ITOH, DROP BY OUR STORE.
WE HAVE SOME OF THAT IZU BREW YOU LIKE, SENSEI!!
IT'S NOT FAR, BUT IT'S NOT THAT CLOSE EITHER.

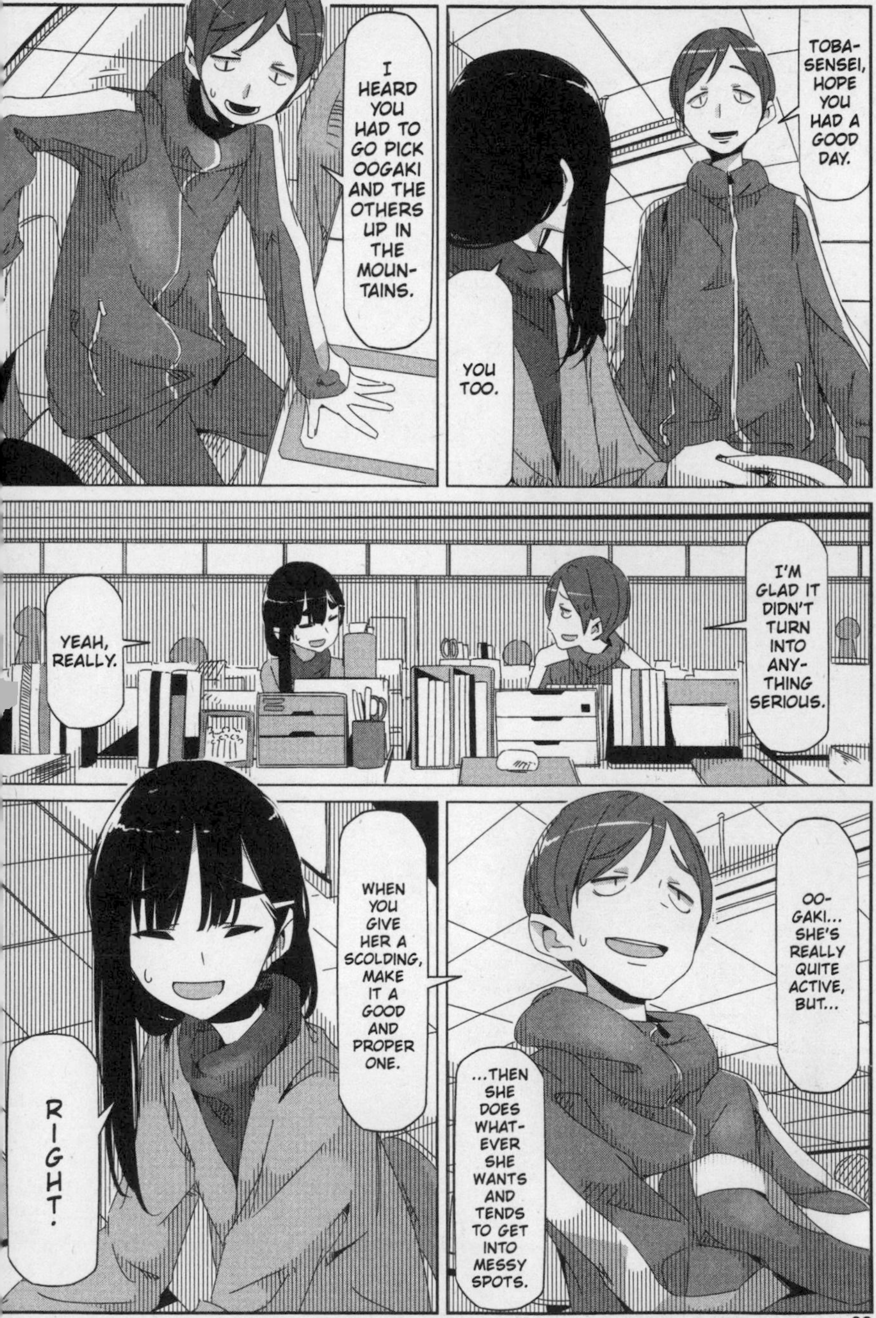
TOBA-SENSEI, HOPE YOU HAD A GOOD DAY.
YOU TOO.
I HEARD YOU HAD TO GO PICK OOGAKI AND THE OTHERS UP IN THE MOUN-TAINS.
I'M GLAD IT DIDN'T TURN INTO ANY-THING SERIOUS.
YEAH, REALLY.
OO-GAKI... SHE'S REALLY QUITE ACTIVE, BUT...
...THEN SHE DOES WHAT-EVER SHE WANTS AND TENDS TO GET INTO MESSY SPOTS.
WHEN YOU GIVE HER A SCOLDING, MAKE IT A GOOD AND PROPER ONE.
RIGHT.

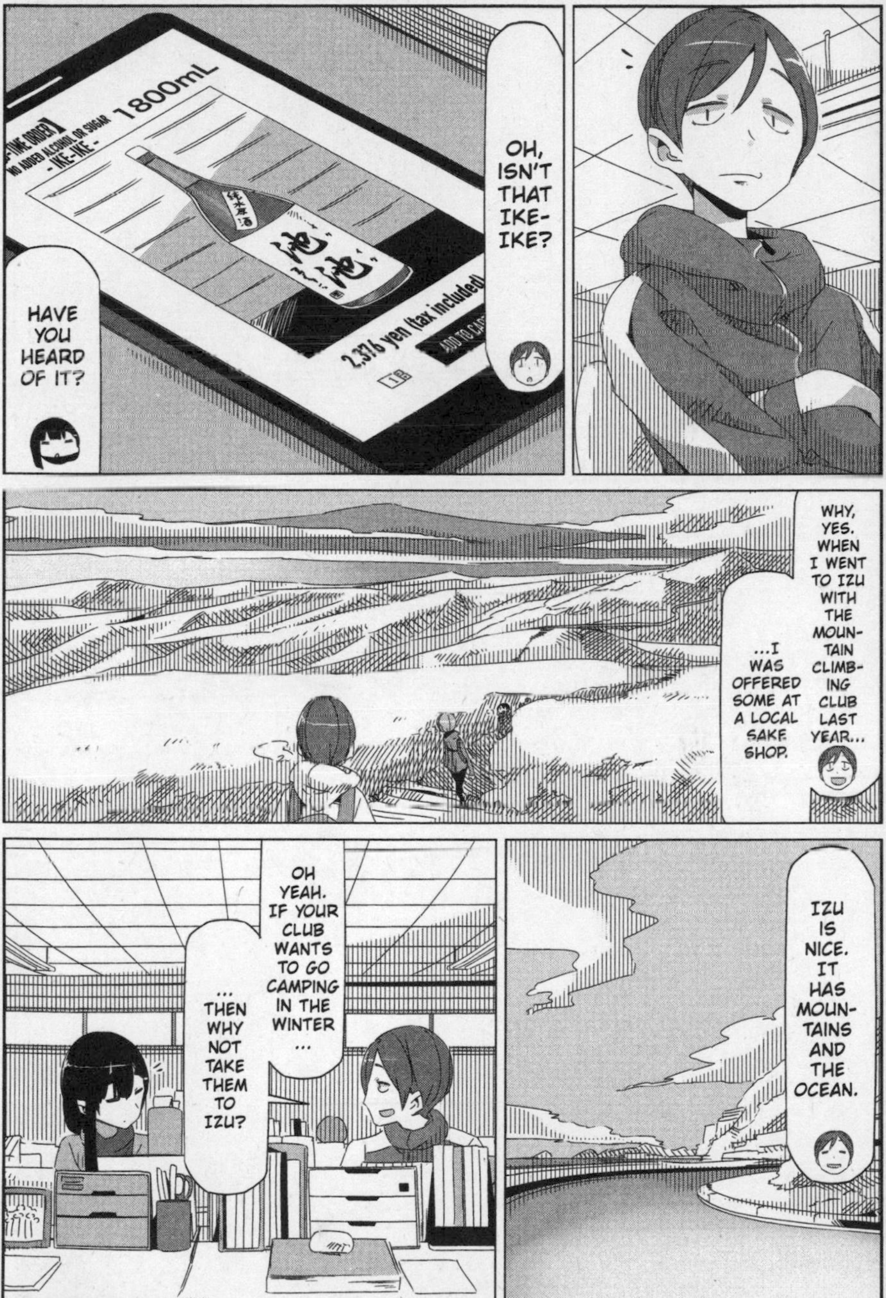
!
OH, ISN'T THAT IKE-IKE?
TIME ORDER
NO ADDED ALCOHOL OR SUGAR
-IKE-IKE-
1800mL
2,376 yen (tax included)
HAVE YOU HEARD OF IT?
WHY, YES. WHEN I WENT TO IZU WITH THE MOUNTAIN-CLIMBING CLUB LAST YEAR...
...I WAS OFFERED SOME AT A LOCAL SAKE SHOP.
IZU IS NICE. IT HAS MOUNTAINS AND THE OCEAN.
OH YEAH. IF YOUR CLUB WANTS TO GO CAMPING IN THE WINTER...
...THEN WHY NOT TAKE THEM TO IZU?

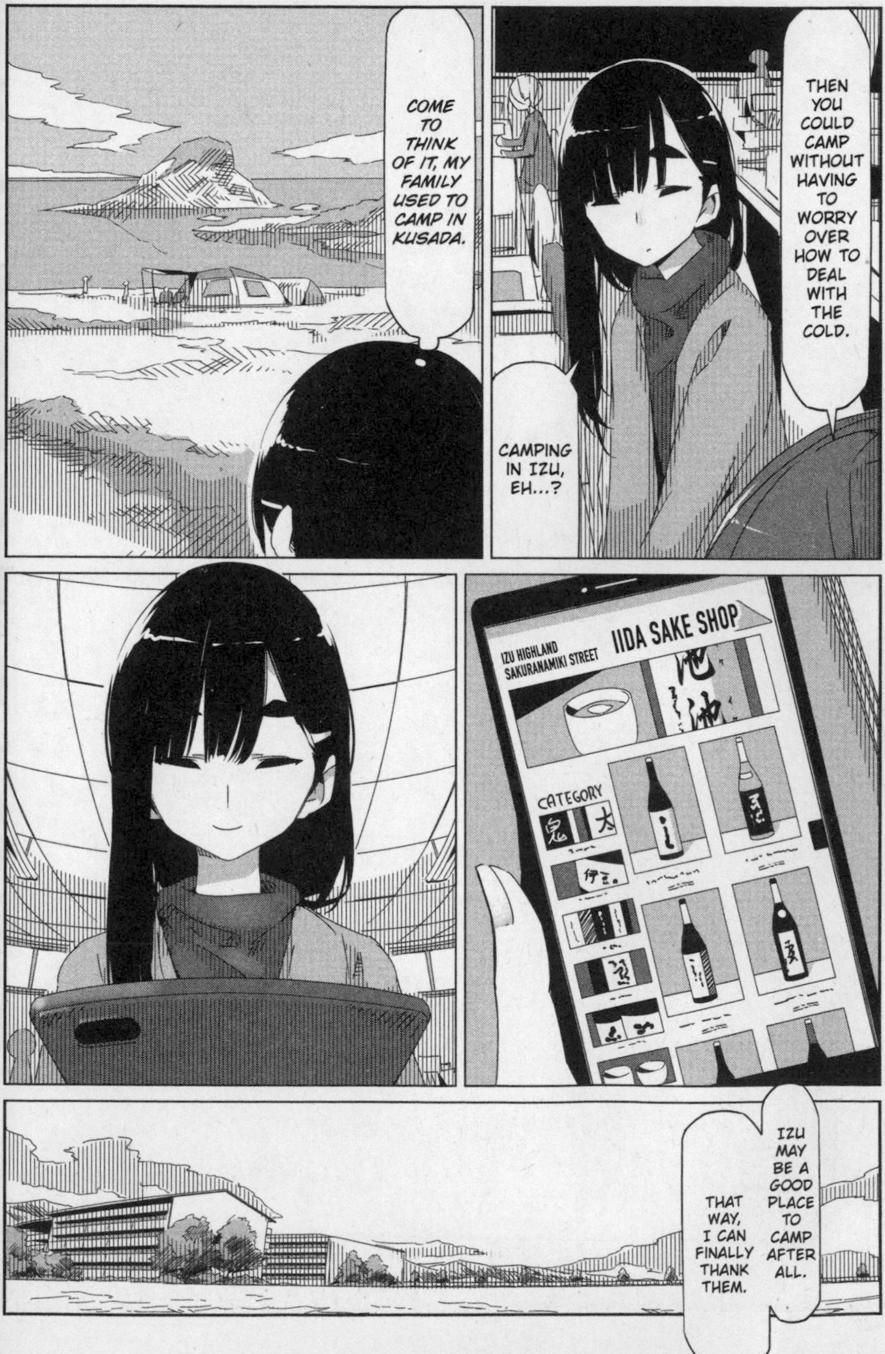
THEN YOU COULD CAMP WITHOUT HAVING TO WORRY OVER HOW TO DEAL WITH THE COLD.
CAMPING IN IZU, EH...?
COME TO THINK OF IT, MY FAMILY USED TO CAMP IN KUSADA.
IIDA SAKE SHOP
IZU HIGHLAND SAKURANAMIKI STREET
CATEGORY
IZU MAY BE A GOOD PLACE TO CAMP AFTER ALL.
THAT WAY, I CAN FINALLY THANK THEM.

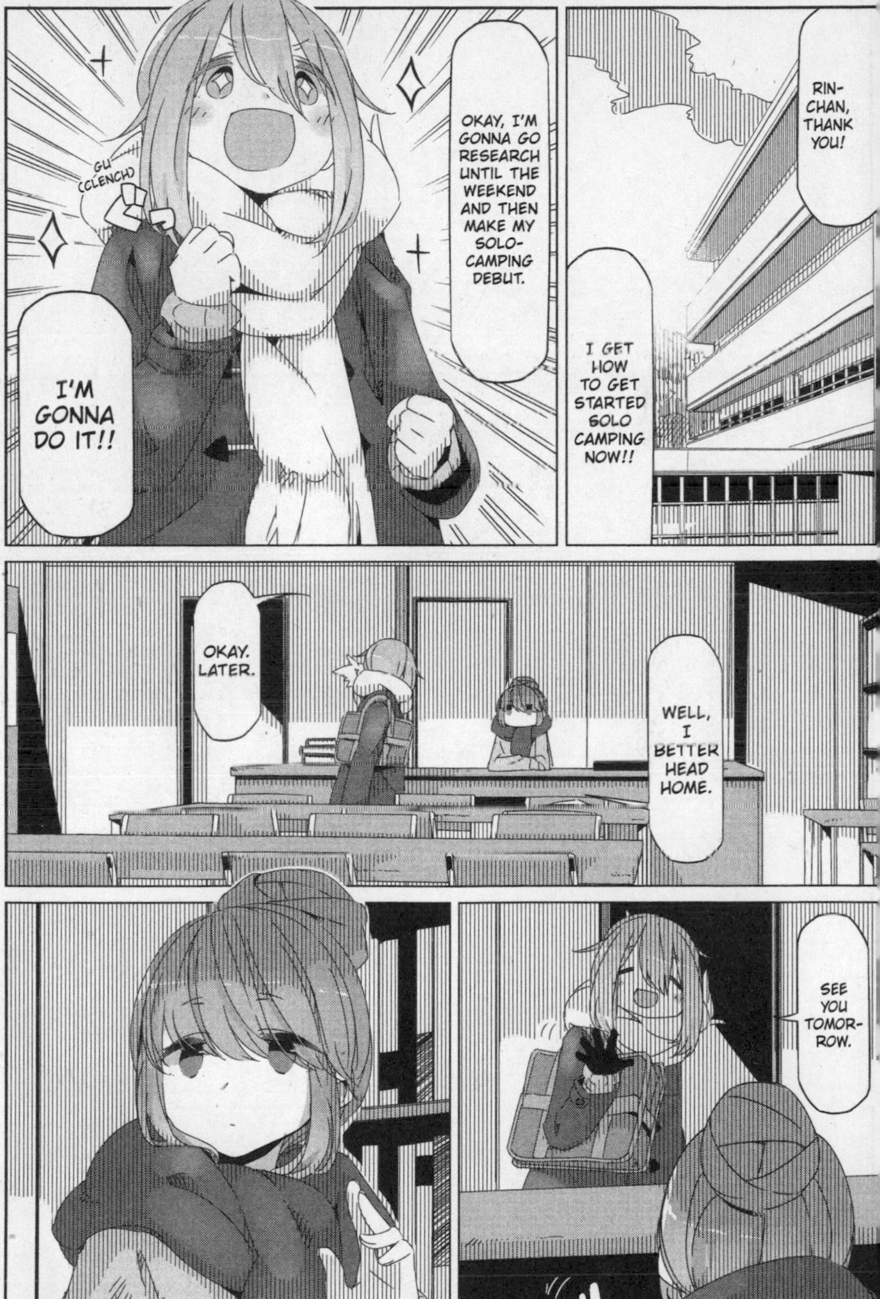
RIN-CHAN, THANK YOU!
I GET HOW TO GET STARTED SOLO CAMPING NOW!!
OKAY, I'M GONNA GO RESEARCH UNTIL THE WEEKEND AND THEN MAKE MY SOLO-CAMPING DEBUT.
GU (CLENCH)
I'M GONNA DO IT!!
WELL, I BETTER HEAD HOME.
OKAY. LATER.
SEE YOU TOMOR-ROW.

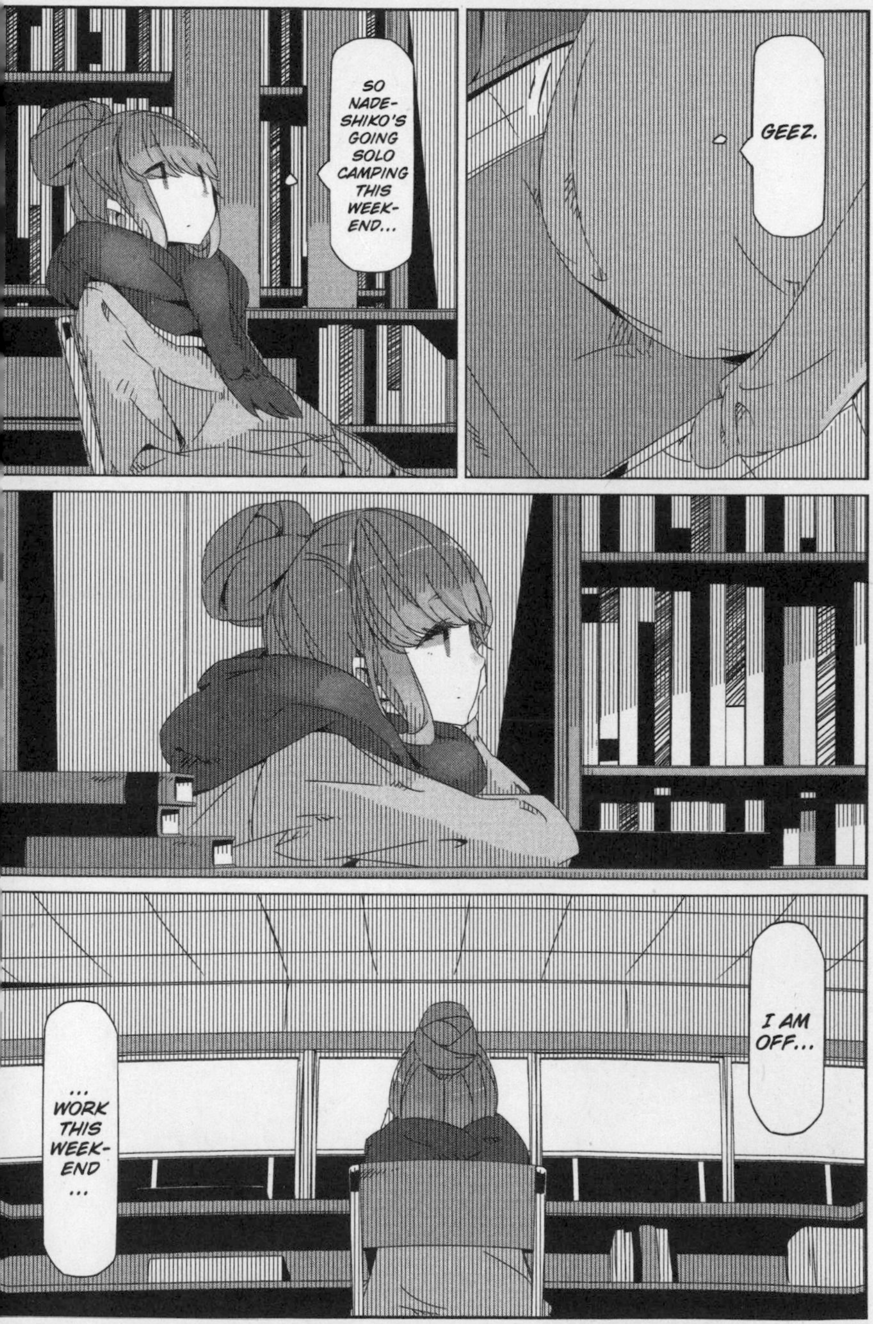
GEEZ.
SO NADE-SHIKO'S GOING SOLO CAMPING THIS WEEK-END...
I AM OFF...
...WORK THIS WEEK-END ...

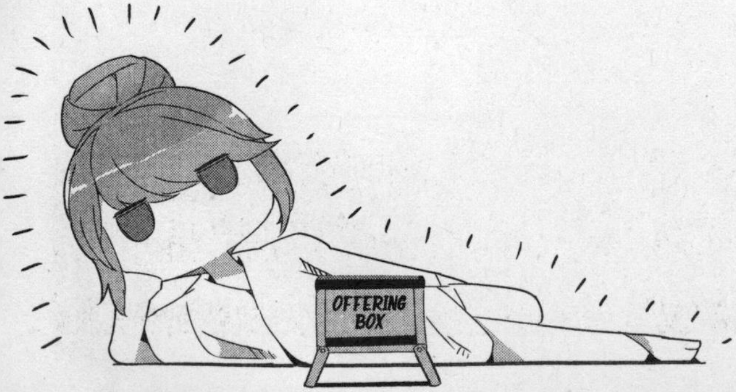
OFFERING BOX

WOOF! WOOF!

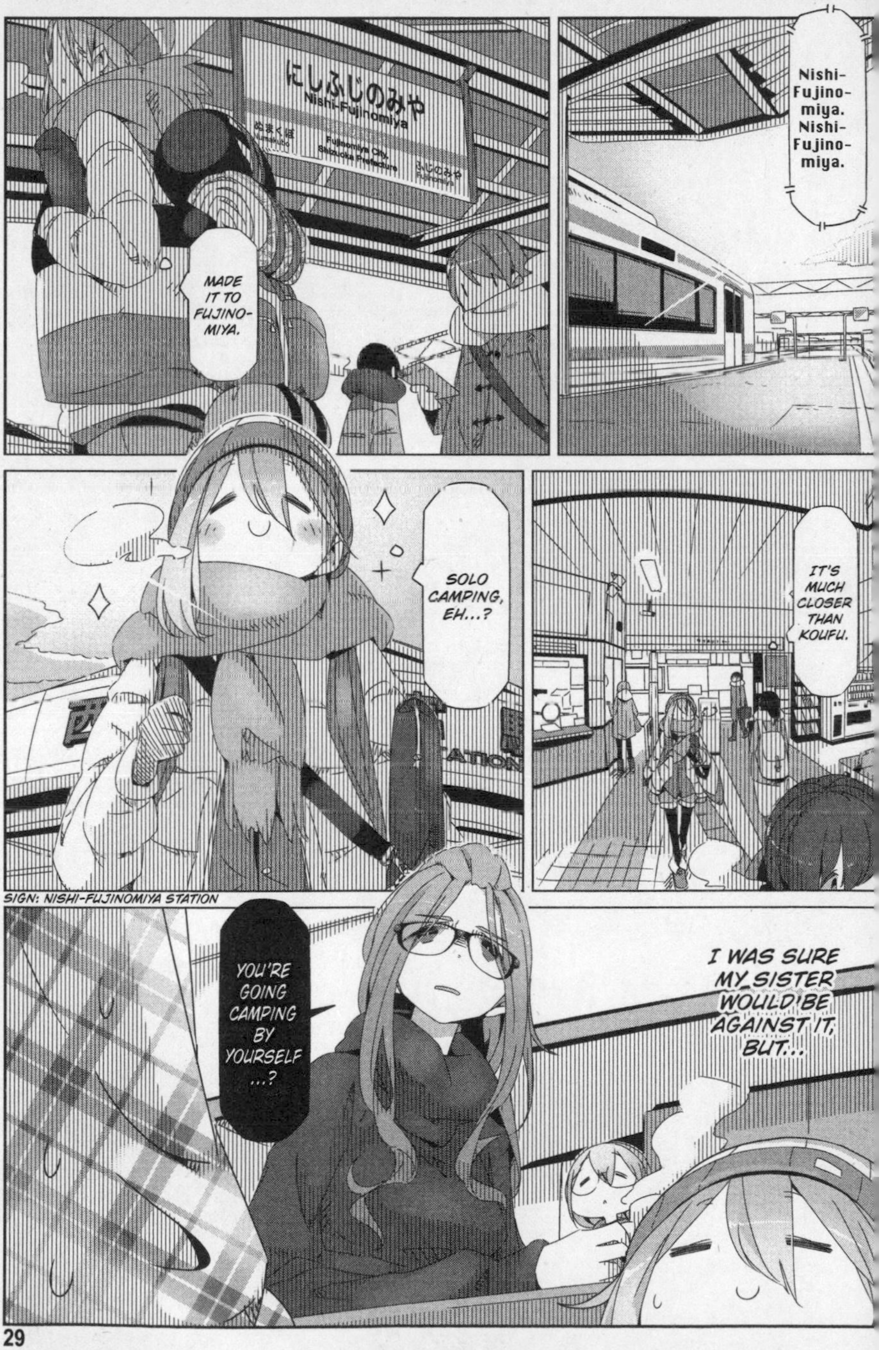
Nishi-Fujinomiya. Nishi-Fujinomiya.
にしふじのみや
Nishi-Fujinomiya
ぬまくぼ
Fujinomiya City, Shizuoka Prefecture
ふじのみや
MADE IT TO FUJINOMIYA.
IT'S MUCH CLOSER THAN KOUFU.
SOLO CAMPING, EH...?
SIGN: NISHI-FUJINOMIYA STATION
I WAS SURE MY SISTER WOULD BE AGAINST IT, BUT...
YOU'RE GOING CAMPING BY YOURSELF...?

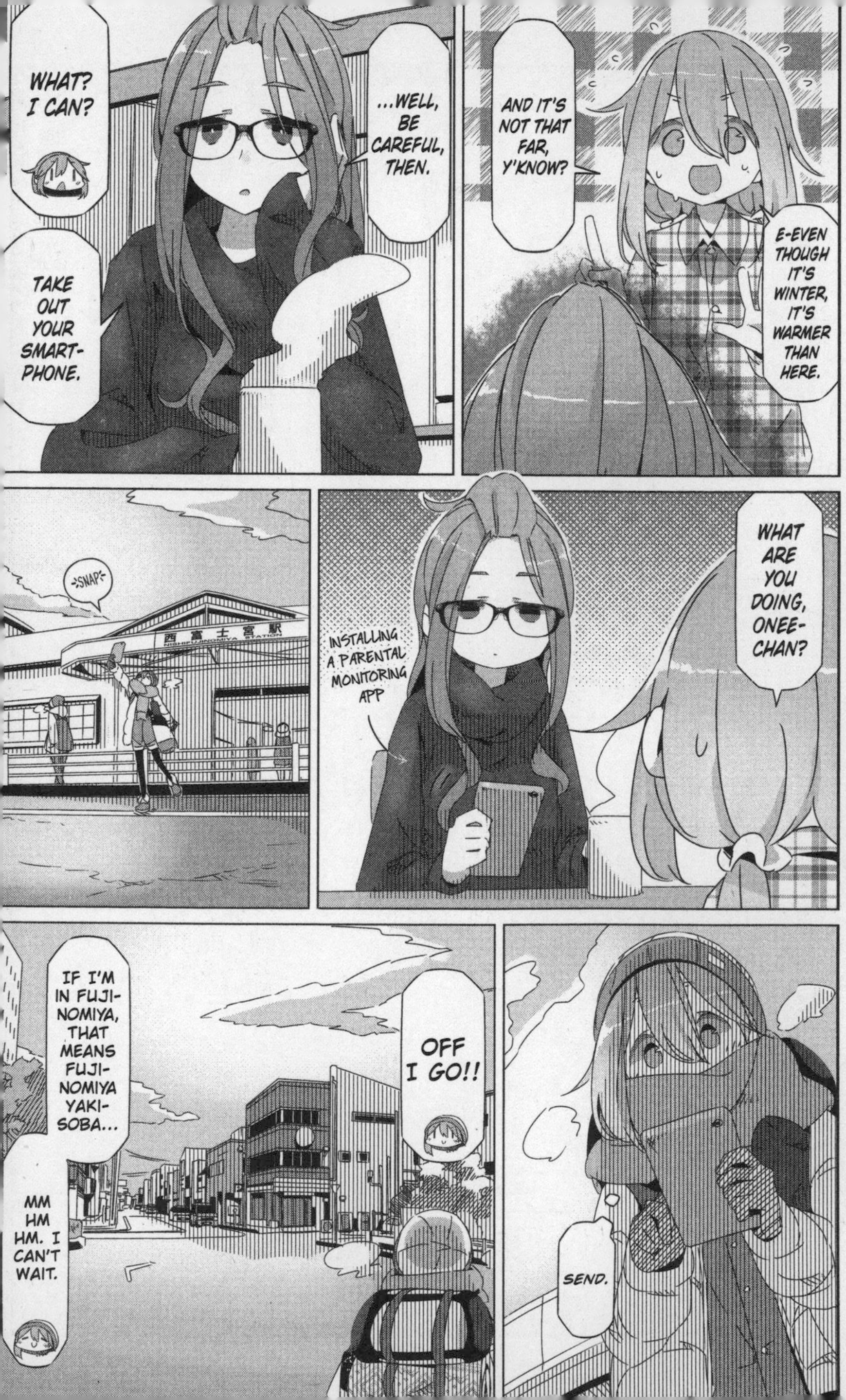
E-EVEN THOUGH IT'S WINTER, IT'S WARMER THAN HERE.
AND IT'S NOT THAT FAR, Y'KNOW?
...WELL, BE CAREFUL, THEN.
WHAT? I CAN?
TAKE OUT YOUR SMARTPHONE.
WHAT ARE YOU DOING, ONEE-CHAN?
INSTALLING A PARENTAL MONITORING APP
SNAP
西富士宮駅
NISHIFUJINOMIYA STATION
SEND.
OFF I GO!!
IF I'M IN FUJI-NOMIYA, THAT MEANS FUJI-NOMIYA YAKI-SOBA...
MM HM HM. I CAN'T WAIT.

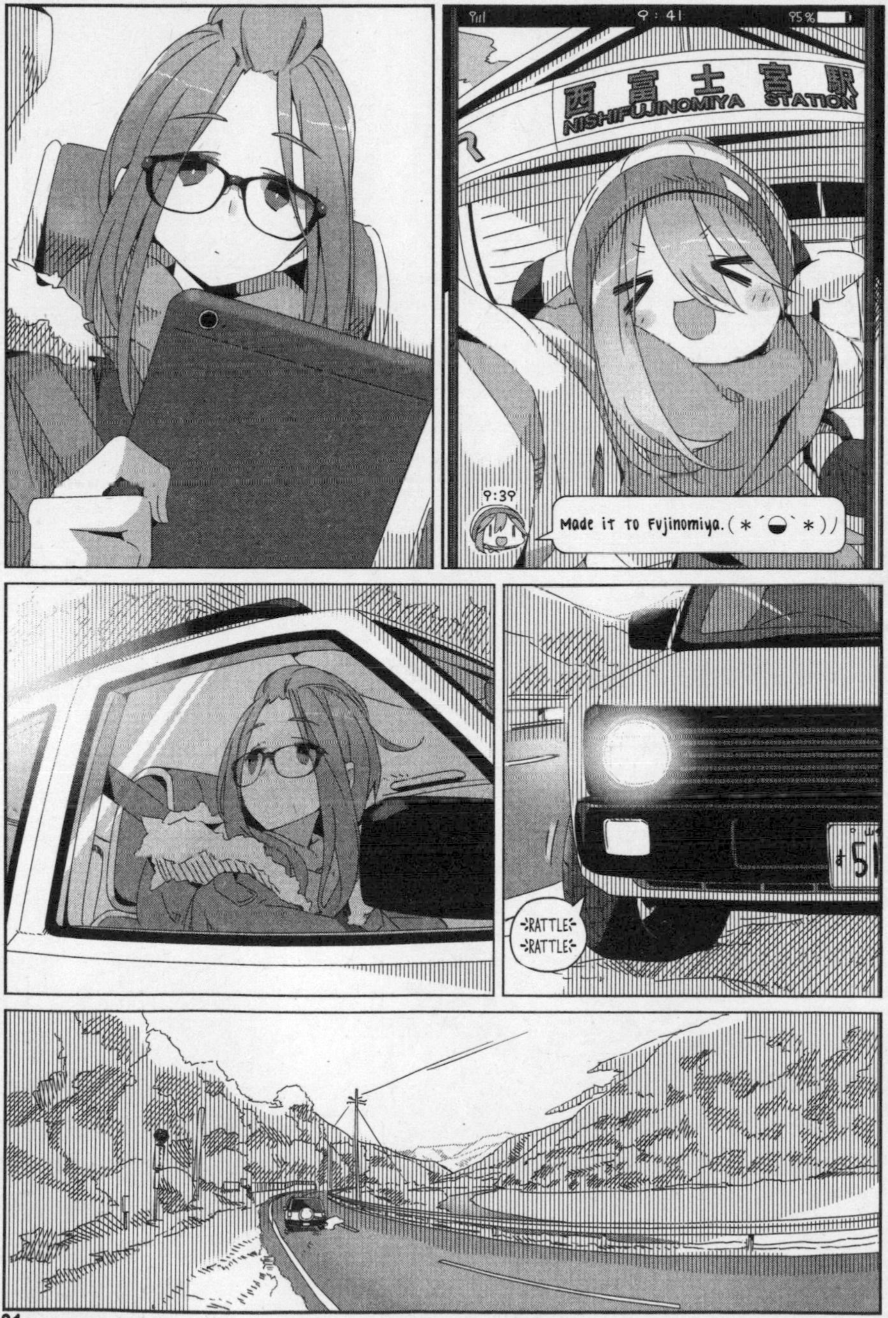
9:41
95%
西富士宮駅
NISHIFUJINOMIYA STATION
9:39
Made it to Fujinomiya.(＊´◒`＊)
RATTLE
RATTLE

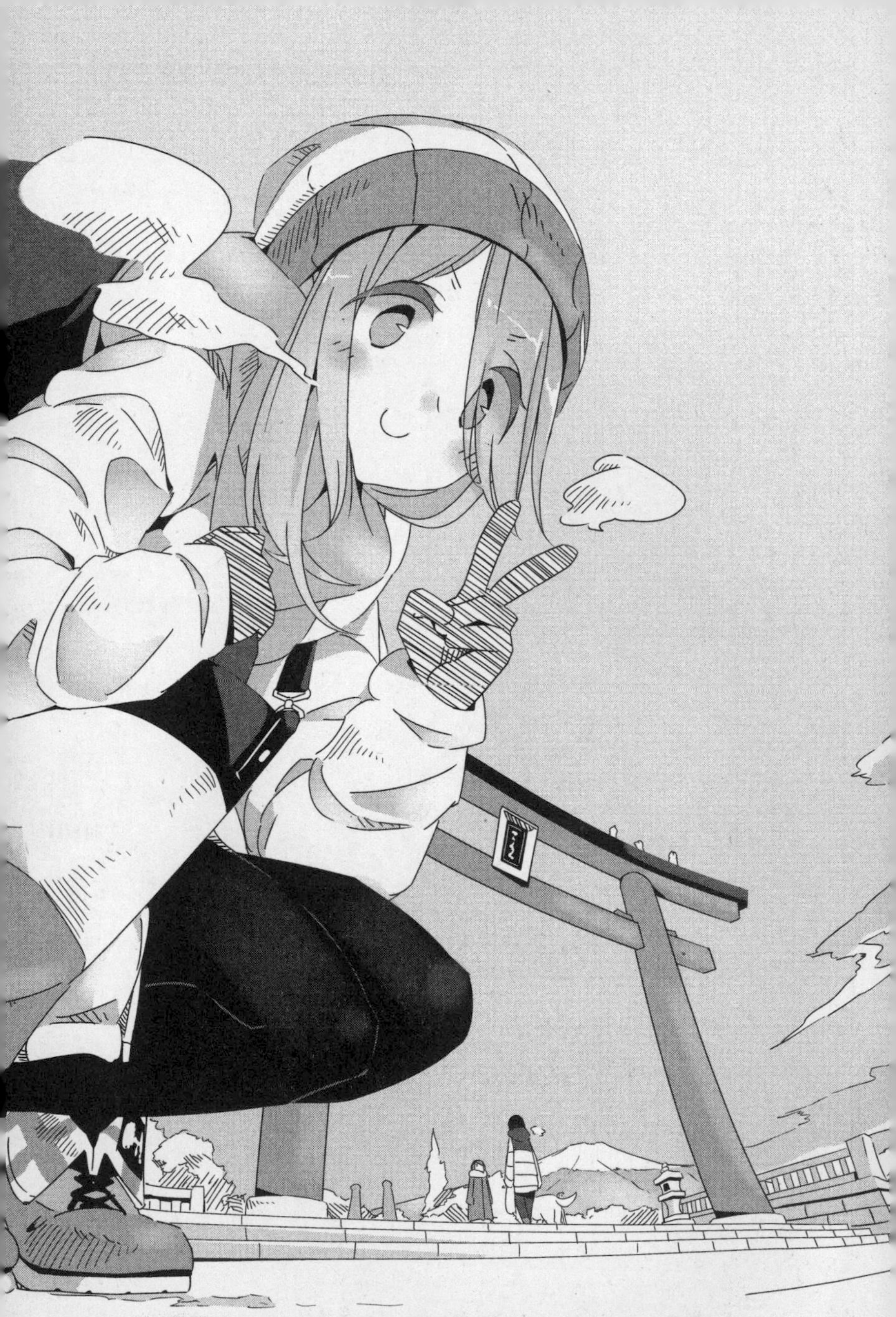

CHAPTER 36 NADESHIKO'S WALK AND SHIMARIN'S WALK

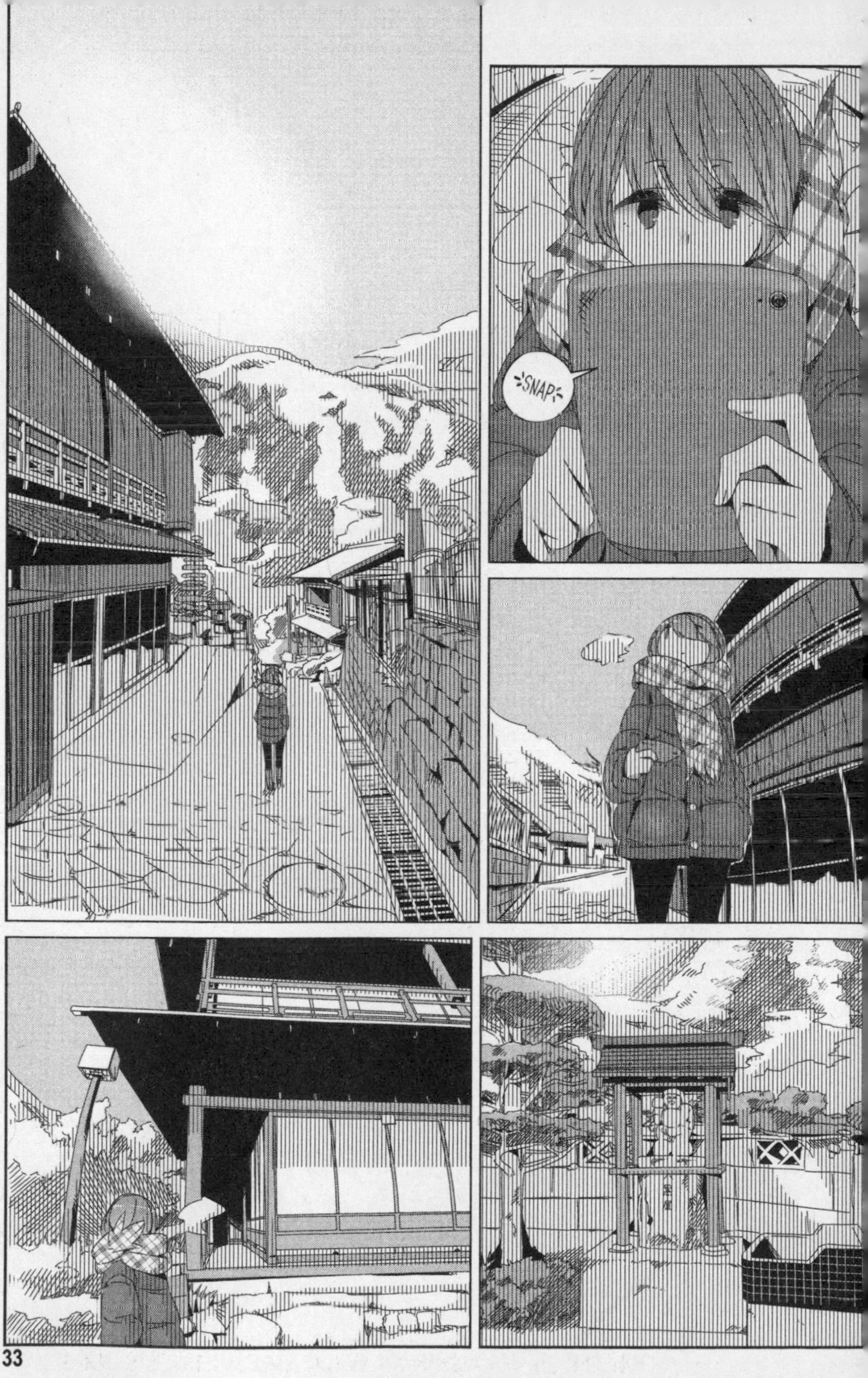
SNAP

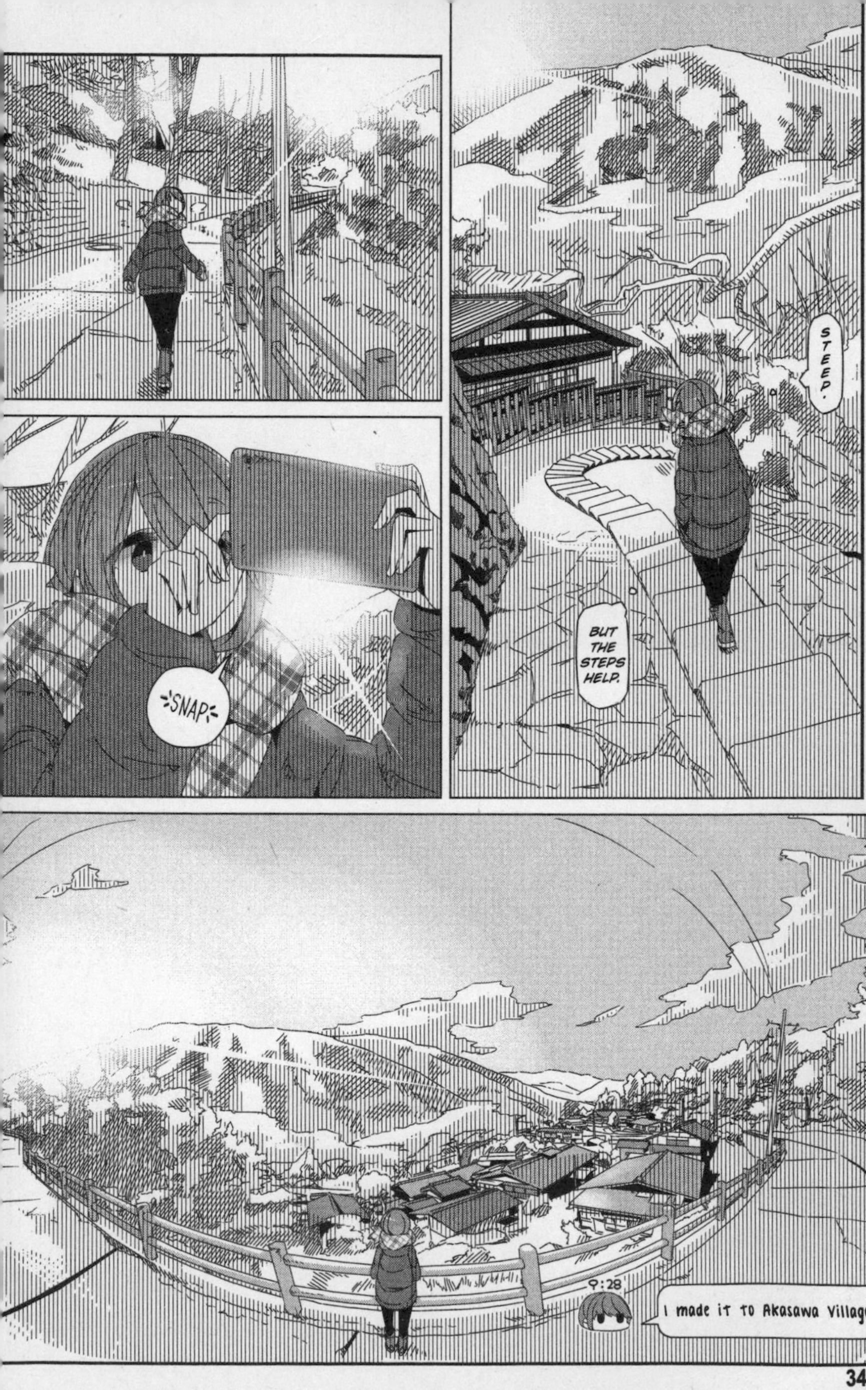
STEEP.
BUT THE STEPS HELP.
SNAP
9:28
I made it to Akasawa Village.

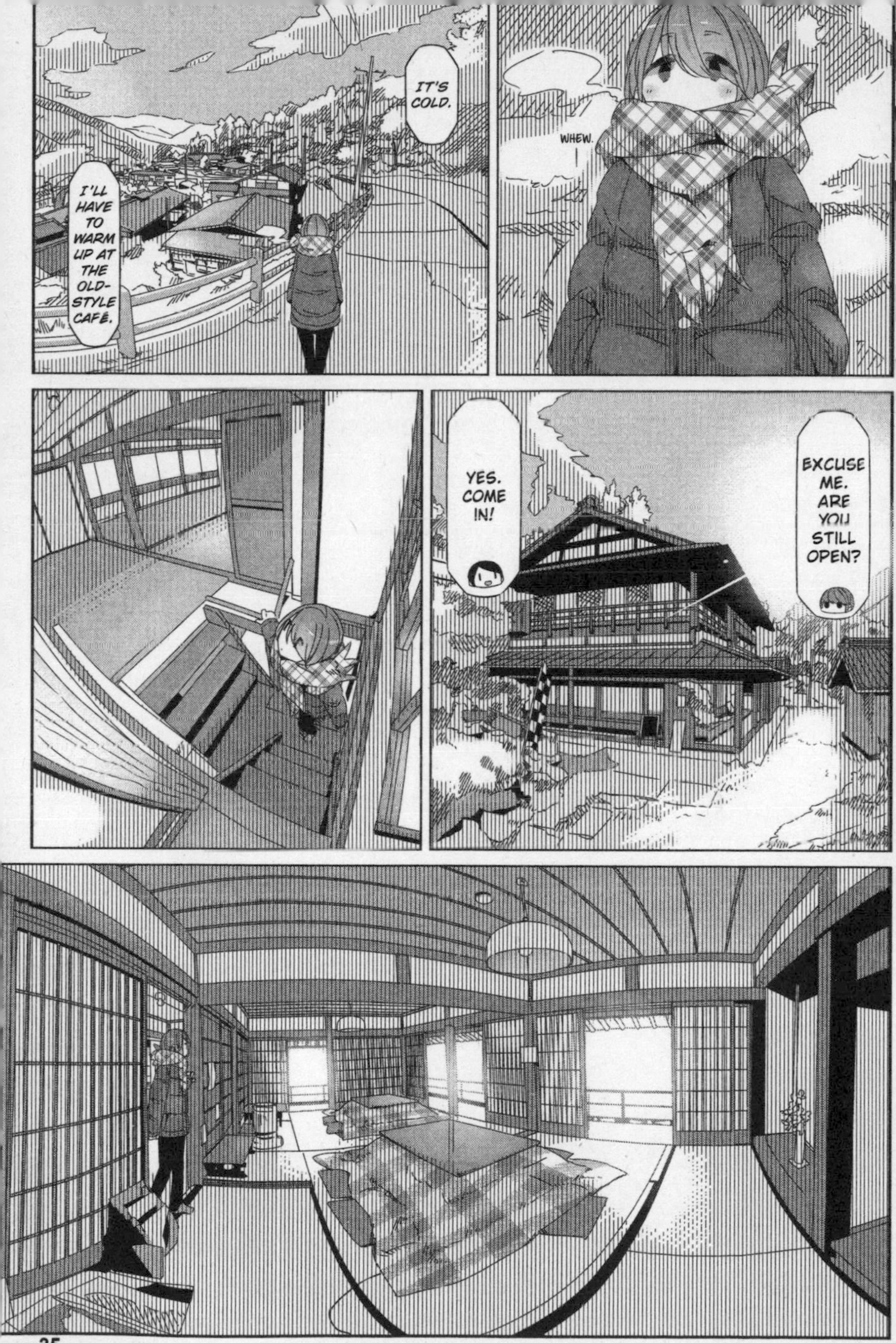
WHEW.
IT'S COLD.
I'LL HAVE TO WARM UP AT THE OLD-STYLE CAFÉ.
EXCUSE ME. ARE YOU STILL OPEN?
YES. COME IN!

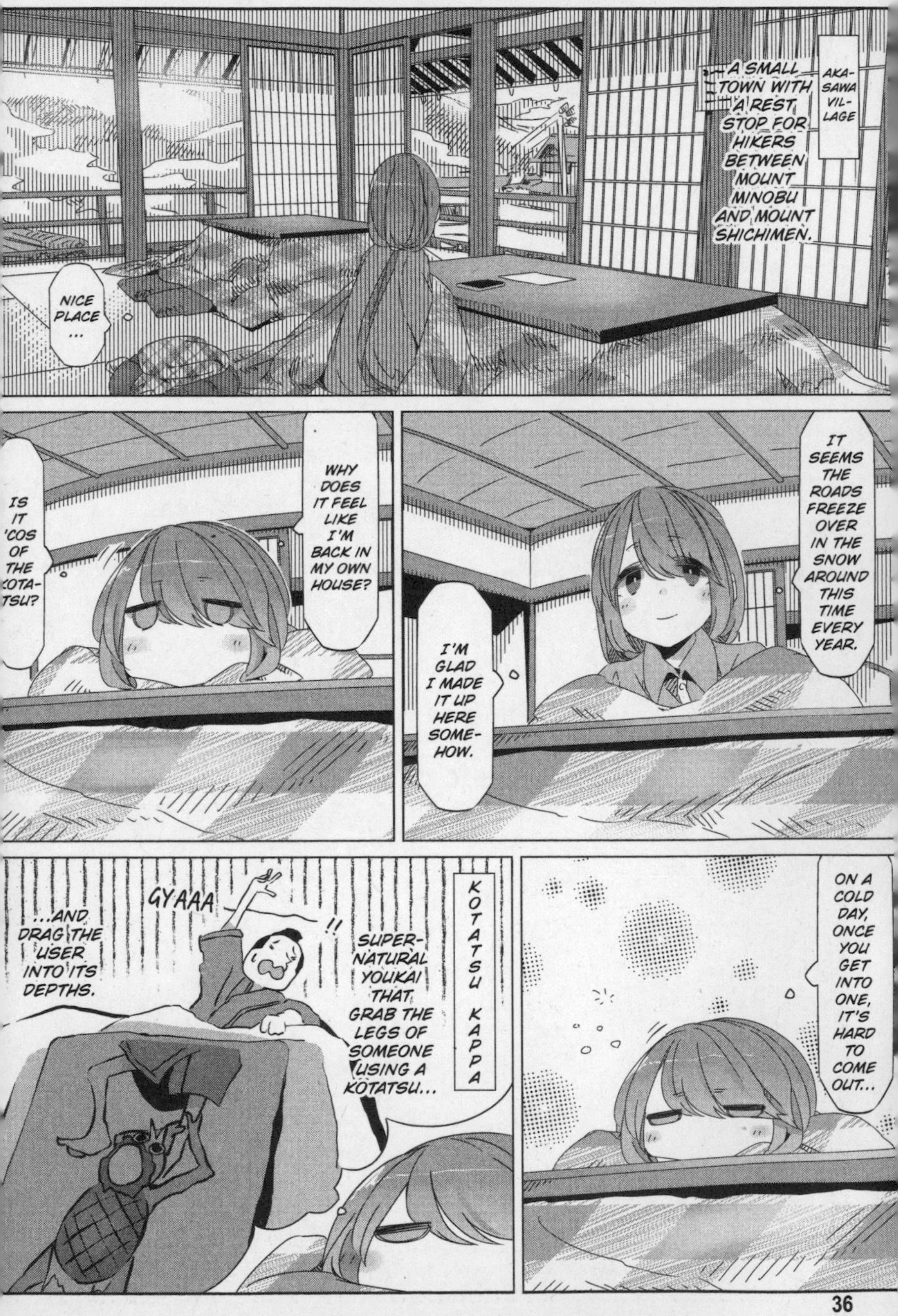
AKASAWA VILLAGE
A SMALL TOWN WITH A REST STOP FOR HIKERS BETWEEN MOUNT MINOBU AND MOUNT SHICHIMEN.
NICE PLACE...
IT SEEMS THE ROADS FREEZE OVER IN THE SNOW AROUND THIS TIME EVERY YEAR.
I'M GLAD I MADE IT UP HERE SOMEHOW.
WHY DOES IT FEEL LIKE I'M BACK IN MY OWN HOUSE?
IS IT 'COS OF THE KOTATSU?
ON A COLD DAY, ONCE YOU GET INTO ONE, IT'S HARD TO COME OUT...
KOTATSU KAPPA
SUPERNATURAL YOUKAI THAT GRAB THE LEGS OF SOMEONE USING A KOTATSU...
GYAAA
!!
...AND DRAG THE USER INTO ITS DEPTHS.

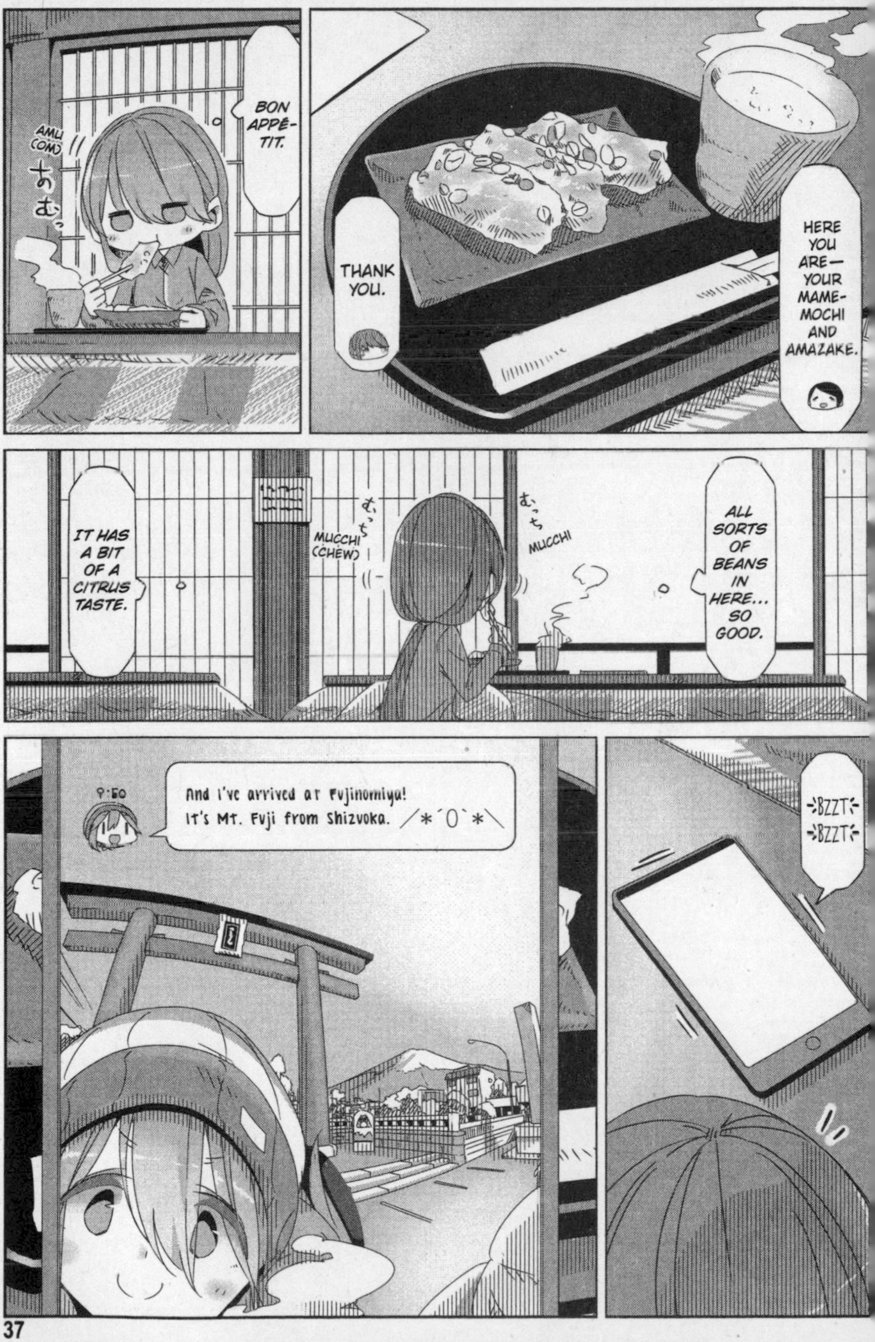
HERE YOU ARE—YOUR MAME-MOCHI AND AMAZAKE.
THANK YOU.
BON APPÉTIT.
あむっ
AMU (OM)
ALL SORTS OF BEANS IN HERE... SO GOOD.
むっち
MUCCHI
むっち
MUCCHI (CHEW)
IT HAS A BIT OF A CITRUS TASTE.
BZZT
BZZT
9:50
And I've arrived at Fujinomiya! It's Mt. Fuji from Shizuoka. ／*´O`*＼

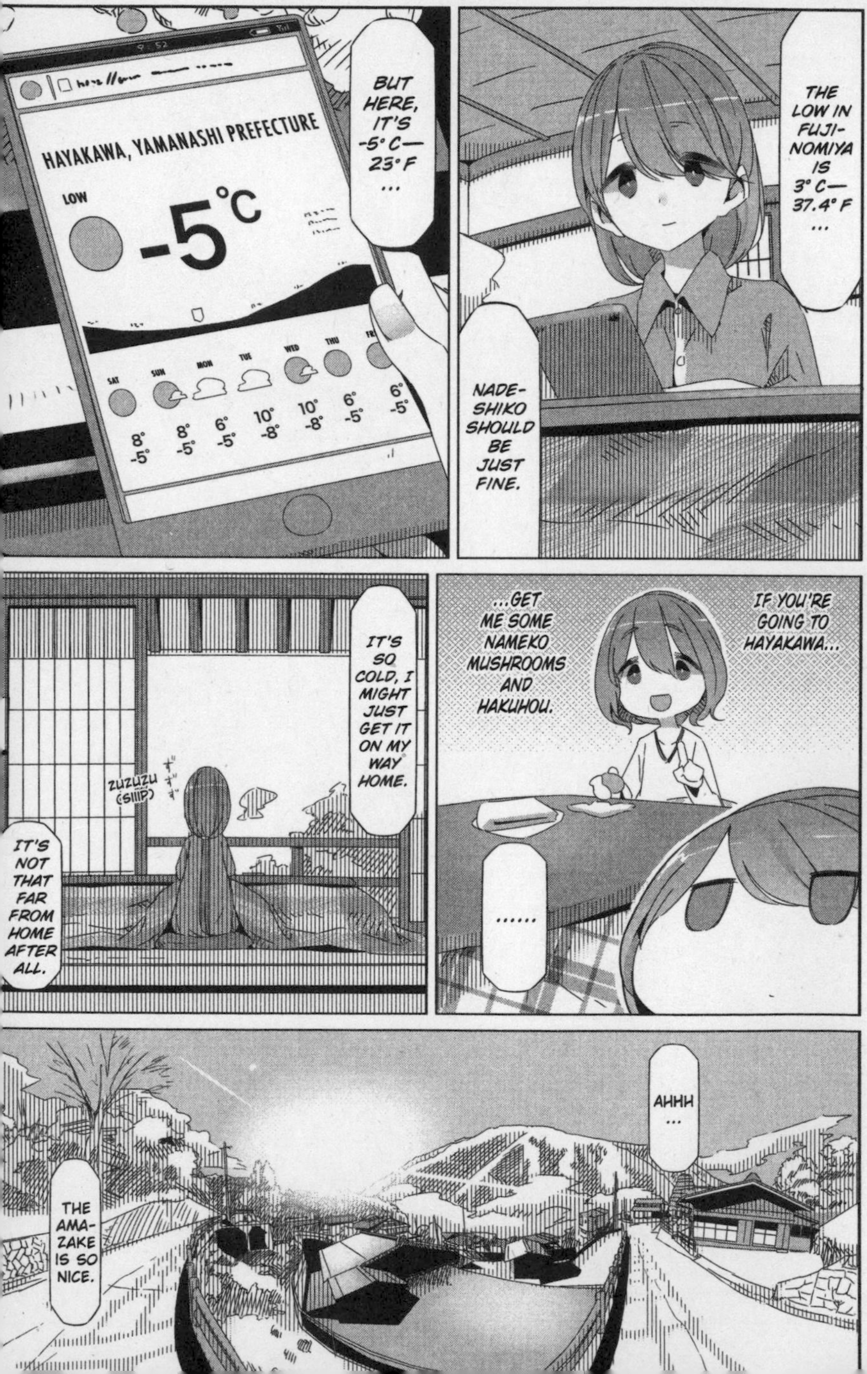
THE LOW IN FUJI-NOMIYA IS 3° C—37.4° F ...
NADE-SHIKO SHOULD BE JUST FINE.
BUT HERE, IT'S -5° C—23° F ...
HAYAKAWA, YAMANASHI PREFECTURE
LOW
-5°C
SAT 8° -5°
SUN 8° -5°
MON 6° -5°
TUE 10° -8°
WED 10° -8°
THU 6° -5°
6° -5°
IF YOU'RE GOING TO HAYAKAWA...
...GET ME SOME NAMEKO MUSHROOMS AND HAKUHOU.
......
IT'S SO COLD, I MIGHT JUST GET IT ON MY WAY HOME.
ZUZUZU (SIIIP)
IT'S NOT THAT FAR FROM HOME AFTER ALL.
AHHH ...
THE AMA-ZAKE IS SO NICE.

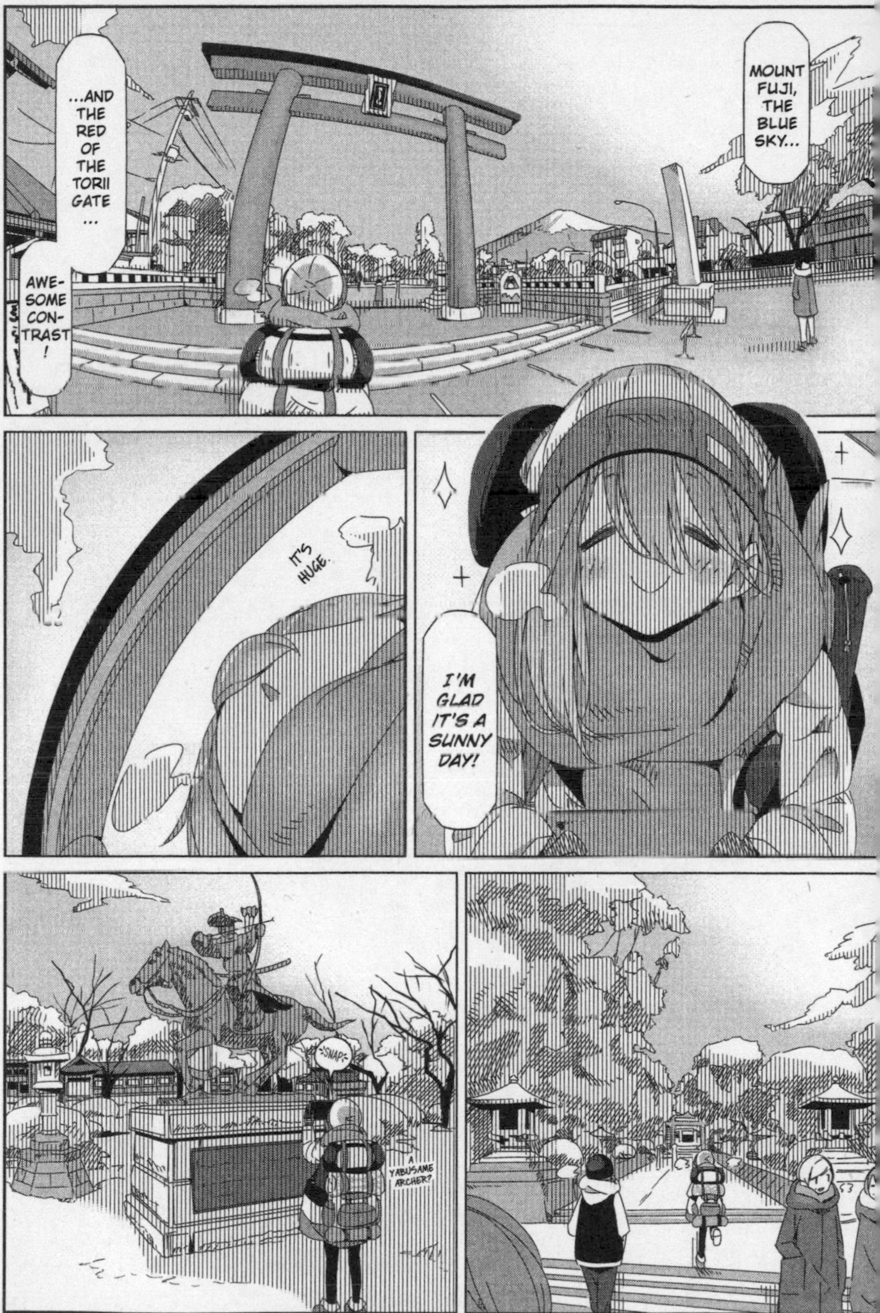
MOUNT FUJI, THE BLUE SKY...
...AND THE RED OF THE TORII GATE ...
AWE-SOME CON-TRAST!
I'M GLAD IT'S A SUNNY DAY!
IT'S HUGE.
SNAP
A YABUSAME ARCHER?

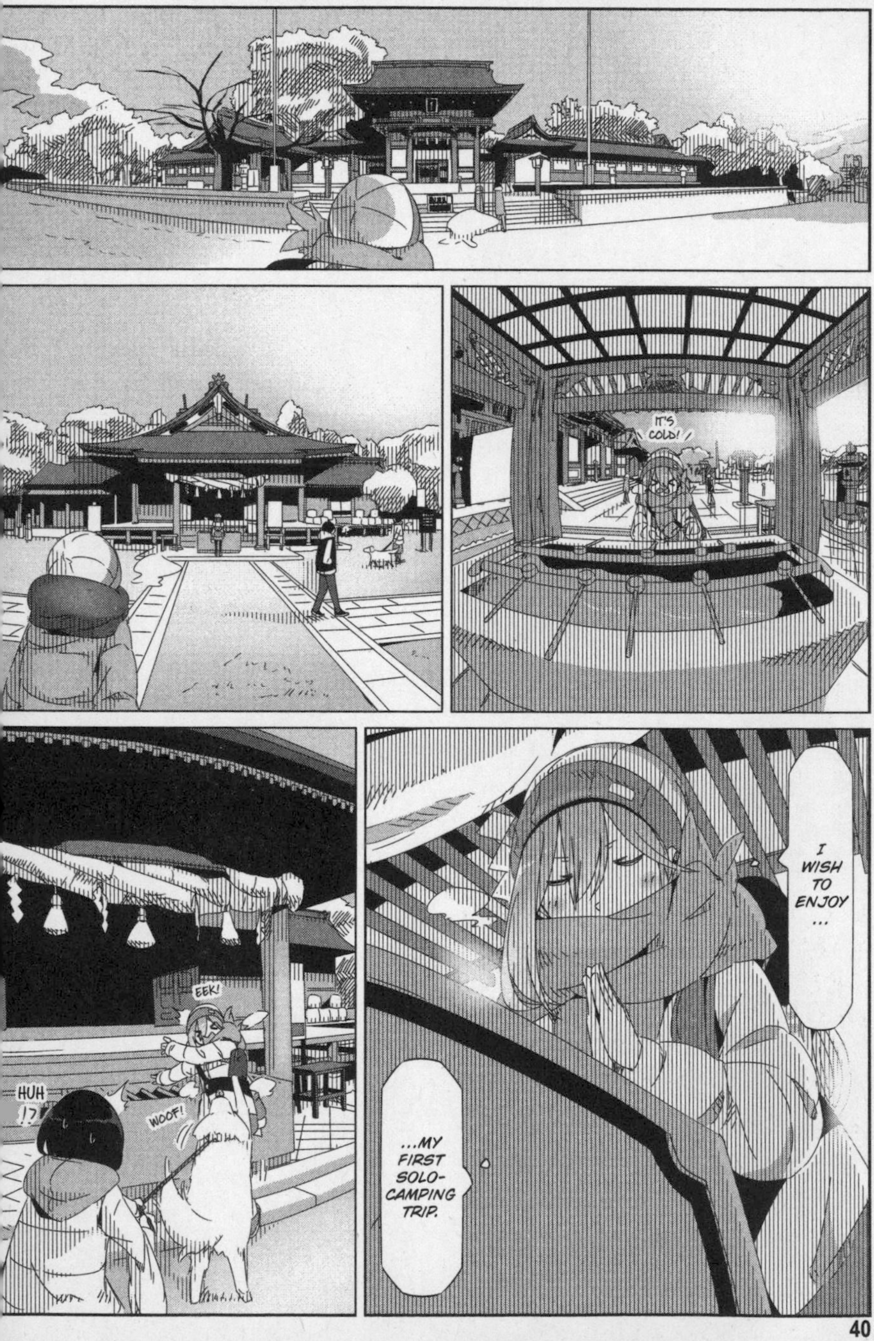

IT'S COLD!
I WISH TO ENJOY ...
...MY FIRST SOLO-CAMPING TRIP.
EEK!
WOOF!
HUH !?

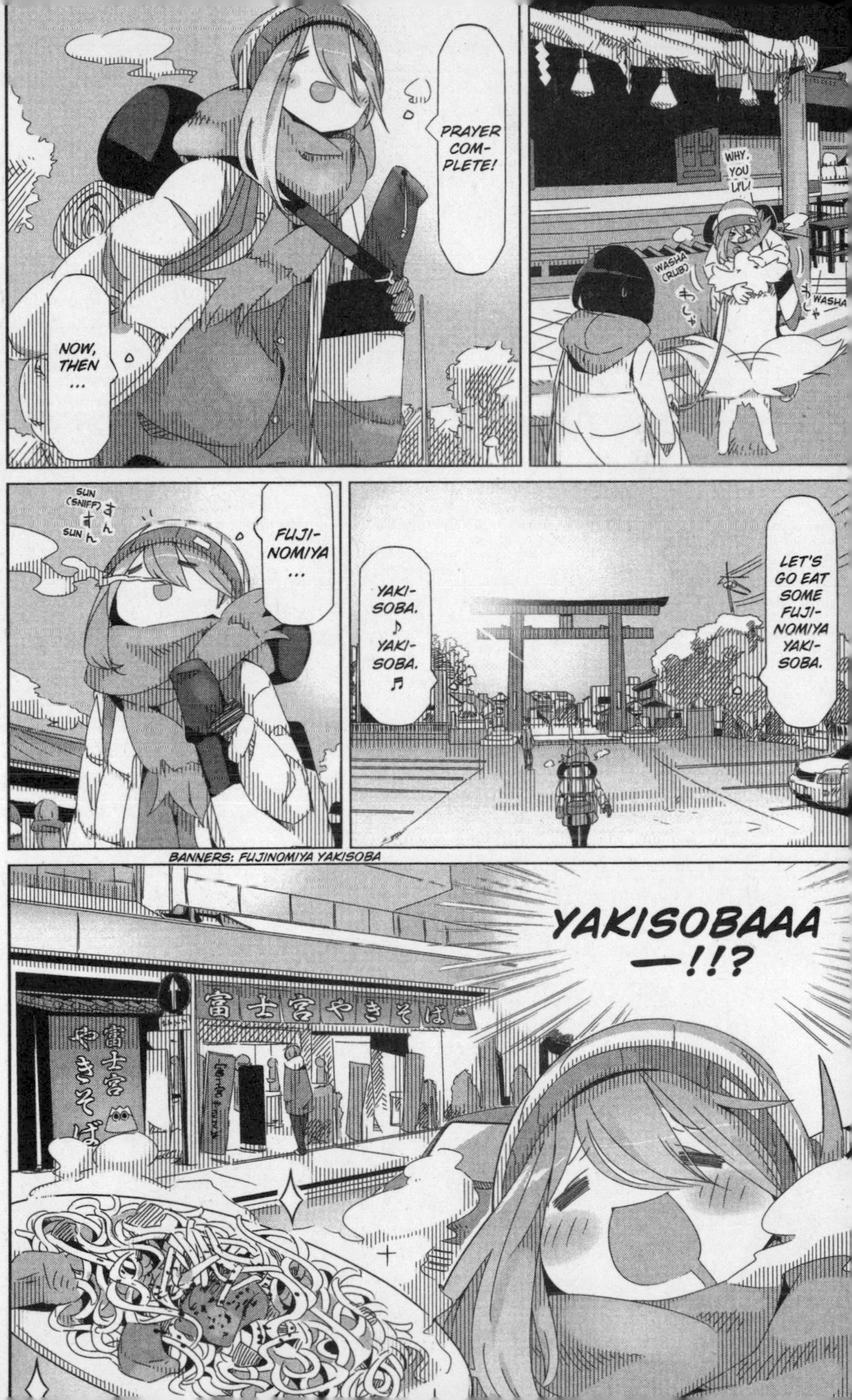
WHY, YOU LI'L!
WASHA (RUB)
わしゃ
WASHA
PRAYER COMPLETE!
NOW, THEN ...
LET'S GO EAT SOME FUJI-NOMIYA YAKI-SOBA.
YAKI-SOBA. ♪ YAKI-SOBA. ♬
FUJI-NOMIYA ...
SUN (SNIFF) すん
SUN すん
BANNERS: FUJINOMIYA YAKISOBA
YAKISOBAAA—!!?
富士宮やきそば
富士宮やきそば

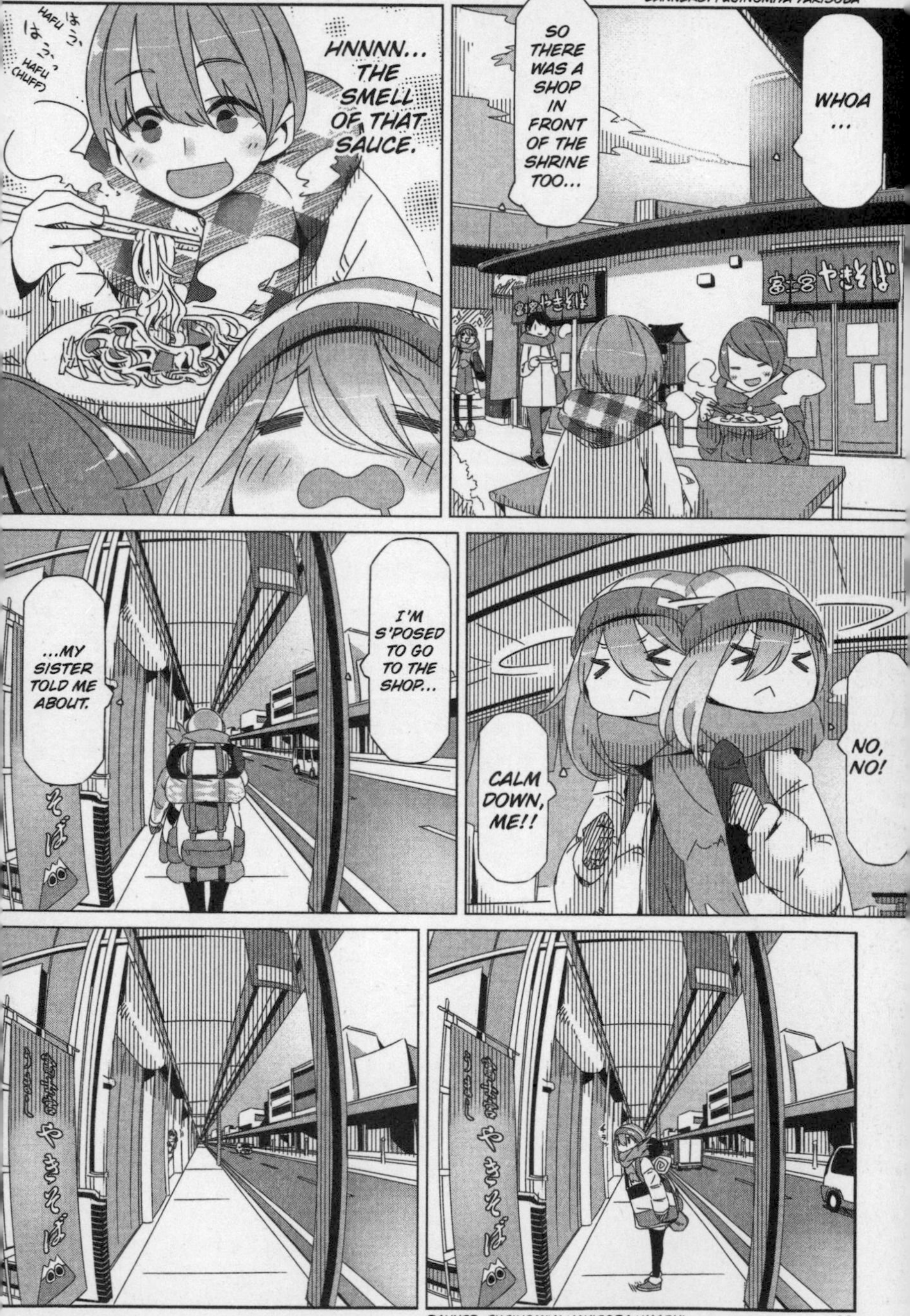
WHOA ...
SO THERE WAS A SHOP IN FRONT OF THE SHRINE TOO...
富士宮やきそば
HNNNN... THE SMELL OF THAT SAUCE.
はふ はふっ
HAFU HAFU (HUFF)
NO, NO!
CALM DOWN, ME!!
I'M S'POSED TO GO TO THE SHOP...
...MY SISTER TOLD ME ABOUT.
そば
やきそば
やきそば

BANNER: FUJINOMIYA YAKISOBA UMASHI

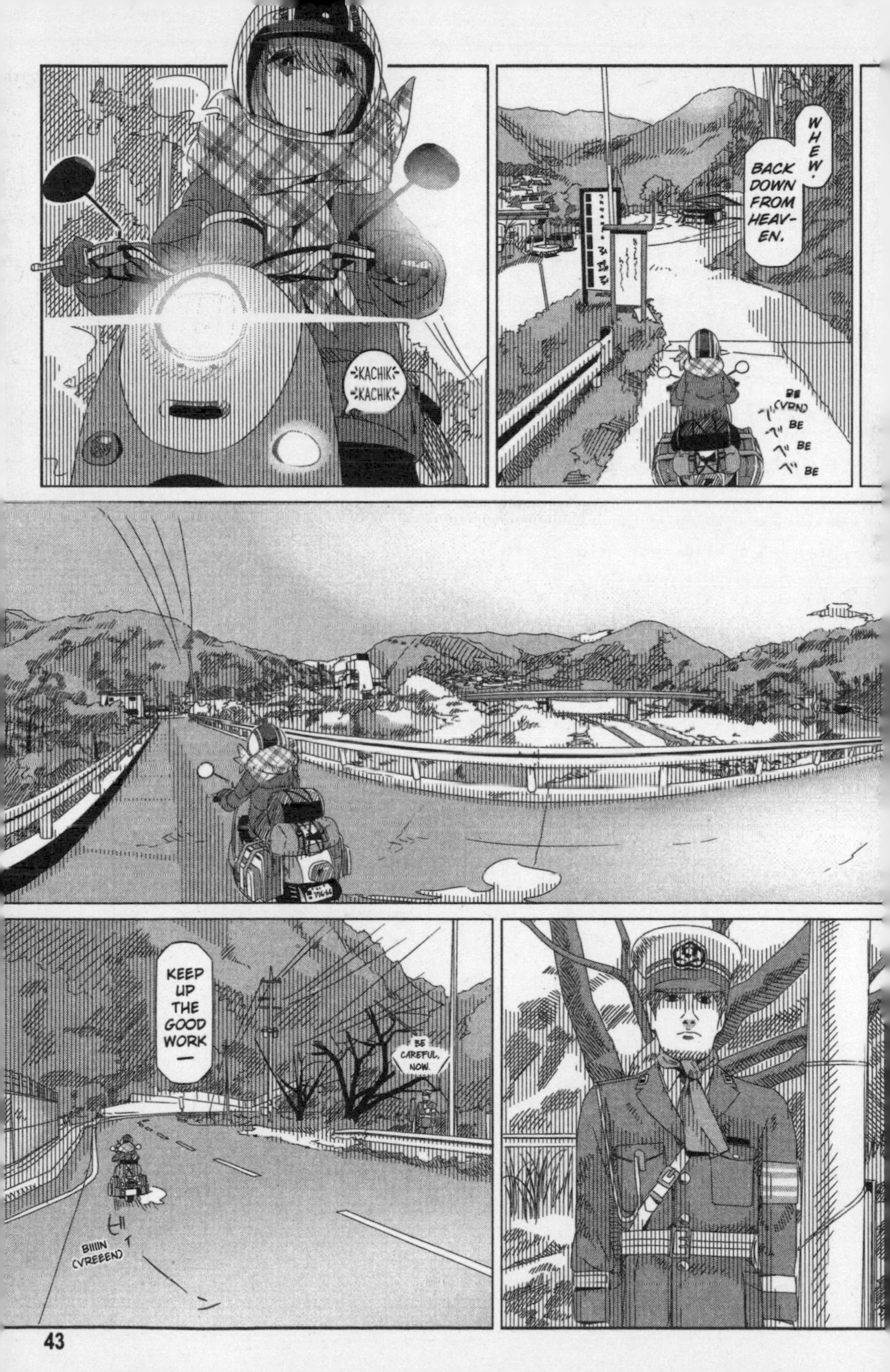
WHEW. BACK DOWN FROM HEAV-EN.
BE (VRN) BE BE BE
KACHIK KACHIK
KEEP UP THE GOOD WORK—
BE CAREFUL, NOW.
BIIIN (VREEEN)

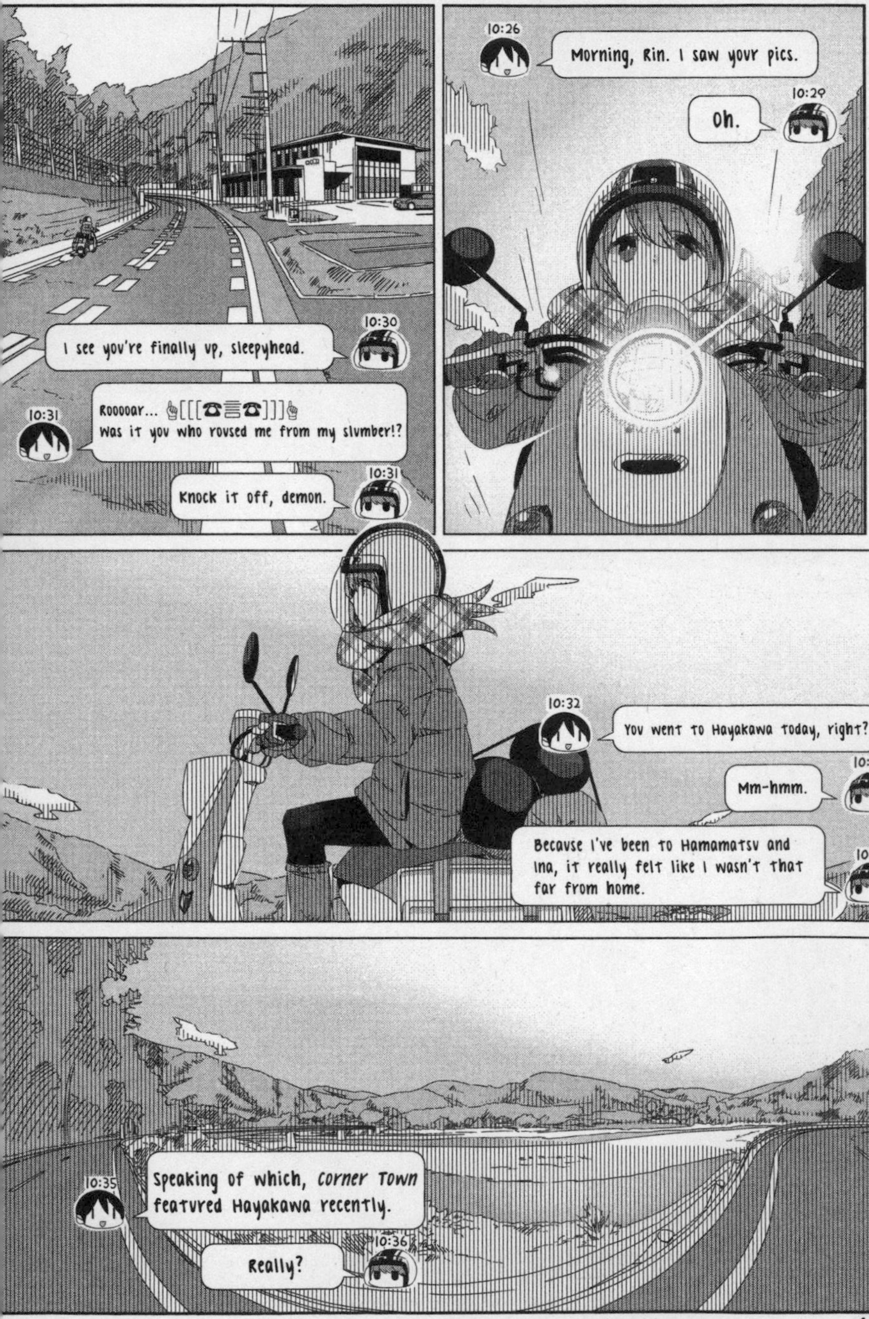
10:26
Morning, Rin. I saw your pics.
10:29
Oh.
10:30
I see you're finally up, sleepyhead.
10:31
Rooooar... ☝[[[☎☰☎]]]☝
Was it you who roused me from my slumber!?
10:31
Knock it off, demon.
10:32
You went to Hayakawa today, right?
10:33
Mm-hmm.
10:34
Because I've been to Hamamatsu and Ina, it really felt like I wasn't that far from home.
10:35
Speaking of which, *Corner Town* featured Hayakawa recently.
10:36
Really?

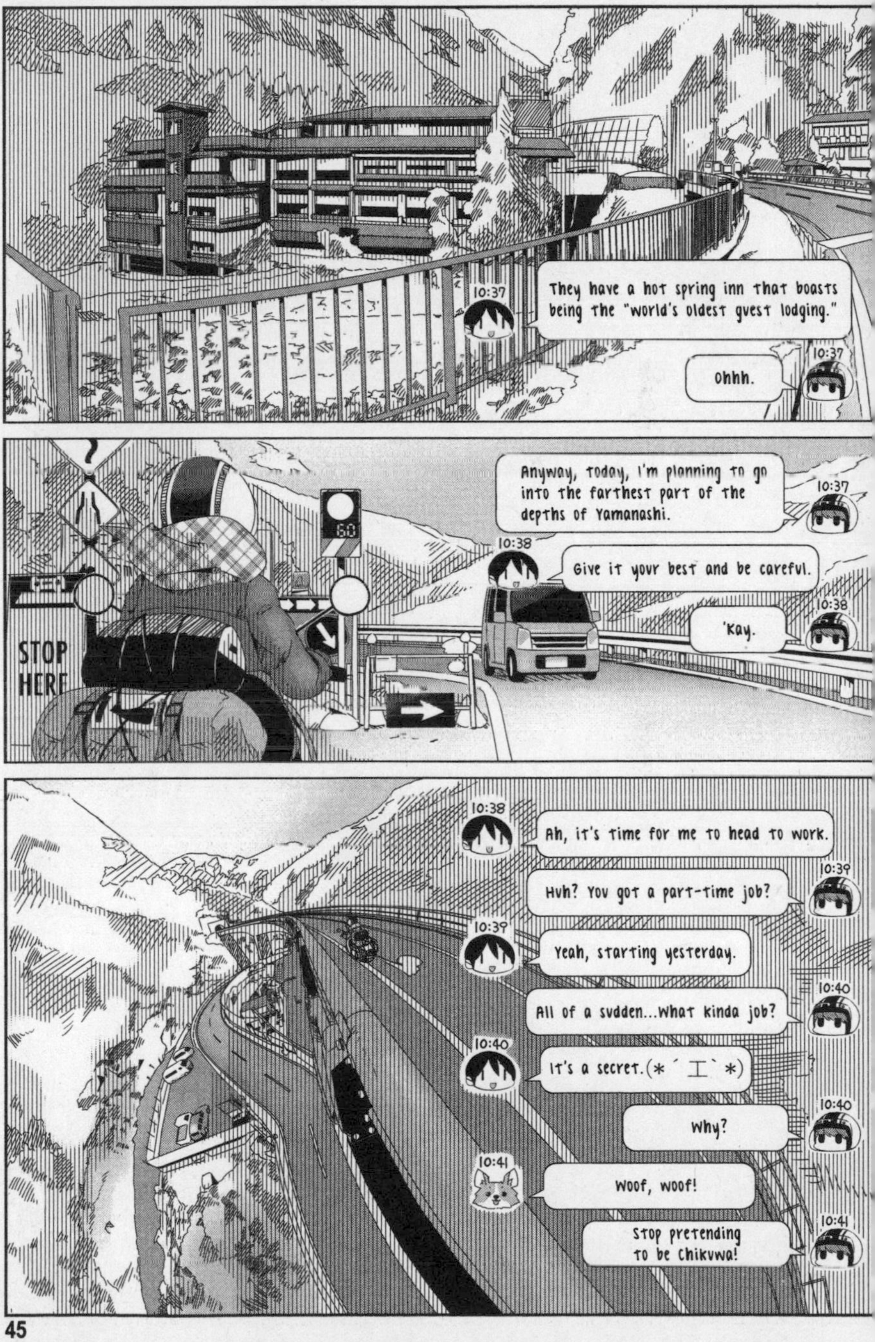
10:37
They have a hot spring inn that boasts being the "world's oldest guest lodging."
10:37
Ohhh.
10:37
Anyway, today, I'm planning to go into the farthest part of the depths of Yamanashi.
10:38
Give it your best and be careful.
10:38
'Kay.
60
STOP HERE
10:38
Ah, it's time for me to head to work.
10:39
Huh? You got a part-time job?
10:39
Yeah, starting yesterday.
10:40
All of a sudden...What kinda job?
10:40
It's a secret.(* ´工` *)
10:40
Why?
10:41
Woof, woof!
10:41
Stop pretending to be Chikuwa!

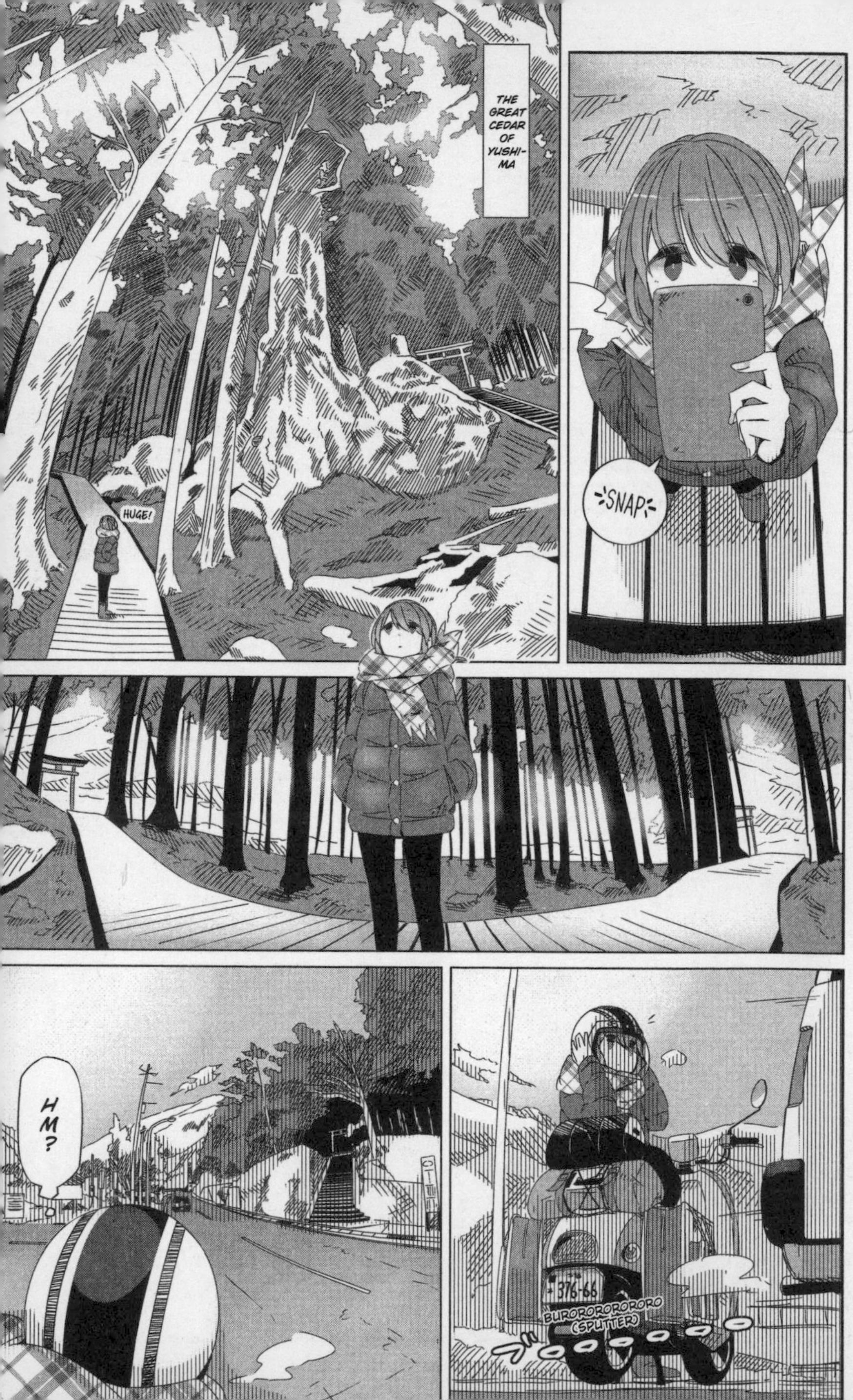
SNAP
THE GREAT CEDAR OF YUSHIMA
HUGE!
BURORORORORORO (SPUTTER)
HM?

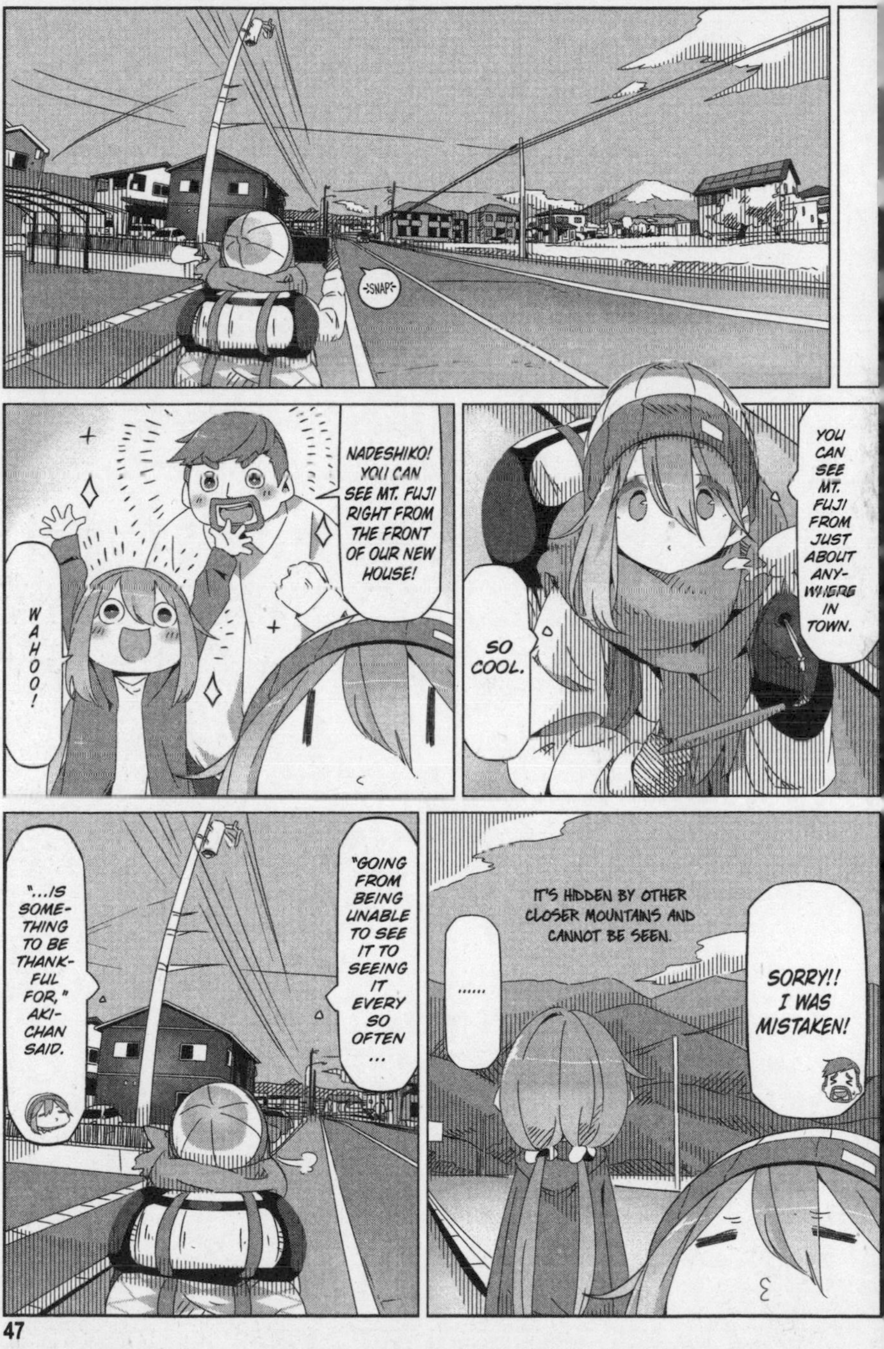
SNAP
YOU CAN SEE MT. FUJI FROM JUST ABOUT ANYWHERE IN TOWN.
SO COOL.
NADESHIKO! YOU CAN SEE MT. FUJI RIGHT FROM THE FRONT OF OUR NEW HOUSE!
WAHOO!
SORRY!! I WAS MISTAKEN!
IT'S HIDDEN BY OTHER CLOSER MOUNTAINS AND CANNOT BE SEEN.
......
"GOING FROM BEING UNABLE TO SEE IT TO SEEING IT EVERY SO OFTEN...
"...IS SOMETHING TO BE THANKFUL FOR," AKI-CHAN SAID.

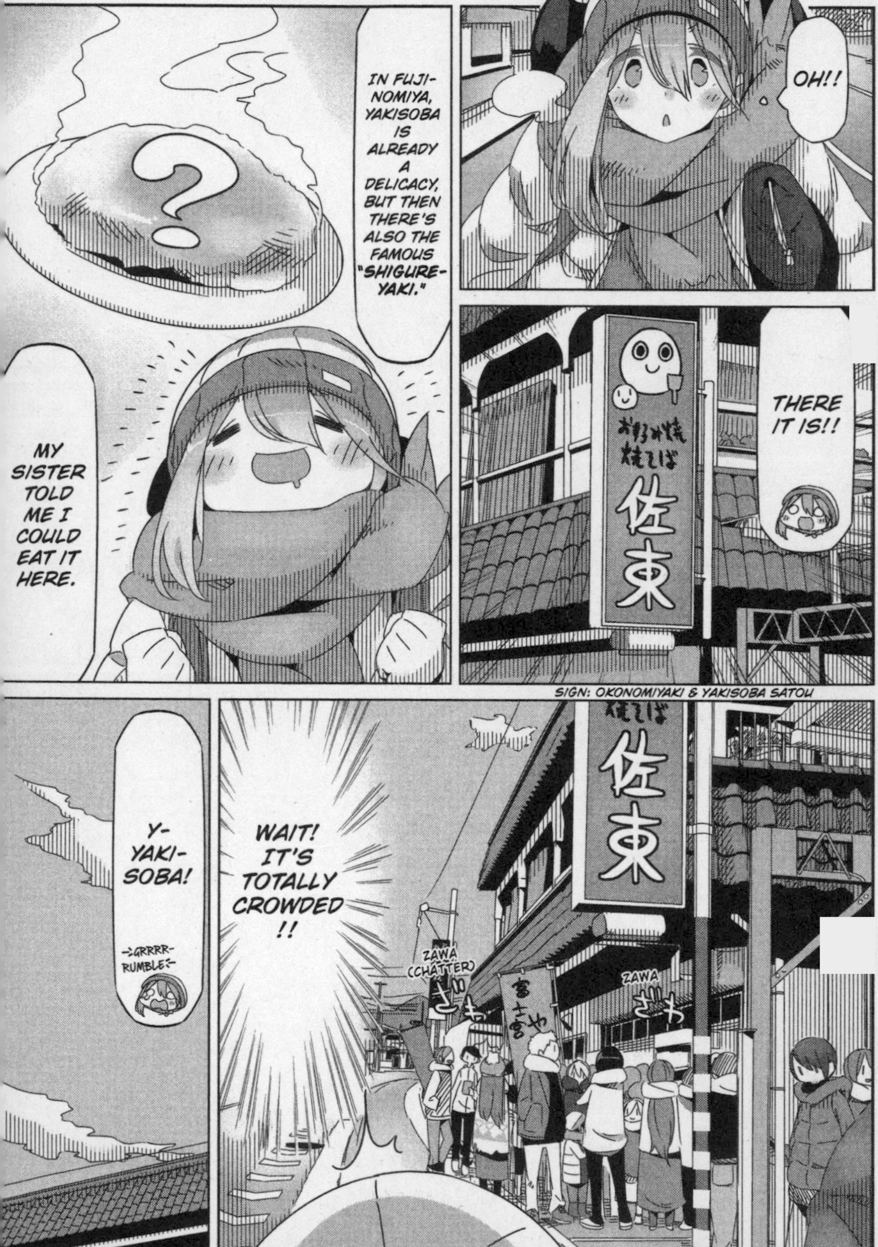
OH!!
THERE IT IS!!
お好み焼 焼そば 佐東
SIGN: OKONOMIYAKI & YAKISOBA SATOU
IN FUJI-NOMIYA, YAKISOBA IS ALREADY A DELICACY, BUT THEN THERE'S ALSO THE FAMOUS "SHIGURE-YAKI."
MY SISTER TOLD ME I COULD EAT IT HERE.
焼そば 佐東
WAIT! IT'S TOTALLY CROWDED!!
ZAWA (CHATTER)
ZAWA
Y-YAKI-SOBA!
GRRRR RUMBLE

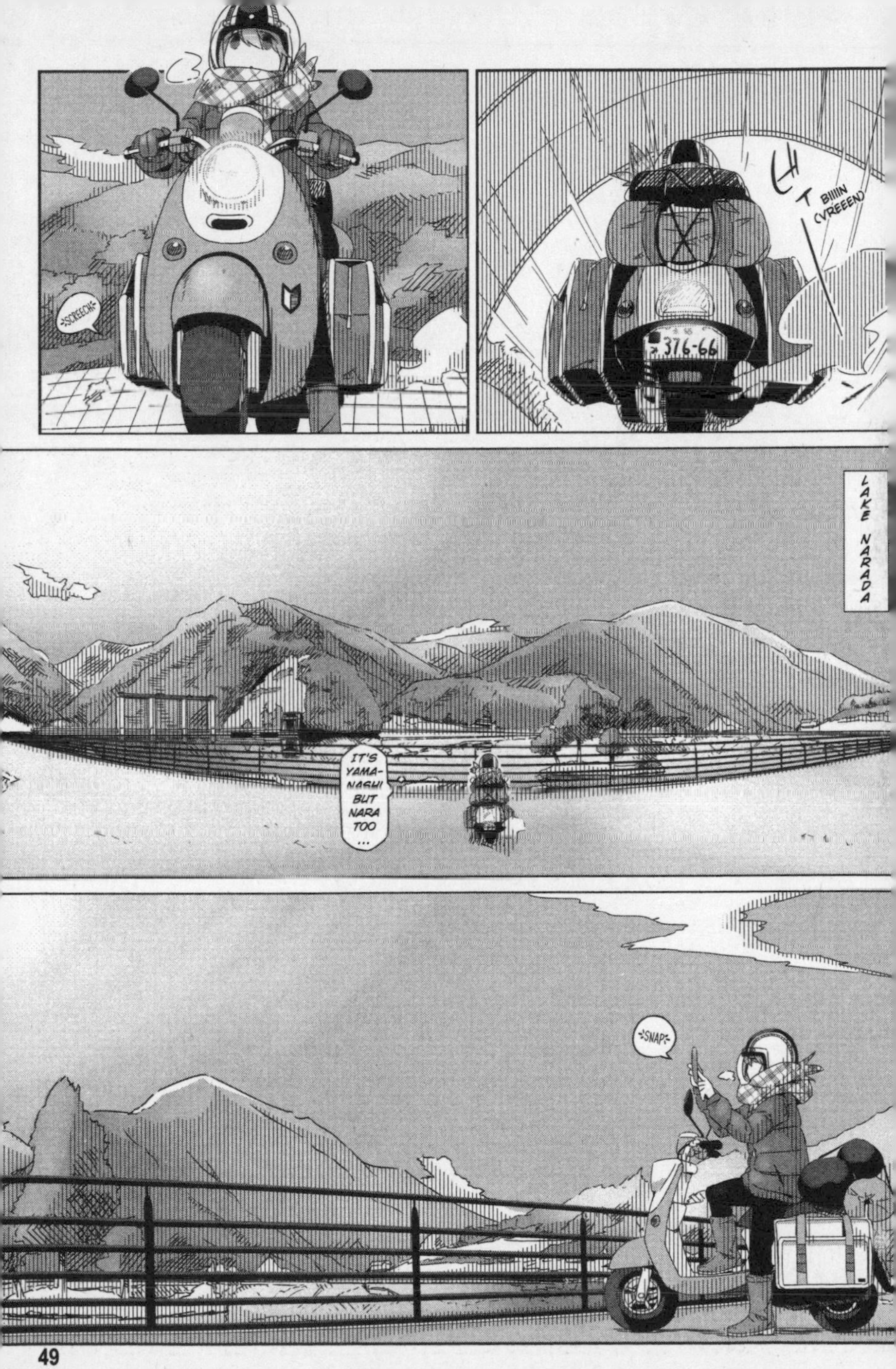
BIIIN (VREEEN)
376-66
SCREECH
LAKE NARADA
IT'S YAMANASHI BUT NARA TOO...
SNAP

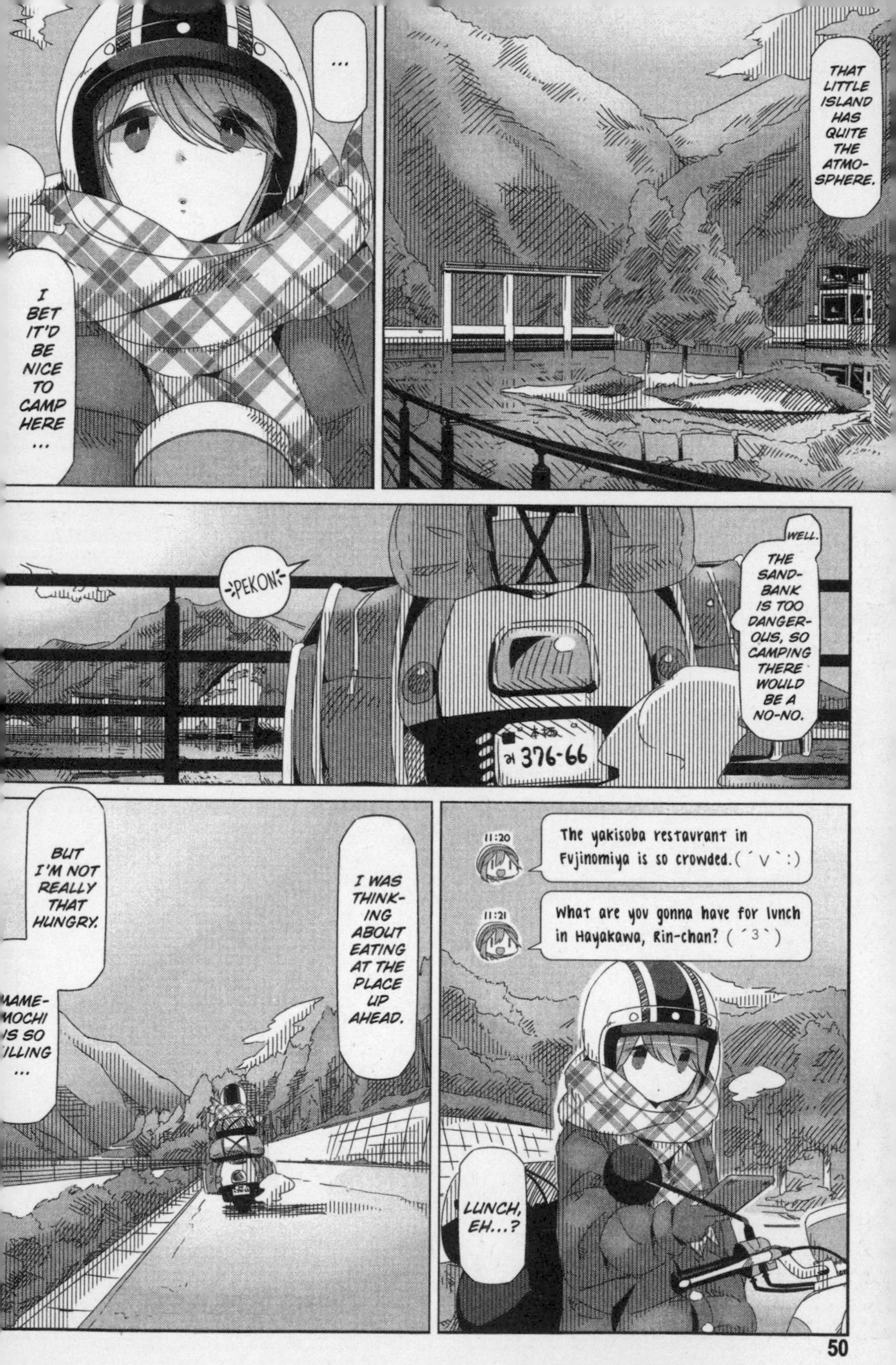
THAT LITTLE ISLAND HAS QUITE THE ATMOSPHERE.
...
I BET IT'D BE NICE TO CAMP HERE...
WELL.
THE SANDBANK IS TOO DANGEROUS, SO CAMPING THERE WOULD BE A NO-NO.
PEKON
11:20
The yakisoba restaurant in Fujinomiya is so crowded. (´∨`;)
11:21
What are you gonna have for lunch in Hayakawa, Rin-chan? (´3`)
LUNCH, EH...?
I WAS THINKING ABOUT EATING AT THE PLACE UP AHEAD.
BUT I'M NOT REALLY THAT HUNGRY.
MAME-MOCHI IS SO ILLING...

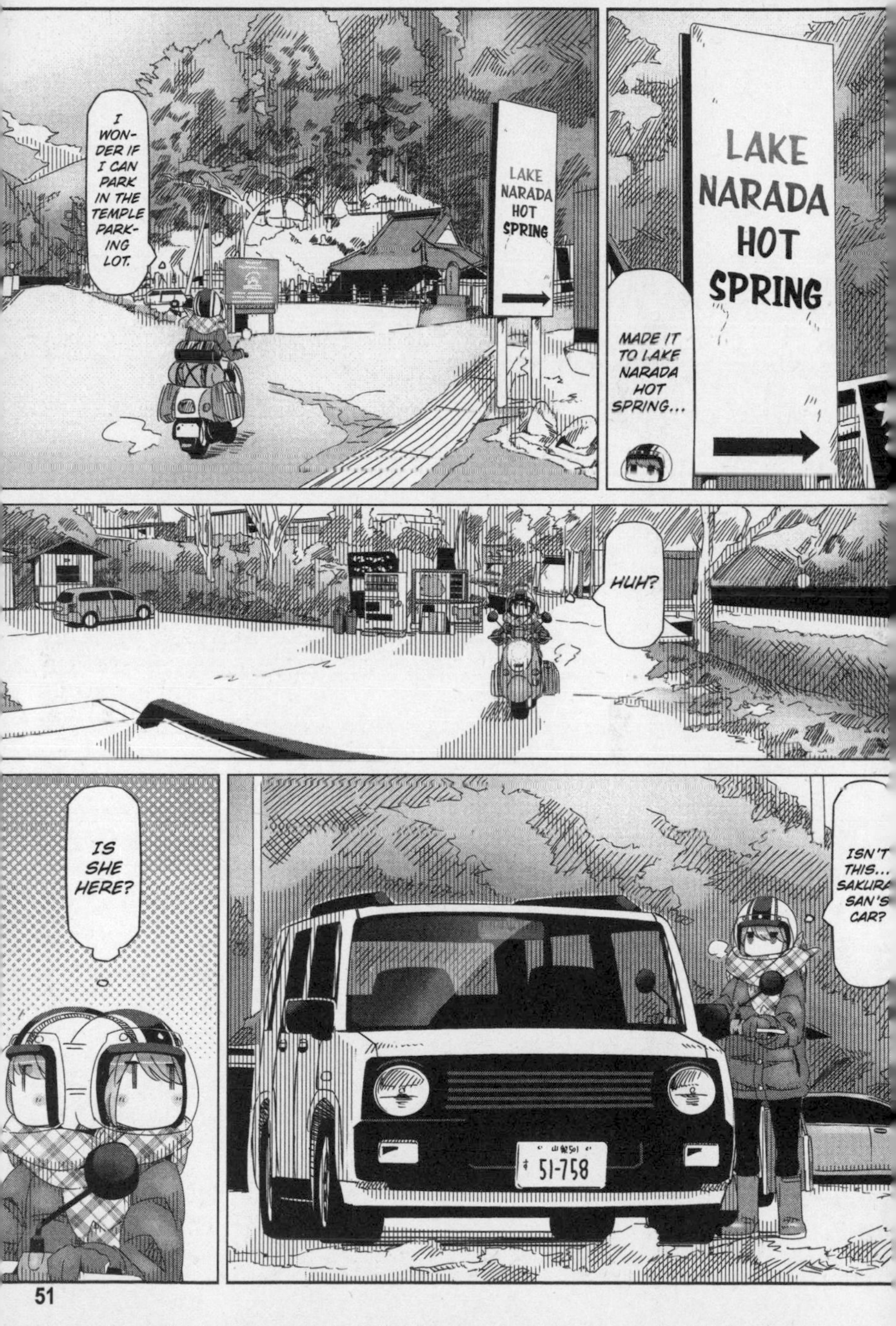
LAKE NARADA HOT SPRING
MADE IT TO LAKE NARADA HOT SPRING...
LAKE NARADA HOT SPRING
I WONDER IF I CAN PARK IN THE TEMPLE PARKING LOT.
HUH?
ISN'T THIS... SAKURA-SAN'S CAR?
51-758
IS SHE HERE?

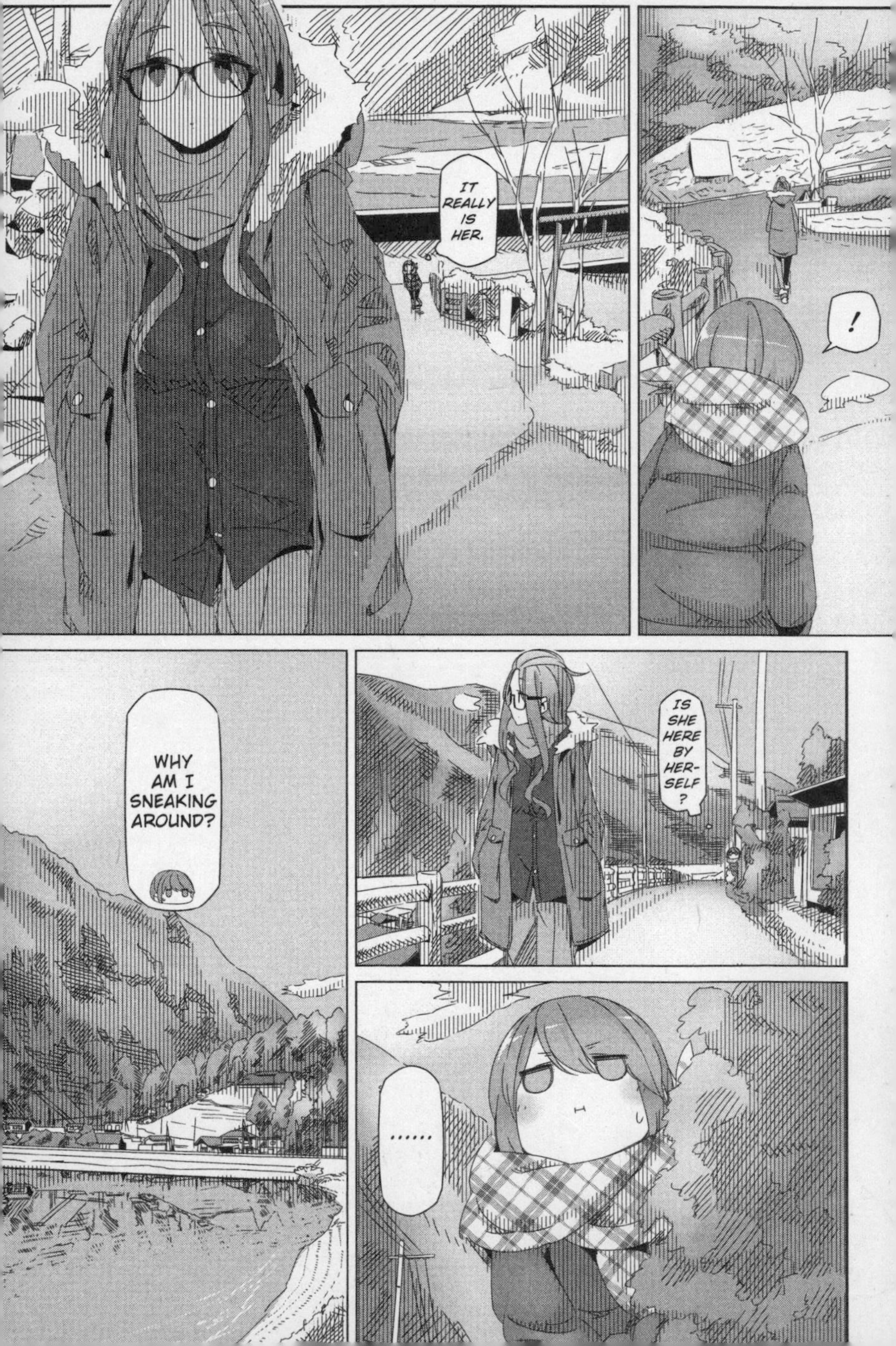
!
IT REALLY IS HER.
IS SHE HERE BY HER-SELF?
......
WHY AM I SNEAKING AROUND?

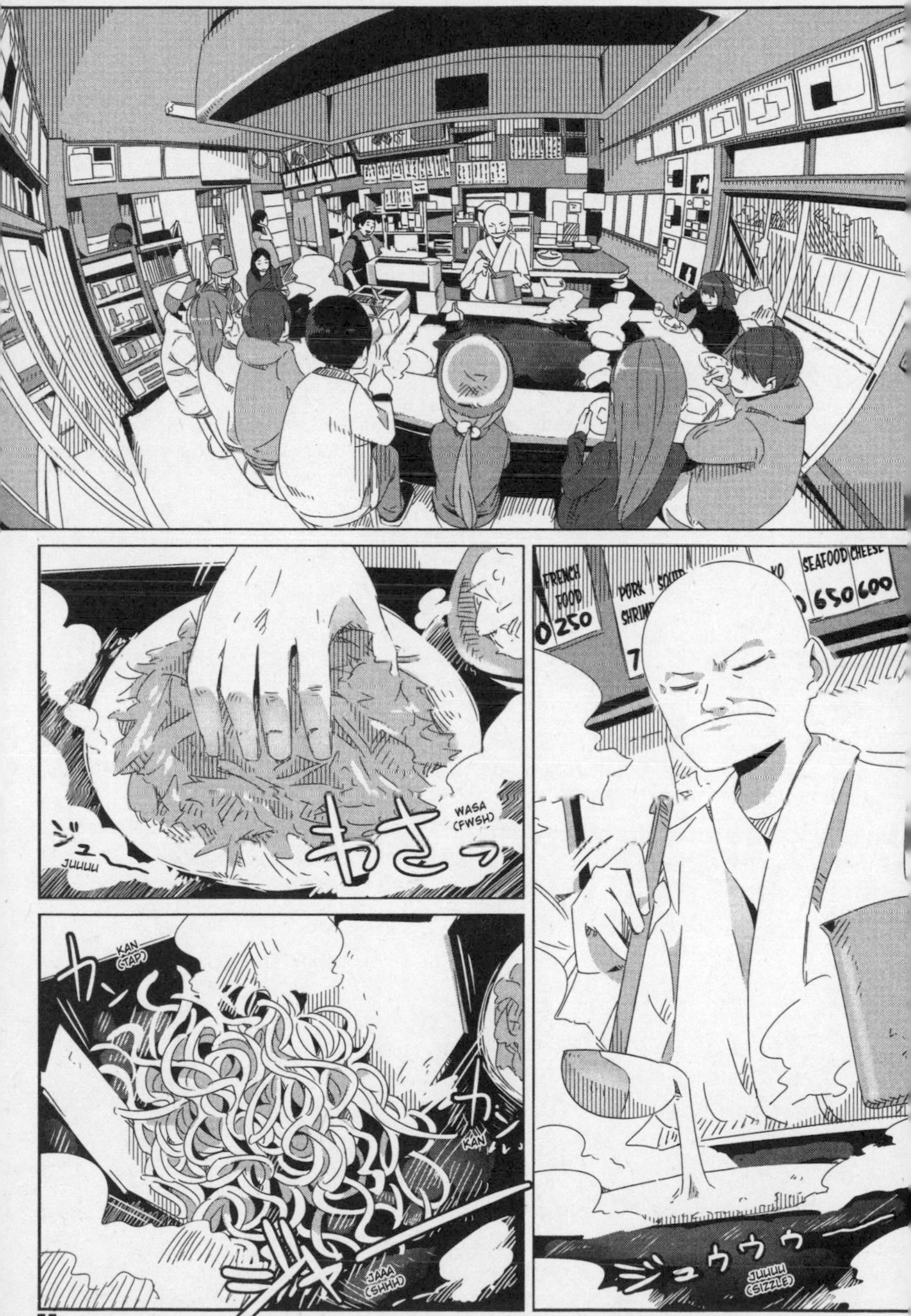
SEAFOOD CHEESE
650 600
FRENCH FOOD
250
PORK
SHRIMP
ジュウウウー
JUUUU (SIZZLE)
わさっ
WASA (FWSH)
ジュ
JUUUU
カン
KAN (TAP)
カン
KAN
ジャ
JAAA (SHHH)

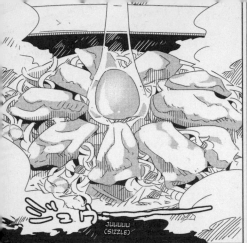

JUUUUU
(SIZZLE)

JIII
(STAAARE)

PORK
SHRIMP

650 600

SEAFOOD

JIII

WAIT TIME: 30 MINUTES

GUUUU
(GURGLE)

GU

NOT
LONG
NOW.

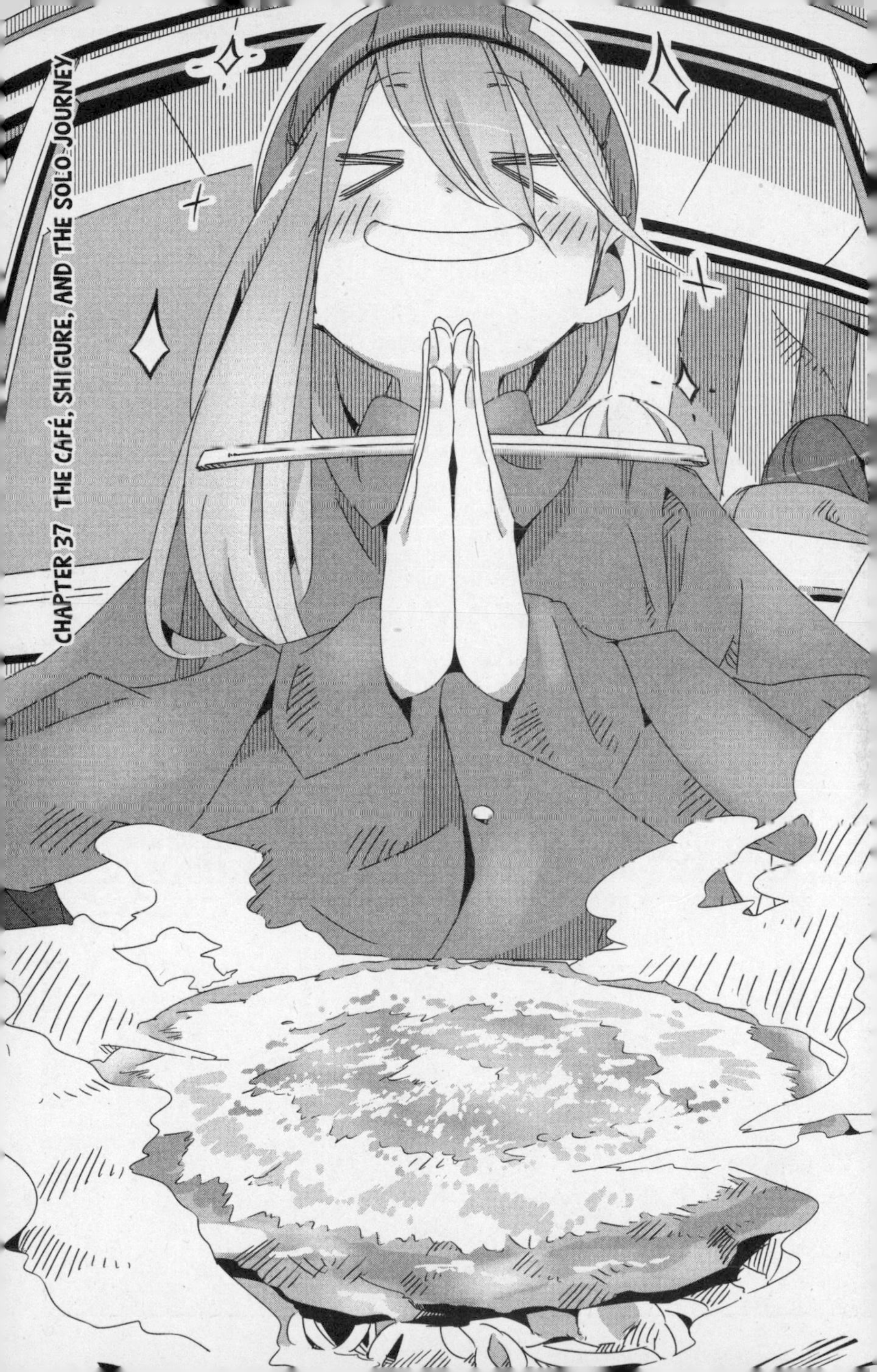
CHAPTER 37 THE CAFÉ, SHIGURE, AND THE SOLO JOURNEY

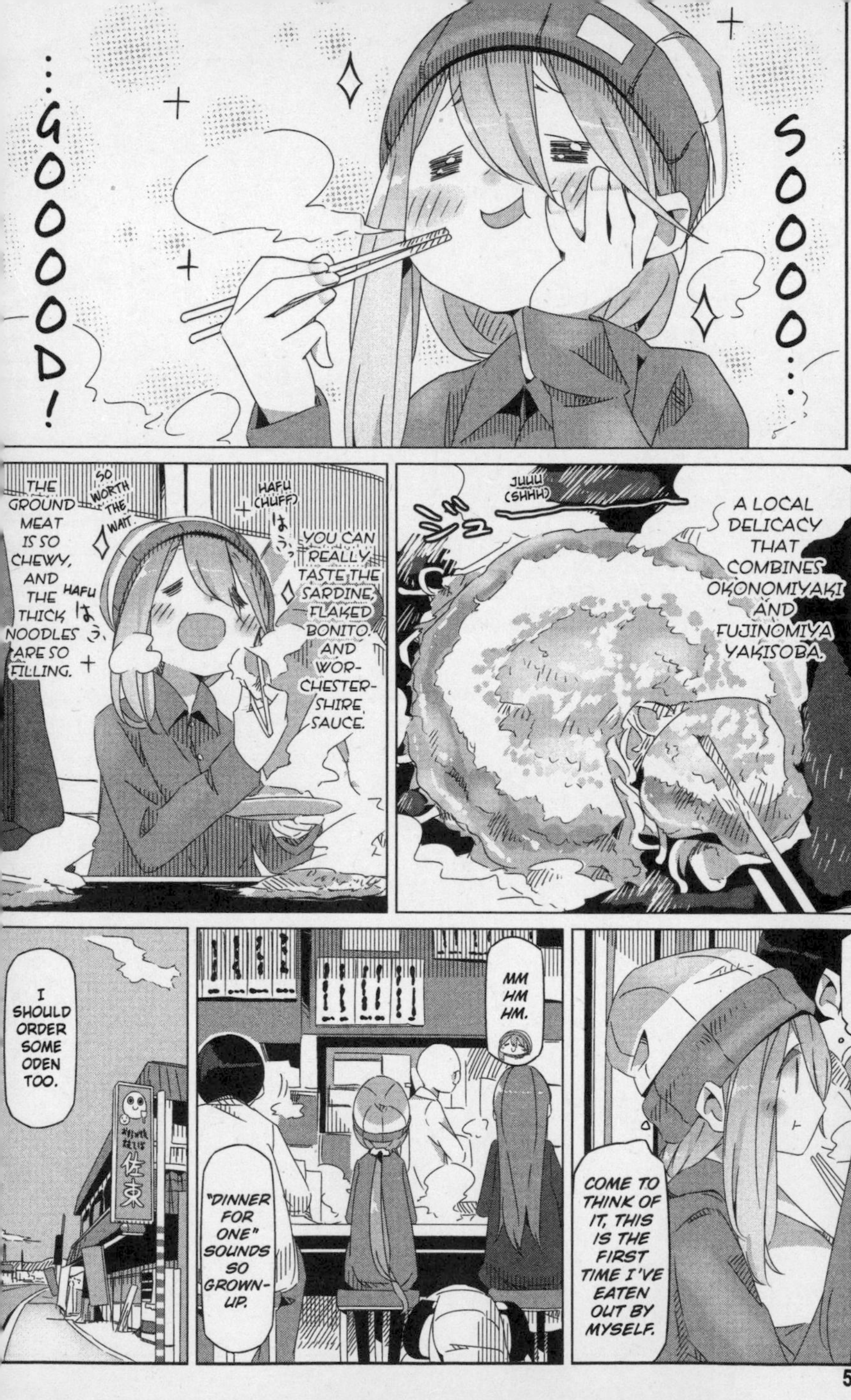
SOOOO...
...GOOOOD!
SHIGUREYAKI
JUUU (SHHH)
A LOCAL DELICACY THAT COMBINES OKONOMIYAKI AND FUJINOMIYA YAKISOBA.
YOU CAN REALLY TASTE THE SARDINE, FLAKED BONITO, AND WORCHESTERSHIRE SAUCE.
HAFU (CHUFF) はふ
SO WORTH THE WAIT.
HAFU はふ
THE GROUND MEAT IS SO CHEWY, AND THE THICK NOODLES ARE SO FILLING.
HUH?
COME TO THINK OF IT, THIS IS THE FIRST TIME I'VE EATEN OUT BY MYSELF.
MM HM HM.
"DINNER FOR ONE" SOUNDS SO GROWN-UP.
I SHOULD ORDER SOME ODEN TOO.
佐東

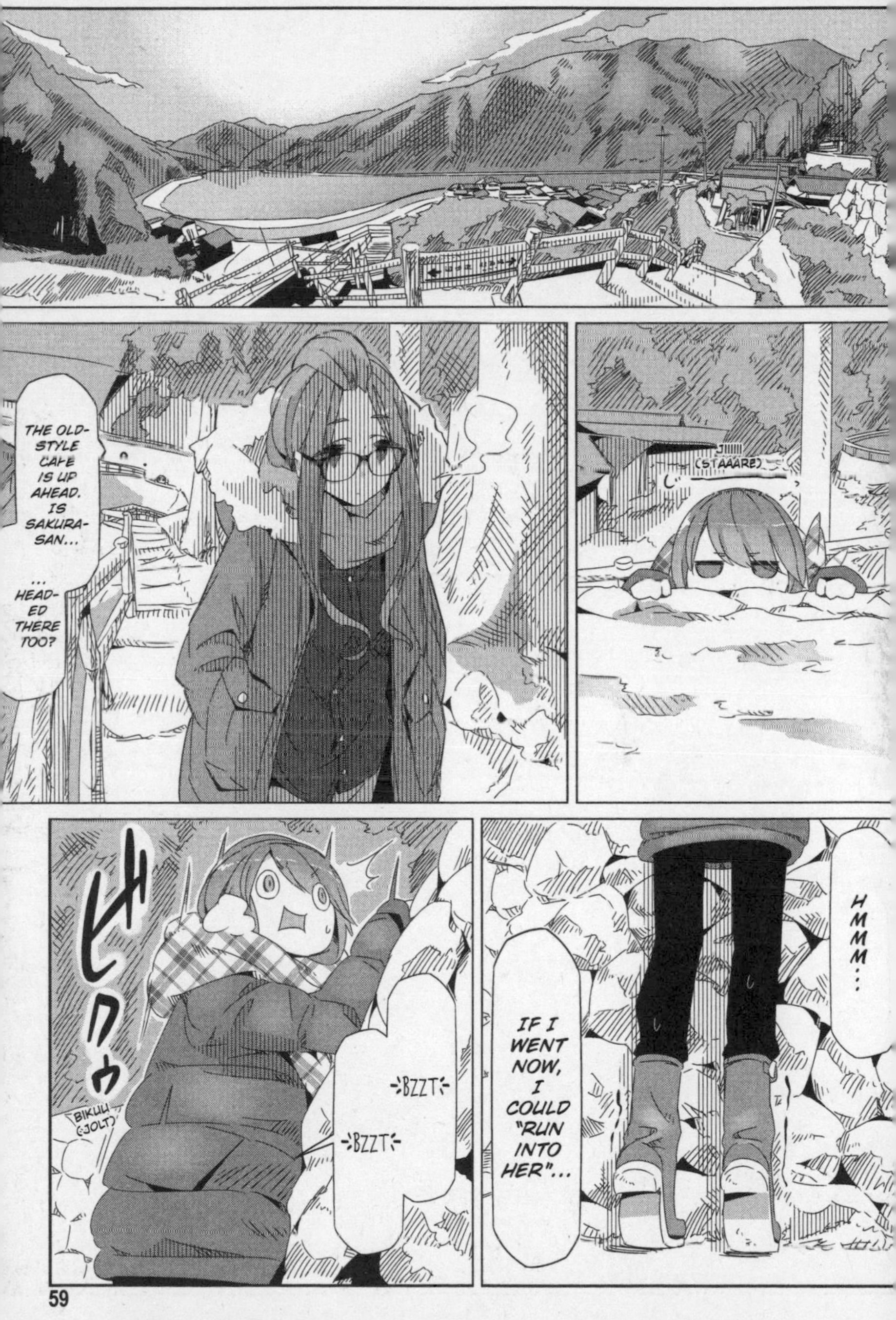
JIIIII (STAAARE)
THE OLD-STYLE CAFE IS UP AHEAD. IS SAKURA-SAN...
...HEADED THERE TOO?
HMMM...
IF I WENT NOW, I COULD "RUN INTO HER"...
ビクゥ
BIKUU (JOLT)
BZZT
BZZT

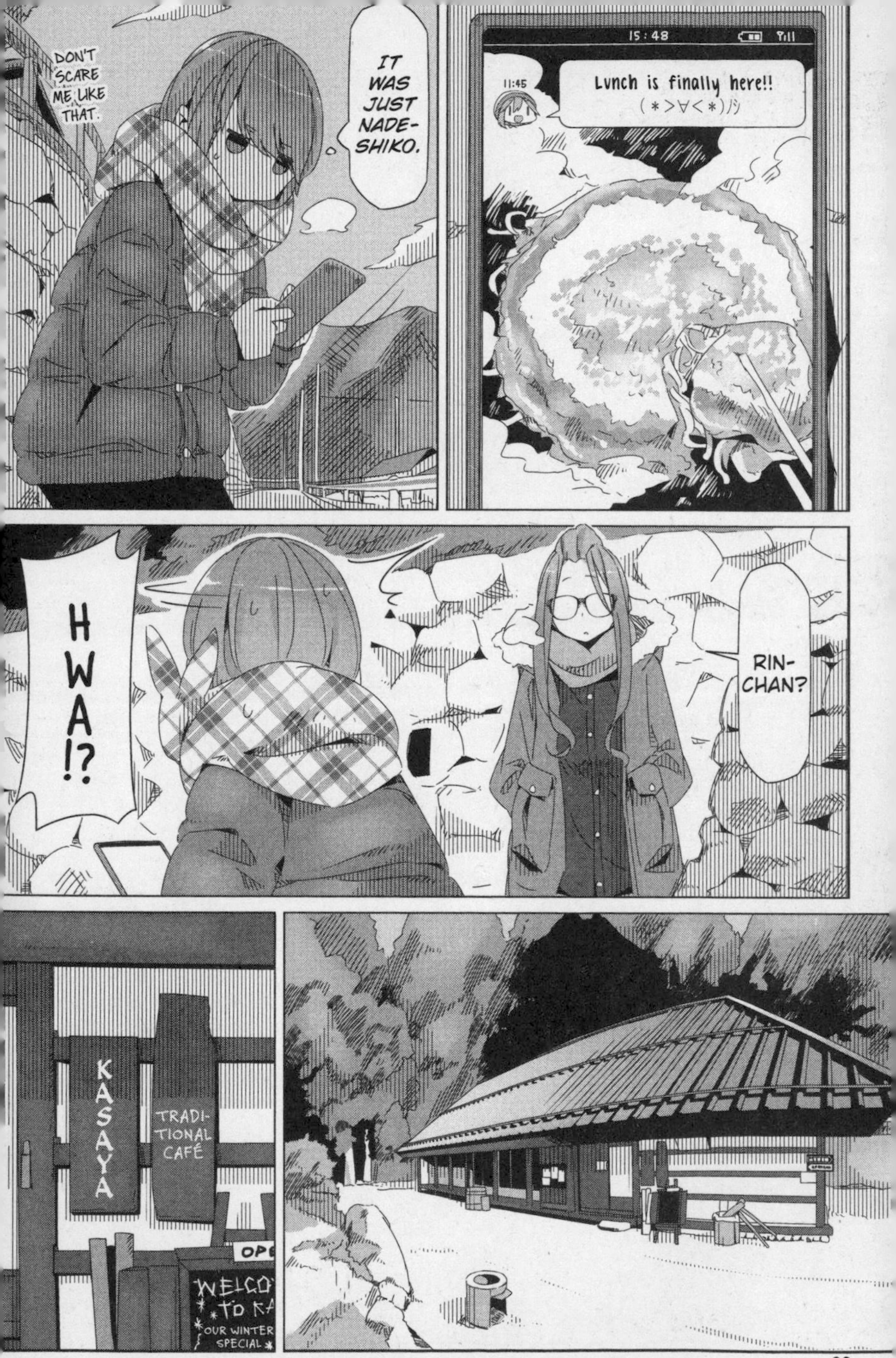
15:48
11:45
Lvnch is finally here!!
(*>∀<*)ﾉｼ
IT WAS JUST NADE-SHIKO.
DON'T SCARE ME LIKE THAT.
RIN-CHAN?
HWA!?
KASAYA
TRADI-TIONAL CAFÉ
OPE
WELCO
TO KA
OUR WINTER SPECIAL

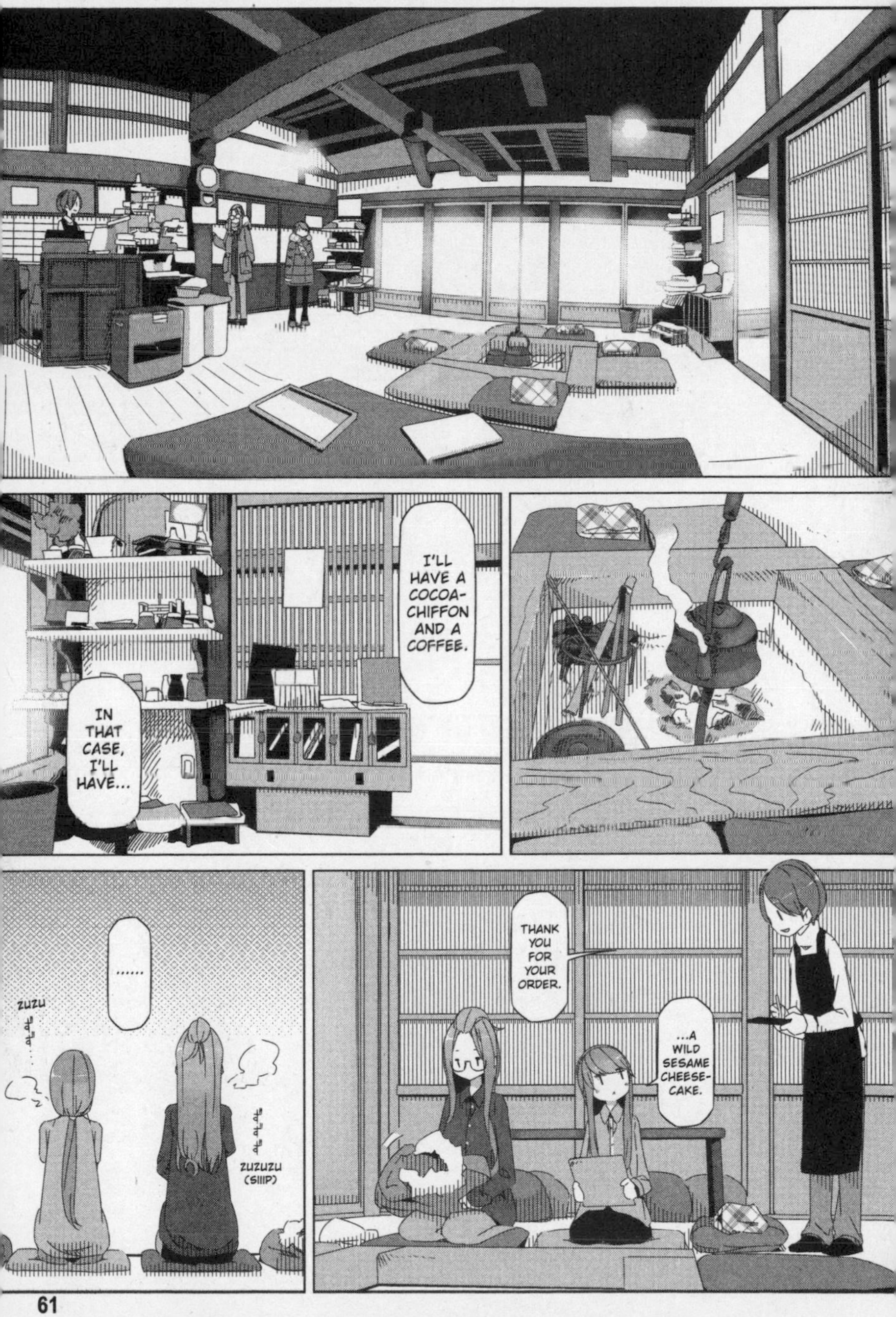
I'LL HAVE A COCOA-CHIFFON AND A COFFEE.
IN THAT CASE, I'LL HAVE...
...A WILD SESAME CHEESE-CAKE.
THANK YOU FOR YOUR ORDER.
......
ZUZU
ZUZUZU (SIIIP)

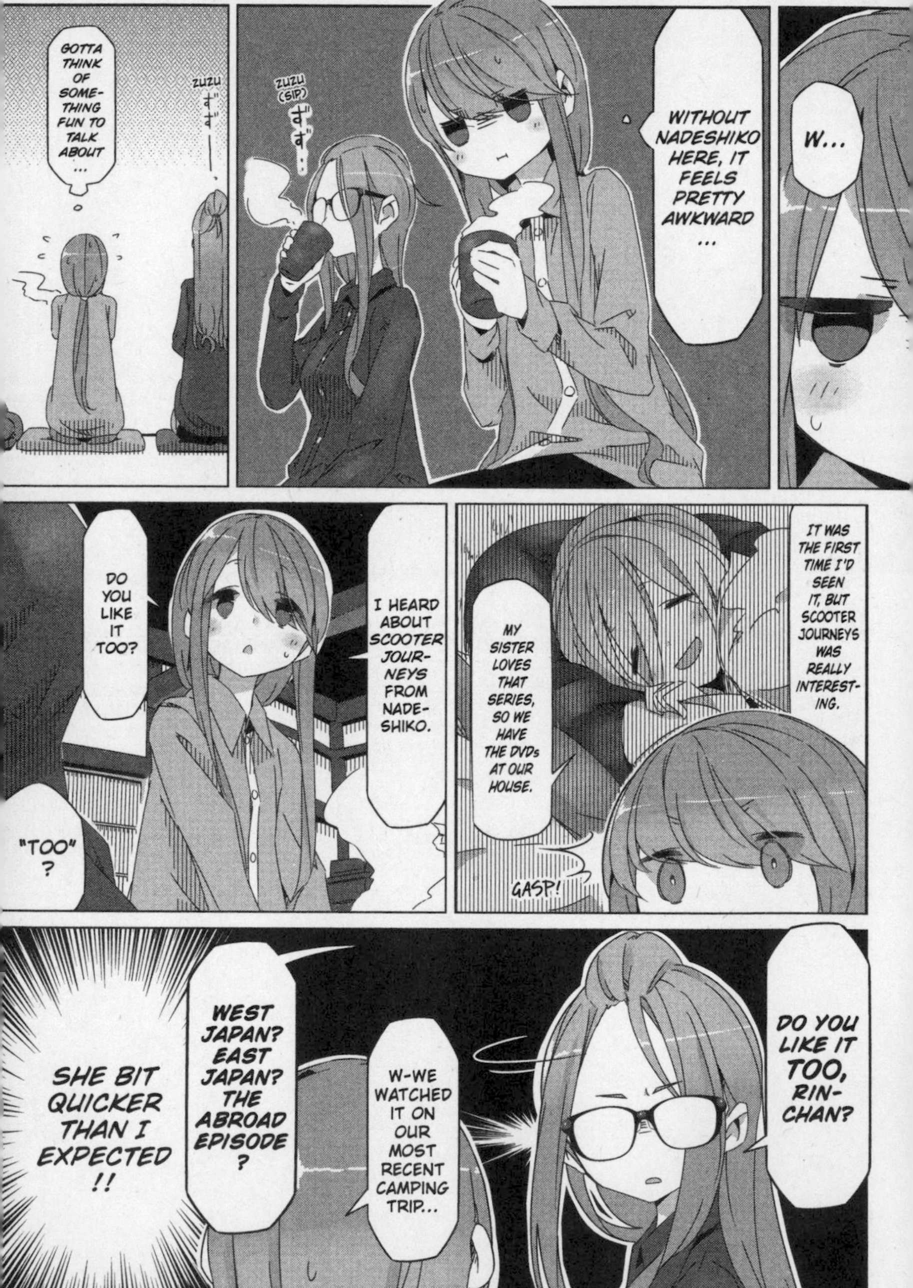
W...
WITHOUT NADESHIKO HERE, IT FEELS PRETTY AWKWARD...
ZUZU (SIP) ずず…
ZUZU ずずー
GOTTA THINK OF SOMETHING FUN TO TALK ABOUT...
IT WAS THE FIRST TIME I'D SEEN IT, BUT SCOOTER JOURNEYS WAS REALLY INTERESTING.
MY SISTER LOVES THAT SERIES, SO WE HAVE THE DVDs AT OUR HOUSE.
GASP!
I HEARD ABOUT SCOOTER JOURNEYS FROM NADESHIKO.
DO YOU LIKE IT TOO?
"TOO"?
DO YOU LIKE IT TOO, RIN-CHAN?
W-WE WATCHED IT ON OUR MOST RECENT CAMPING TRIP...
WEST JAPAN? EAST JAPAN? THE ABROAD EPISODE?
SHE BIT QUICKER THAN I EXPECTED!!

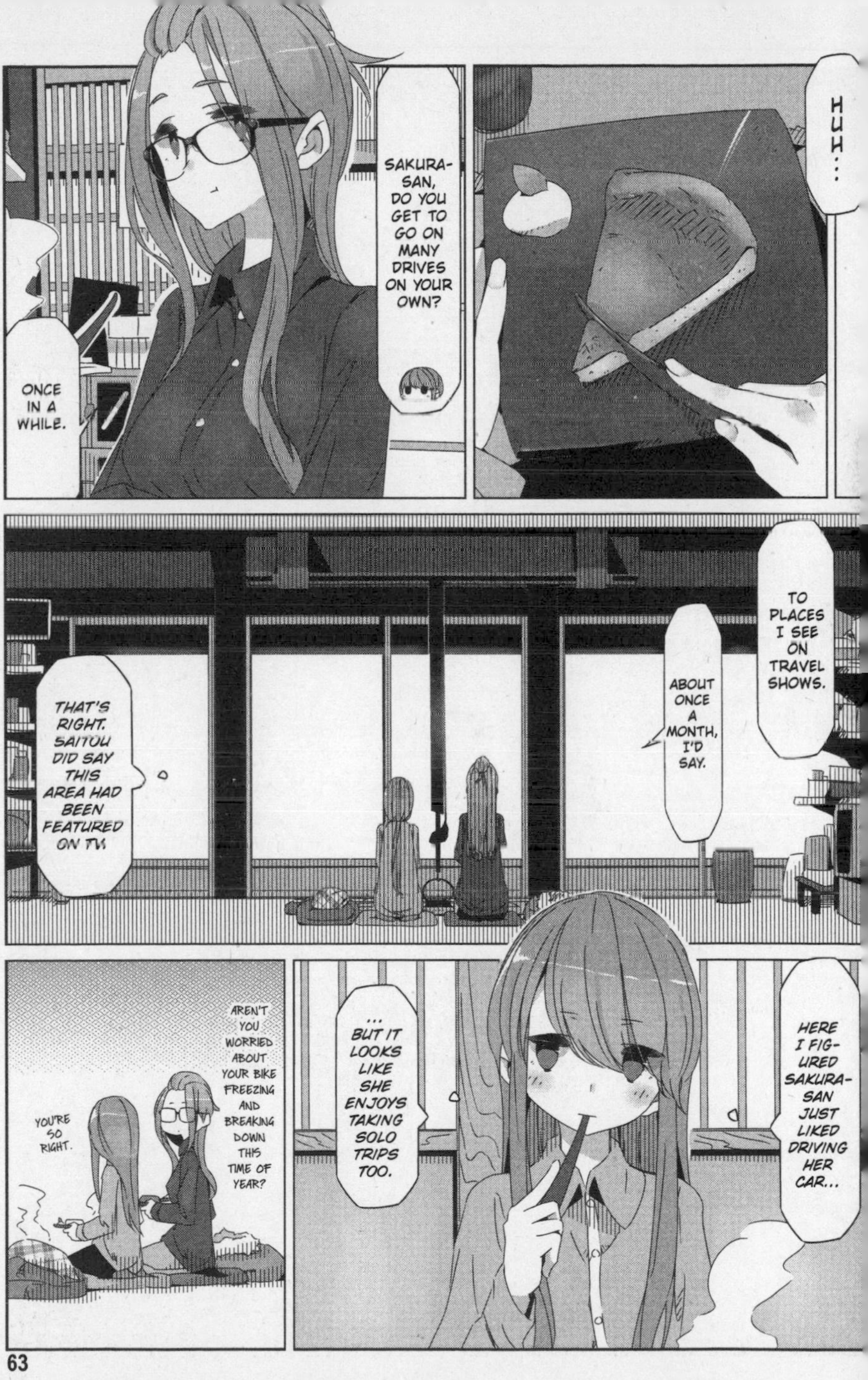
HUH...
SAKURA-SAN, DO YOU GET TO GO ON MANY DRIVES ON YOUR OWN?
ONCE IN A WHILE.
TO PLACES I SEE ON TRAVEL SHOWS.
ABOUT ONCE A MONTH, I'D SAY.
THAT'S RIGHT. SAITOU DID SAY THIS AREA HAD BEEN FEATURED ON TV.
HERE I FIG-URED SAKURA-SAN JUST LIKED DRIVING HER CAR...
...BUT IT LOOKS LIKE SHE ENJOYS TAKING SOLO TRIPS TOO.
AREN'T YOU WORRIED ABOUT YOUR BIKE FREEZING AND BREAKING DOWN THIS TIME OF YEAR?
YOU'RE SO RIGHT.

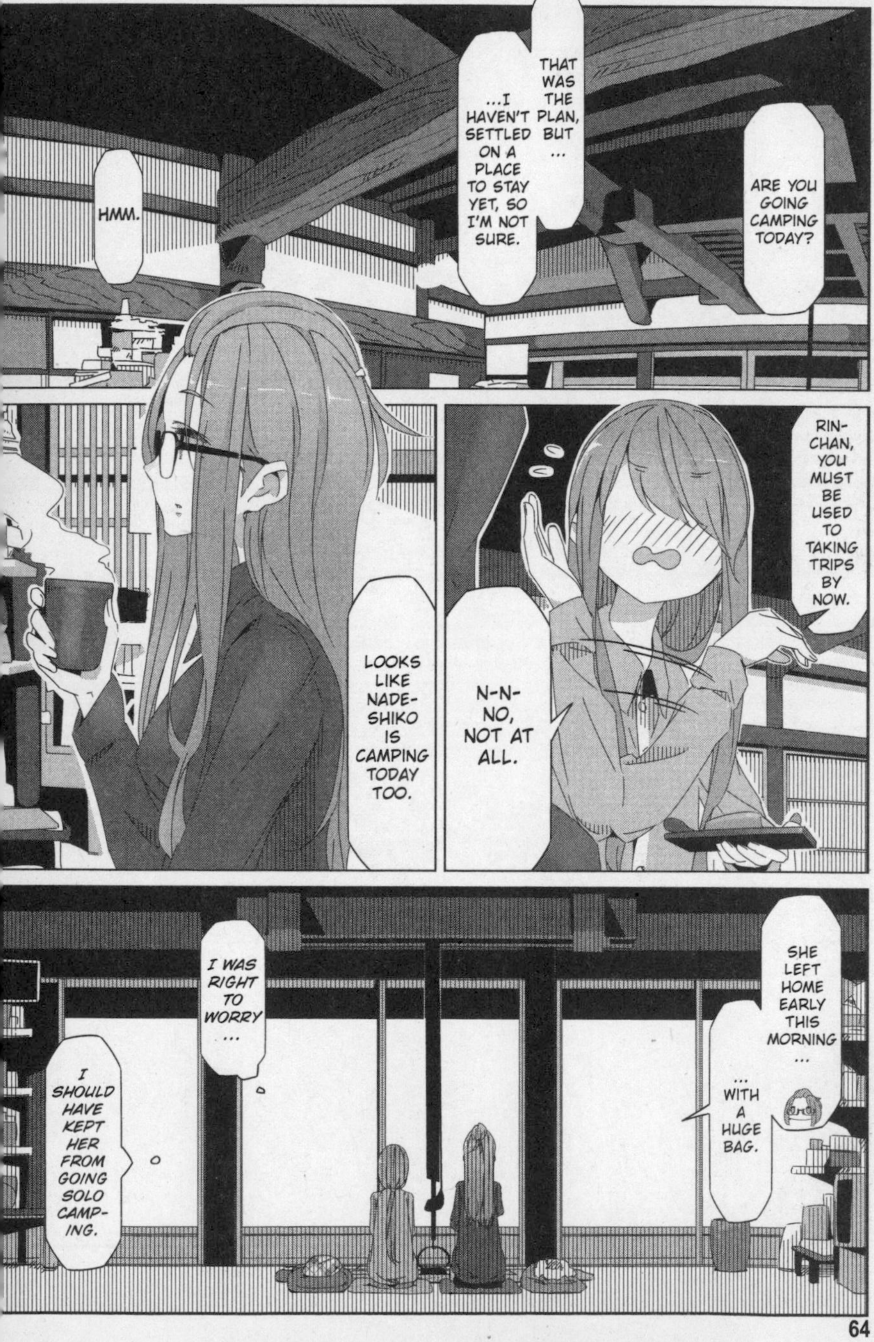
ARE YOU GOING CAMPING TODAY?
THAT WAS THE PLAN, BUT ...
...I HAVEN'T SETTLED ON A PLACE TO STAY YET, SO I'M NOT SURE.
HMM.
RIN-CHAN, YOU MUST BE USED TO TAKING TRIPS BY NOW.
N-N-NO, NOT AT ALL.
LOOKS LIKE NADESHIKO IS CAMPING TODAY TOO.
SHE LEFT HOME EARLY THIS MORNING ...
...WITH A HUGE BAG.
I WAS RIGHT TO WORRY ...
I SHOULD HAVE KEPT HER FROM GOING SOLO CAMPING.

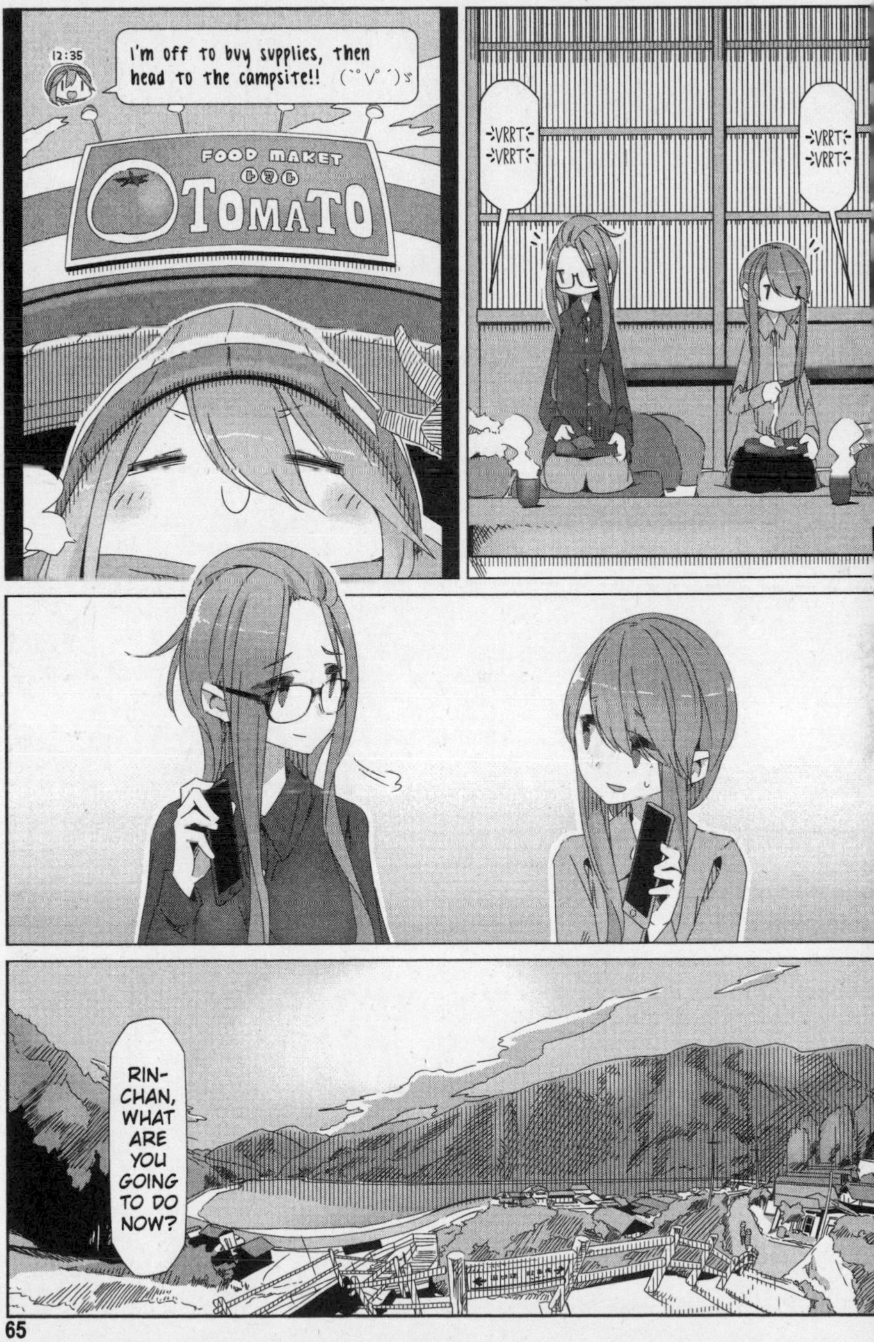

-VRRT- -VRRT-
-VRRT- -VRRT-
12:35
I'm off to buy supplies, then head to the campsite!! (`°V°´)ゞ
FOOD MAKET TOMATO
RIN-CHAN, WHAT ARE YOU GOING TO DO NOW?

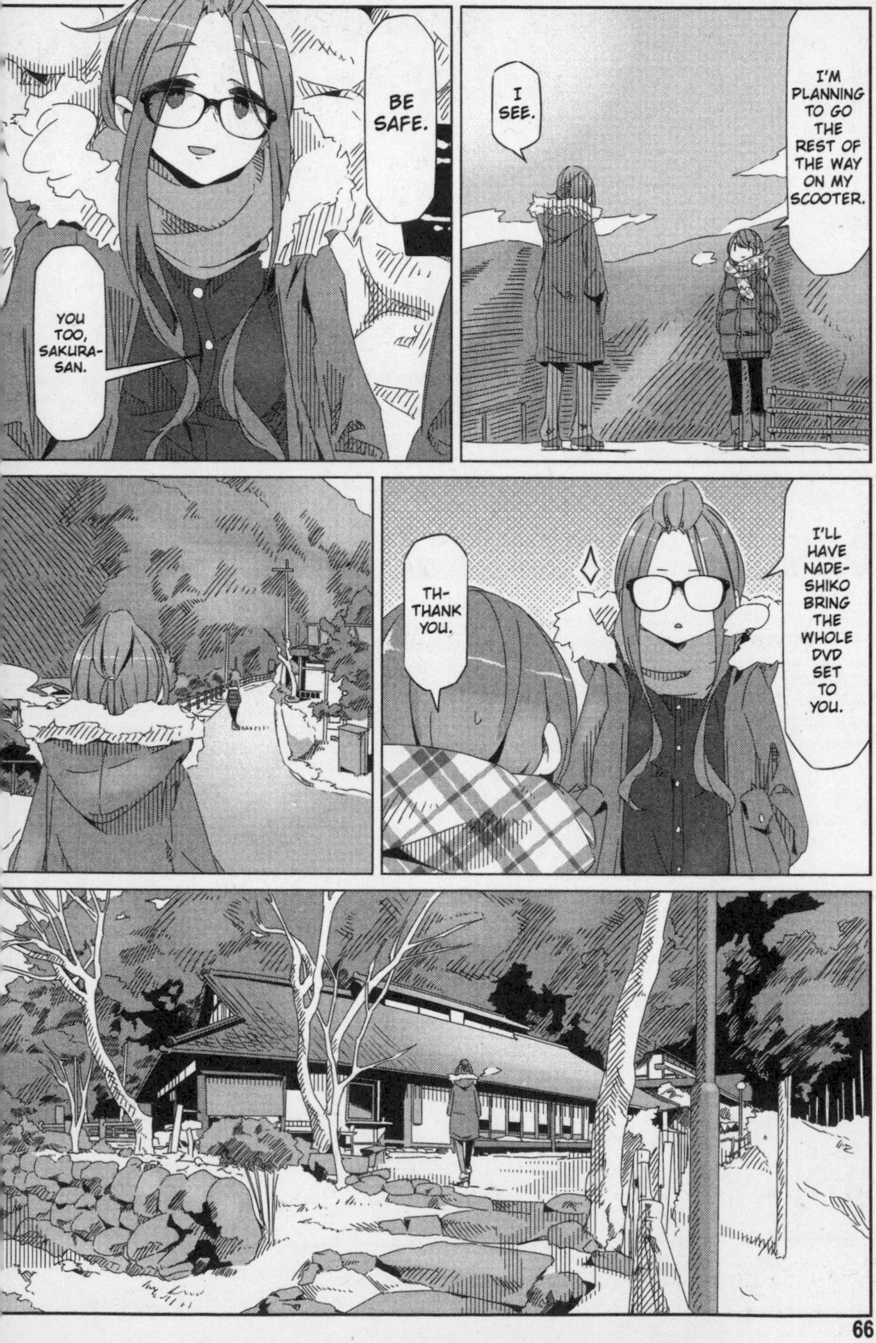
I'M PLANNING TO GO THE REST OF THE WAY ON MY SCOOTER.
I SEE.
BE SAFE.
YOU TOO, SAKURA-SAN.
I'LL HAVE NADE-SHIKO BRING THE WHOLE DVD SET TO YOU.
TH-THANK YOU.

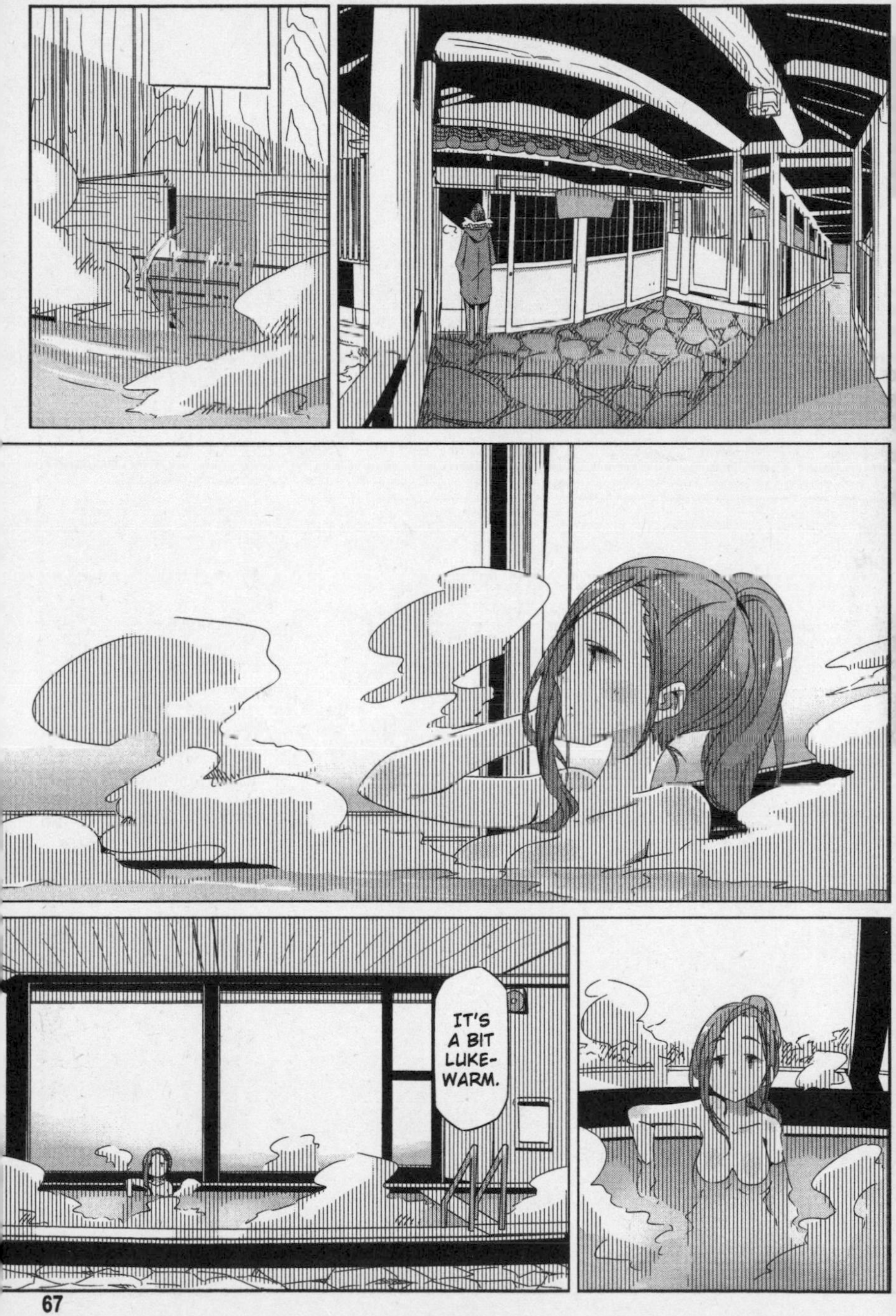
IT'S A BIT LUKE-WARM.

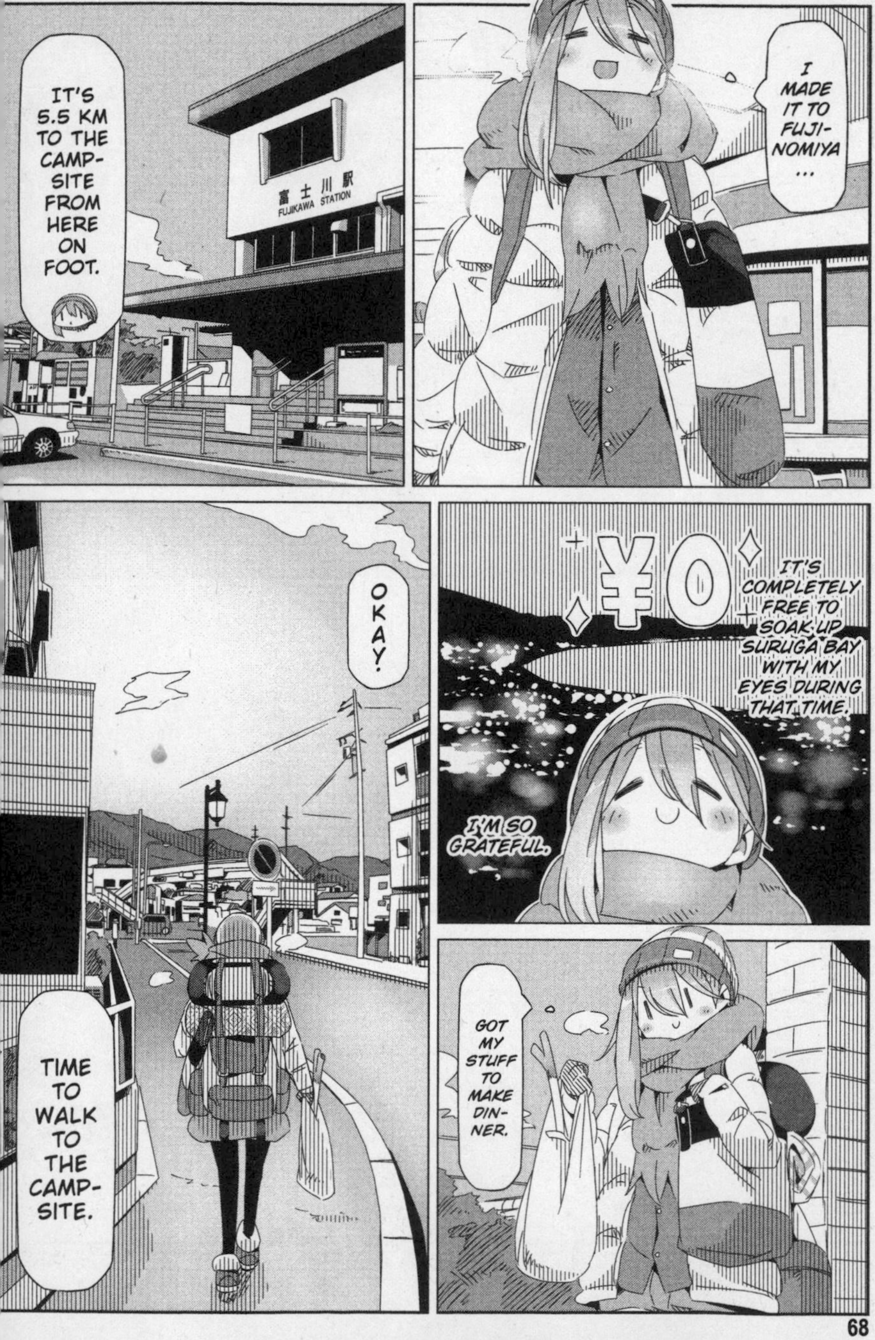
I MADE IT TO FUJI-NOMIYA ...
富士川駅
FUJIKAWA STATION
IT'S 5.5 KM TO THE CAMP-SITE FROM HERE ON FOOT.
¥0
IT'S COMPLETELY FREE TO SOAK UP SURUGA BAY WITH MY EYES DURING THAT TIME.
I'M SO GRATEFUL.
GOT MY STUFF TO MAKE DIN-NER.
OKAY.
TIME TO WALK TO THE CAMP-SITE.

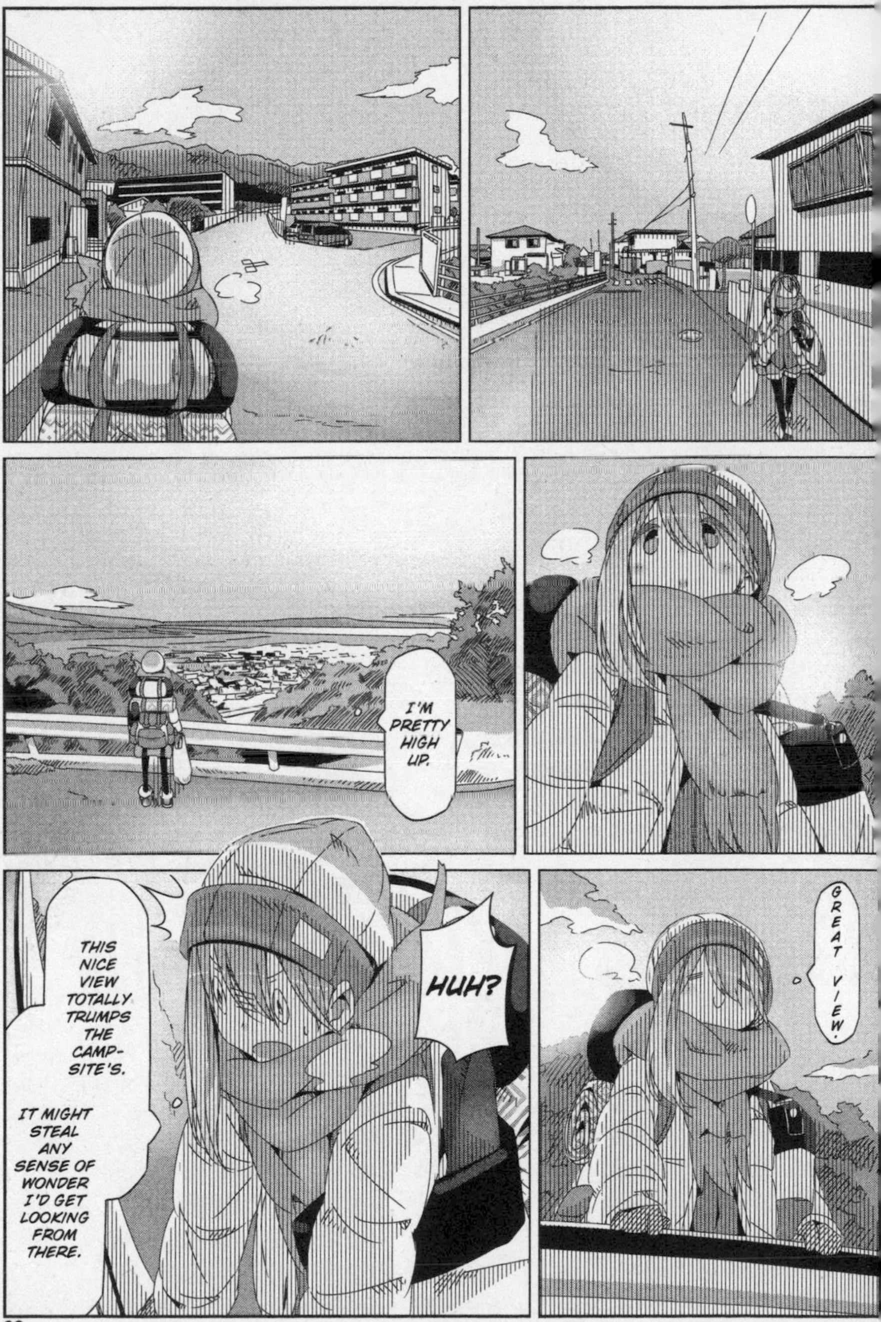
I'M PRETTY HIGH UP.
GREAT VIEW.
HUH?
THIS NICE VIEW TOTALLY TRUMPS THE CAMP-SITE'S.
IT MIGHT STEAL ANY SENSE OF WONDER I'D GET LOOKING FROM THERE.

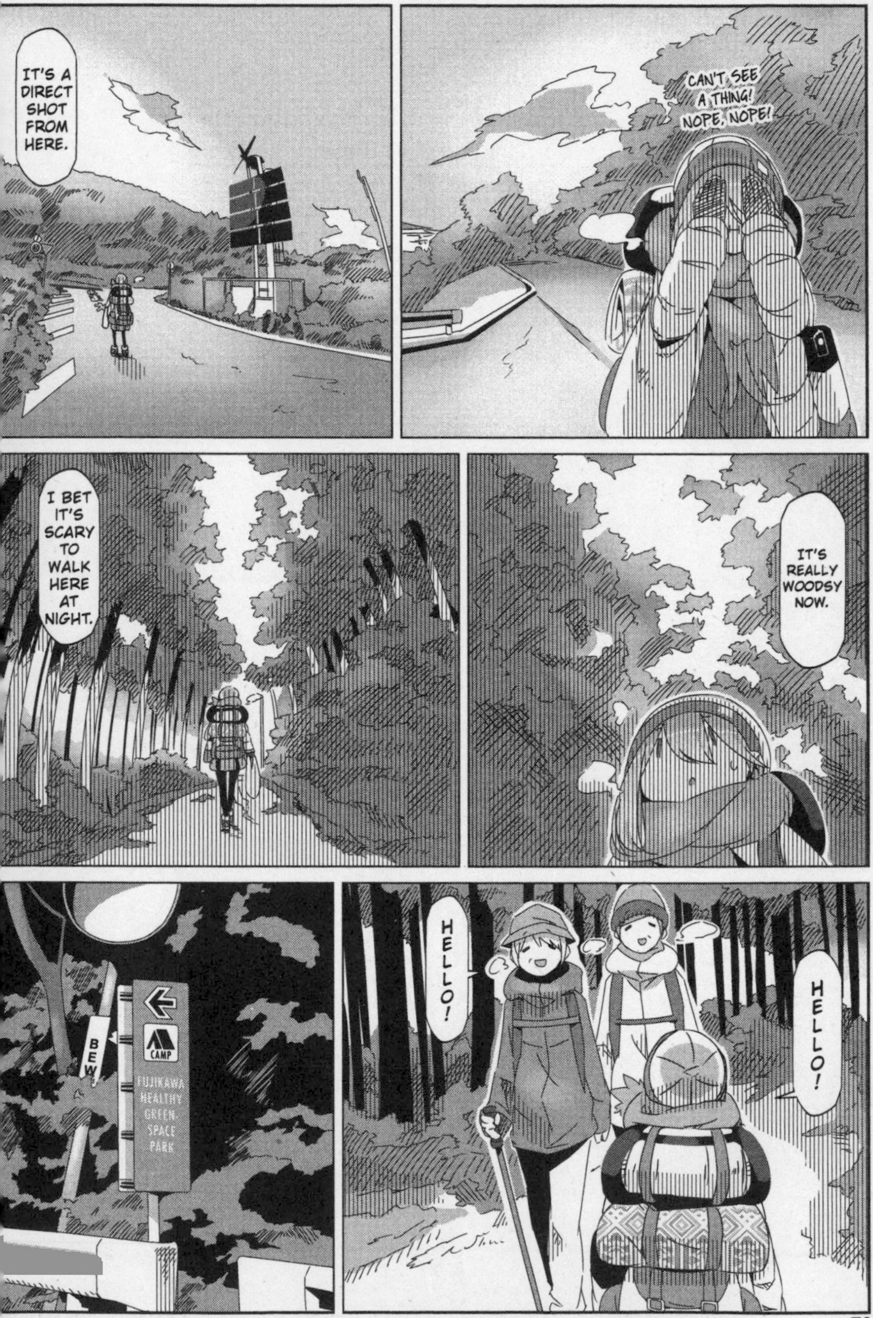
CAN'T SEE A THING! NOPE, NOPE!
IT'S A DIRECT SHOT FROM HERE.
IT'S REALLY WOODSY NOW.
I BET IT'S SCARY TO WALK HERE AT NIGHT.
HELLO!
HELLO!
CAMP
FUJIKAWA HEALTHY GREEN SPACE PARK

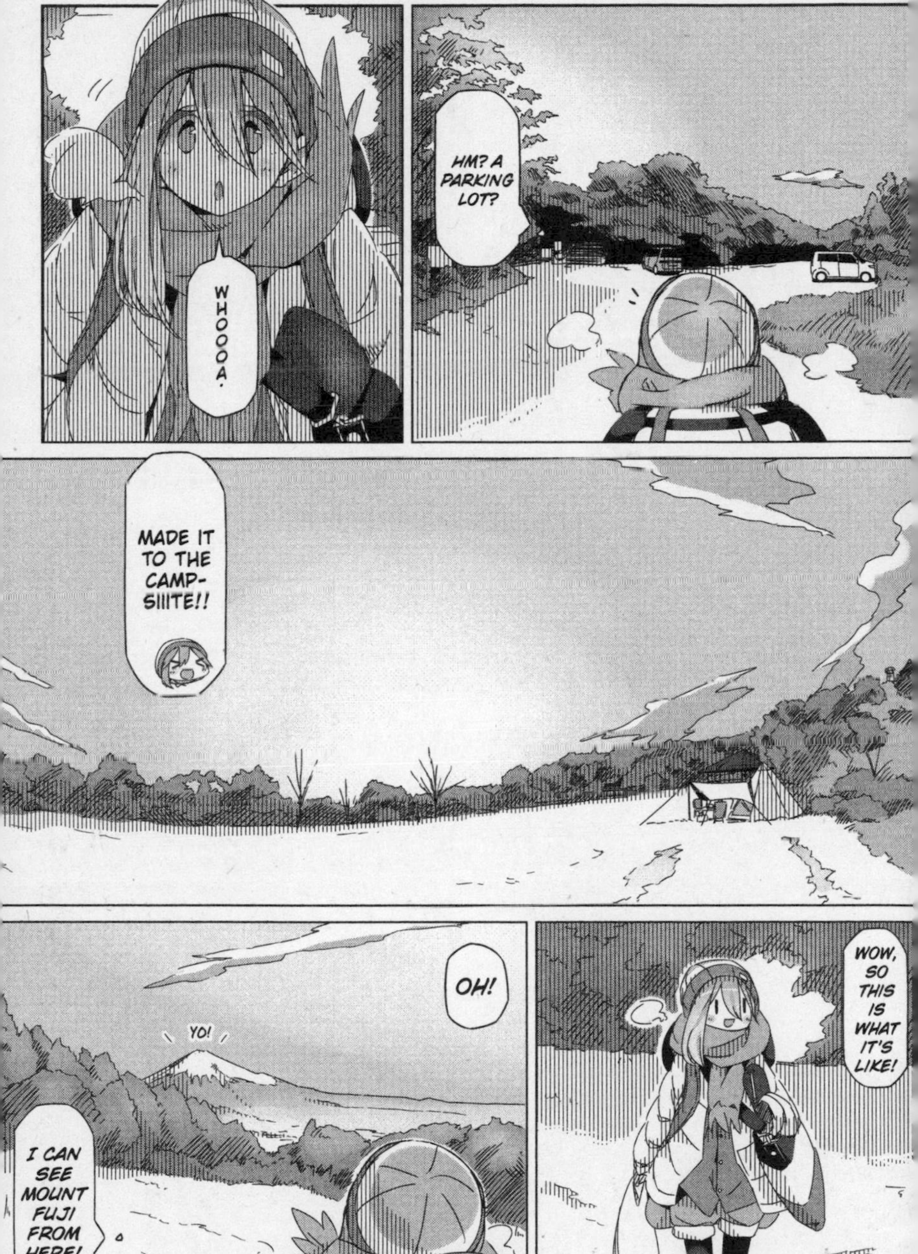
HM? A PARKING LOT?
WHOOOA.
MADE IT TO THE CAMP-SIIITE!!
WOW, SO THIS IS WHAT IT'S LIKE!
OH!
YO!
I CAN SEE MOUNT FUJI FROM HERE!

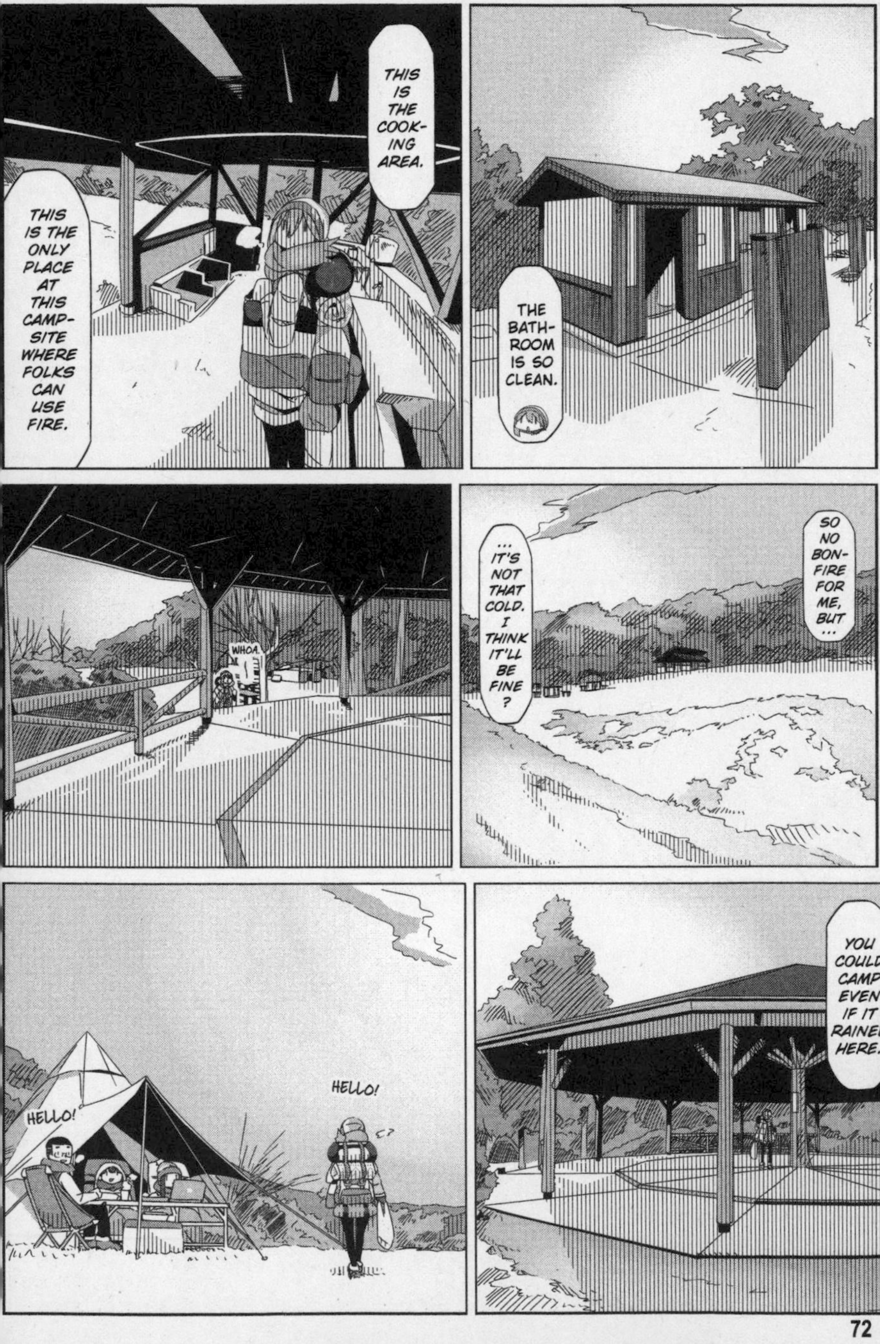
THE BATHROOM IS SO CLEAN.
THIS IS THE COOKING AREA.
THIS IS THE ONLY PLACE AT THIS CAMPSITE WHERE FOLKS CAN USE FIRE.
SO NO BONFIRE FOR ME, BUT...
...IT'S NOT THAT COLD. I THINK IT'LL BE FINE?
WHOA.
YOU COULD CAMP EVEN IF IT RAINED HERE.
HELLO!
HELLO!

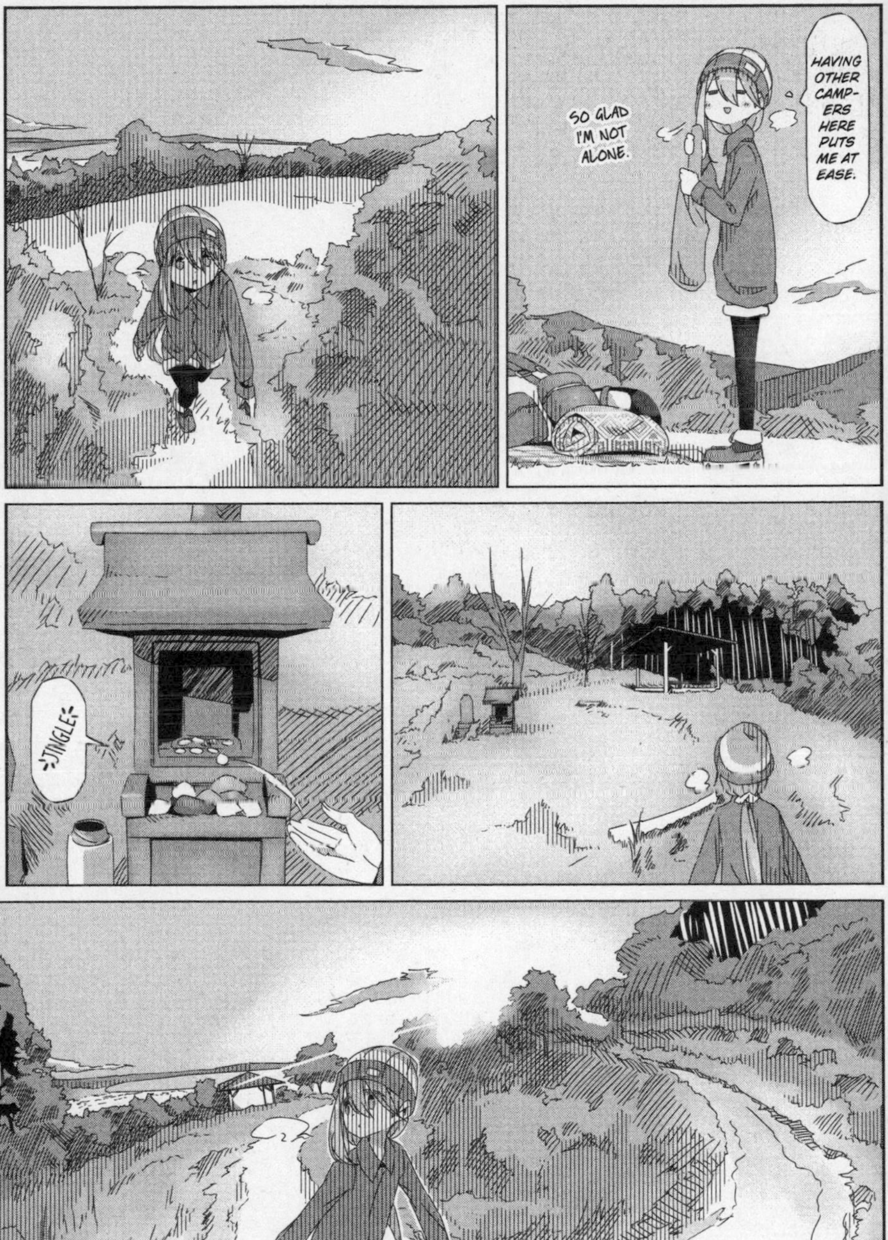
HAVING OTHER CAMPERS HERE PUTS ME AT EASE.
SO GLAD I'M NOT ALONE.
JINGLE

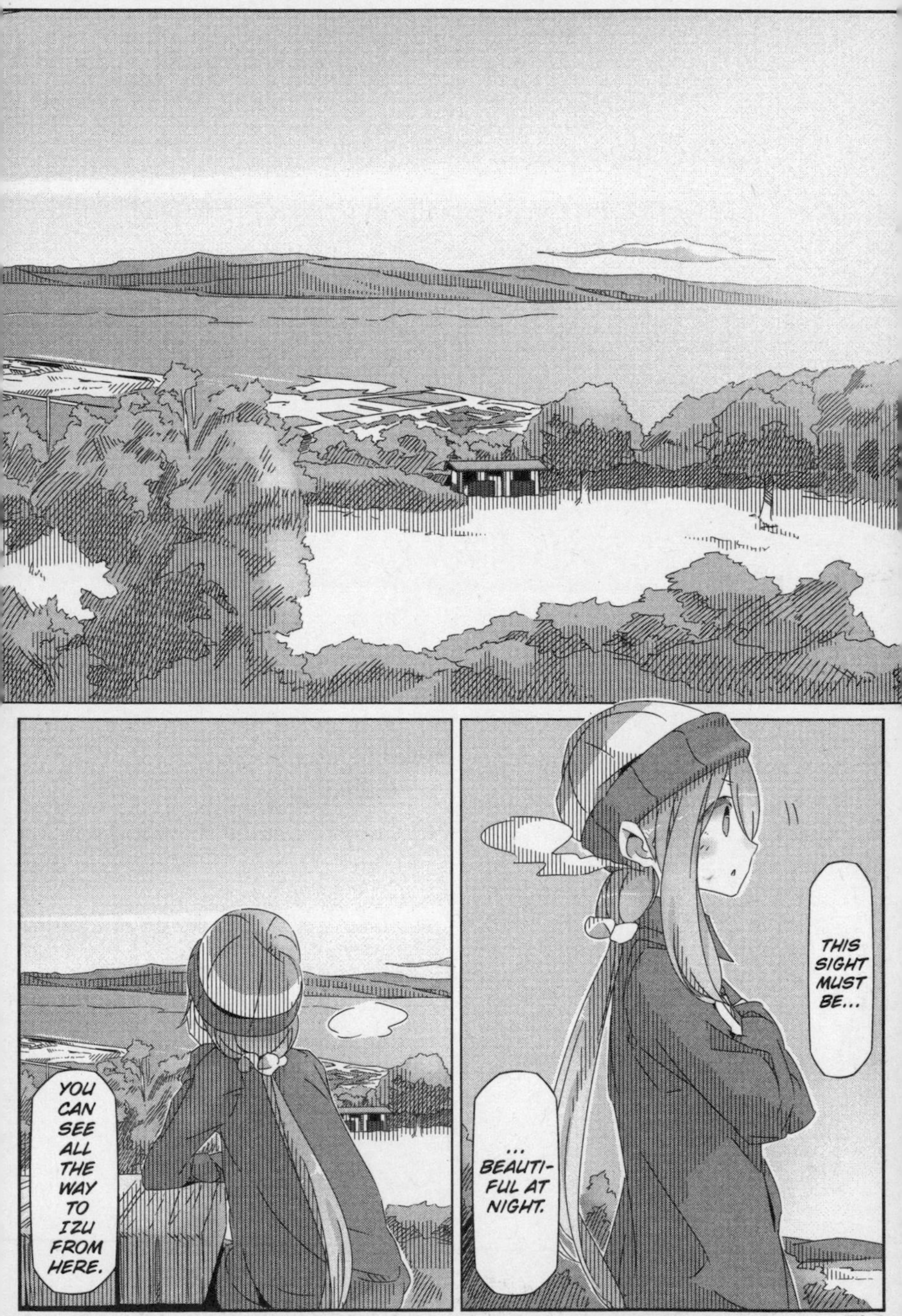
THIS SIGHT MUST BE...
...BEAUTI-FUL AT NIGHT.
YOU CAN SEE ALL THE WAY TO IZU FROM HERE.

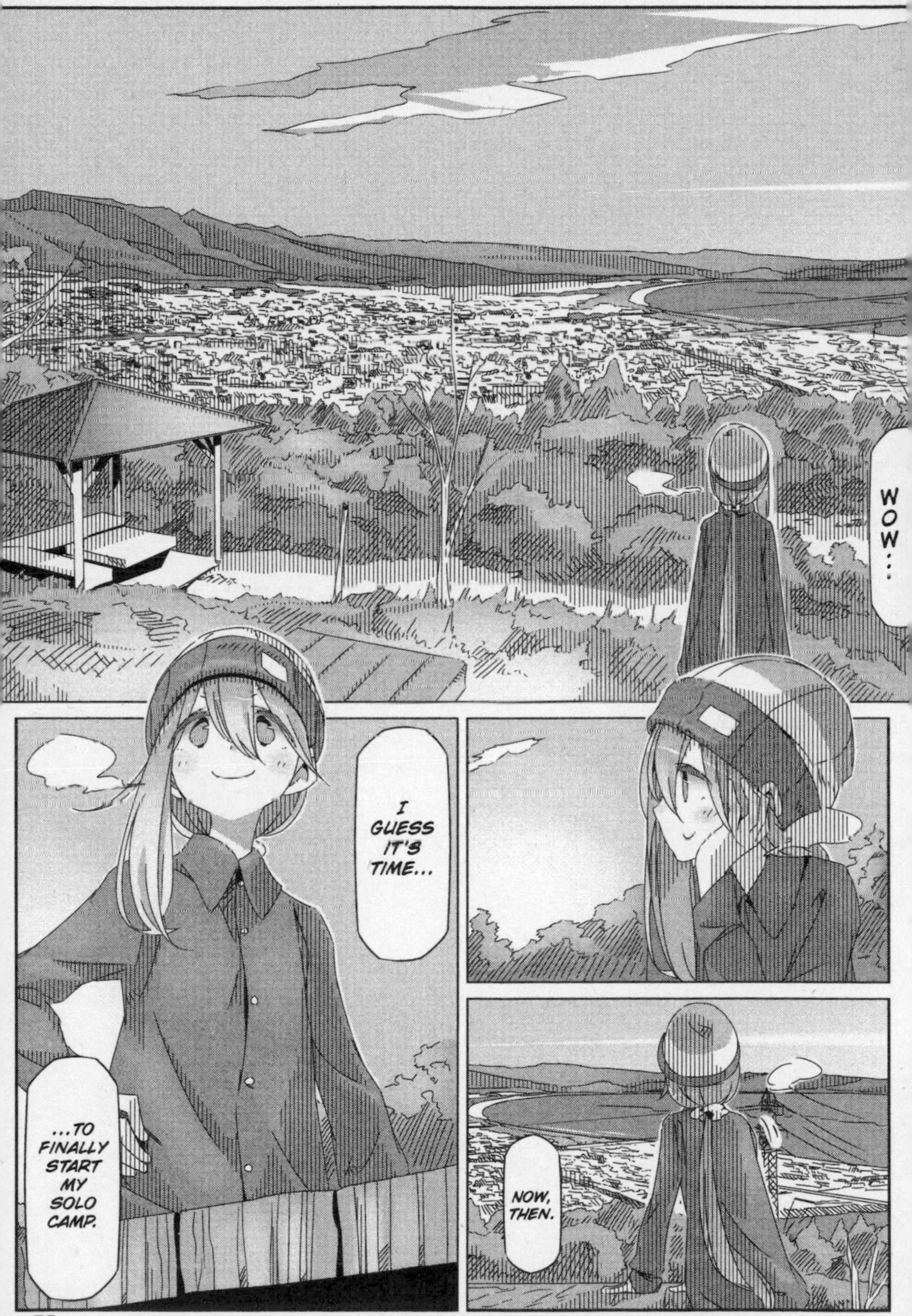
WOW...
NOW, THEN.
I GUESS IT'S TIME...
...TO FINALLY START MY SOLO CAMP.

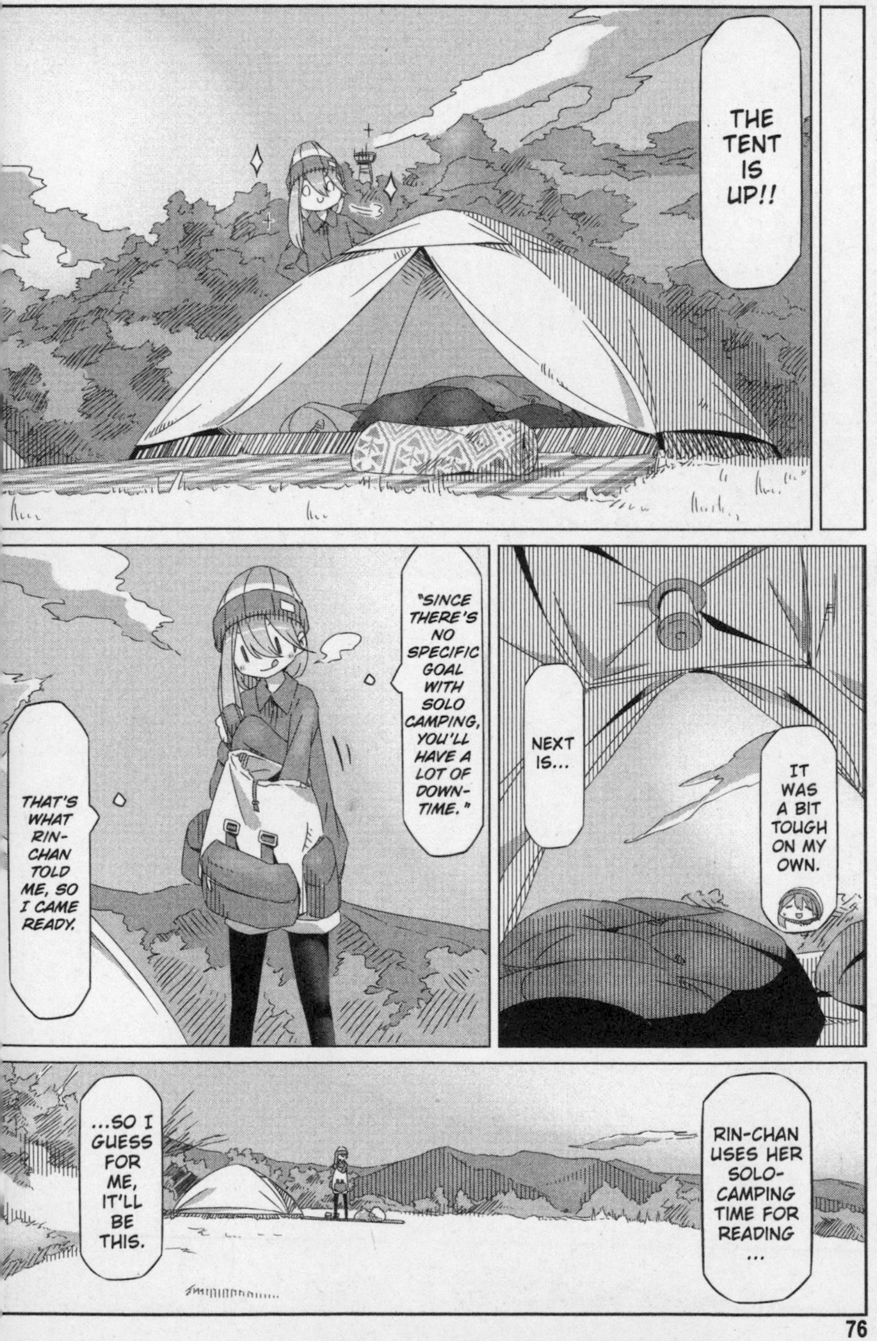
THE TENT IS UP!!
IT WAS A BIT TOUGH ON MY OWN.
NEXT IS...
"SINCE THERE'S NO SPECIFIC GOAL WITH SOLO CAMPING, YOU'LL HAVE A LOT OF DOWN-TIME."
THAT'S WHAT RIN-CHAN TOLD ME, SO I CAME READY.
RIN-CHAN USES HER SOLO-CAMPING TIME FOR READING...
...SO I GUESS FOR ME, IT'LL BE THIS.

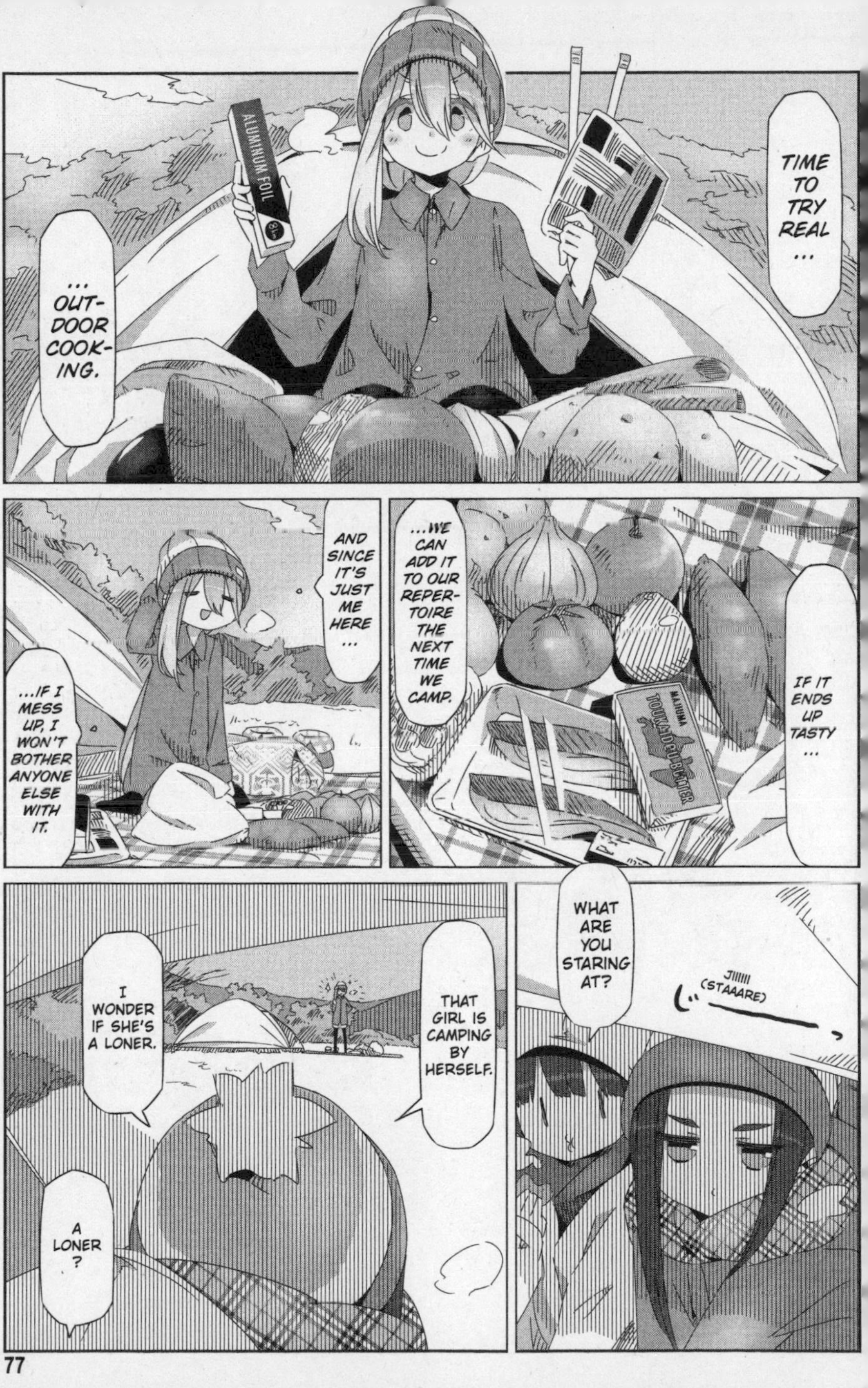
ALUMINUM FOIL
TIME TO TRY REAL ...
... OUT-DOOR COOK-ING.
IF IT ENDS UP TASTY ...
...WE CAN ADD IT TO OUR REPER-TOIRE THE NEXT TIME WE CAMP.
AND SINCE IT'S JUST ME HERE ...
...IF I MESS UP, I WON'T BOTHER ANYONE ELSE WITH IT.
WHAT ARE YOU STARING AT?
JIIIIII (STAAARE)
THAT GIRL IS CAMPING BY HERSELF.
I WONDER IF SHE'S A LONER.
A LONER ?

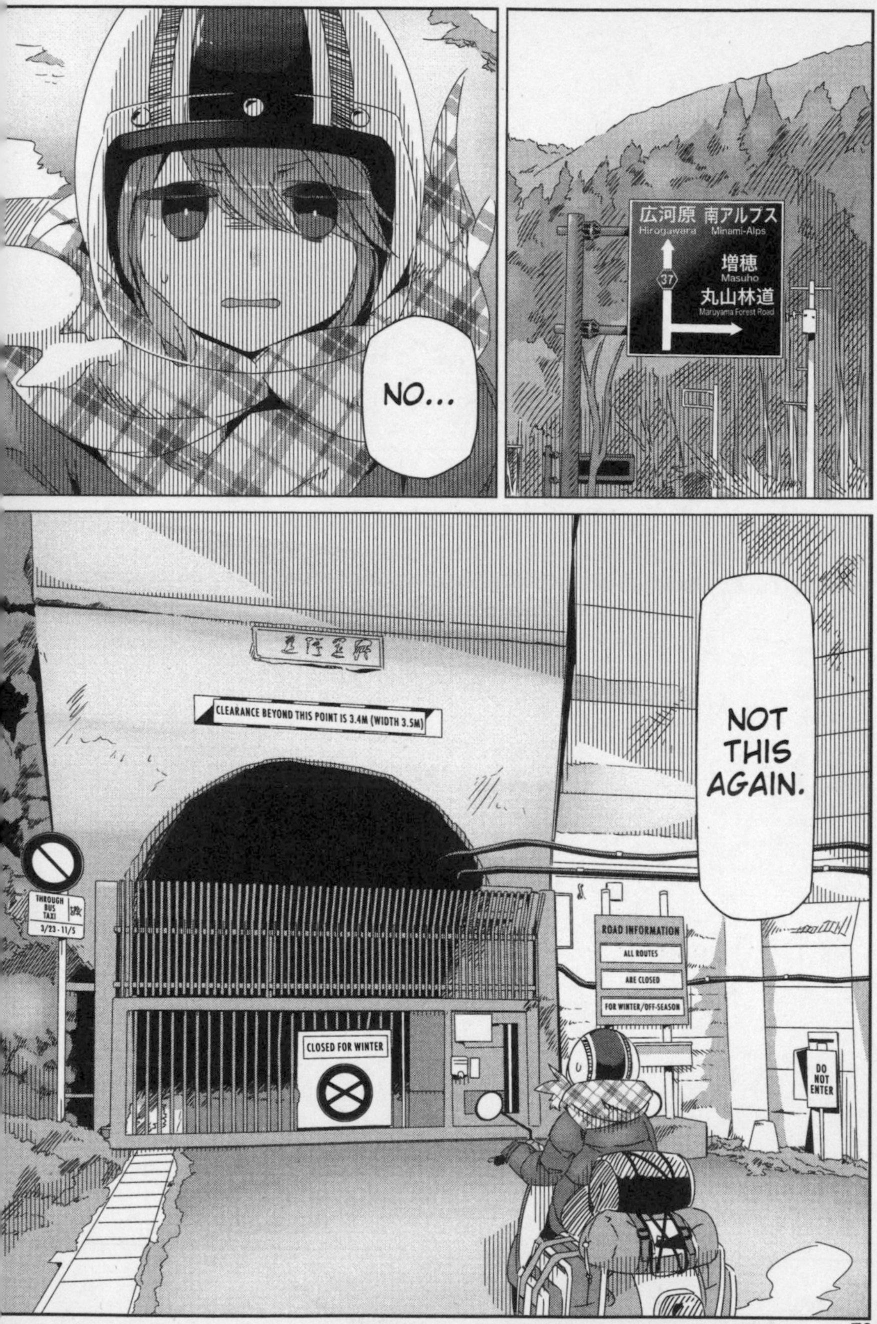
広河原 南アルプス
Hirogawara Minami-Alps
37
増穂
Masuho
丸山林道
Maruyama Forest Road
NO...
NOT THIS AGAIN.
CLEARANCE BEYOND THIS POINT IS 3.4M (WIDTH 3.5M)
ROAD INFORMATION
ALL ROUTES
ARE CLOSED
FOR WINTER/OFF-SEASON
DO NOT ENTER
THROUGH BUS TAXI
3/23 - 11/5
CLOSED FOR WINTER

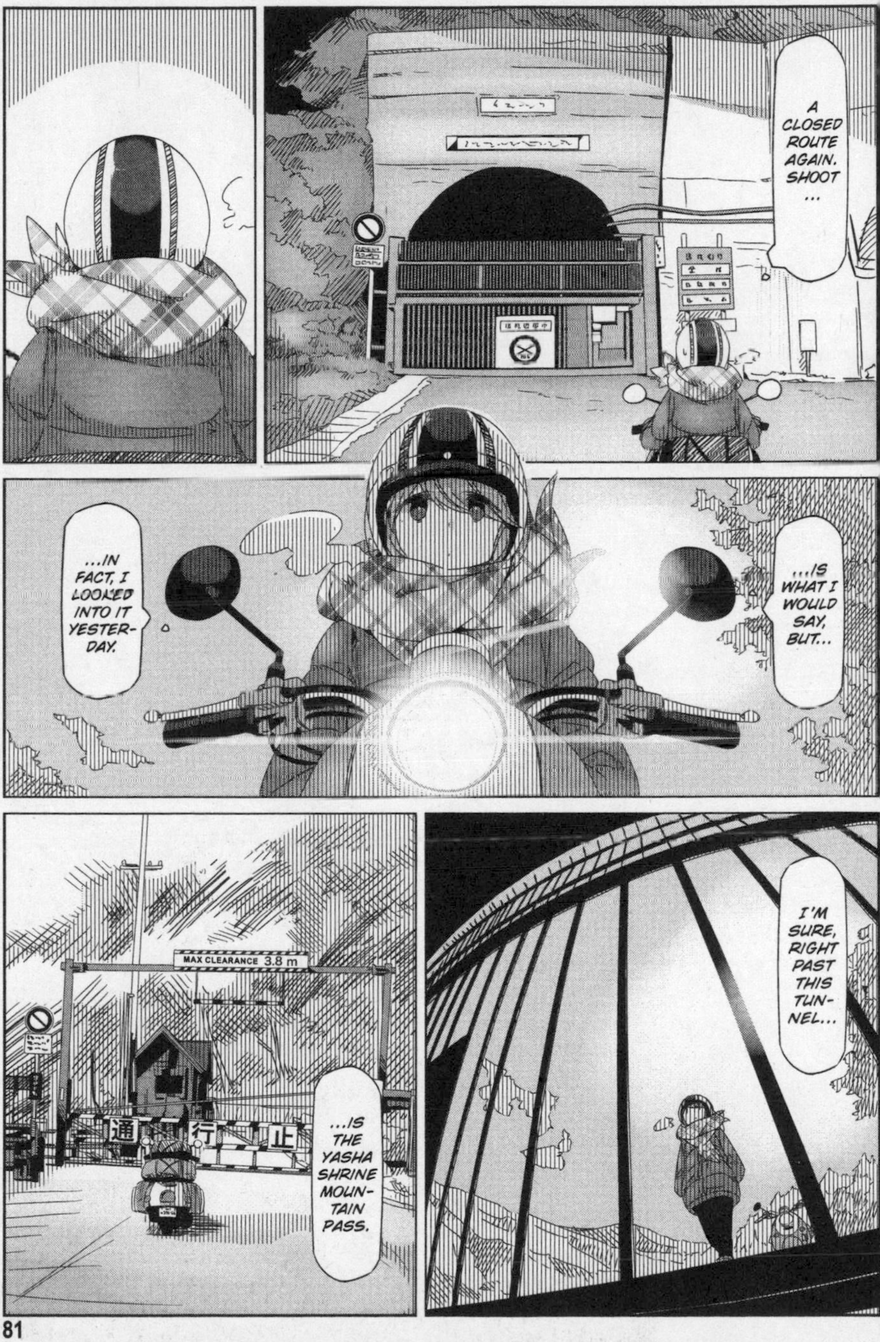
A CLOSED ROUTE AGAIN. SHOOT ...
...IS WHAT I WOULD SAY, BUT...
...IN FACT, I LOOKED INTO IT YESTER-DAY.
I'M SURE, RIGHT PAST THIS TUN-NEL...
MAX CLEARANCE 3.8 m
通行止
...IS THE YASHA SHRINE MOUN-TAIN PASS.

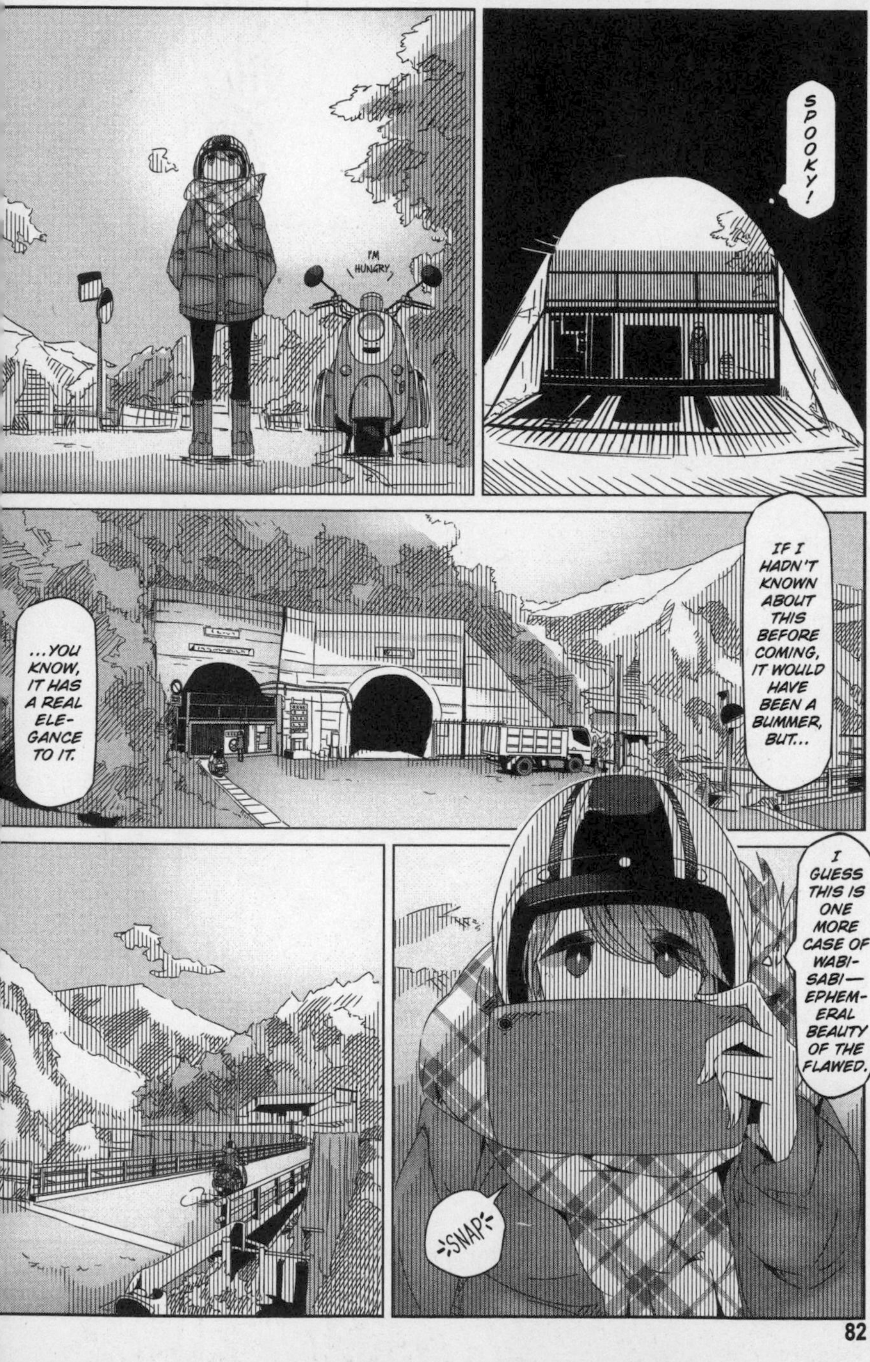
SPOOKY!
I'M HUNGRY
IF I HADN'T KNOWN ABOUT THIS BEFORE COMING, IT WOULD HAVE BEEN A BUMMER, BUT...
...YOU KNOW, IT HAS A REAL ELEGANCE TO IT.
I GUESS THIS IS ONE MORE CASE OF WABI-SABI—EPHEMERAL BEAUTY OF THE FLAWED.
SNAP

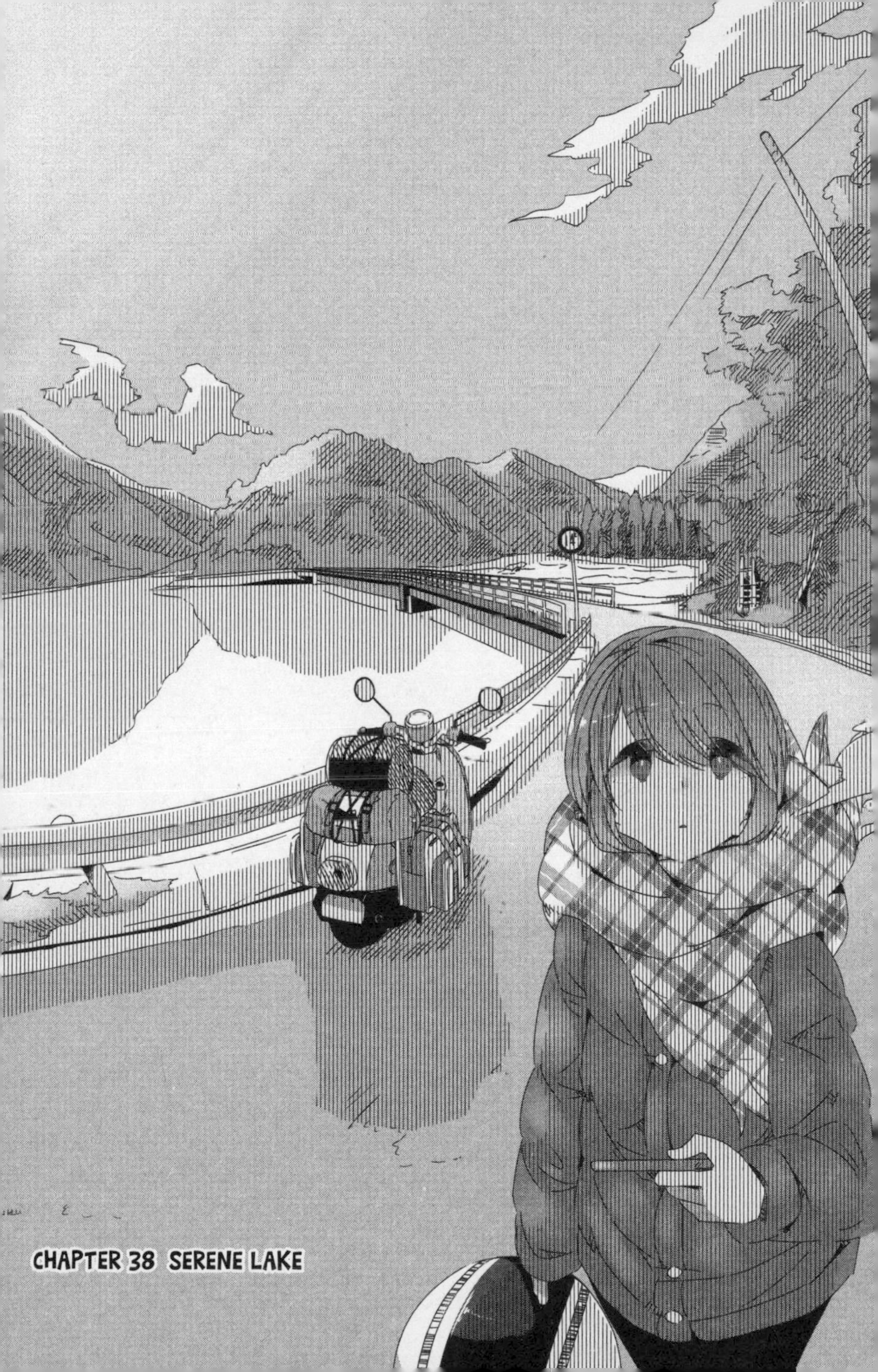
CHAPTER 38 SERENE LAKE

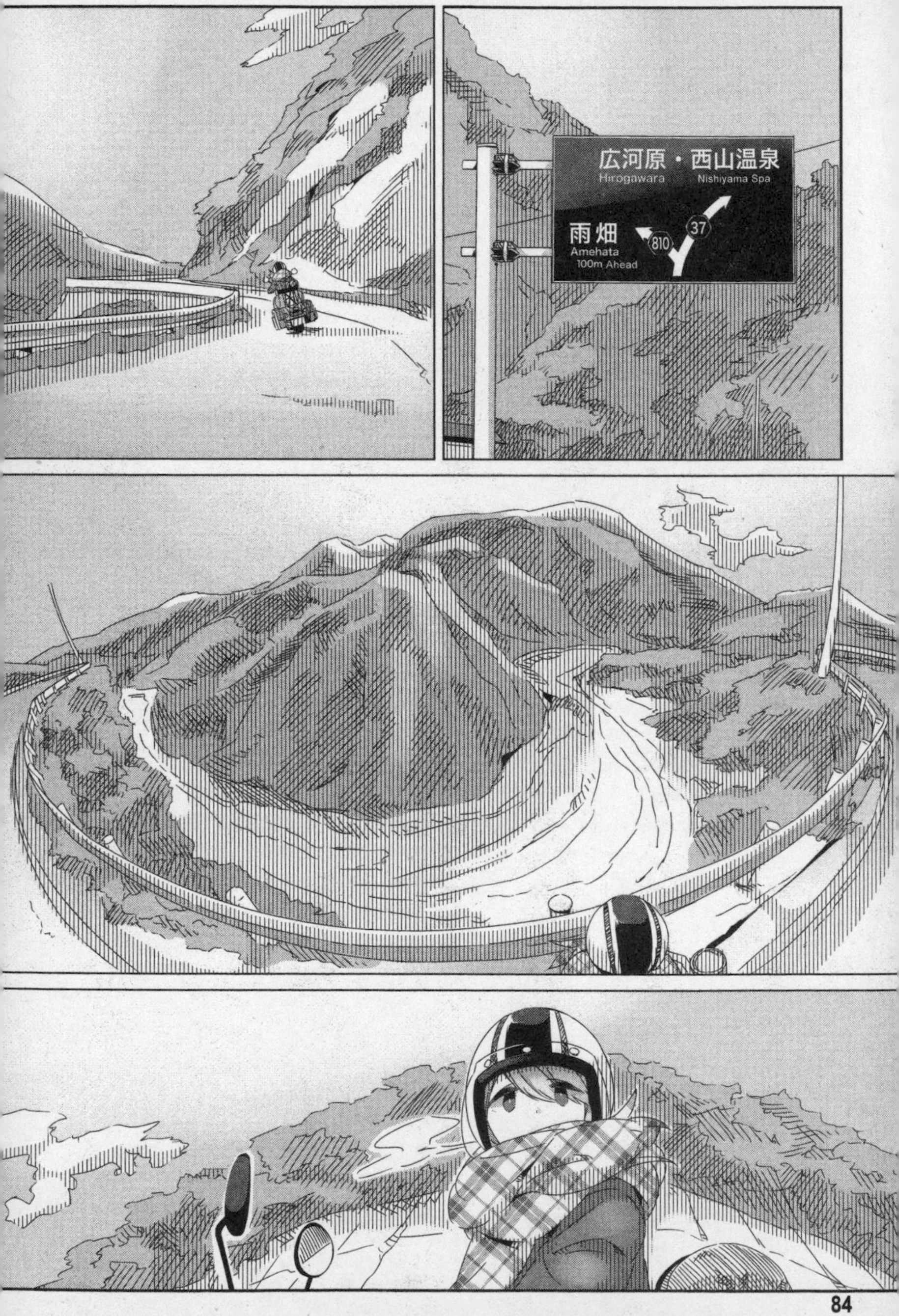
広河原・西山温泉
Hirogawara
Nishiyama Spa
37
雨畑
Amehata
100m Ahead
810

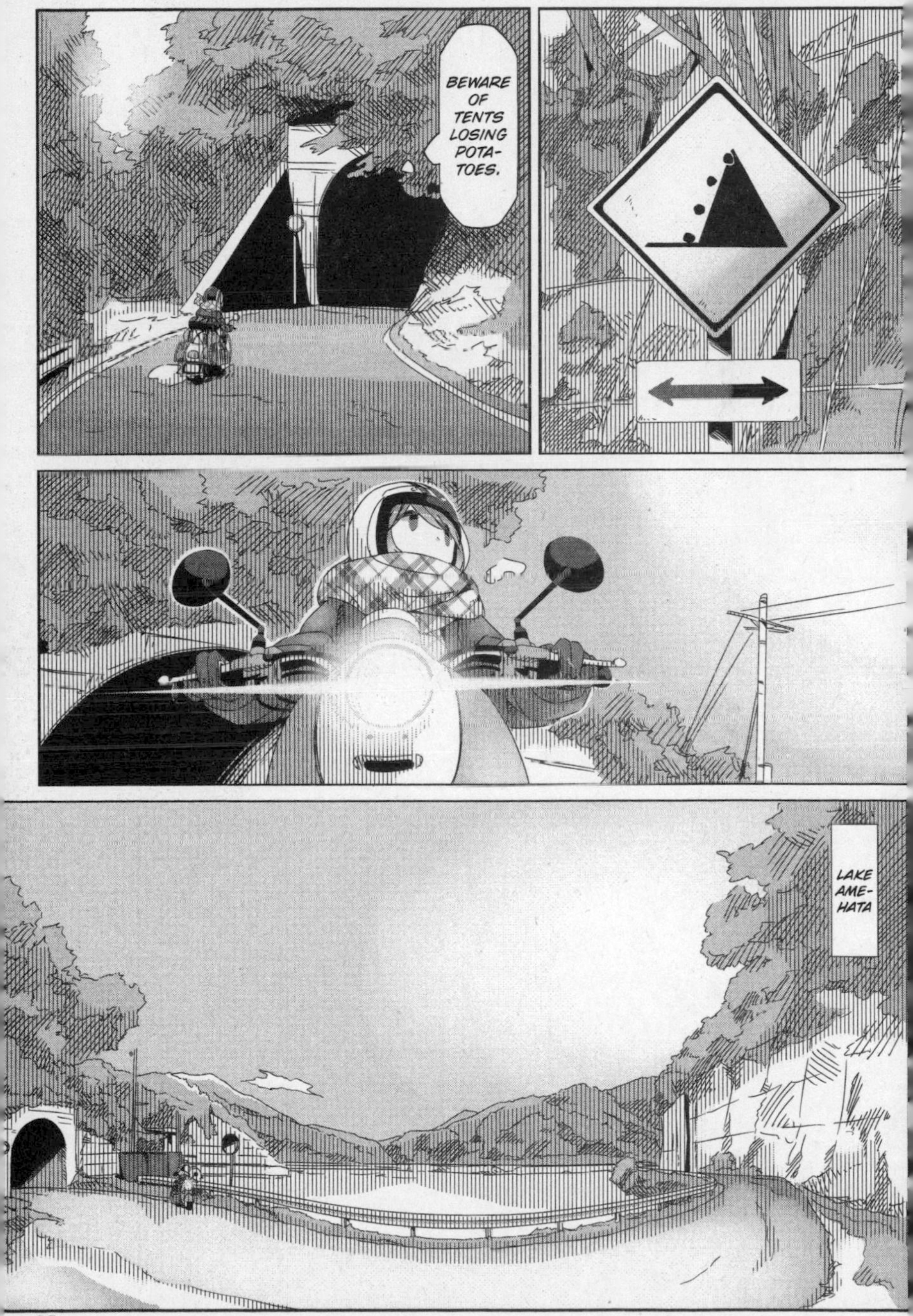
BEWARE OF TENTS LOSING POTA-TOES.
LAKE AME-HATA

BIIIN
(VREEEN)

IT'S EMERALD GREEN, JUST LIKE LAKE NARADA.

A SCHOOL?

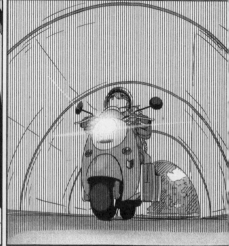

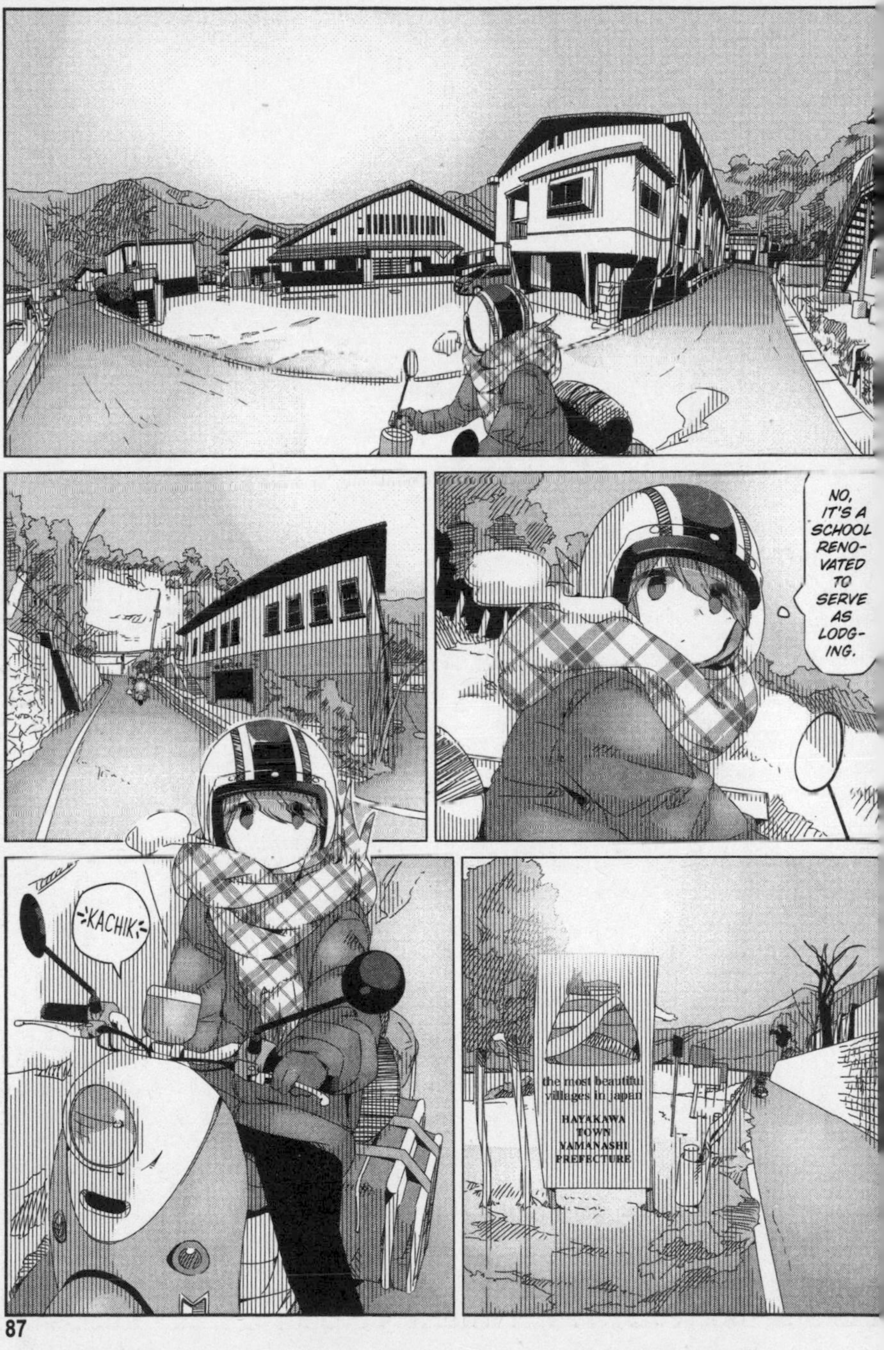
NO, IT'S A SCHOOL RENOVATED TO SERVE AS LODGING.
the most beautiful villages in japan
HAYAKAWA TOWN YAMANASHI PREFECTURE
KACHIK

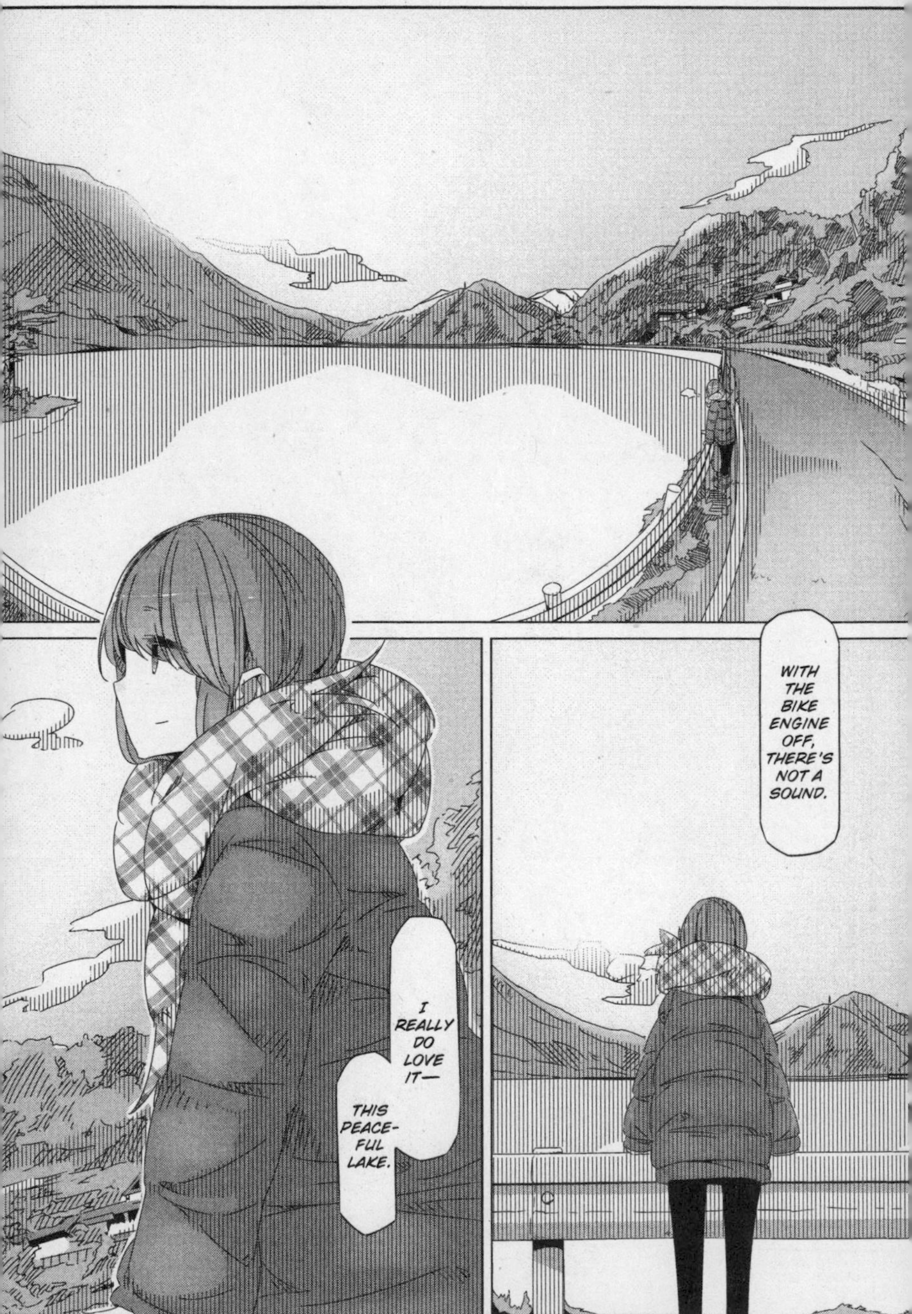
WITH THE BIKE ENGINE OFF, THERE'S NOT A SOUND.
I REALLY DO LOVE IT—
THIS PEACE-FUL LAKE.

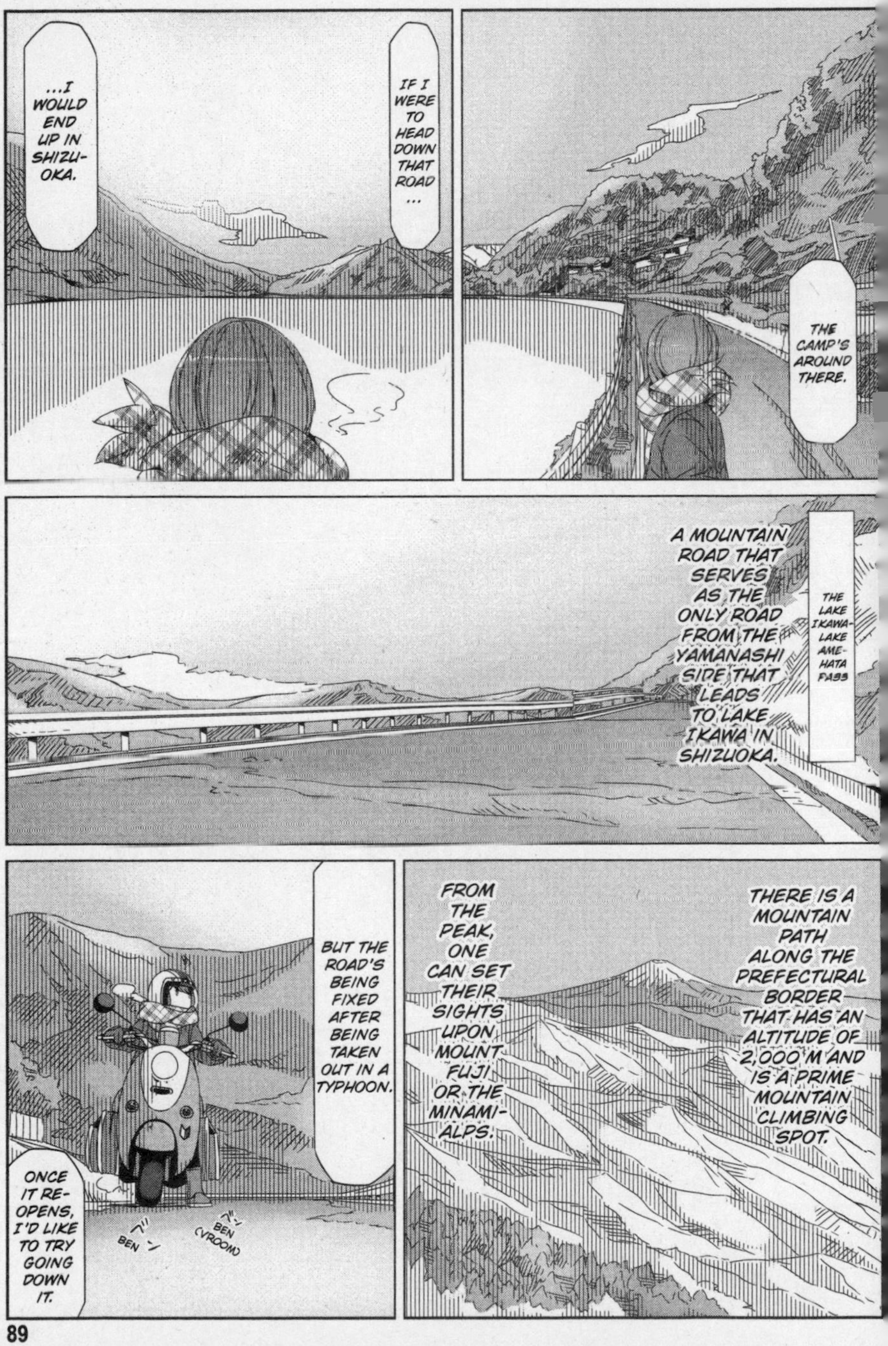
THE CAMP'S AROUND THERE.
IF I WERE TO HEAD DOWN THAT ROAD...
...I WOULD END UP IN SHIZUOKA.
THE LAKE IKAWA-LAKE AMEHATA PASS
A MOUNTAIN ROAD THAT SERVES AS THE ONLY ROAD FROM THE YAMANASHI SIDE THAT LEADS TO LAKE IKAWA IN SHIZUOKA.
THERE IS A MOUNTAIN PATH ALONG THE PREFECTURAL BORDER THAT HAS AN ALTITUDE OF 2,000 M AND IS A PRIME MOUNTAIN CLIMBING SPOT.
FROM THE PEAK, ONE CAN SET THEIR SIGHTS UPON MOUNT FUJI OR THE MINAMI-ALPS.
BUT THE ROAD'S BEING FIXED AFTER BEING TAKEN OUT IN A TYPHOON.
ONCE IT REOPENS, I'D LIKE TO TRY GOING DOWN IT.
ベン BEN (VROOM)
ベン BEN

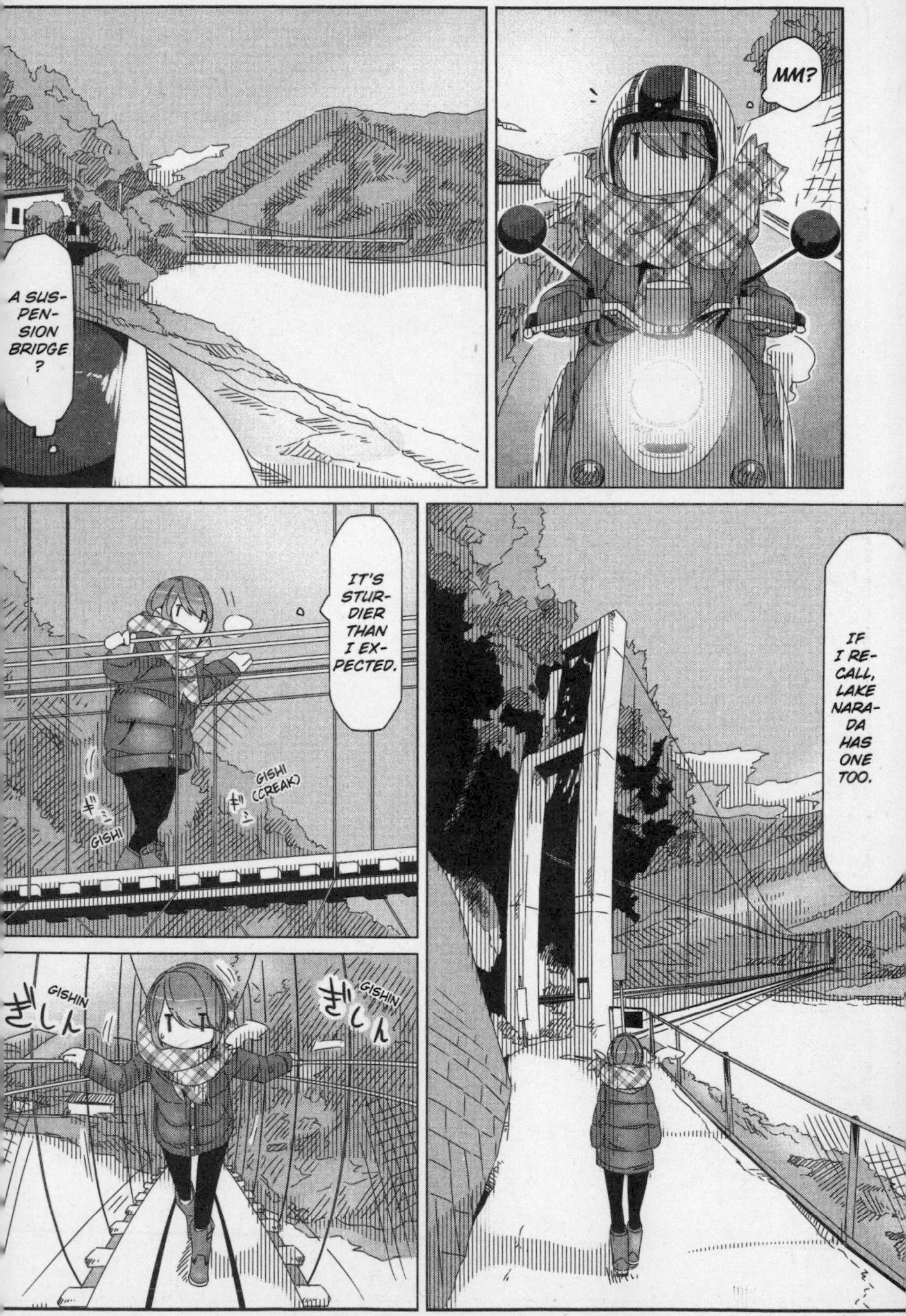
MM?
A SUSPENSION BRIDGE?
IF I RECALL, LAKE NARADA HAS ONE TOO.
IT'S STURDIER THAN I EXPECTED.
ギシ
GISHI (CREAK)
ギシ
GISHI
ぎしん
GISHIN
ぎしん
GISHIN

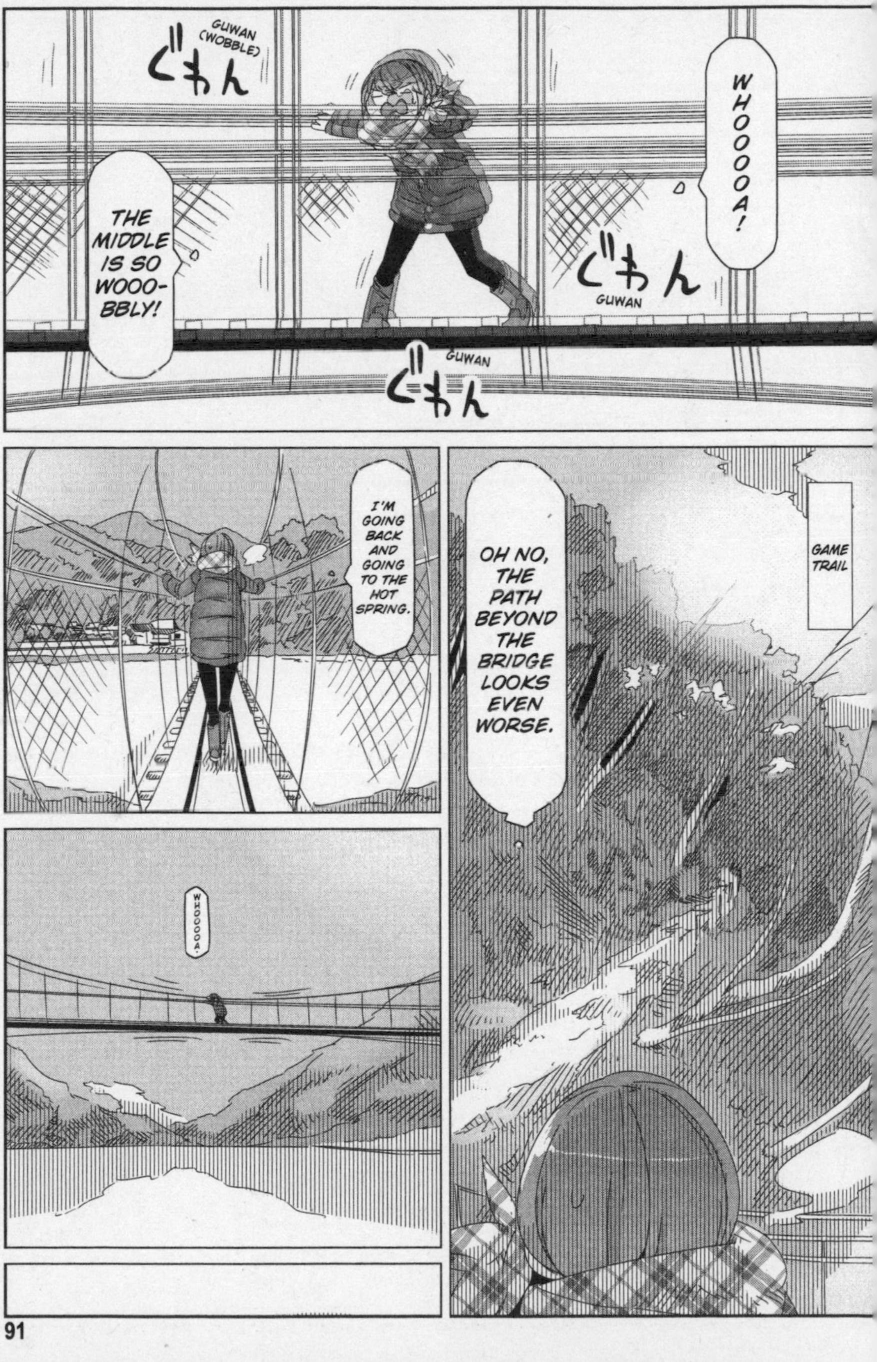
WHOOOOA!
GUWAN (WOBBLE)
ぐわん
THE MIDDLE IS SO WOOO-BBLY!
ぐわん
GUWAN
GUWAN
ぐわん
GAME TRAIL
OH NO, THE PATH BEYOND THE BRIDGE LOOKS EVEN WORSE.
I'M GOING BACK AND GOING TO THE HOT SPRING.
WHOOOOA.

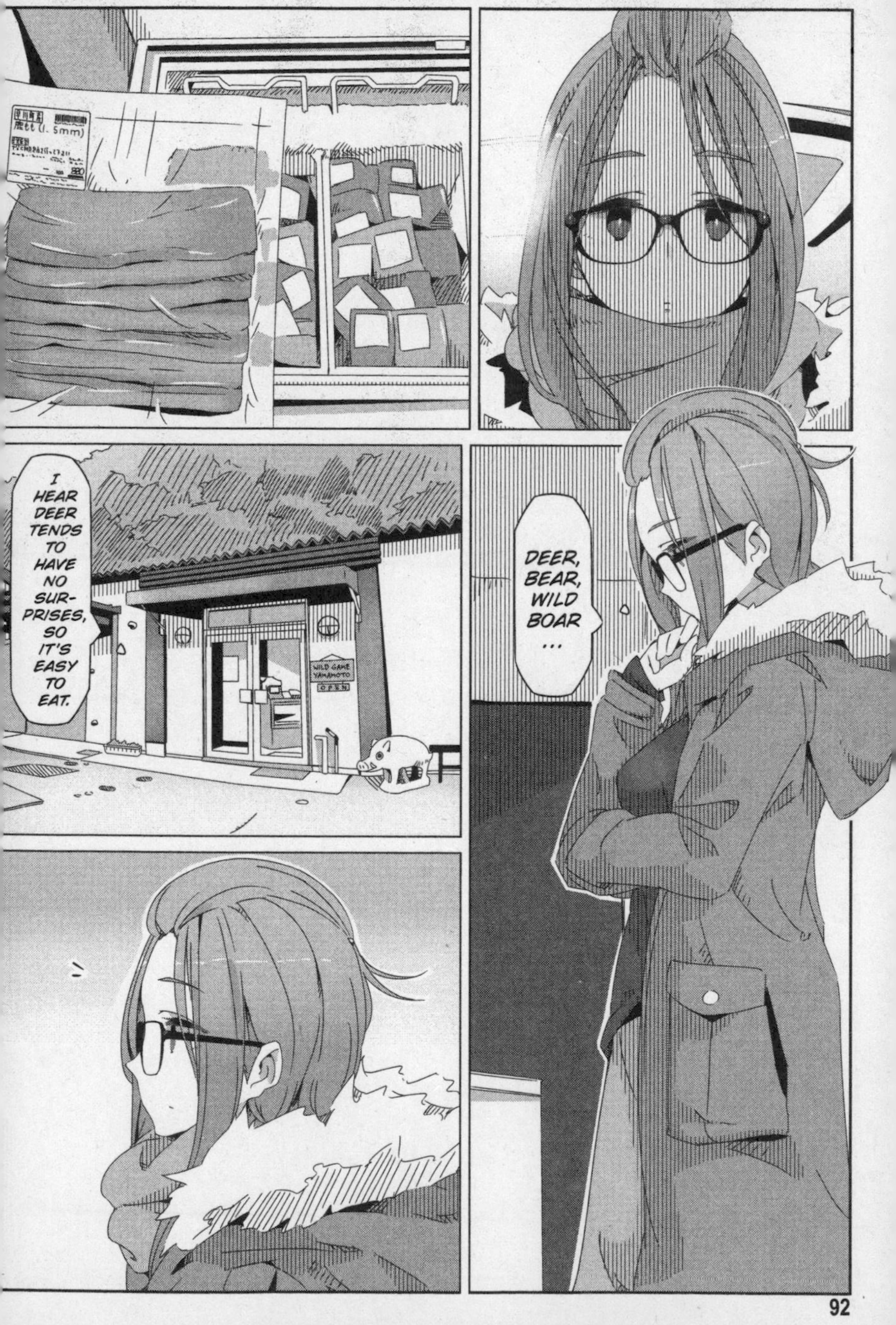
鹿もも(1.5mm)
DEER, BEAR, WILD BOAR ...
I HEAR DEER TENDS TO HAVE NO SURPRISES, SO IT'S EASY TO EAT.
WILD GAME YAMAMOTO
OPEN

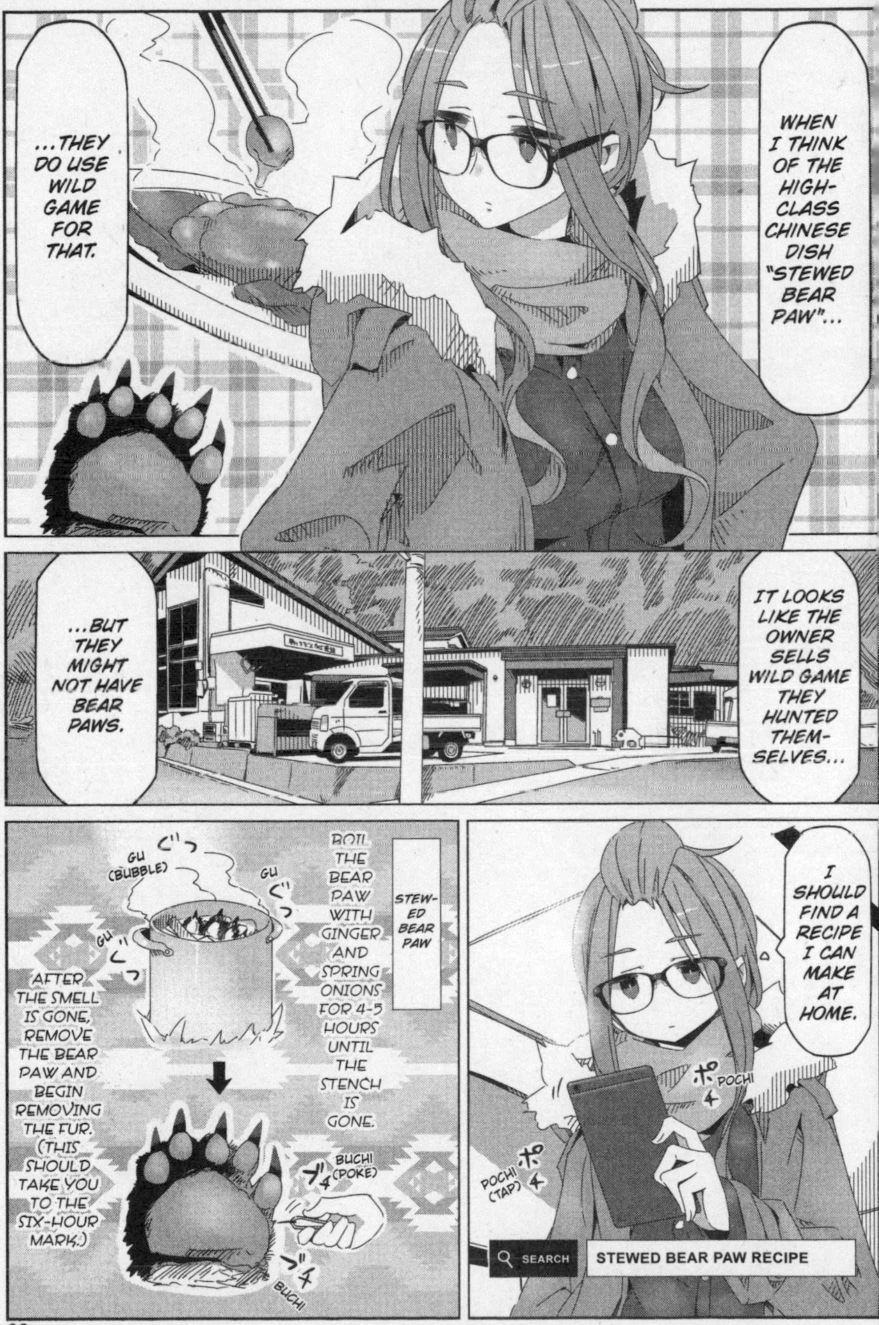
WHEN I THINK OF THE HIGH-CLASS CHINESE DISH "STEWED BEAR PAW"...
...THEY DO USE WILD GAME FOR THAT.
IT LOOKS LIKE THE OWNER SELLS WILD GAME THEY HUNTED THEMSELVES...
...BUT THEY MIGHT NOT HAVE BEAR PAWS.
I SHOULD FIND A RECIPE I CAN MAKE AT HOME.
POCHI
POCHI (TAP)
SEARCH
STEWED BEAR PAW RECIPE
STEWED BEAR PAW
BOIL THE BEAR PAW WITH GINGER AND SPRING ONIONS FOR 4-5 HOURS UNTIL THE STENCH IS GONE.
GU (BUBBLE)
GU
GU
AFTER THE SMELL IS GONE, REMOVE THE BEAR PAW AND BEGIN REMOVING THE FUR. (THIS SHOULD TAKE YOU TO THE SIX-HOUR MARK.)
BUCHI (POKE)
BUCHI

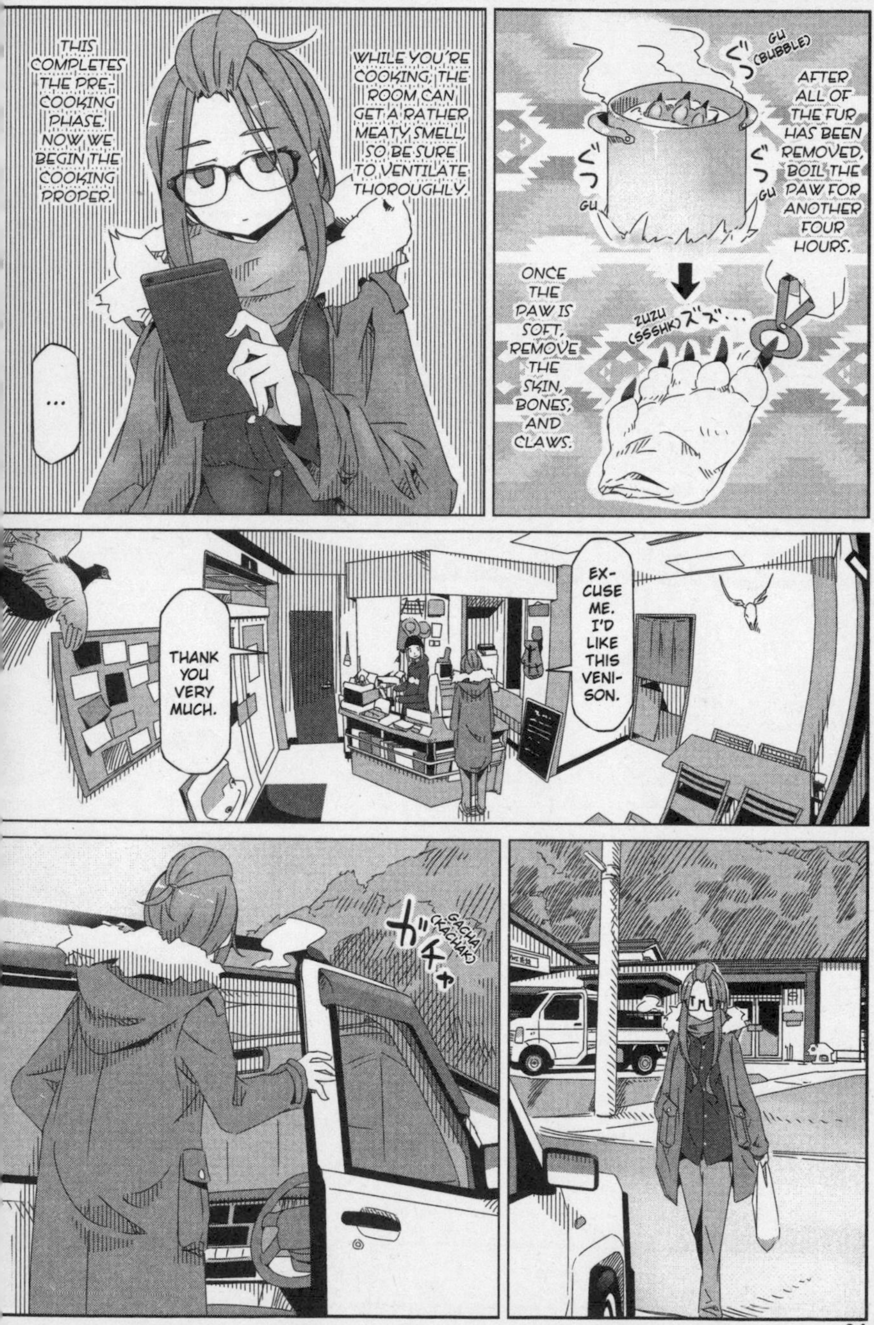
ぐつ GU (BUBBLE)
AFTER ALL OF THE FUR HAS BEEN REMOVED, BOIL THE PAW FOR ANOTHER FOUR HOURS.
ぐつ GU
ぐつ GU
ONCE THE PAW IS SOFT, REMOVE THE SKIN, BONES, AND CLAWS.
ZUZU (SSSHK) ズズ…
WHILE YOU'RE COOKING, THE ROOM CAN GET A RATHER MEATY SMELL, SO BE SURE TO VENTILATE THOROUGHLY.
THIS COMPLETES THE PRE-COOKING PHASE. NOW WE BEGIN THE COOKING PROPER.
…
EX-CUSE ME. I'D LIKE THIS VENI-SON.
THANK YOU VERY MUCH.
ガチャ GACHA (KACHAK)

BATAN
(SHUT)
バタン

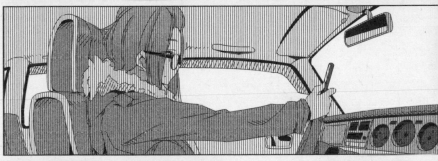

BURORO
(VROOOOM)
ブロロ

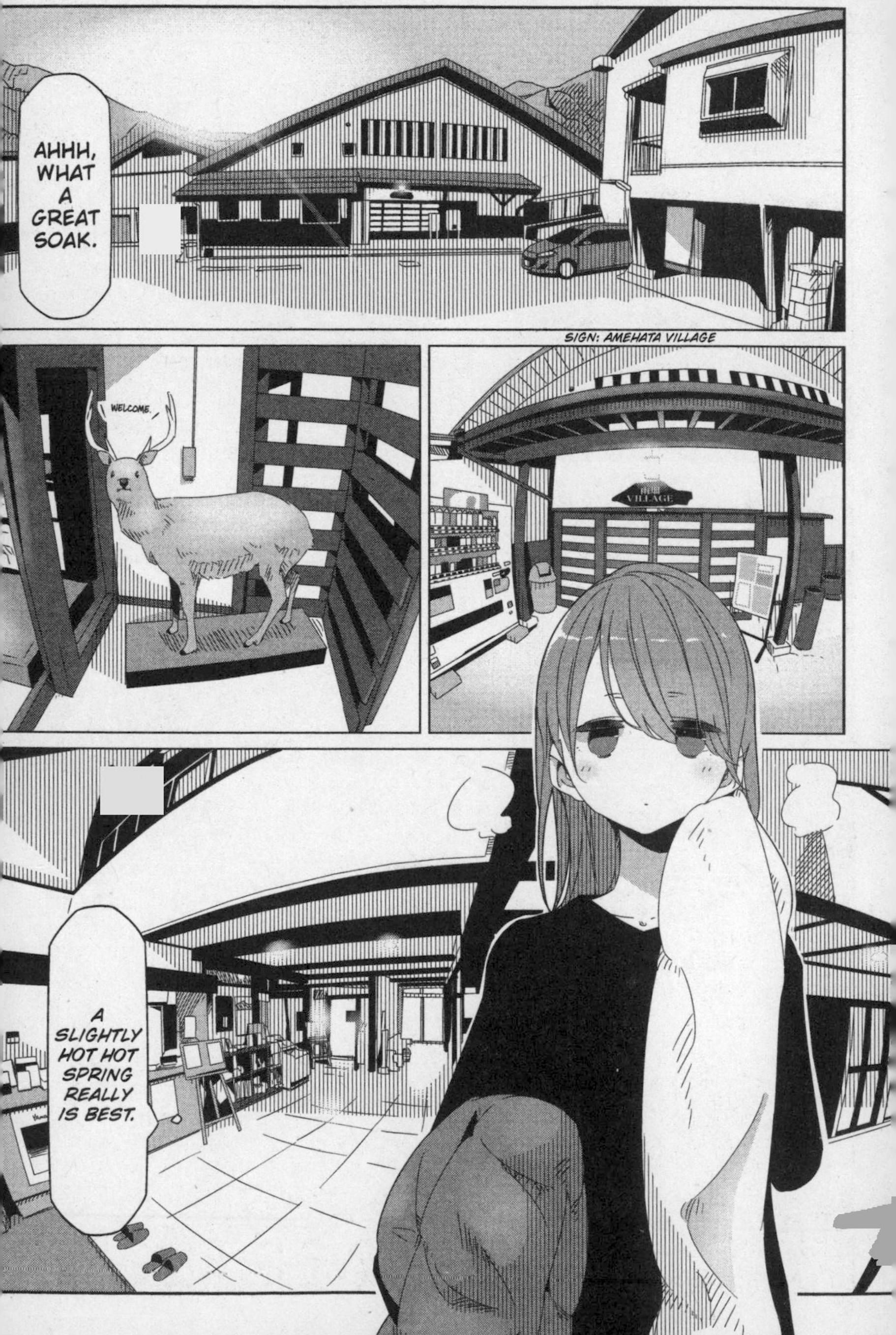
AHHH, WHAT A GREAT SOAK.
SIGN: AMEHATA VILLAGE
VILLAGE
WELCOME.
A SLIGHTLY HOT HOT SPRING REALLY IS BEST.

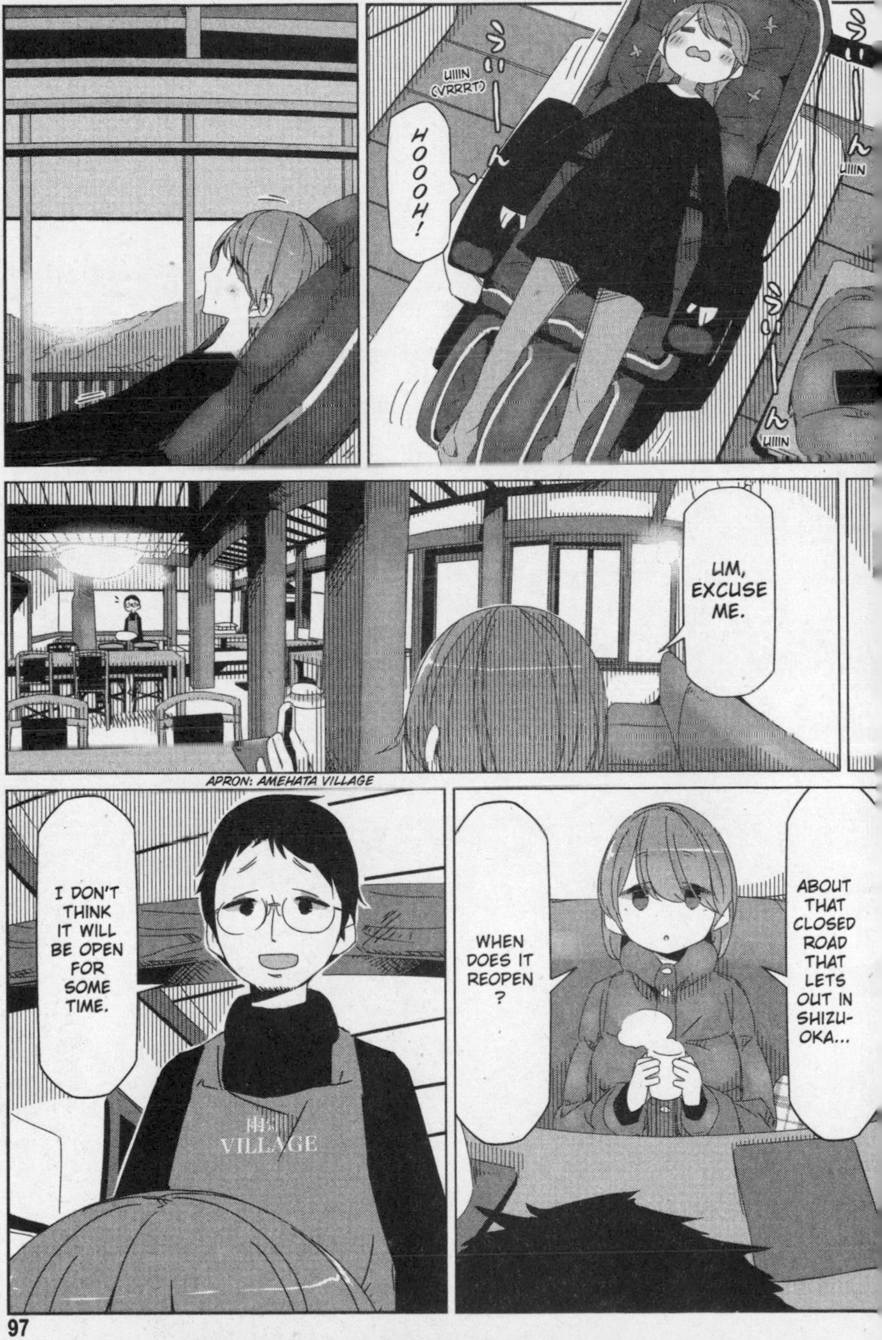
UIIIN
UIIIN (VRRRT)
HOOOOH!
UIIIN
UM, EXCUSE ME.
APRON: AMEHATA VILLAGE
ABOUT THAT CLOSED ROAD THAT LETS OUT IN SHIZUOKA...
WHEN DOES IT REOPEN?
I DON'T THINK IT WILL BE OPEN FOR SOME TIME.
VILLAGE

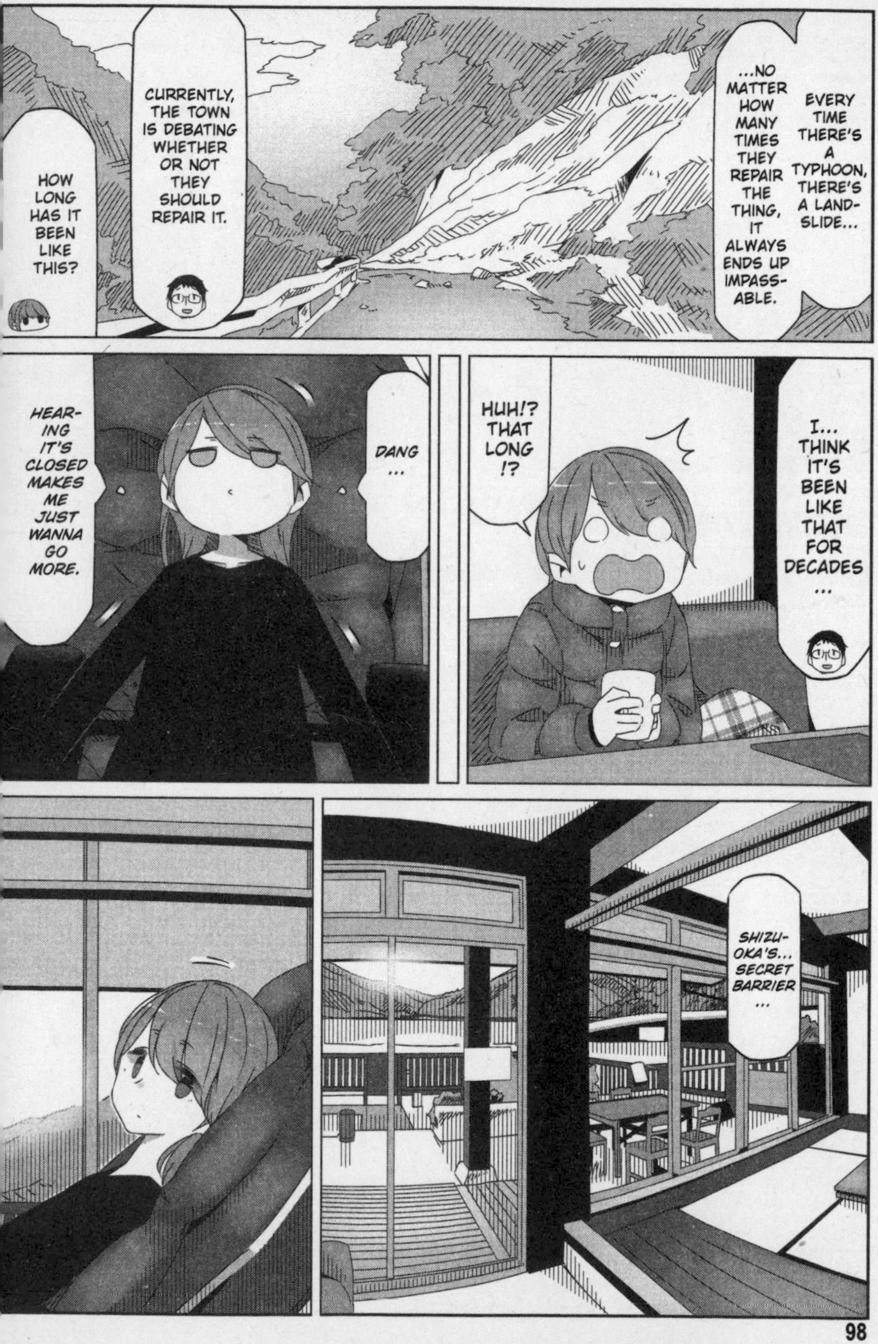
EVERY TIME THERE'S A TYPHOON, THERE'S A LAND-SLIDE...
...NO MATTER HOW MANY TIMES THEY REPAIR THE THING, IT ALWAYS ENDS UP IMPASS-ABLE.
CURRENTLY, THE TOWN IS DEBATING WHETHER OR NOT THEY SHOULD REPAIR IT.
HOW LONG HAS IT BEEN LIKE THIS?
I... THINK IT'S BEEN LIKE THAT FOR DECADES...
HUH!? THAT LONG!?
DANG...
HEAR-ING IT'S CLOSED MAKES ME JUST WANNA GO MORE.
SHIZU-OKA'S... SECRET BARRIER...

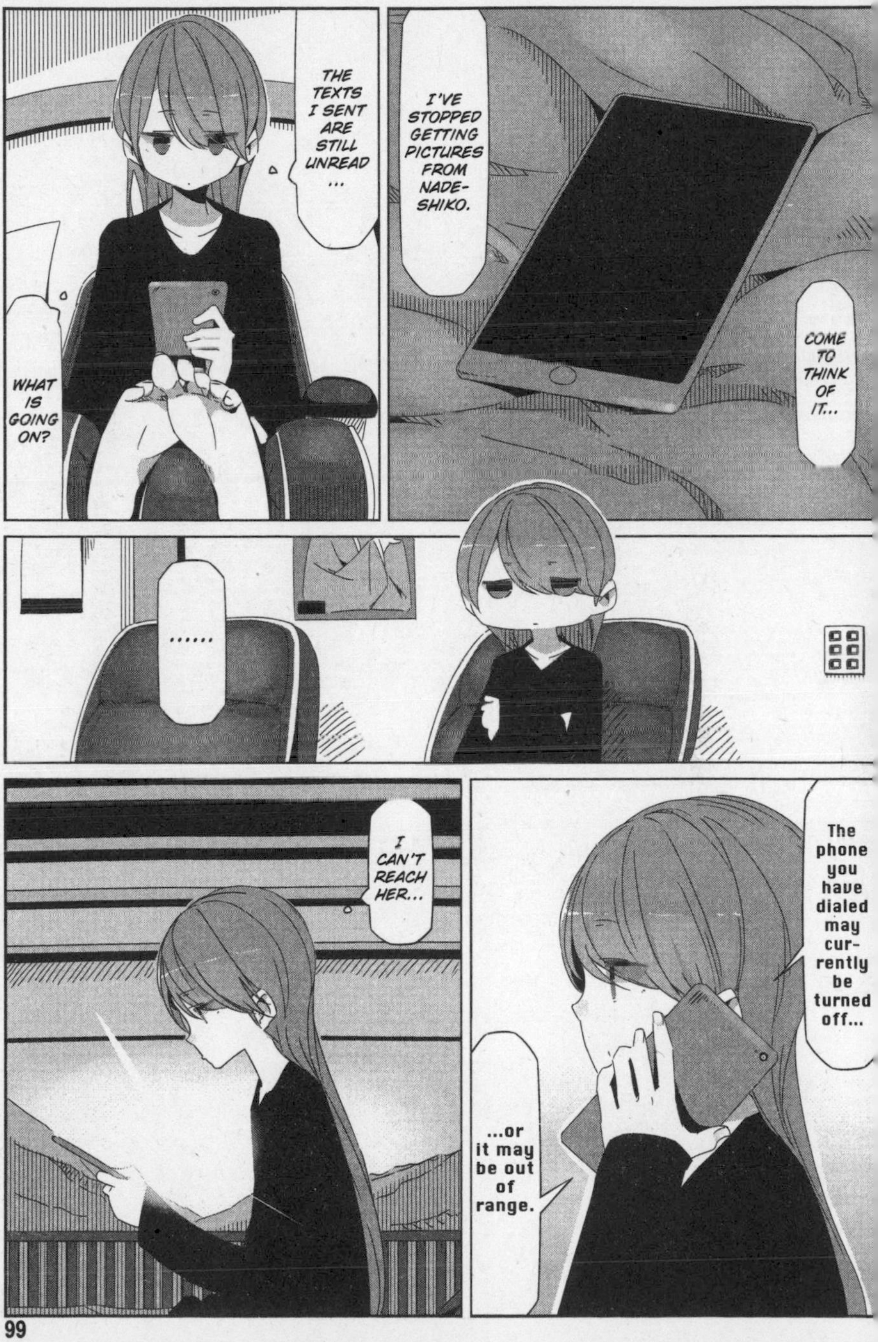
COME TO THINK OF IT...
I'VE STOPPED GETTING PICTURES FROM NADE-SHIKO.
THE TEXTS I SENT ARE STILL UNREAD...
WHAT IS GOING ON?
......
The phone you have dialed may cur-rently be turned off...
...or it may be out of range.
I CAN'T REACH HER...

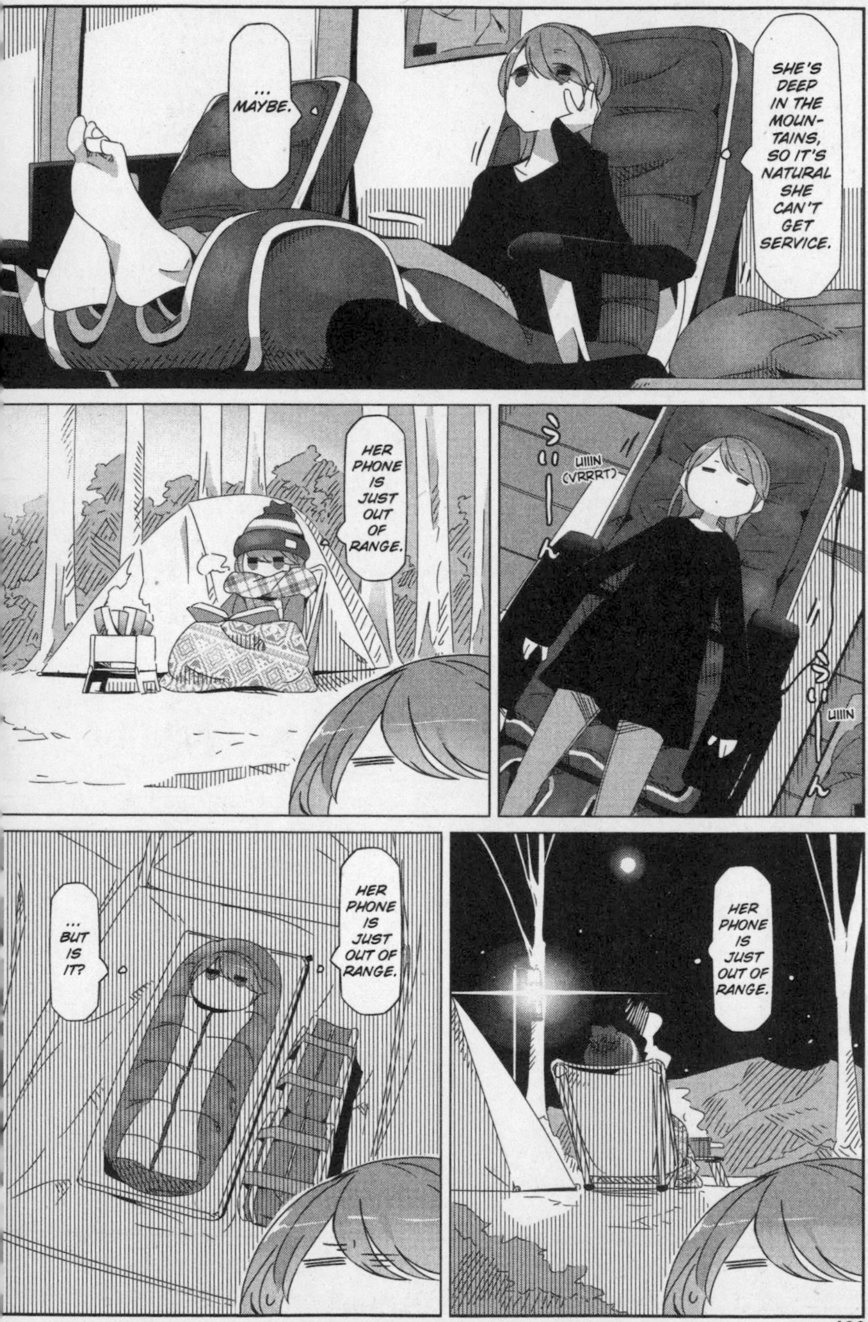
SHE'S DEEP IN THE MOUN- TAINS, SO IT'S NATURAL SHE CAN'T GET SERVICE.
... MAYBE.
ういーん
UIIIN (VRRRT)
ういーん
UIIIN
HER PHONE IS JUST OUT OF RANGE.
HER PHONE IS JUST OUT OF RANGE.
HER PHONE IS JUST OUT OF RANGE.
... BUT IS IT?

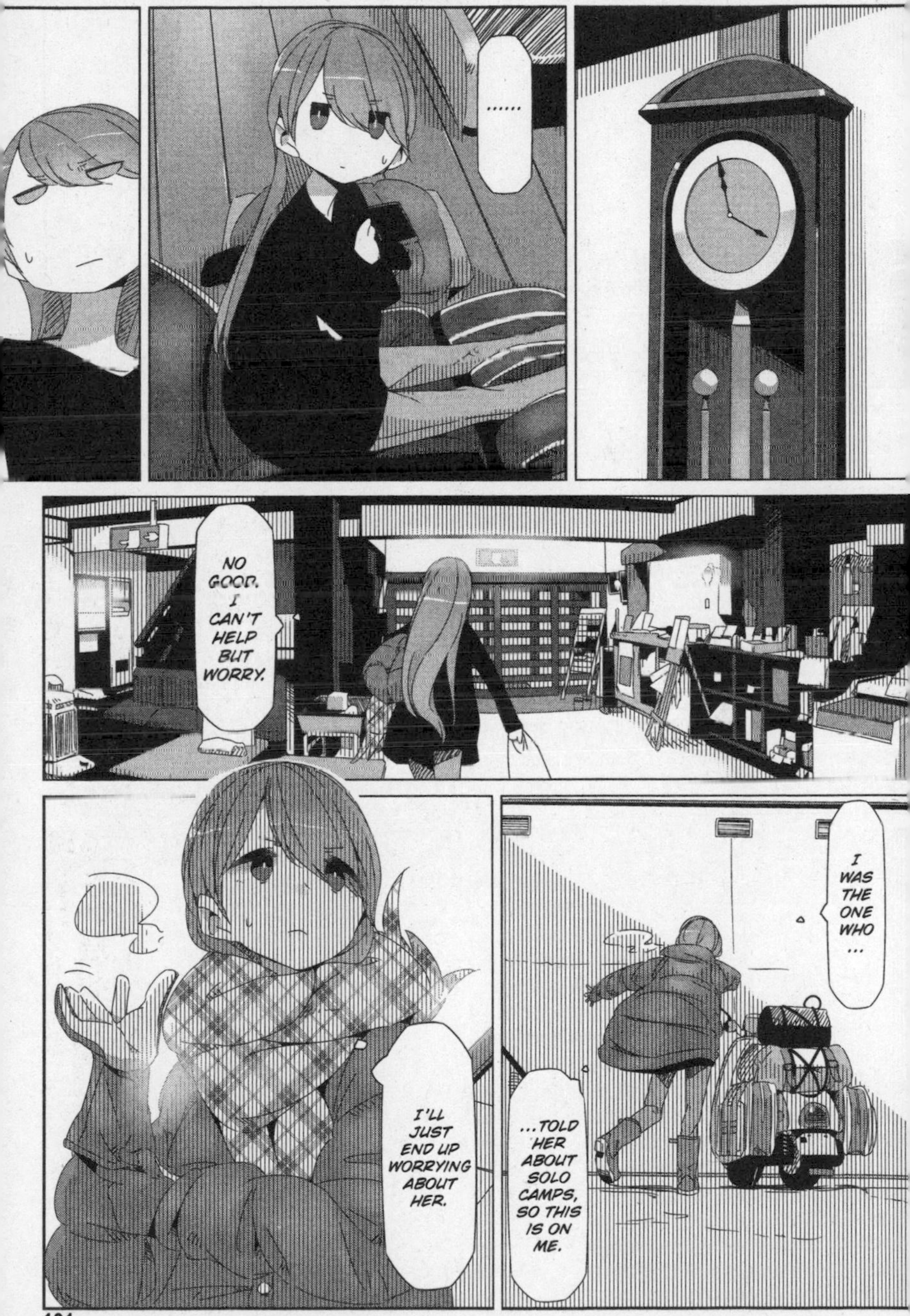
......
NO GOOD. I CAN'T HELP BUT WORRY.
I WAS THE ONE WHO...
...TOLD HER ABOUT SOLO CAMPS, SO THIS IS ON ME.
I'LL JUST END UP WORRYING ABOUT HER.

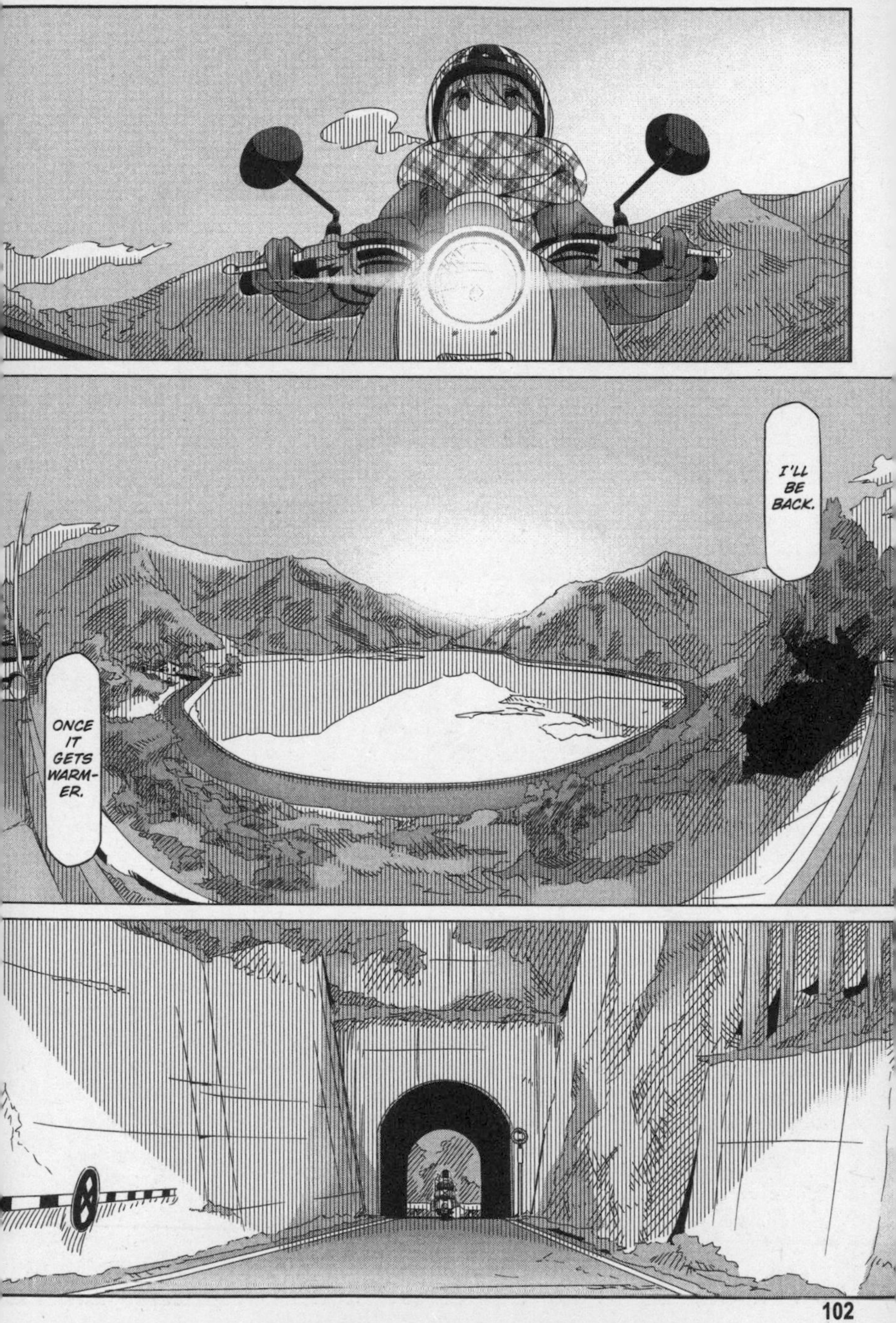
I'LL BE BACK.
ONCE IT GETS WARMER.

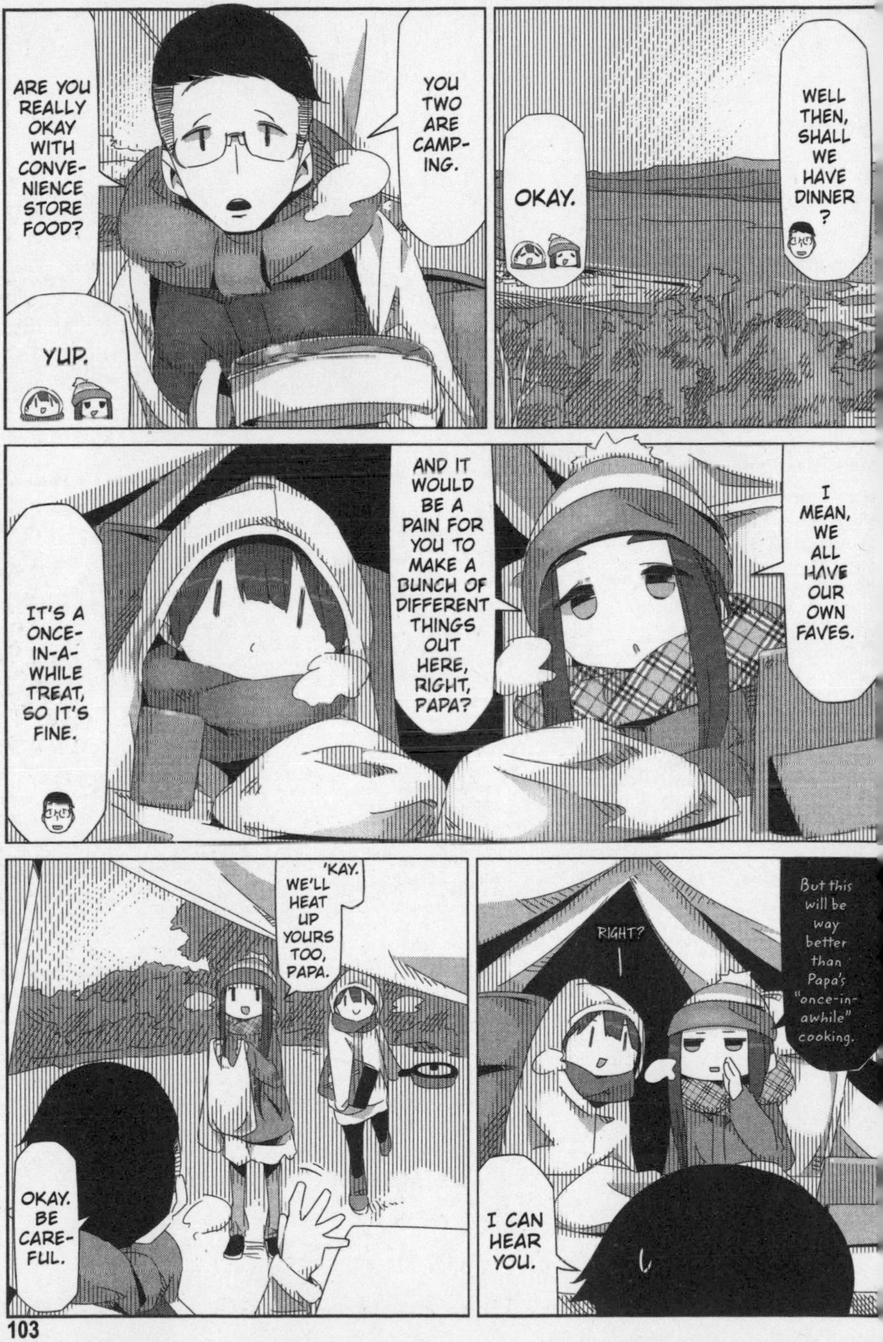
WELL THEN, SHALL WE HAVE DINNER?
OKAY.
YOU TWO ARE CAMPING.
ARE YOU REALLY OKAY WITH CONVENIENCE STORE FOOD?
YUP.
I MEAN, WE ALL HAVE OUR OWN FAVES.
AND IT WOULD BE A PAIN FOR YOU TO MAKE A BUNCH OF DIFFERENT THINGS OUT HERE, RIGHT, PAPA?
IT'S A ONCE-IN-A-WHILE TREAT, SO IT'S FINE.
But this will be way better than Papa's "once-in-awhile" cooking.
RIGHT?
I CAN HEAR YOU.
'KAY. WE'LL HEAT UP YOURS TOO, PAPA.
OKAY. BE CAREFUL.

シュオオ
ォォ
ォ
SHUOOOOO
(FWOOOOSH)

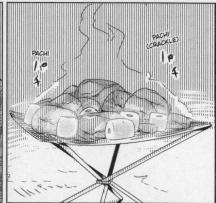

PACHI
(CRACKLE)

PACHI
(CRACKLE)

HEY,
ONEE-
CHAN,
WHAT'S
SHE
DOING?

DUNNO.
MAYBE
SHE'S
PART
OF
SOME
CULT.

BEARS...

I'M...
...HUNGRY.

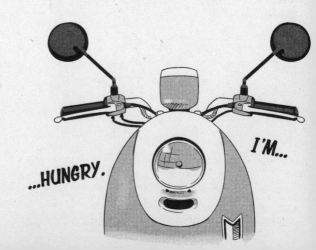

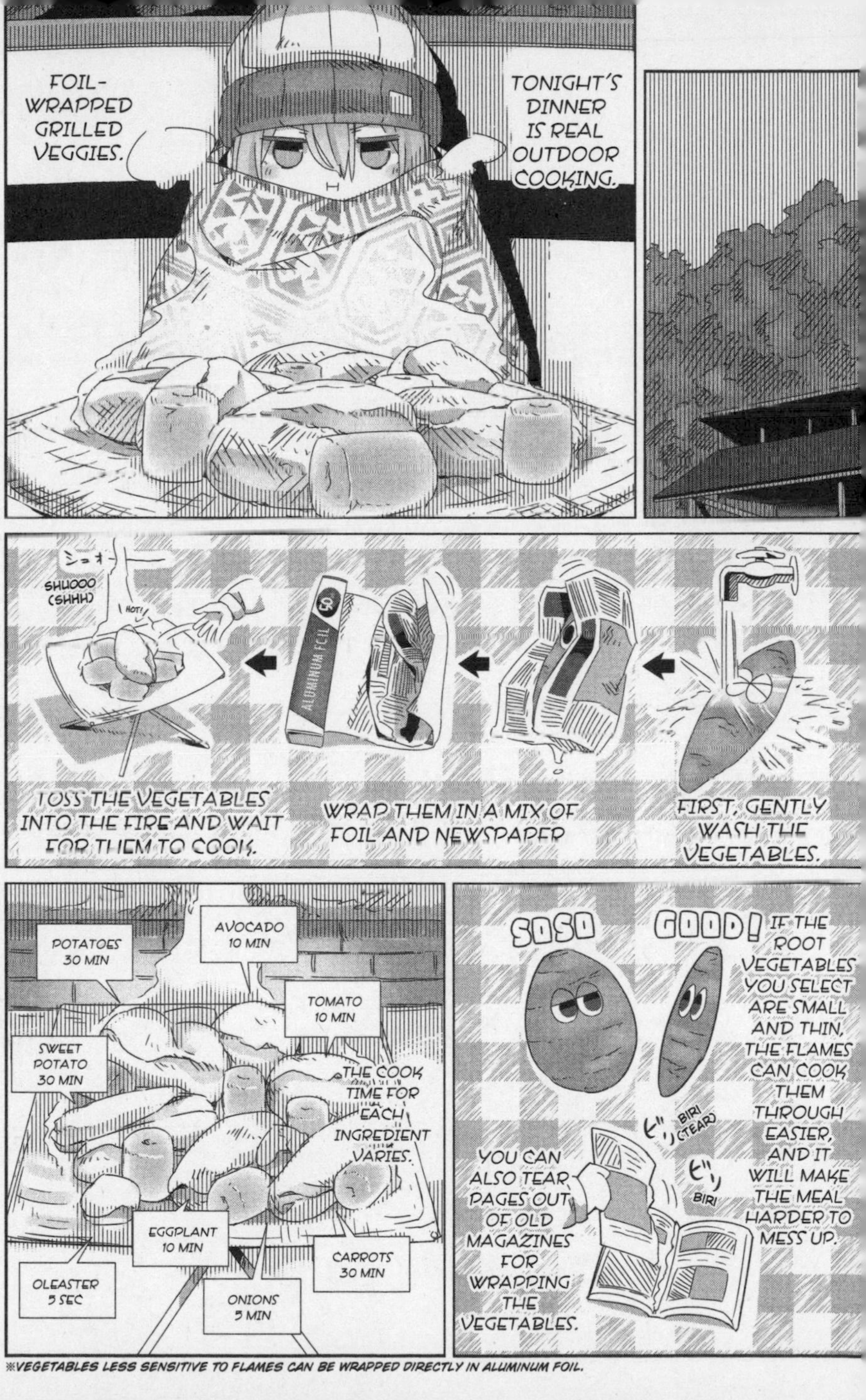
TONIGHT'S DINNER IS REAL OUTDOOR COOKING.
FOIL-WRAPPED GRILLED VEGGIES.
FIRST, GENTLY WASH THE VEGETABLES.
WRAP THEM IN A MIX OF FOIL AND NEWSPAPER
ALUMINUM FOIL
TOSS THE VEGETABLES INTO THE FIRE AND WAIT FOR THEM TO COOK.
シュオー
SHUOOO (SHHH)
HOT!
GOOD!
SOSO
IF THE ROOT VEGETABLES YOU SELECT ARE SMALL AND THIN, THE FLAMES CAN COOK THEM THROUGH EASIER, AND IT WILL MAKE THE MEAL HARDER TO MESS UP.
ビリ BIRI (TEAR)
ビリ BIRI
YOU CAN ALSO TEAR PAGES OUT OF OLD MAGAZINES FOR WRAPPING THE VEGETABLES.
AVOCADO 10 MIN
POTATOES 30 MIN
TOMATO 10 MIN
SWEET POTATO 30 MIN
THE COOK TIME FOR EACH INGREDIENT VARIES.
EGGPLANT 10 MIN
CARROTS 30 MIN
OLEASTER 5 SEC
ONIONS 5 MIN

※VEGETABLES LESS SENSITIVE TO FLAMES CAN BE WRAPPED DIRECTLY IN ALUMINUM FOIL.

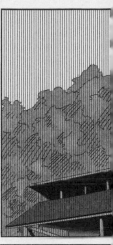

BA
(FWIP)

BA

BA
(FWIP)

TAKE THEM OUT AT THE RIGHT TIME SO THEY DON'T OVER-COOK.

SET A TIMER.

PIKYUUN (JOLT)

→BEEBEE←
→BEEBEE←
→BEEBEE←
→BEEBEE←

LIGHTLY SEASON.

OLIVE OIL

TOROO (DROOP)

PA (SHAKE)
PA
PA

HERB. SALT

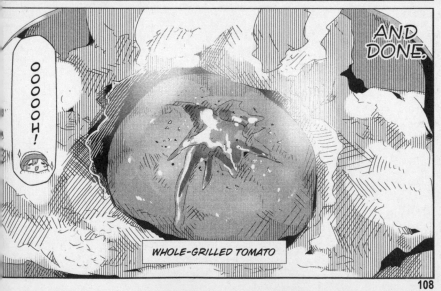

OOOOOH!

AND DONE.

WHOLE-GRILLED TOMATO

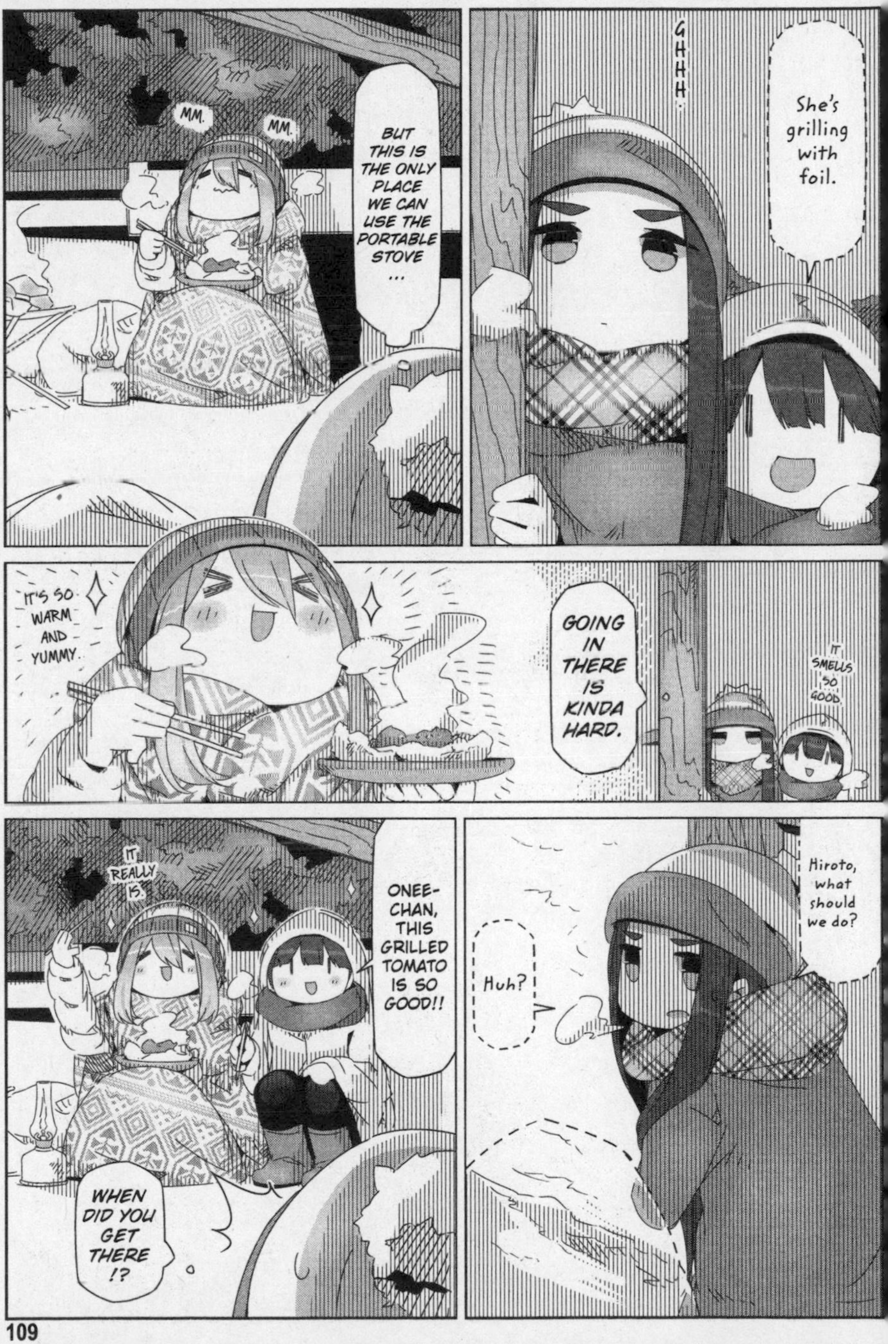
GHHH...
She's grilling with foil.
MM.
MM.
BUT THIS IS THE ONLY PLACE WE CAN USE THE PORTABLE STOVE...
GOING IN THERE IS KINDA HARD.
IT SMELLS SO GOOD.
IT'S SO WARM AND YUMMY.
Hiroto, what should we do?
Huh?
ONEE-CHAN, THIS GRILLED TOMATO IS SO GOOD!!
IT REALLY IS.
WHEN DID YOU GET THERE!?

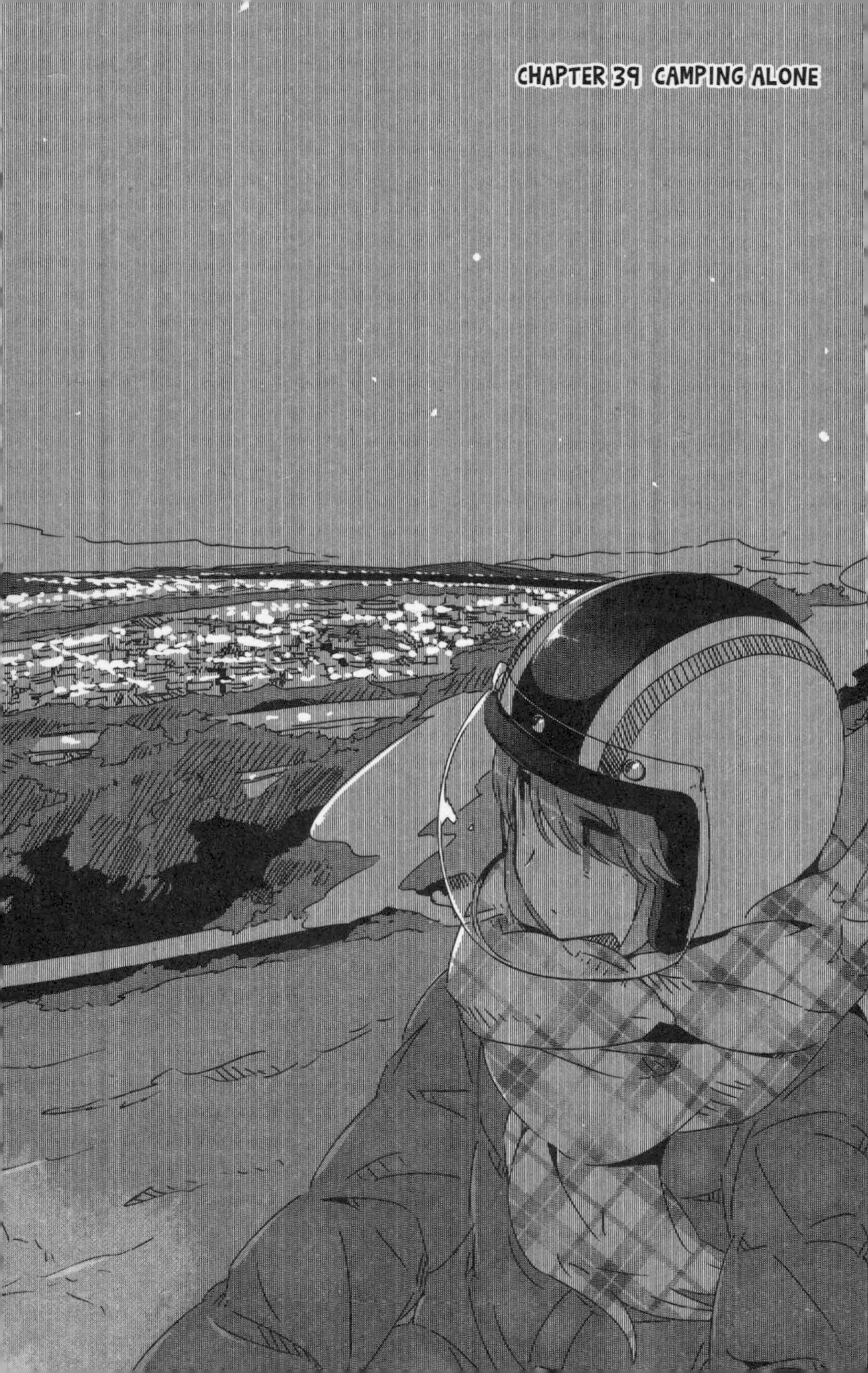
CHAPTER 39 CAMPING ALONE

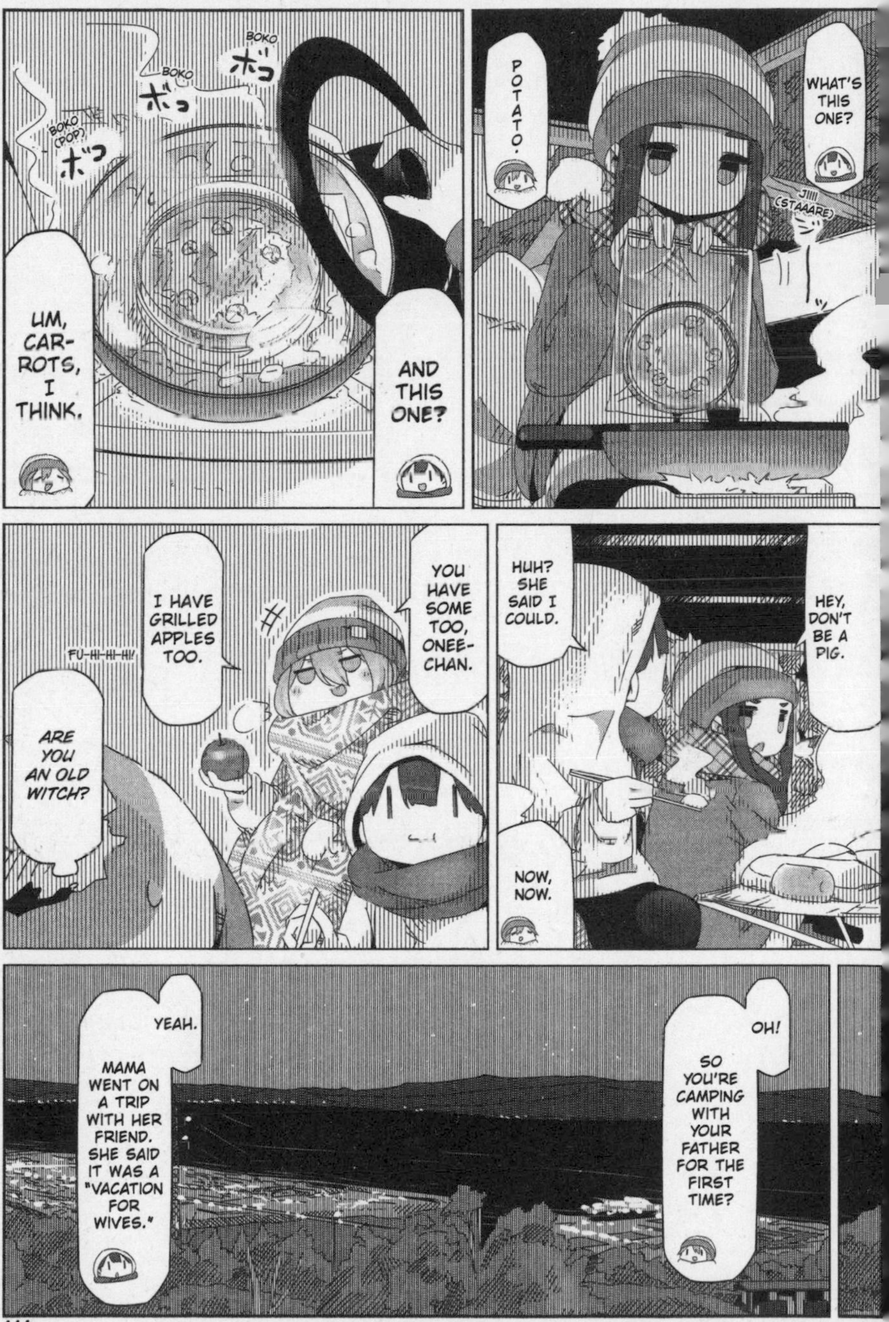
WHAT'S THIS ONE?
JIIII (STAAARE)
POTATO.
BOKO ボコ
BOKO ボコ
BOKO (POP) ボコ
AND THIS ONE?
UM, CAR-ROTS, I THINK.
HEY, DON'T BE A PIG.
HUH? SHE SAID I COULD.
NOW, NOW.
YOU HAVE SOME TOO, ONEE-CHAN.
I HAVE GRILLED APPLES TOO.
FU-HI-HI-HI!
ARE YOU AN OLD WITCH?
OH!
SO YOU'RE CAMPING WITH YOUR FATHER FOR THE FIRST TIME?
YEAH.
MAMA WENT ON A TRIP WITH HER FRIEND. SHE SAID IT WAS A "VACATION FOR WIVES."

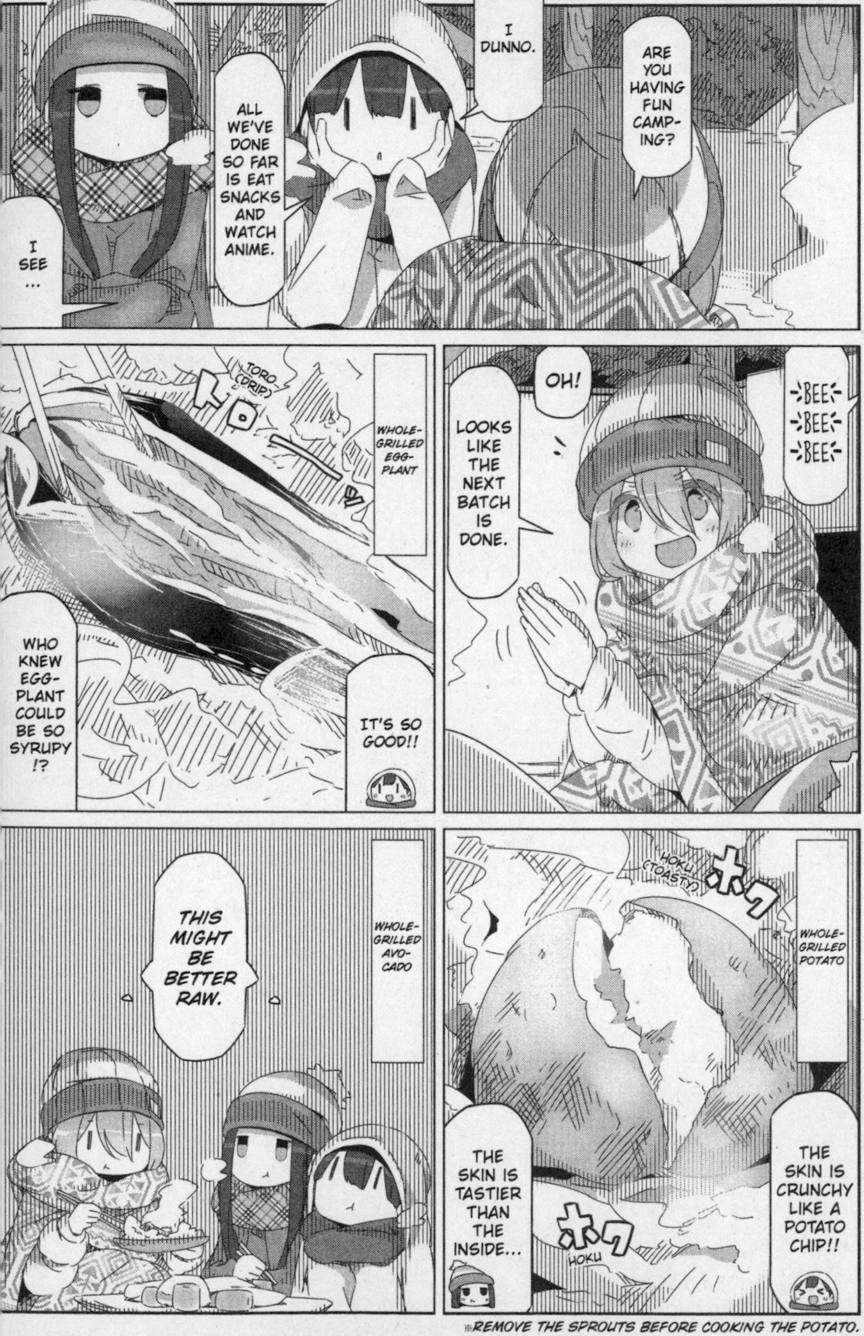
ARE YOU HAVING FUN CAMPING?
I DUNNO.
ALL WE'VE DONE SO FAR IS EAT SNACKS AND WATCH ANIME.
I SEE ...
BEE BEE BEE
OH!
LOOKS LIKE THE NEXT BATCH IS DONE.
WHOLE-GRILLED EGGPLANT
TORO (DRIP)
IT'S SO GOOD!!
WHO KNEW EGGPLANT COULD BE SO SYRUPY !?
WHOLE-GRILLED POTATO
HOKU (TOASTY)
THE SKIN IS CRUNCHY LIKE A POTATO CHIP!!
HOKU
THE SKIN IS TASTIER THAN THE INSIDE...
WHOLE-GRILLED AVOCADO
THIS MIGHT BE BETTER RAW.

※REMOVE THE SPROUTS BEFORE COOKING THE POTATO.

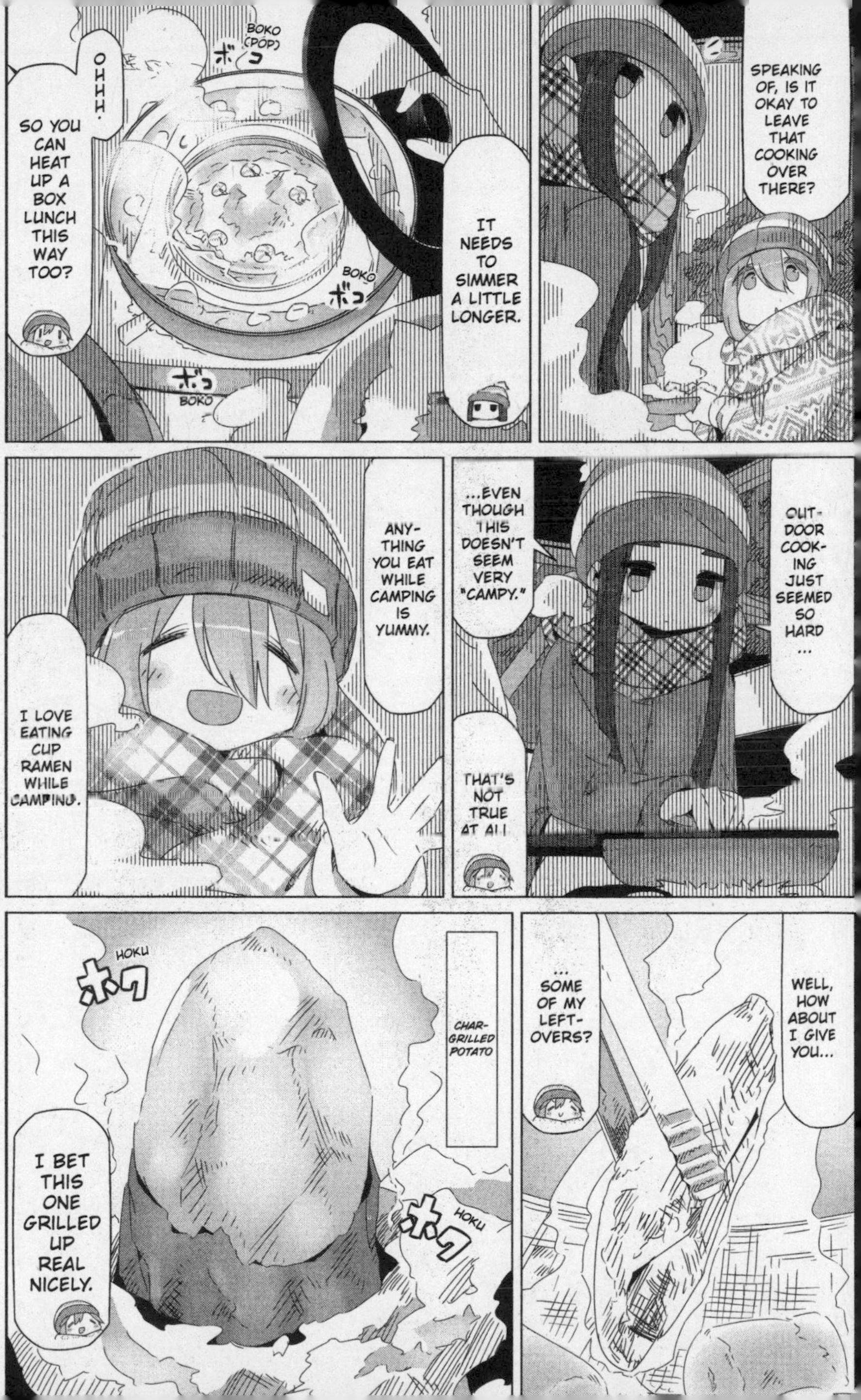
SPEAKING OF, IS IT OKAY TO LEAVE THAT COOKING OVER THERE?
IT NEEDS TO SIMMER A LITTLE LONGER.
BOKO (POP)
ボコ
OHHH.
SO YOU CAN HEAT UP A BOX LUNCH THIS WAY TOO?
BOKO
ボコ
ボコ
BOKO
OUT-DOOR COOK-ING JUST SEEMED SO HARD...
...EVEN THOUGH THIS DOESN'T SEEM VERY "CAMPY."
THAT'S NOT TRUE AT ALL.
ANY-THING YOU EAT WHILE CAMPING IS YUMMY.
I LOVE EATING CUP RAMEN WHILE CAMPING.
WELL, HOW ABOUT I GIVE YOU...
...SOME OF MY LEFT-OVERS?
CHAR-GRILLED POTATO
HOKU
ホク
HOKU
ホク
I BET THIS ONE GRILLED UP REAL NICELY.

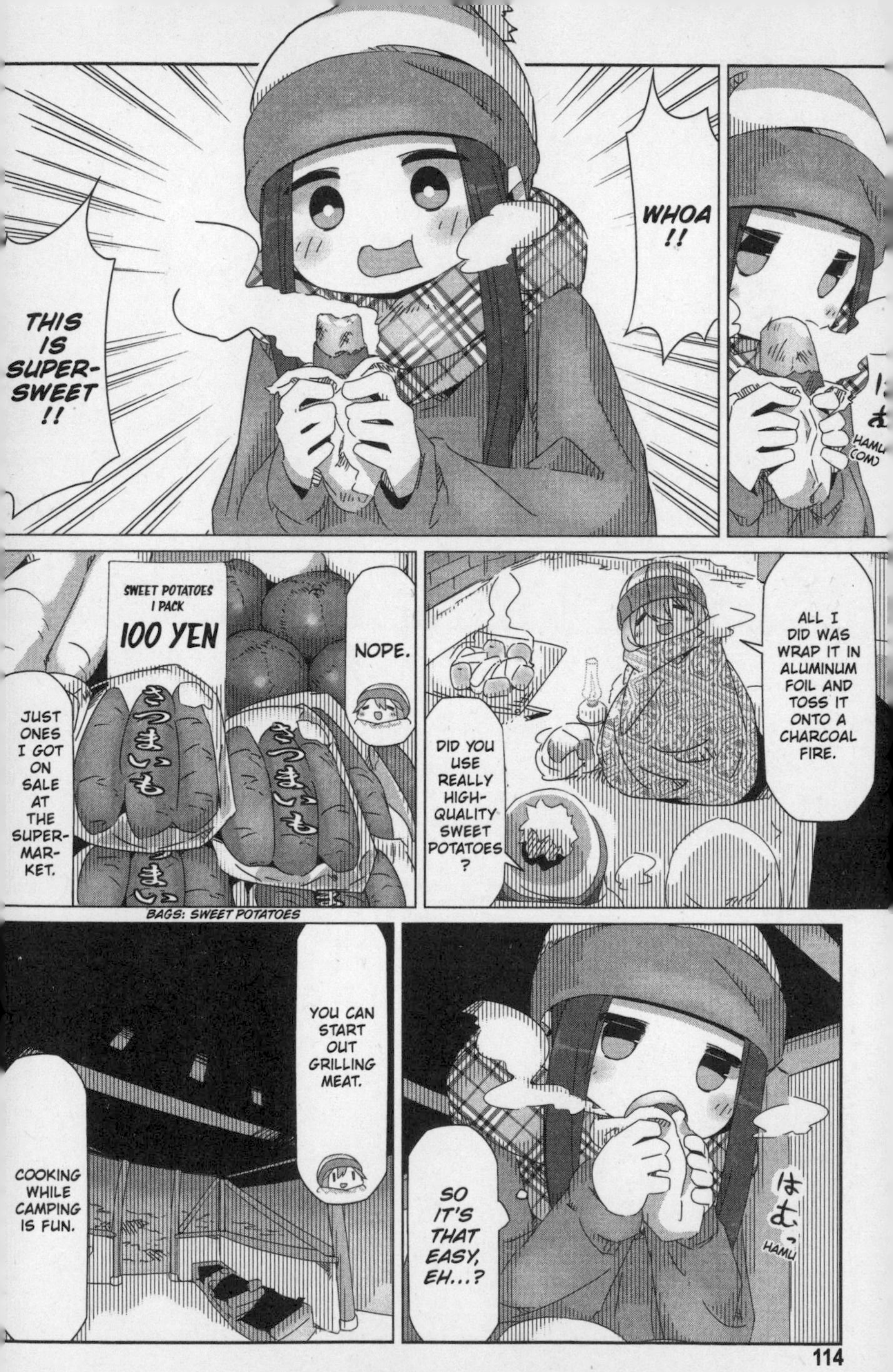
HAMU
WHOA !!
THIS IS SUPER-SWEET !!
ALL I DID WAS WRAP IT IN ALUMINUM FOIL AND TOSS IT ONTO A CHARCOAL FIRE.
DID YOU USE REALLY HIGH-QUALITY SWEET POTATOES ?
NOPE.
SWEET POTATOES 1 PACK
100 YEN
さつまいも
さつまいも
JUST ONES I GOT ON SALE AT THE SUPER-MARKET.
BAGS: SWEET POTATOES
はむっ
HAMU
SO IT'S THAT EASY, EH...?
YOU CAN START OUT GRILLING MEAT.
COOKING WHILE CAMPING IS FUN.

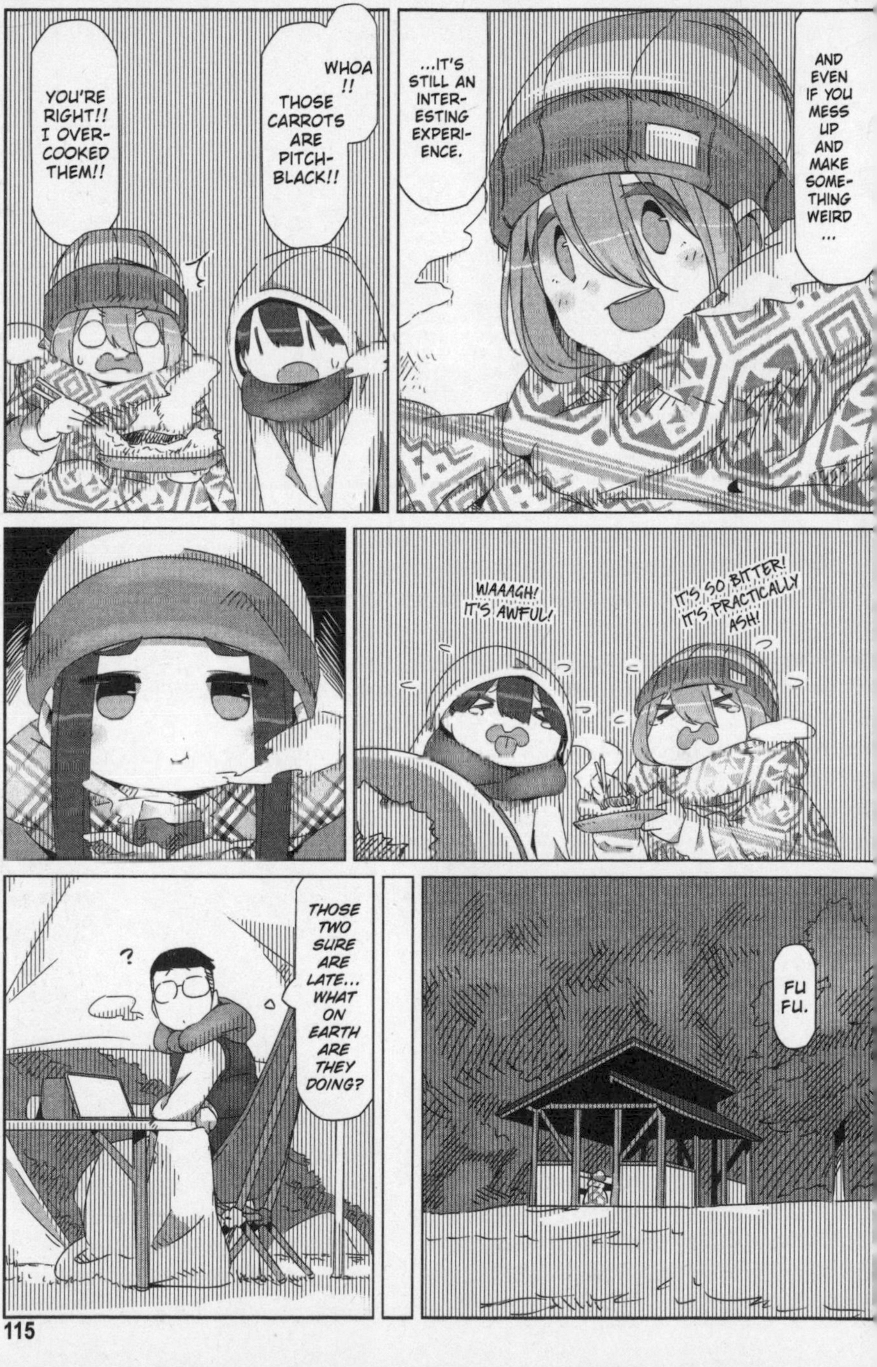
AND EVEN IF YOU MESS UP AND MAKE SOMETHING WEIRD...
...IT'S STILL AN INTERESTING EXPERIENCE.
WHOA!! THOSE CARROTS ARE PITCH-BLACK!!
YOU'RE RIGHT!! I OVERCOOKED THEM!!
IT'S SO BITTER! IT'S PRACTICALLY ASH!
WAAAGH! IT'S AWFUL!
FU FU.
THOSE TWO SURE ARE LATE... WHAT ON EARTH ARE THEY DOING?

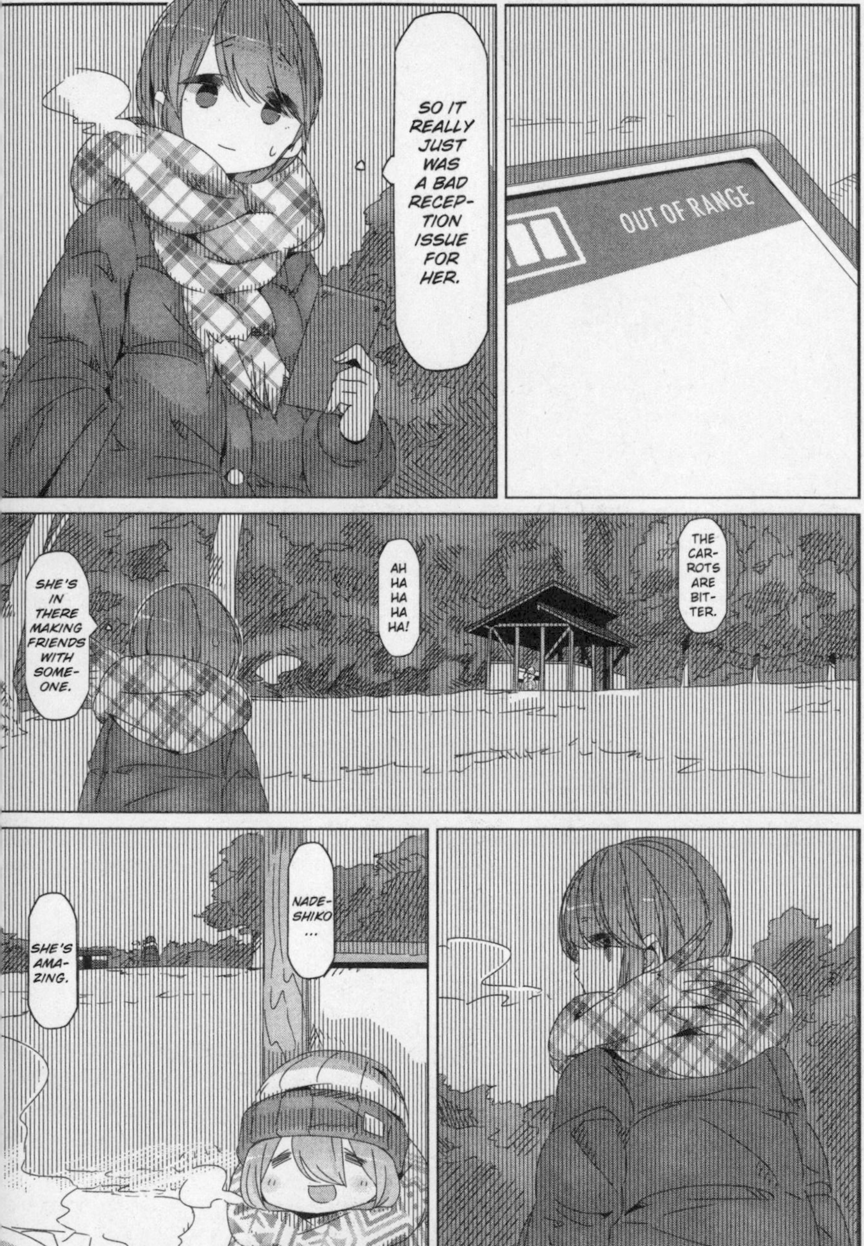
OUT OF RANGE
SO IT REALLY JUST WAS A BAD RECEPTION ISSUE FOR HER.
THE CARROTS ARE BITTER.
AH HA HA HA HA!
SHE'S IN THERE MAKING FRIENDS WITH SOMEONE.
NADESHIKO...
SHE'S AMAZING.

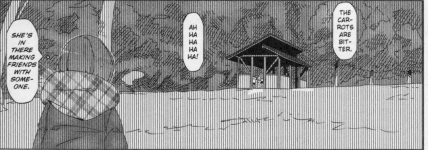

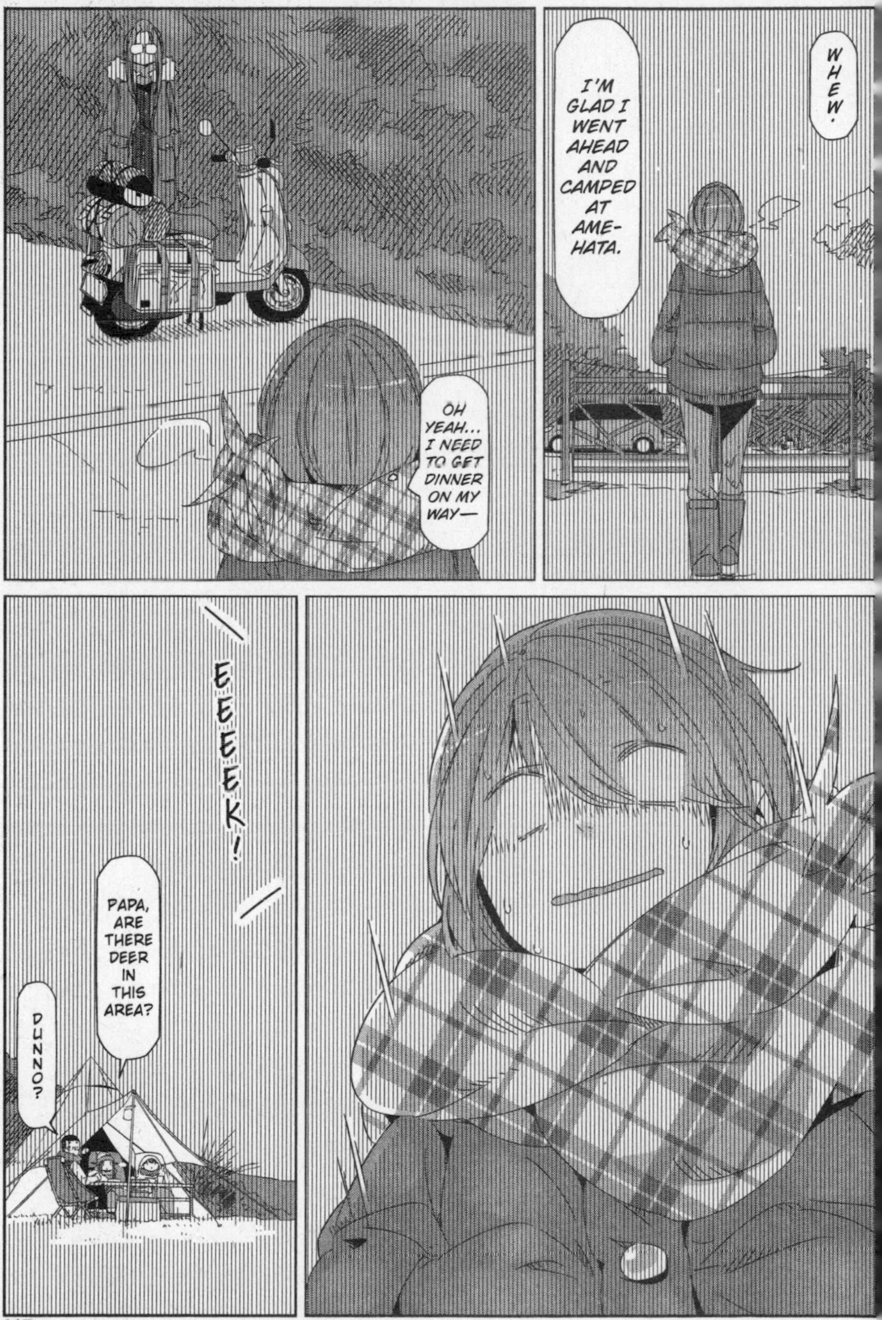
WHEW.
I'M GLAD I WENT AHEAD AND CAMPED AT AME-HATA.
OH YEAH... I NEED TO GET DINNER ON MY WAY—
EEEEK!
PAPA, ARE THERE DEER IN THIS AREA?
DUNNO?

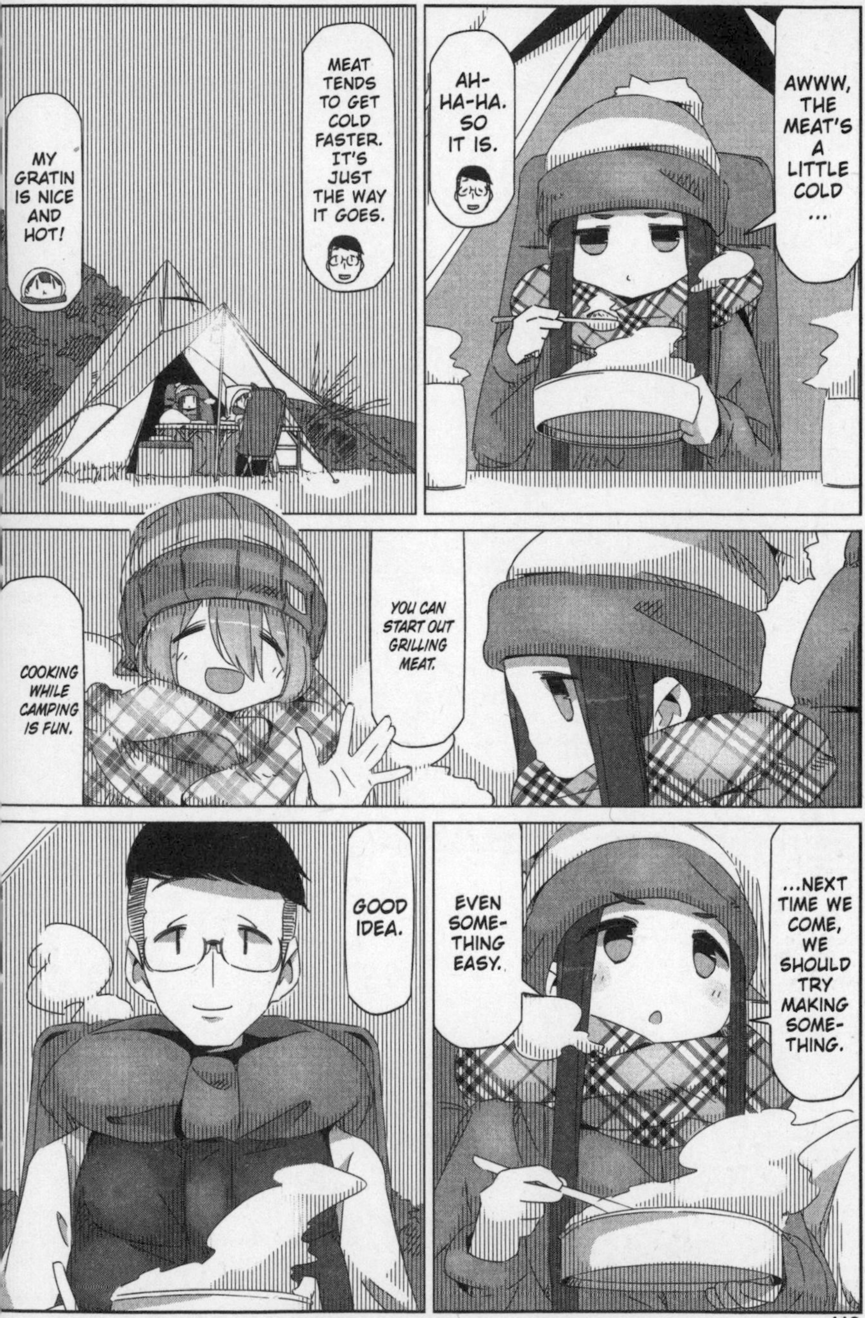
AWWW, THE MEAT'S A LITTLE COLD ...
AH-HA-HA. SO IT IS.
MEAT TENDS TO GET COLD FASTER. IT'S JUST THE WAY IT GOES.
MY GRATIN IS NICE AND HOT!
YOU CAN START OUT GRILLING MEAT.
COOKING WHILE CAMPING IS FUN.
...NEXT TIME WE COME, WE SHOULD TRY MAKING SOME-THING.
EVEN SOME-THING EASY.
GOOD IDEA.

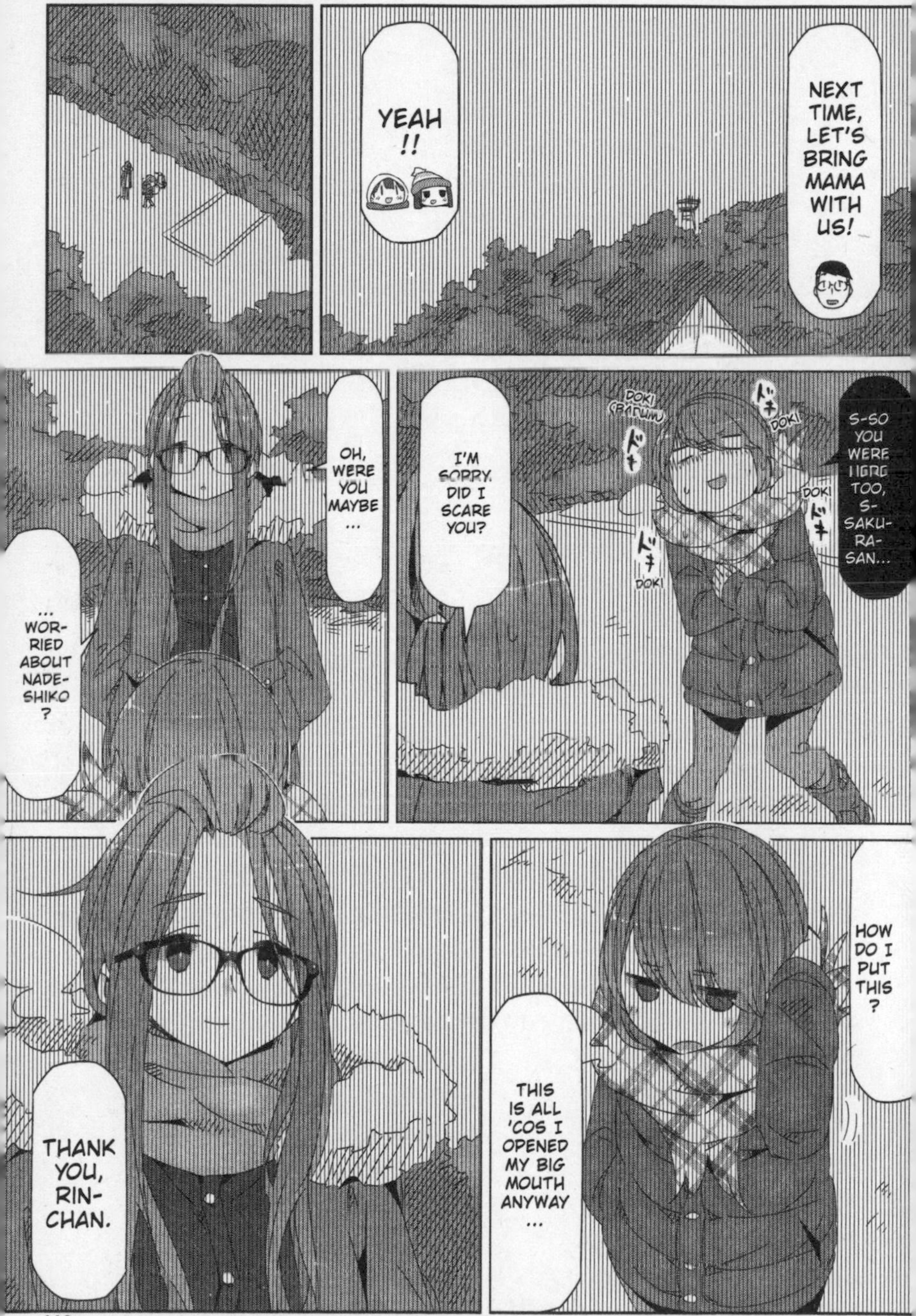
NEXT TIME, LET'S BRING MAMA WITH US!
YEAH!!
S-SO YOU WERE HERE TOO, S-SAKURA-SAN...
ドキ DOKI
DOKI (BADUM) ドキ
DOKI ドキ
ドキ DOKI
I'M SORRY. DID I SCARE YOU?
OH, WERE YOU MAYBE...
...WORRIED ABOUT NADESHIKO?
HOW DO I PUT THIS?
THIS IS ALL 'COS I OPENED MY BIG MOUTH ANYWAY...
THANK YOU, RIN-CHAN.

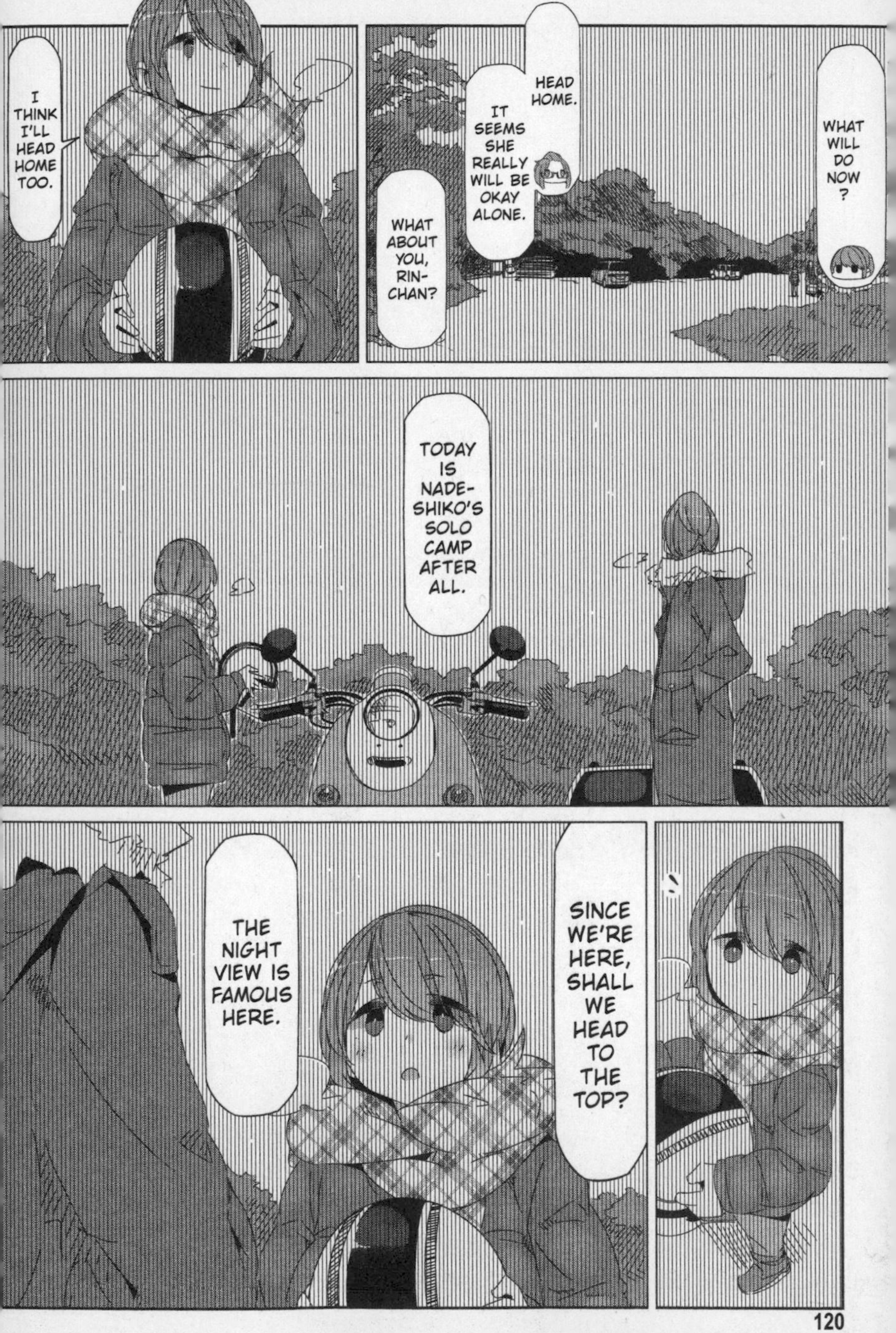
WHAT WILL DO NOW ?
HEAD HOME.
IT SEEMS SHE REALLY WILL BE OKAY ALONE.
WHAT ABOUT YOU, RIN-CHAN?
I THINK I'LL HEAD HOME TOO.
TODAY IS NADE-SHIKO'S SOLO CAMP AFTER ALL.
!
SINCE WE'RE HERE, SHALL WE HEAD TO THE TOP?
THE NIGHT VIEW IS FAMOUS HERE.

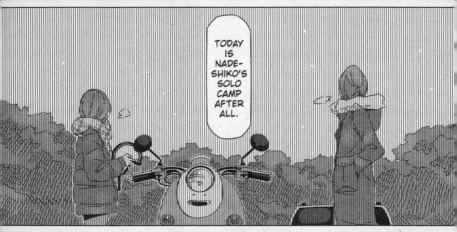

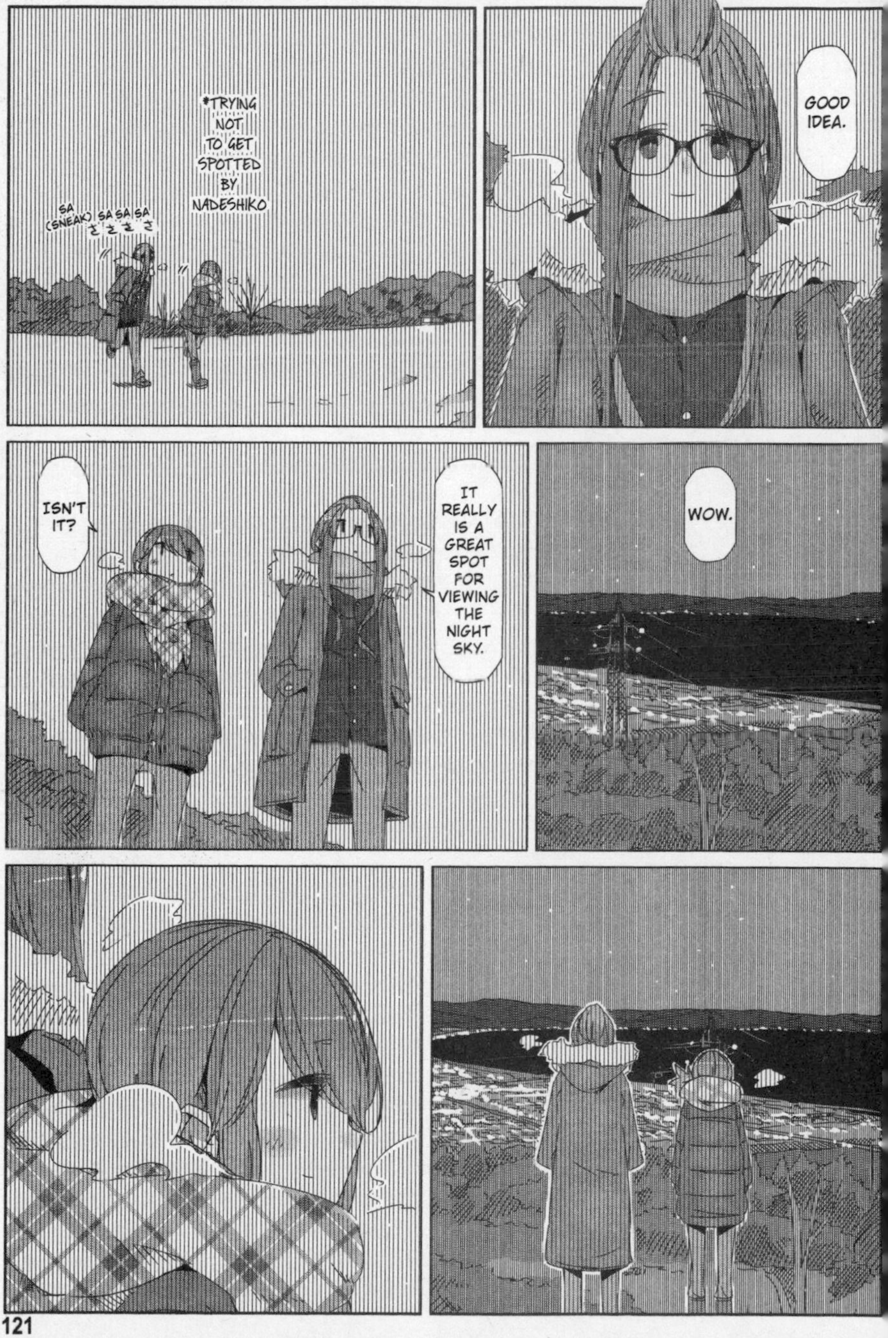
GOOD IDEA.
*TRYING NOT TO GET SPOTTED BY NADESHIKO
SA (SNEAK) SA SA SA
ささささ
WOW.
IT REALLY IS A GREAT SPOT FOR VIEWING THE NIGHT SKY.
ISN'T IT?

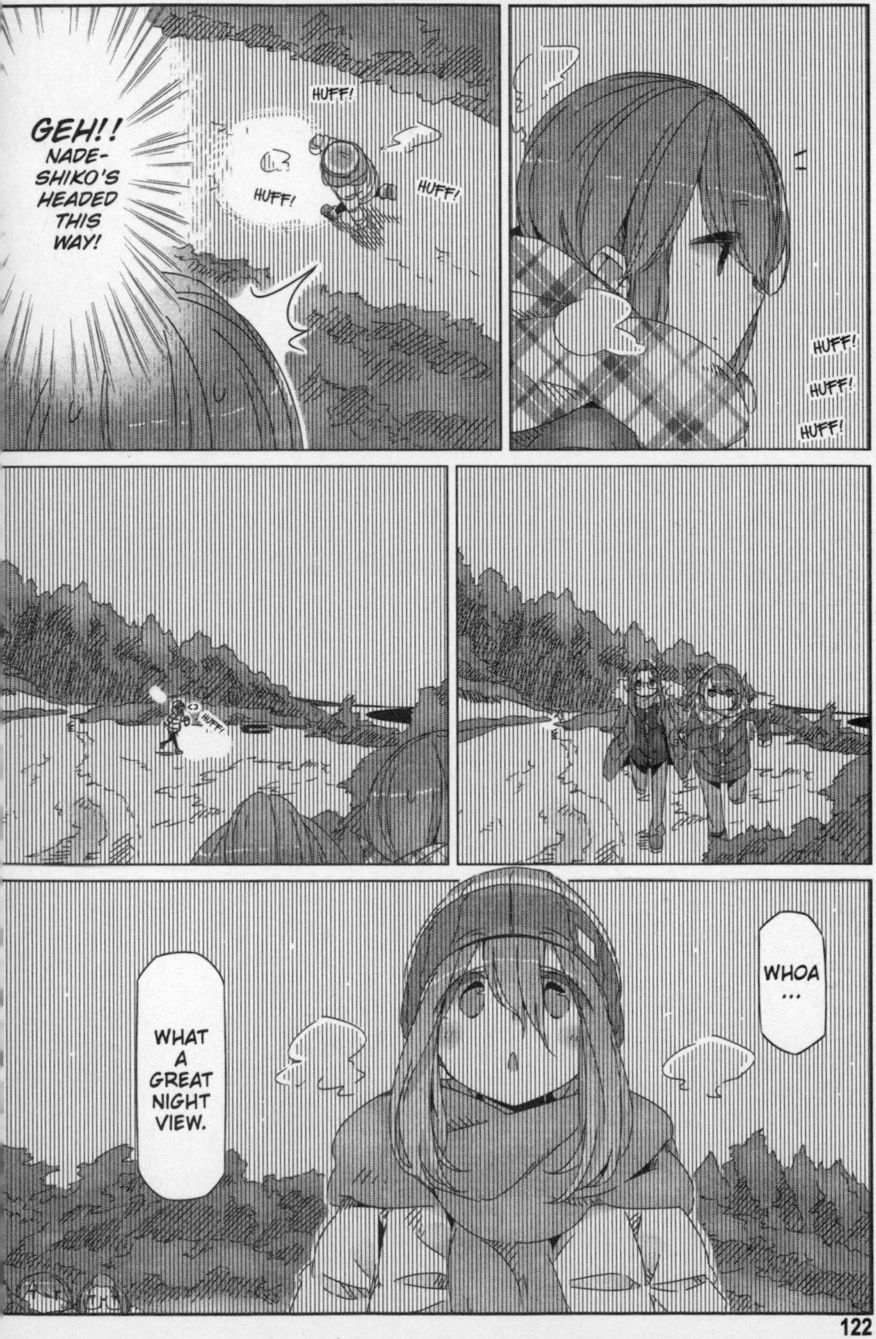
HUFF!
HUFF!
HUFF!
HUFF!
HUFF!
HUFF!
GEH!! NADE-SHIKO'S HEADED THIS WAY!
HUFF!
WHOA...
WHAT A GREAT NIGHT VIEW.

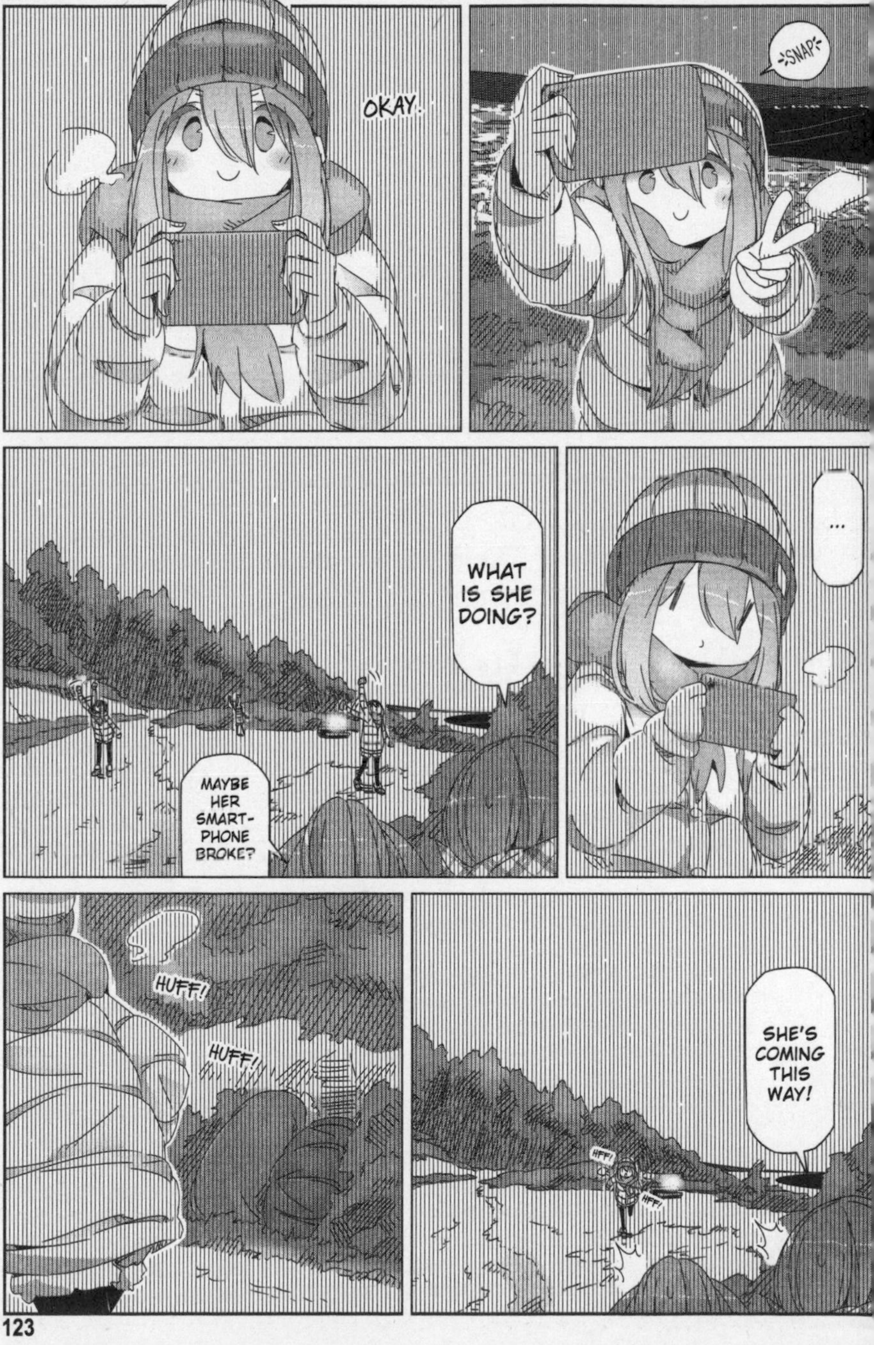
SNAP
OKAY.
...
WHAT IS SHE DOING?
MAYBE HER SMARTPHONE BROKE?
SHE'S COMING THIS WAY!
HFF!
HFF!
HUFF!
HUFF!

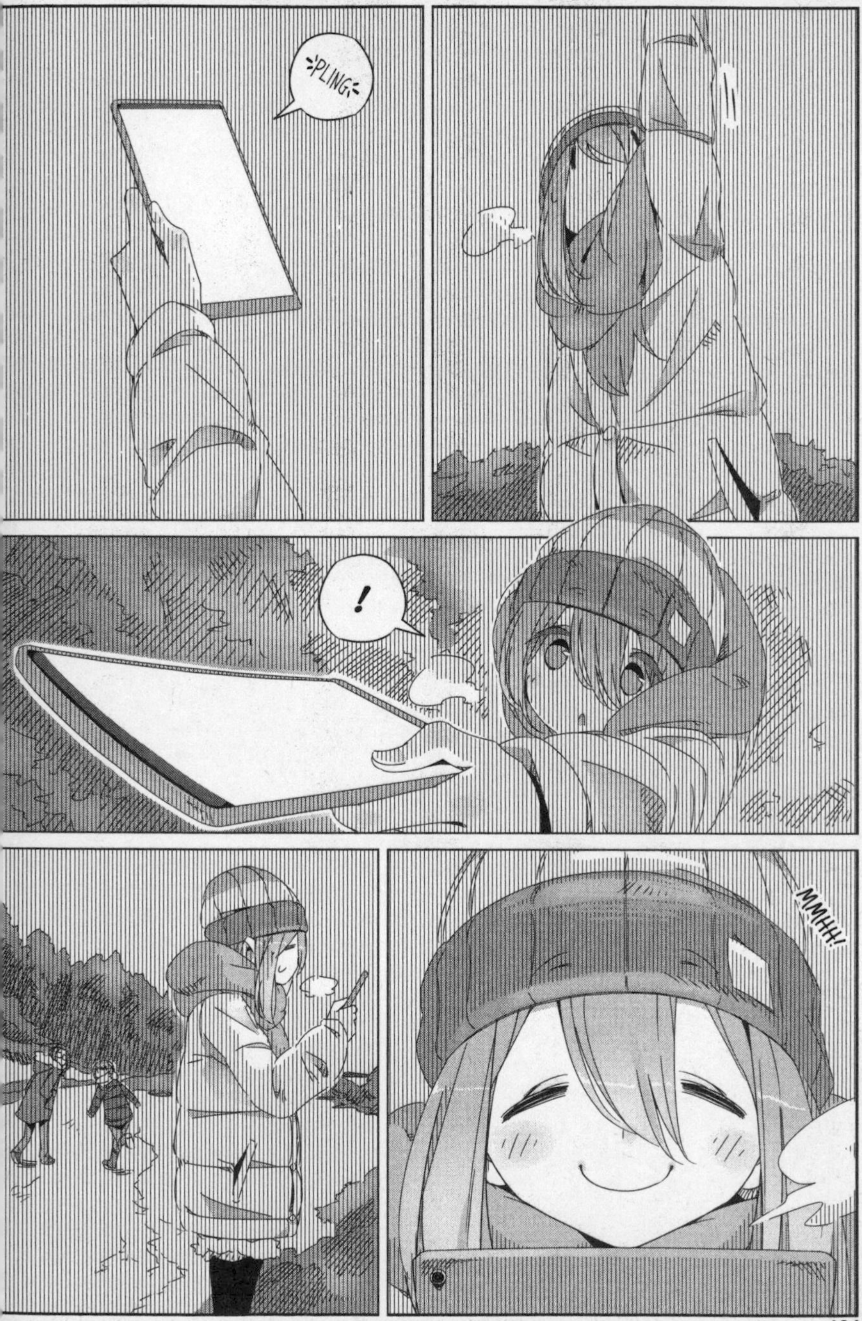
PLING
!
MMHH!

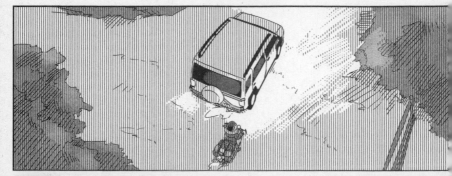

OKAY.

I'LL SEE YOU TO THE BOTTOM, SO TAKE YOUR TIME AND FOLLOW ME.

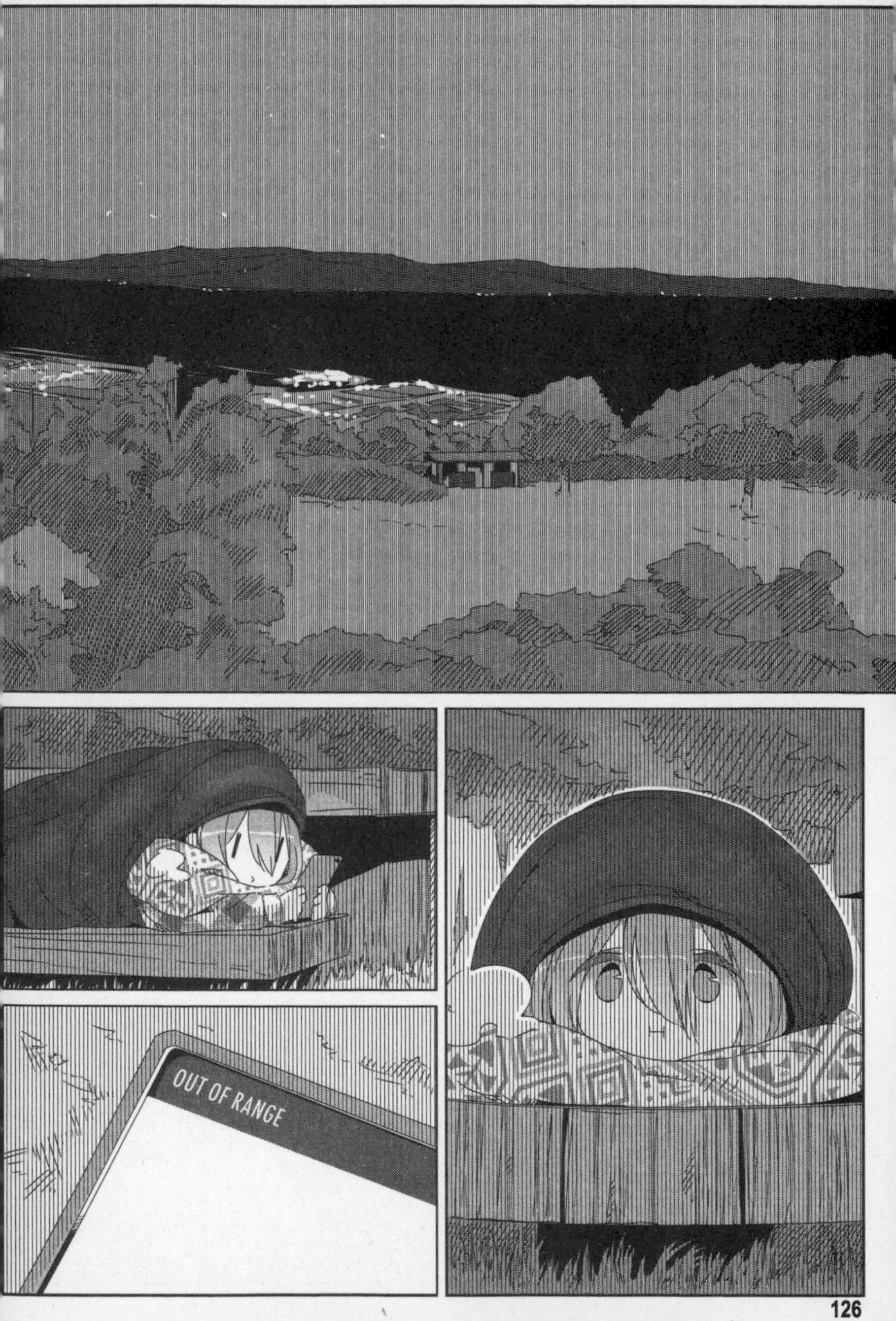
OUT OF RANGE

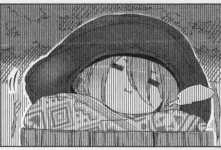

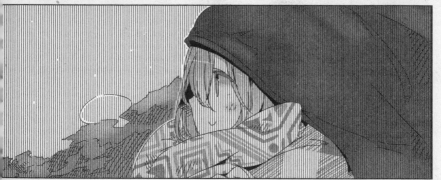

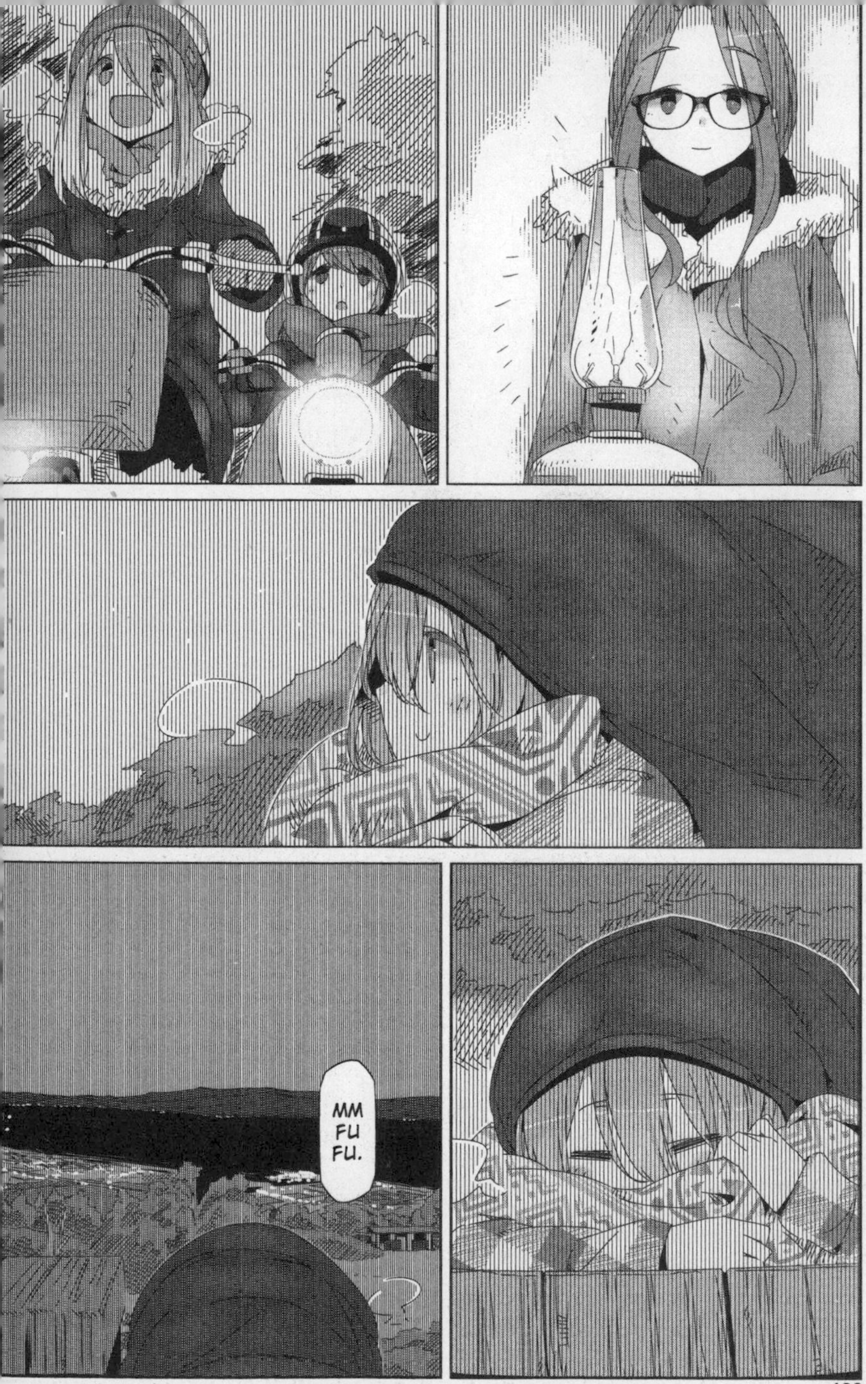
MM
FU
FU.

IS SOME-THING THE MATTER?

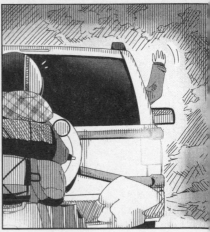

129

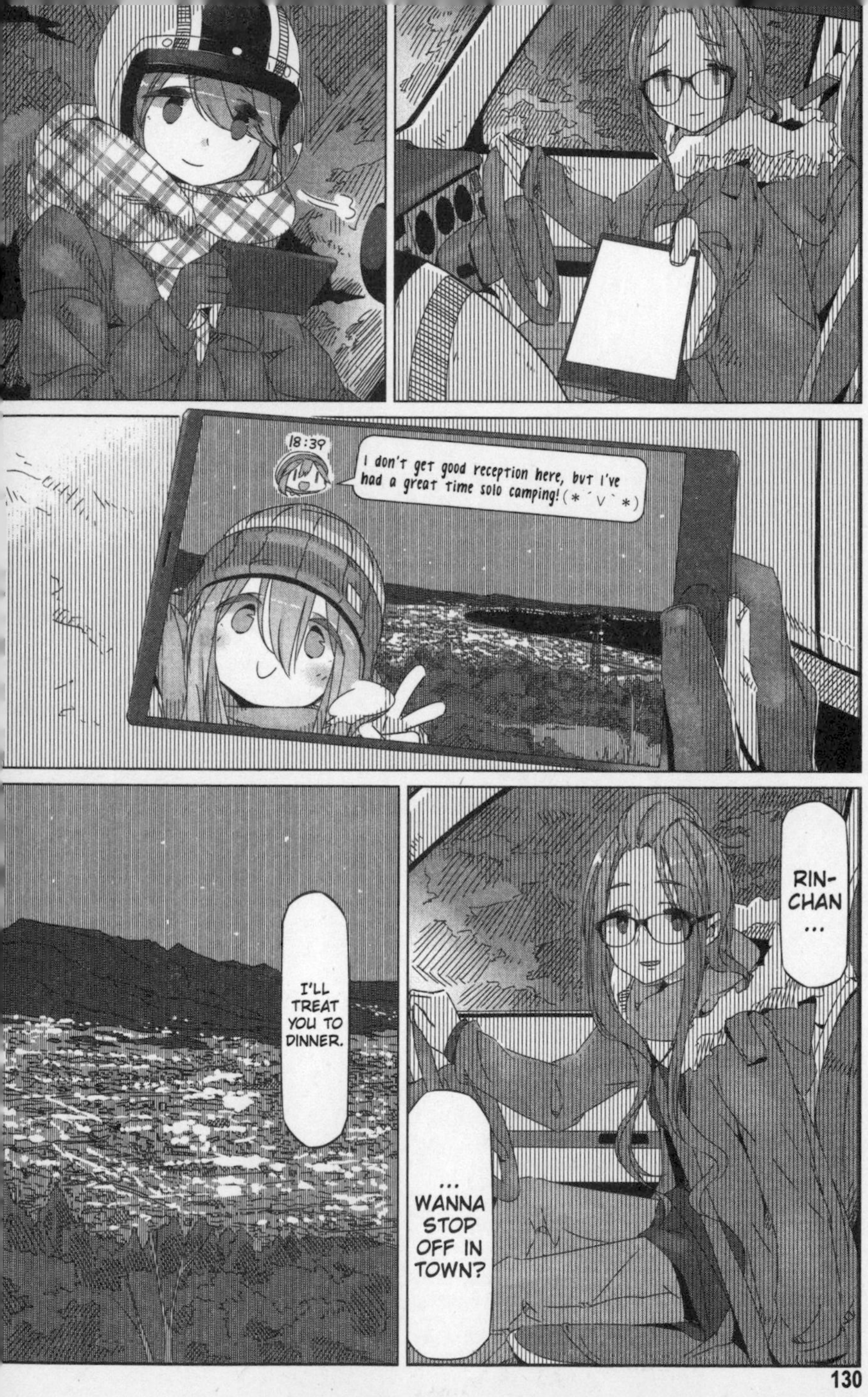
18:39
I don't get good reception here, but I've had a great time solo camping! (*´∀`*)
RIN-CHAN...
...WANNA STOP OFF IN TOWN?
I'LL TREAT YOU TO DINNER.

I'VE BEEN TRYING TO TELL YOU...
...I'M HUNGRY.

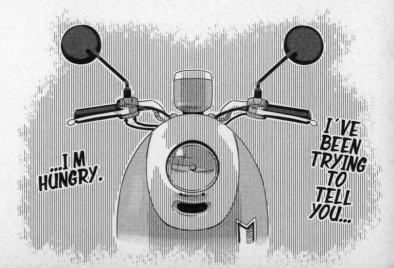

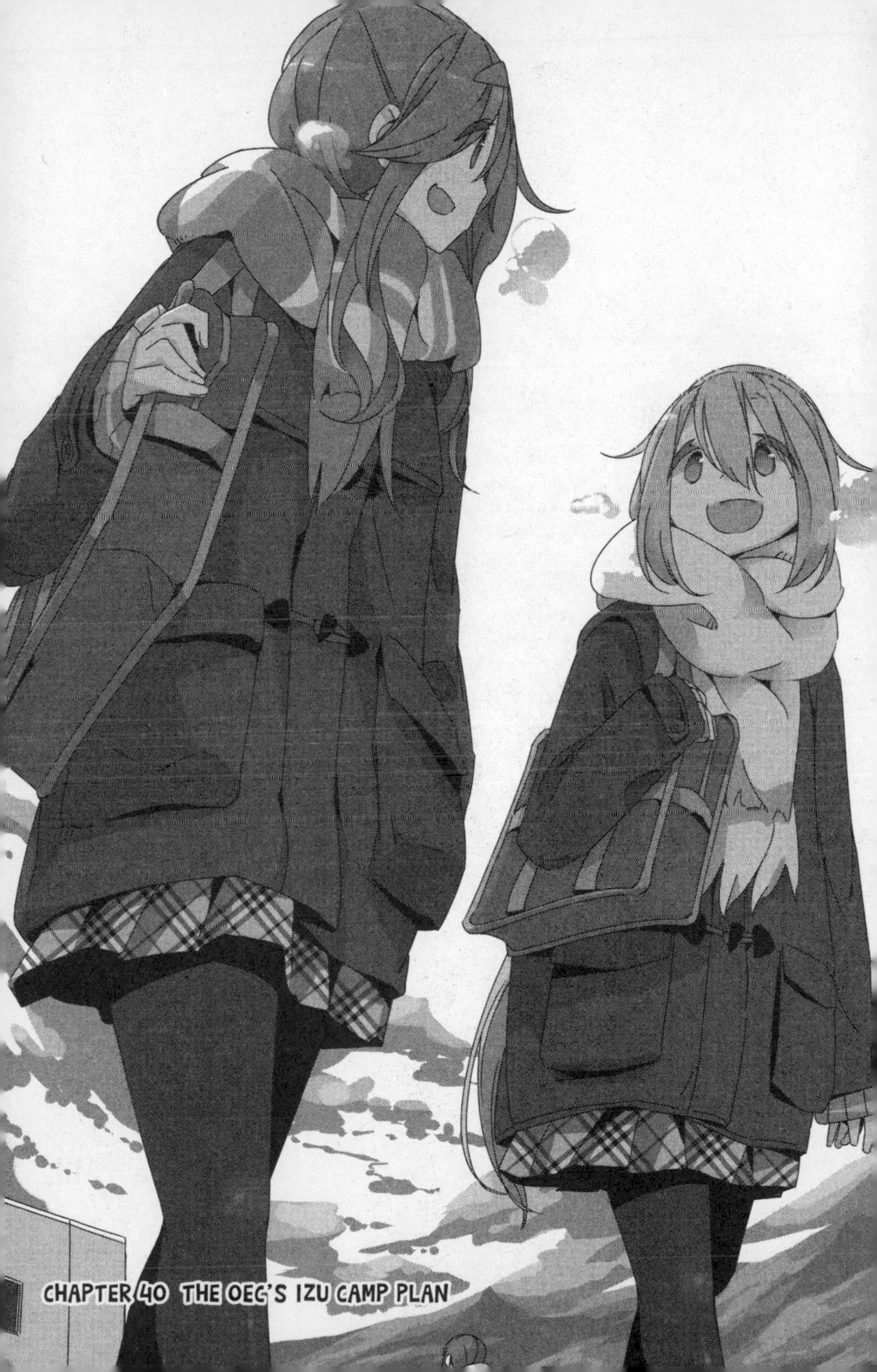

CHAPTER 40 THE OEC'S IZU CAMP PLAN

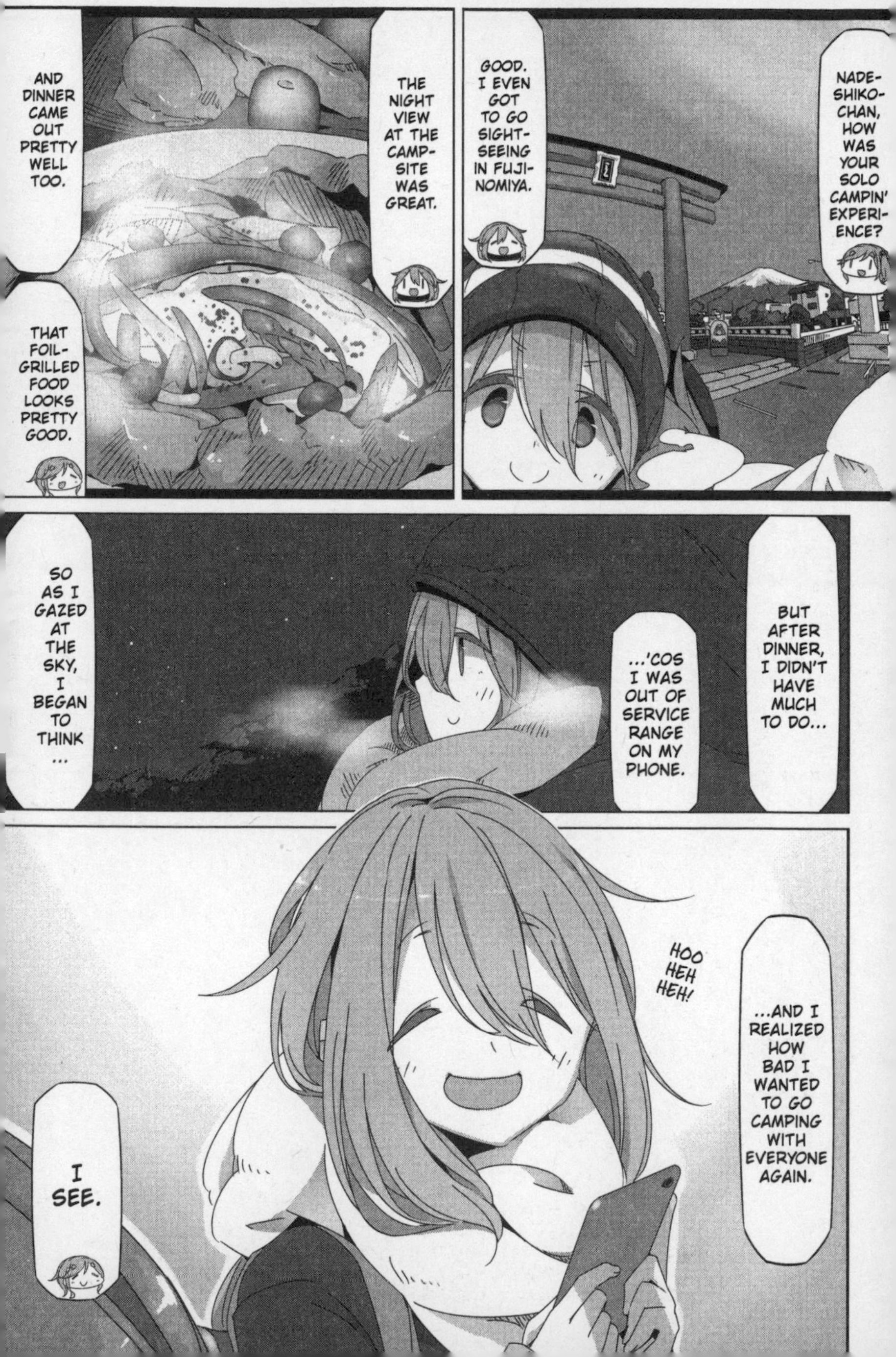
NADE-SHIKO-CHAN, HOW WAS YOUR SOLO CAMPIN' EXPERI-ENCE?
GOOD. I EVEN GOT TO GO SIGHT-SEEING IN FUJI-NOMIYA.
THE NIGHT VIEW AT THE CAMP-SITE WAS GREAT.
AND DINNER CAME OUT PRETTY WELL TOO.
THAT FOIL-GRILLED FOOD LOOKS PRETTY GOOD.
BUT AFTER DINNER, I DIDN'T HAVE MUCH TO DO...
...'COS I WAS OUT OF SERVICE RANGE ON MY PHONE.
SO AS I GAZED AT THE SKY, I BEGAN TO THINK...
...AND I REALIZED HOW BAD I WANTED TO GO CAMPING WITH EVERYONE AGAIN.
HOO HEH HEH!
I SEE.

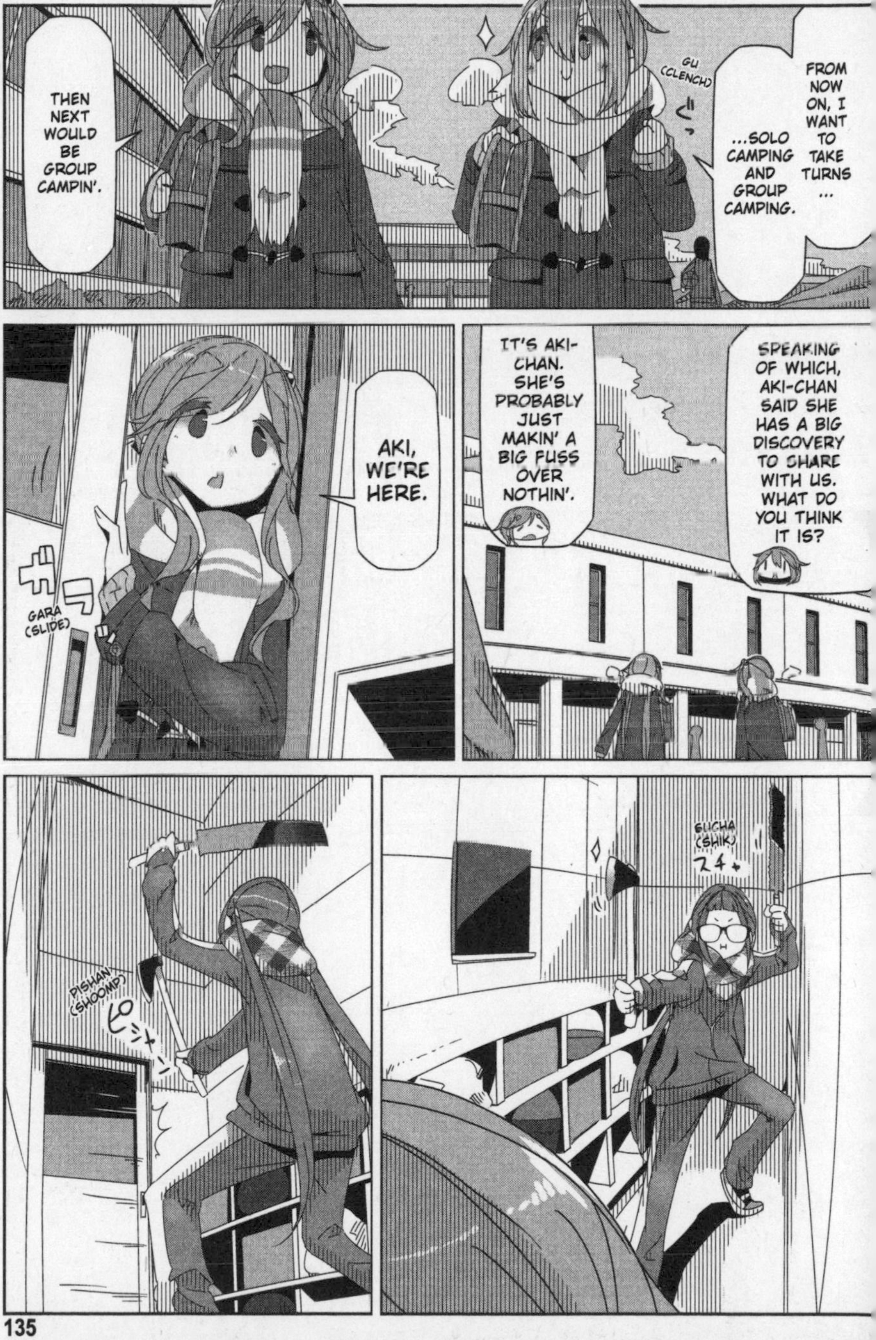
FROM NOW ON, I WANT TO TAKE TURNS...
...SOLO CAMPING AND GROUP CAMPING.
GU (CLENCH)
THEN NEXT WOULD BE GROUP CAMPIN'.
SPEAKING OF WHICH, AKI-CHAN SAID SHE HAS A BIG DISCOVERY TO SHARE WITH US. WHAT DO YOU THINK IT IS?
IT'S AKI-CHAN. SHE'S PROBABLY JUST MAKIN' A BIG FUSS OVER NOTHIN'.
AKI, WE'RE HERE.
GARA (SLIDE)
SUCHA (SHIK)
PISHAN (SHOOMP)

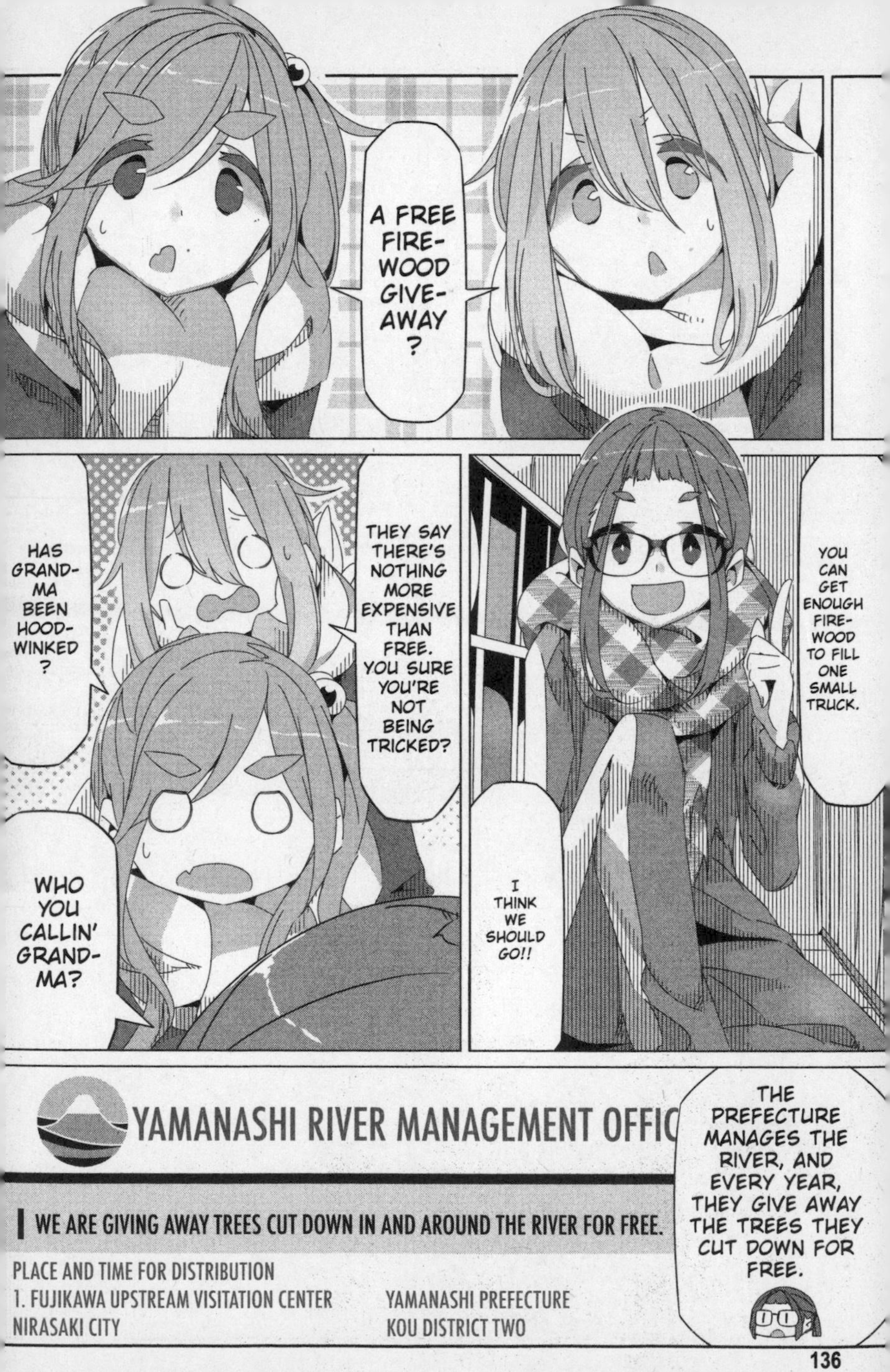
A FREE FIRE-WOOD GIVE-AWAY?
YOU CAN GET ENOUGH FIRE-WOOD TO FILL ONE SMALL TRUCK.
I THINK WE SHOULD GO!!
THEY SAY THERE'S NOTHING MORE EXPENSIVE THAN FREE. YOU SURE YOU'RE NOT BEING TRICKED?
HAS GRAND-MA BEEN HOOD-WINKED?
WHO YOU CALLIN' GRAND-MA?
THE PREFECTURE MANAGES THE RIVER, AND EVERY YEAR, THEY GIVE AWAY THE TREES THEY CUT DOWN FOR FREE.
YAMANASHI RIVER MANAGEMENT OFFIC
WE ARE GIVING AWAY TREES CUT DOWN IN AND AROUND THE RIVER FOR FREE.
PLACE AND TIME FOR DISTRIBUTION
1. FUJIKAWA UPSTREAM VISITATION CENTER
NIRASAKI CITY
YAMANASHI PREFECTURE
KOU DISTRICT TWO

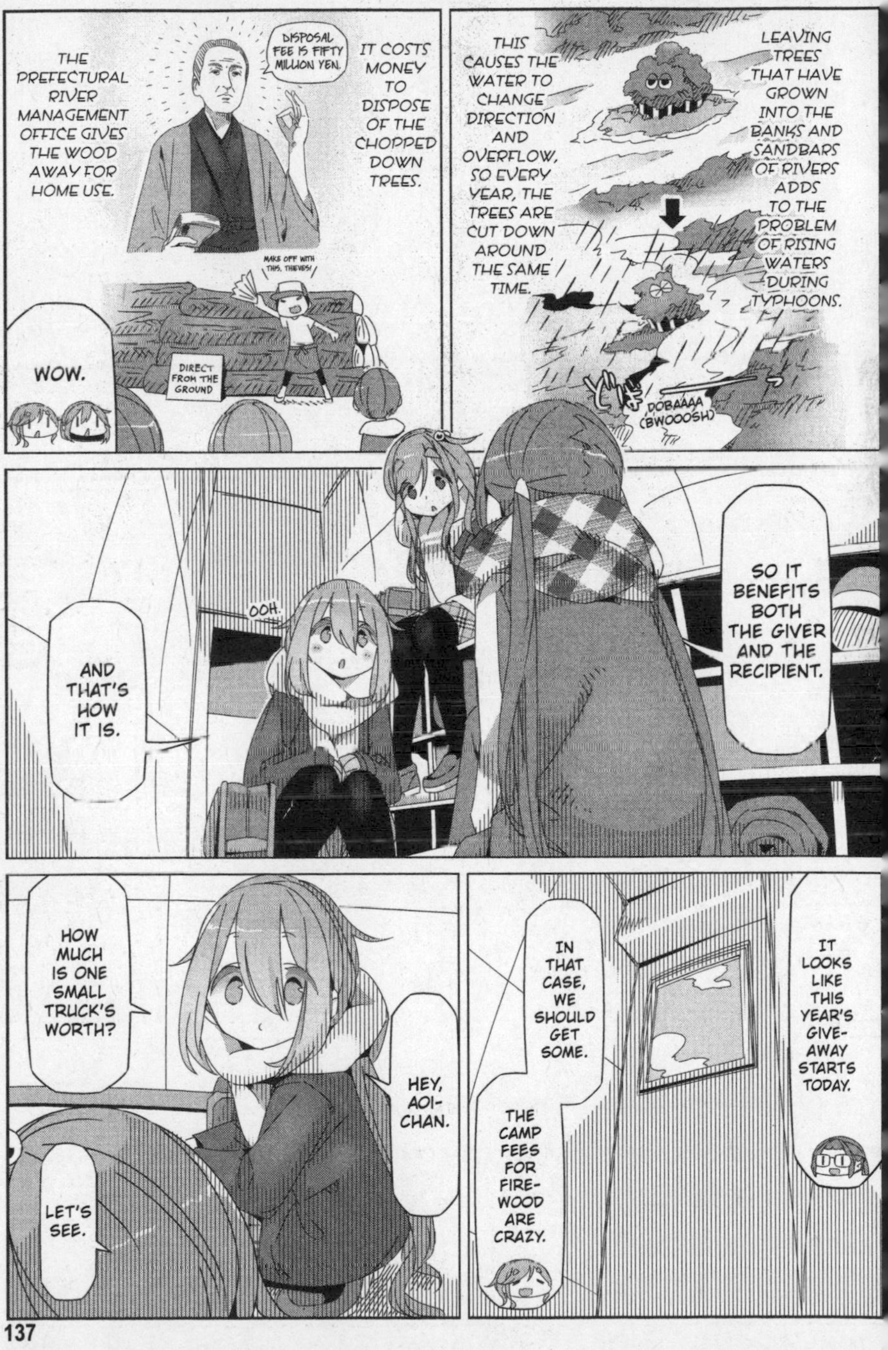
LEAVING TREES THAT HAVE GROWN INTO THE BANKS AND SANDBARS OF RIVERS ADDS TO THE PROBLEM OF RISING WATERS DURING TYPHOONS.
THIS CAUSES THE WATER TO CHANGE DIRECTION AND OVERFLOW, SO EVERY YEAR, THE TREES ARE CUT DOWN AROUND THE SAME TIME.
DOBAAAA (BWOOOSH)
IT COSTS MONEY TO DISPOSE OF THE CHOPPED DOWN TREES.
DISPOSAL FEE IS FIFTY MILLION YEN.
THE PREFECTURAL RIVER MANAGEMENT OFFICE GIVES THE WOOD AWAY FOR HOME USE.
MAKE OFF WITH THIS, THIEVES!
DIRECT FROM THE GROUND
WOW.
SO IT BENEFITS BOTH THE GIVER AND THE RECIPIENT.
OOH.
AND THAT'S HOW IT IS.
IT LOOKS LIKE THIS YEAR'S GIVE-AWAY STARTS TODAY.
IN THAT CASE, WE SHOULD GET SOME.
THE CAMP FEES FOR FIRE-WOOD ARE CRAZY.
HEY, AOI-CHAN.
HOW MUCH IS ONE SMALL TRUCK'S WORTH?
LET'S SEE.

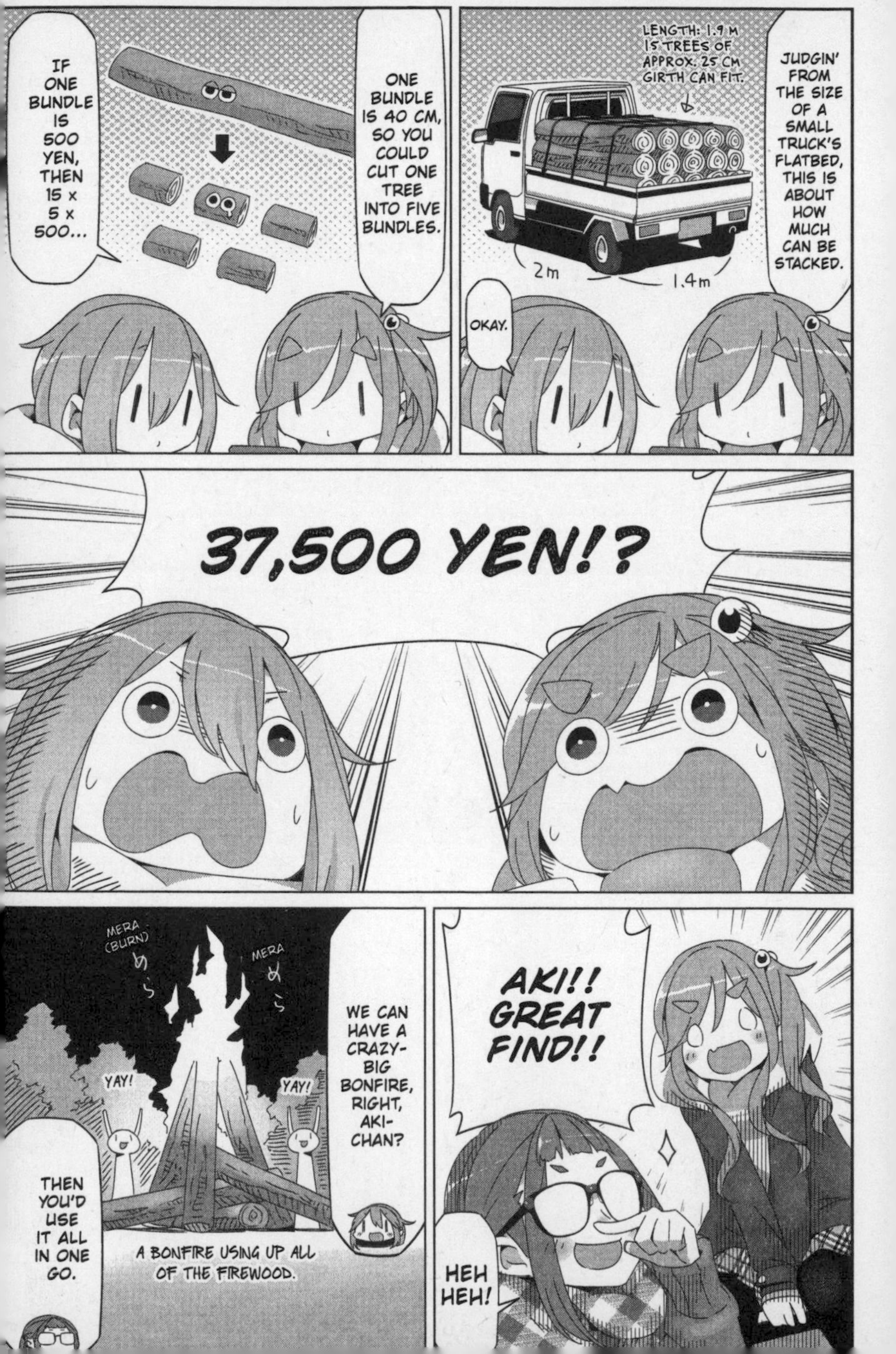

JUDGIN' FROM THE SIZE OF A SMALL TRUCK'S FLATBED, THIS IS ABOUT HOW MUCH CAN BE STACKED.
LENGTH: 1.9 M
15 TREES OF APPROX. 25 CM GIRTH CAN FIT.
2m
1.4m
OKAY.
ONE BUNDLE IS 40 CM, SO YOU COULD CUT ONE TREE INTO FIVE BUNDLES.
IF ONE BUNDLE IS 500 YEN, THEN 15 x 5 x 500...
37,500 YEN!?
AKI!! GREAT FIND!!
HEH HEH!
WE CAN HAVE A CRAZY-BIG BONFIRE, RIGHT, AKI-CHAN?
MERA
めら
MERA (BURN)
めら
YAY!
YAY!
A BONFIRE USING UP ALL OF THE FIREWOOD.
THEN YOU'D USE IT ALL IN ONE GO.

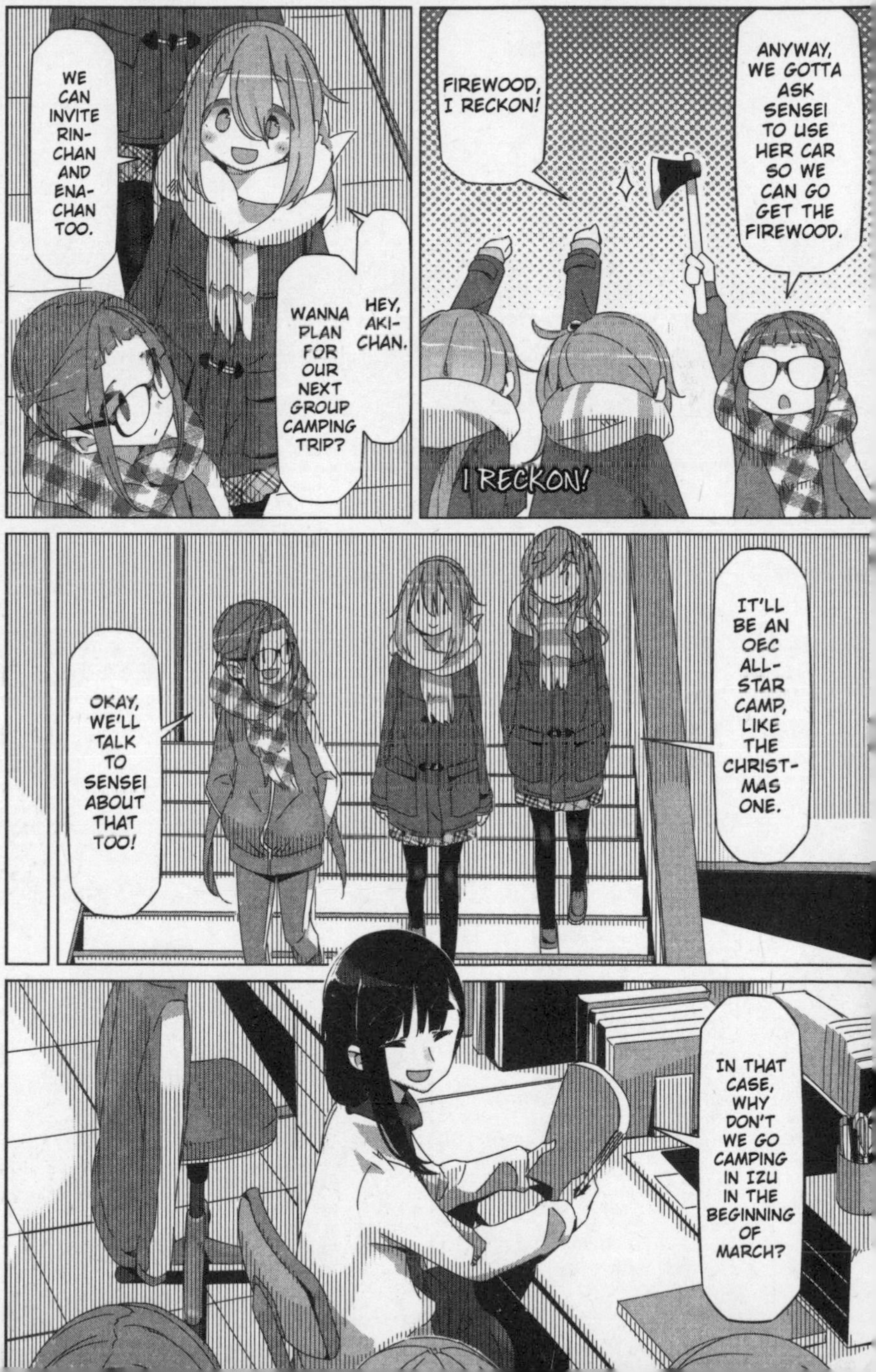
ANYWAY, WE GOTTA ASK SENSEI TO USE HER CAR SO WE CAN GO GET THE FIREWOOD.
FIREWOOD, I RECKON!
I RECKON!
HEY, AKI-CHAN.
WANNA PLAN FOR OUR NEXT GROUP CAMPING TRIP?
WE CAN INVITE RIN-CHAN AND ENA-CHAN TOO.
IT'LL BE AN OEC ALL-STAR CAMP, LIKE THE CHRISTMAS ONE.
OKAY, WE'LL TALK TO SENSEI ABOUT THAT TOO!
IN THAT CASE, WHY DON'T WE GO CAMPING IN IZU IN THE BEGINNING OF MARCH?

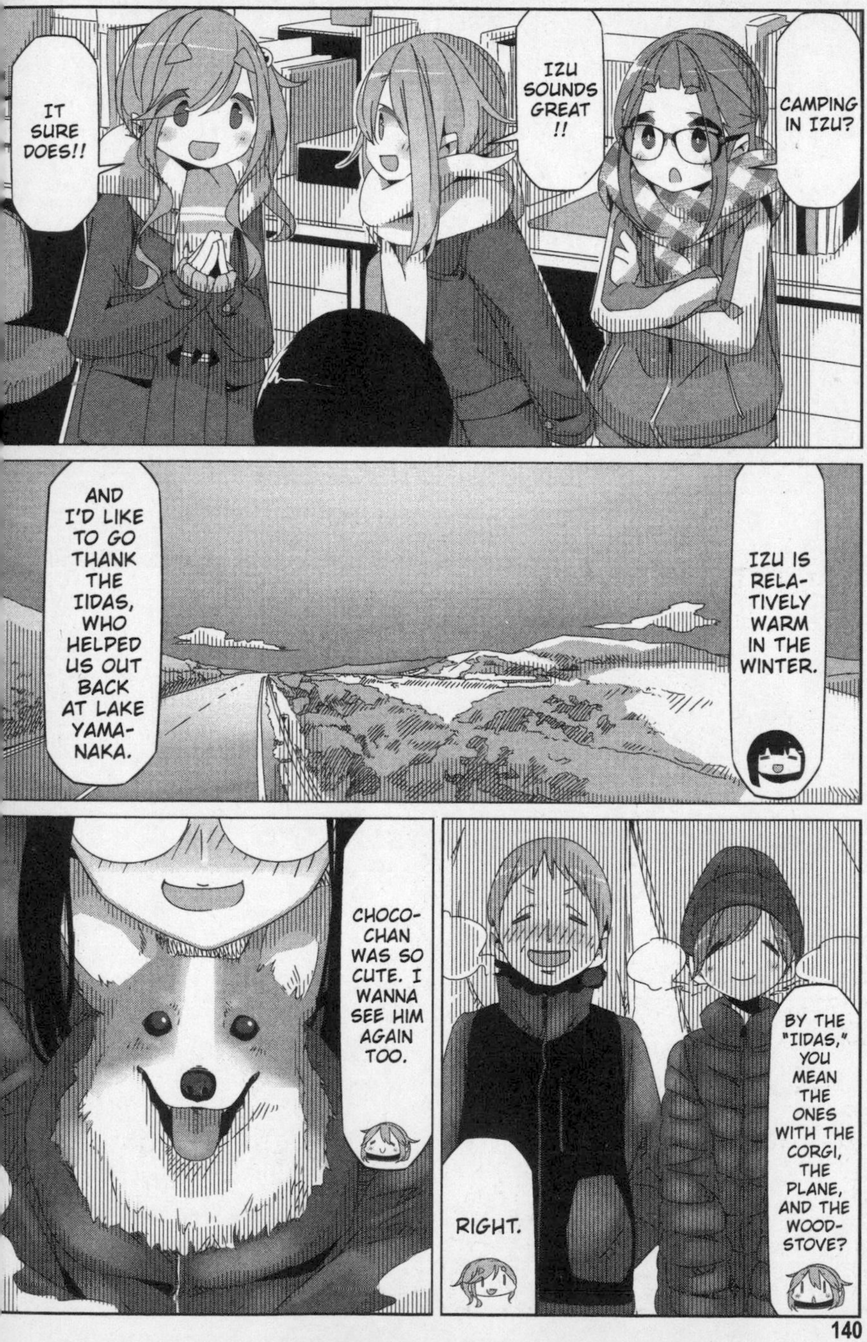
CAMPING IN IZU?
IZU SOUNDS GREAT !!
IT SURE DOES!!
IZU IS RELA-TIVELY WARM IN THE WINTER.
AND I'D LIKE TO GO THANK THE IIDAS, WHO HELPED US OUT BACK AT LAKE YAMA-NAKA.
BY THE "IIDAS," YOU MEAN THE ONES WITH THE CORGI, THE PLANE, AND THE WOOD-STOVE?
RIGHT.
CHOCO-CHAN WAS SO CUTE. I WANNA SEE HIM AGAIN TOO.

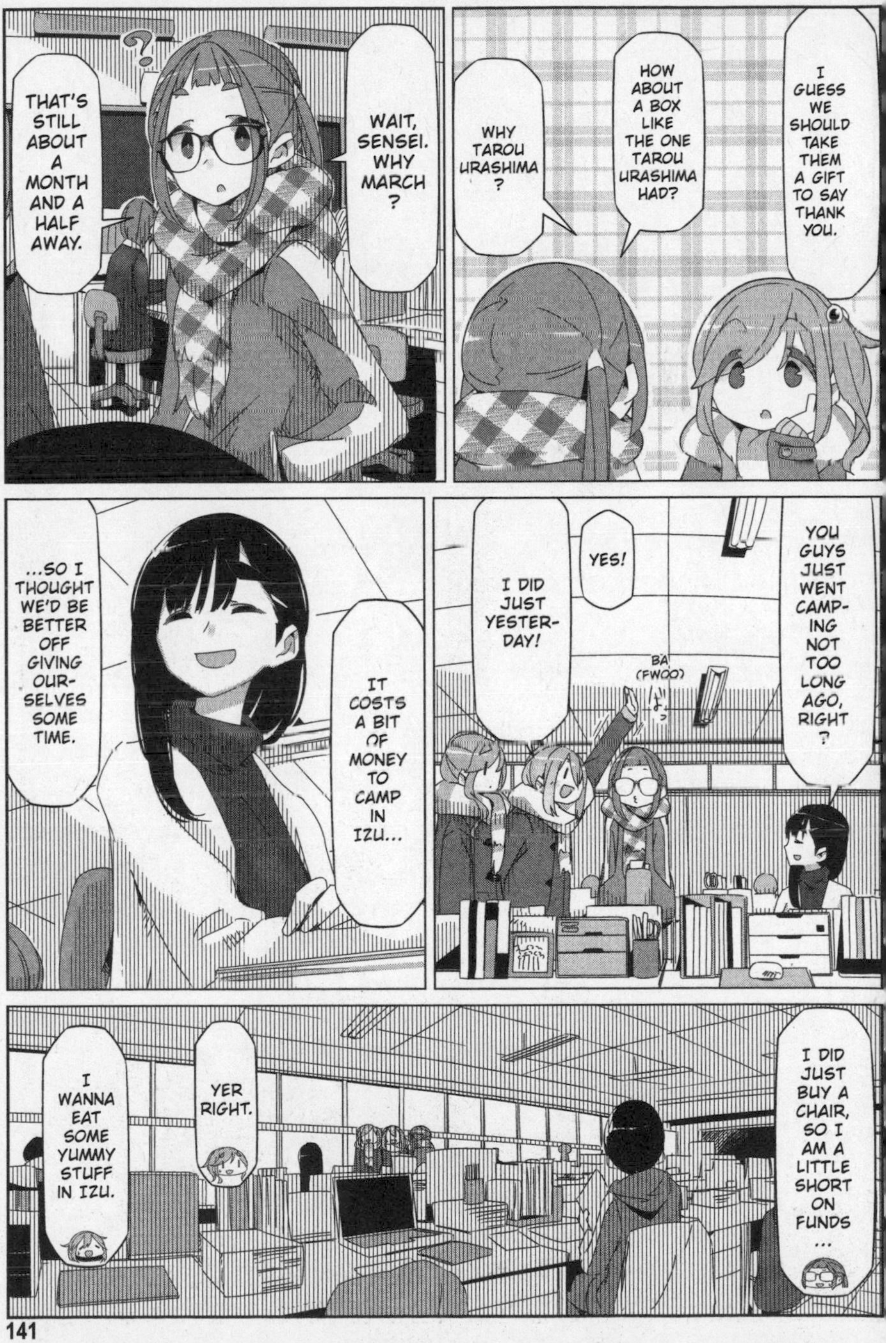
I GUESS WE SHOULD TAKE THEM A GIFT TO SAY THANK YOU.
HOW ABOUT A BOX LIKE THE ONE TAROU URASHIMA HAD?
WHY TAROU URASHIMA?
WAIT, SENSEI. WHY MARCH?
THAT'S STILL ABOUT A MONTH AND A HALF AWAY.
YOU GUYS JUST WENT CAMPING NOT TOO LONG AGO, RIGHT?
YES!
I DID JUST YESTERDAY!
BA (FWOO)
IT COSTS A BIT OF MONEY TO CAMP IN IZU...
...SO I THOUGHT WE'D BE BETTER OFF GIVING OURSELVES SOME TIME.
I DID JUST BUY A CHAIR, SO I AM A LITTLE SHORT ON FUNDS...
YER RIGHT.
I WANNA EAT SOME YUMMY STUFF IN IZU.

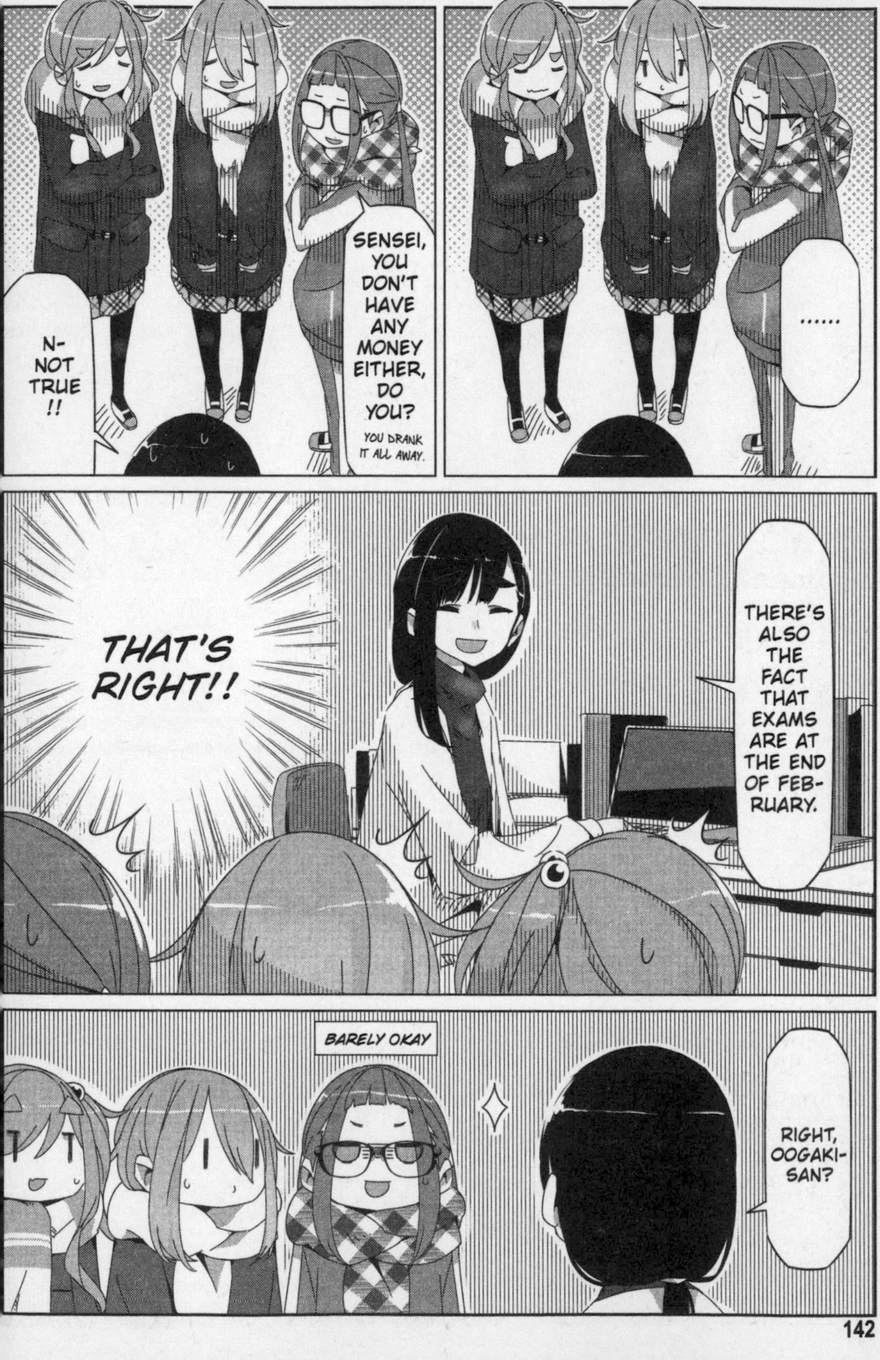
……
SENSEI, YOU DON'T HAVE ANY MONEY EITHER, DO YOU?
YOU DRANK IT ALL AWAY.
N-NOT TRUE!!
THERE'S ALSO THE FACT THAT EXAMS ARE AT THE END OF FEB-RUARY.
THAT'S RIGHT!!
RIGHT, OOGAKI-SAN?
BARELY OKAY

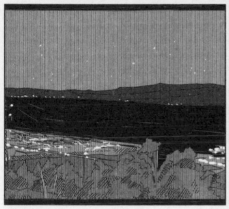

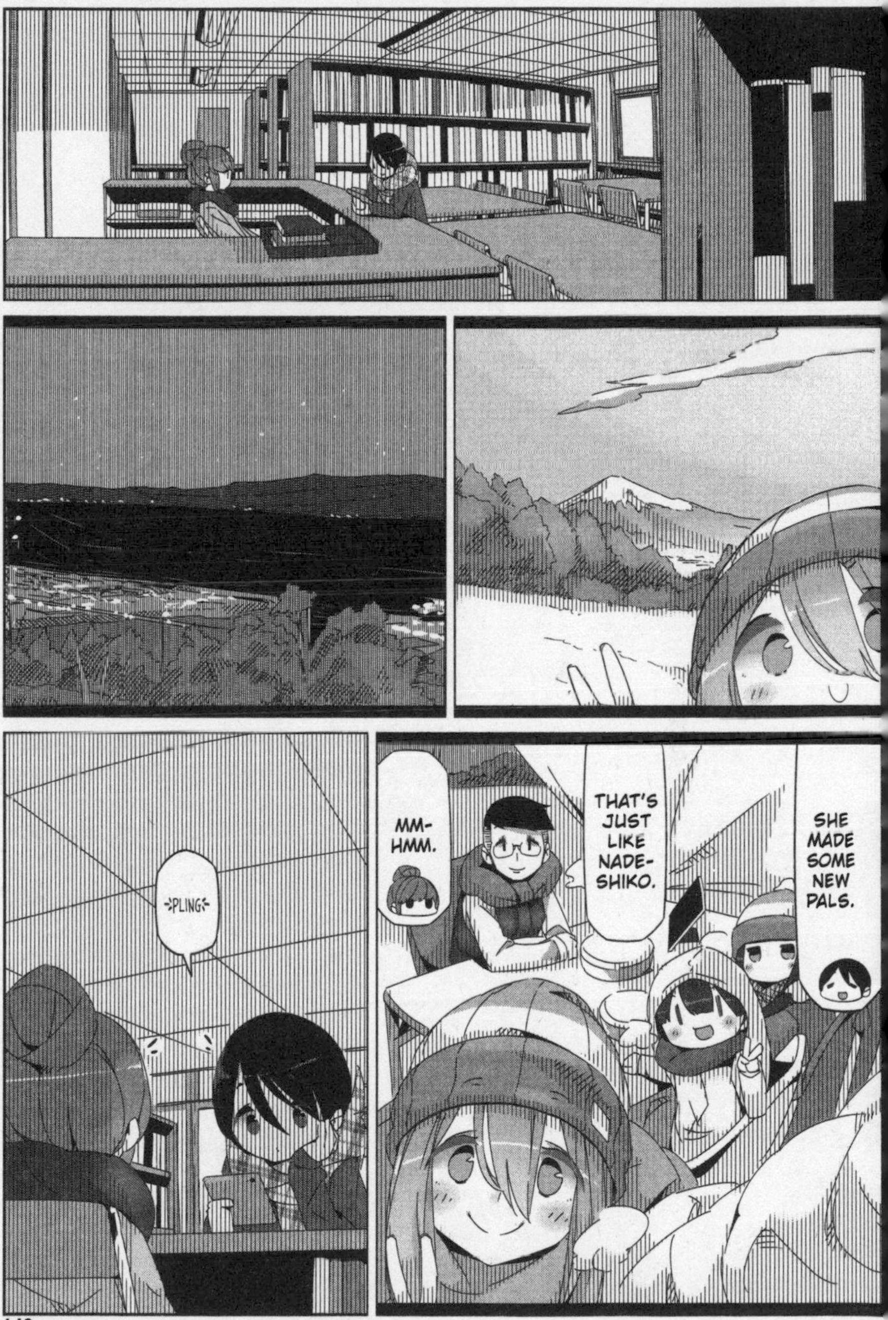
SHE MADE SOME NEW PALS.
THAT'S JUST LIKE NADE-SHIKO.
MM-HMM.
PLING

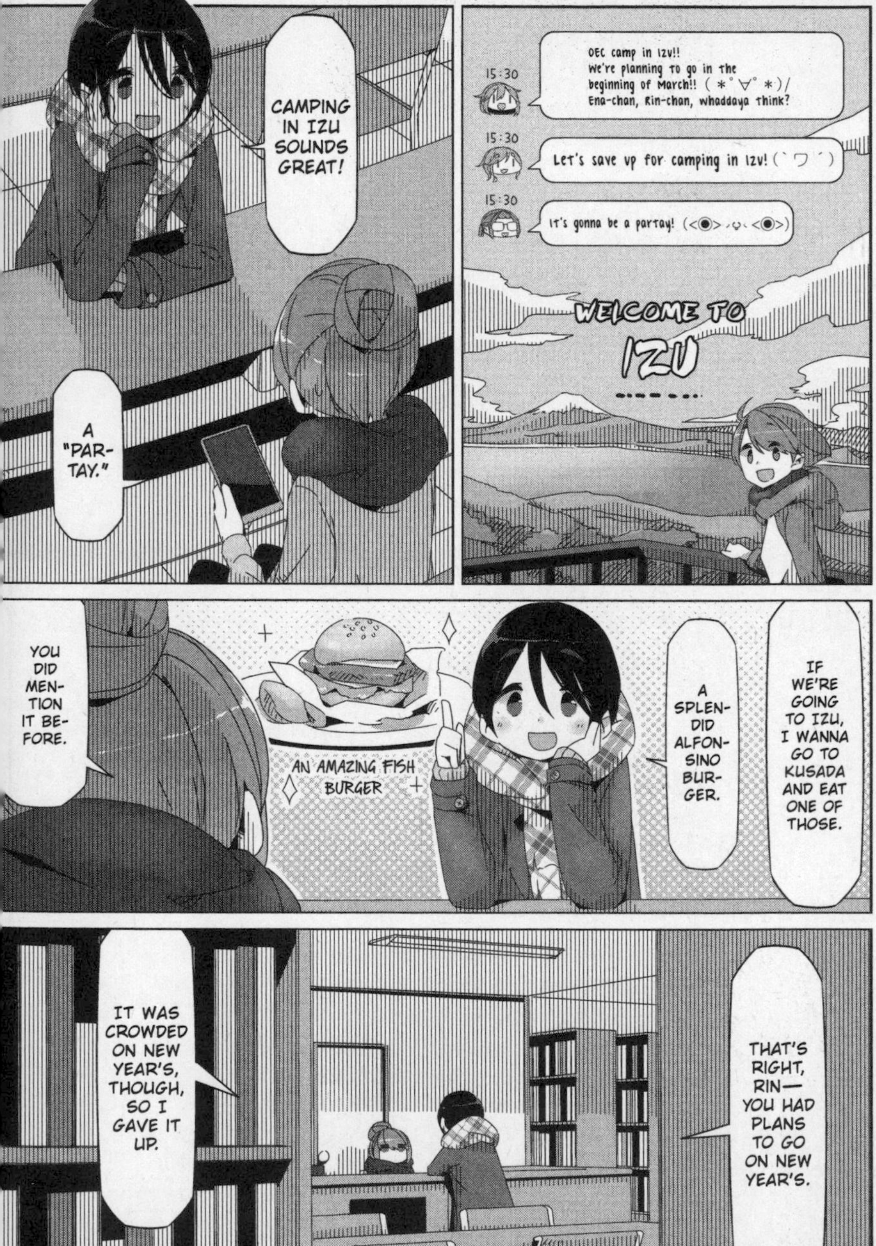
15:30
OEC camp in Izu!! We're planning to go in the beginning of March!! (＊ﾟ∀ﾟ＊)/ Ena-chan, Rin-chan, whaddaya think?
15:30
Let's save up for camping in Izu! (`ワ´)
15:30
It's gonna be a partay! (<◉>ｏωｏ<◉>)
WELCOME TO IZU ......
CAMPING IN IZU SOUNDS GREAT!
A "PARTAY."
IF WE'RE GOING TO IZU, I WANNA GO TO KUSADA AND EAT ONE OF THOSE.
A SPLENDID ALFONSINO BURGER.
AN AMAZING FISH BURGER
YOU DID MENTION IT BEFORE.
THAT'S RIGHT, RIN—YOU HAD PLANS TO GO ON NEW YEAR'S.
IT WAS CROWDED ON NEW YEAR'S, THOUGH, SO I GAVE IT UP.

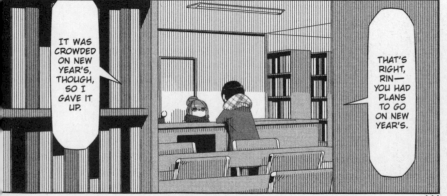

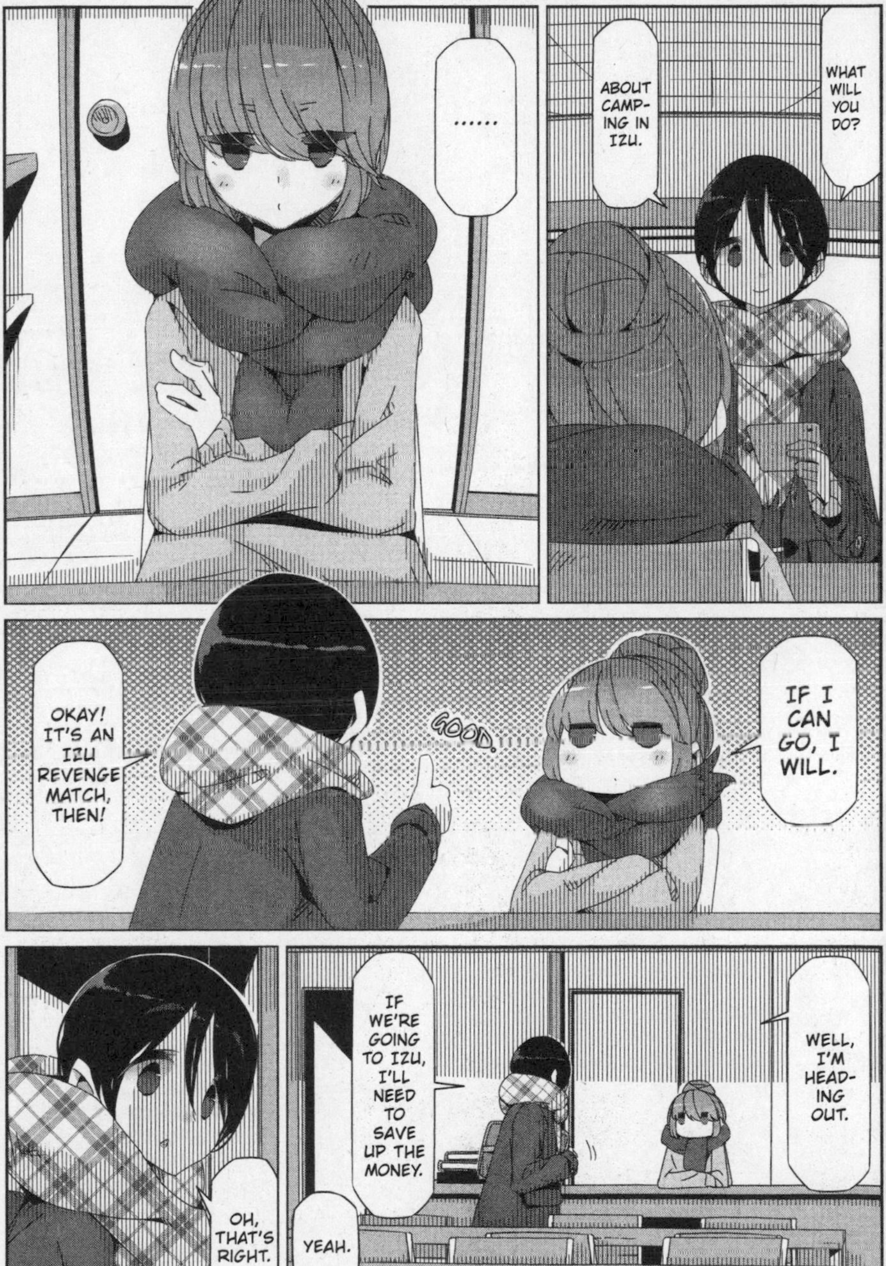
WHAT WILL YOU DO?
ABOUT CAMPING IN IZU.
......
IF I CAN GO, I WILL.
GOOD.
OKAY! IT'S AN IZU REVENGE MATCH, THEN!
WELL, I'M HEADING OUT.
IF WE'RE GOING TO IZU, I'LL NEED TO SAVE UP THE MONEY.
YEAH.
OH, THAT'S RIGHT.

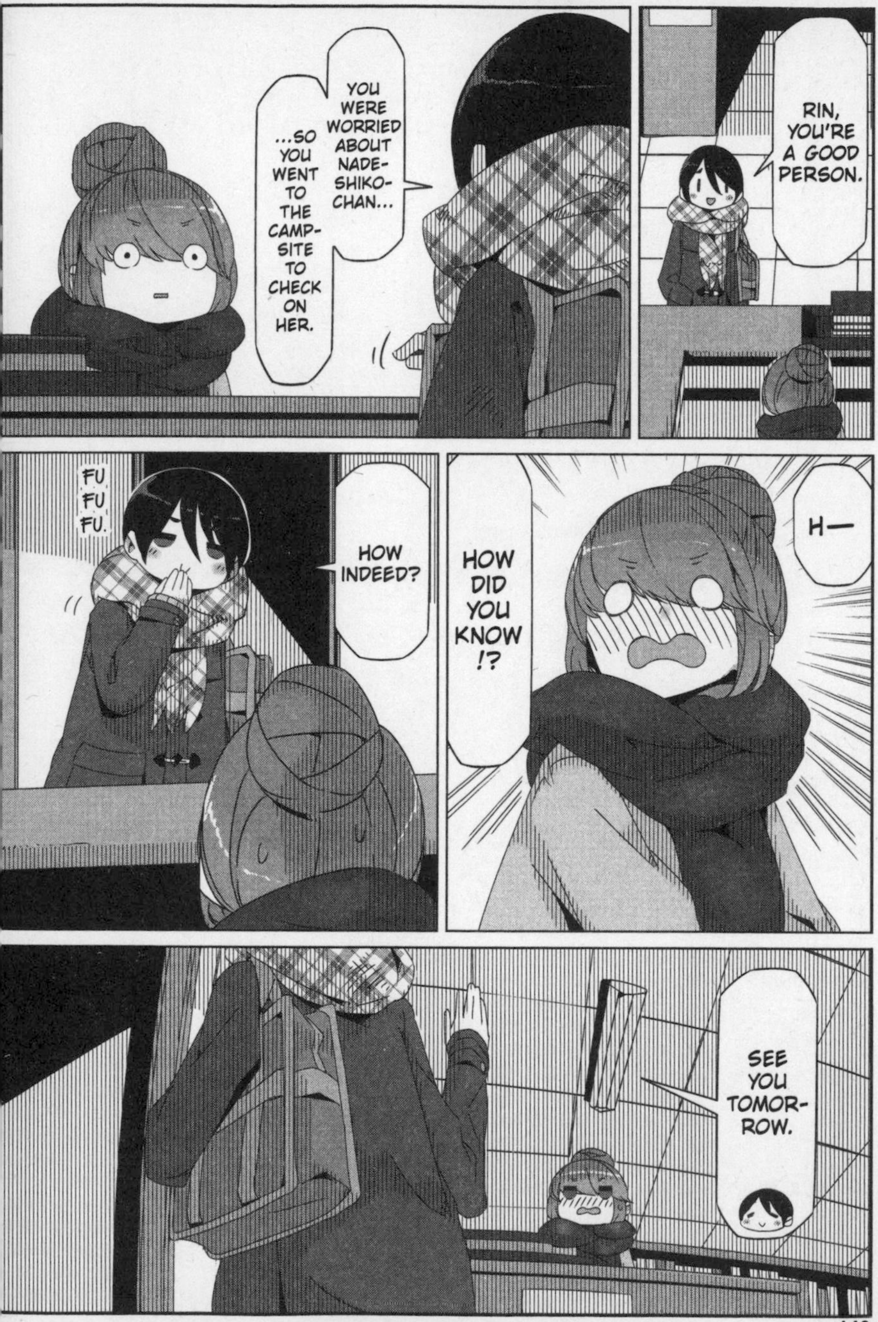
RIN, YOU'RE A GOOD PERSON.
YOU WERE WORRIED ABOUT NADE-SHIKO-CHAN...
...SO YOU WENT TO THE CAMP-SITE TO CHECK ON HER.
H—
HOW DID YOU KNOW!?
HOW INDEED?
FU FU FU.
SEE YOU TOMOR-ROW.

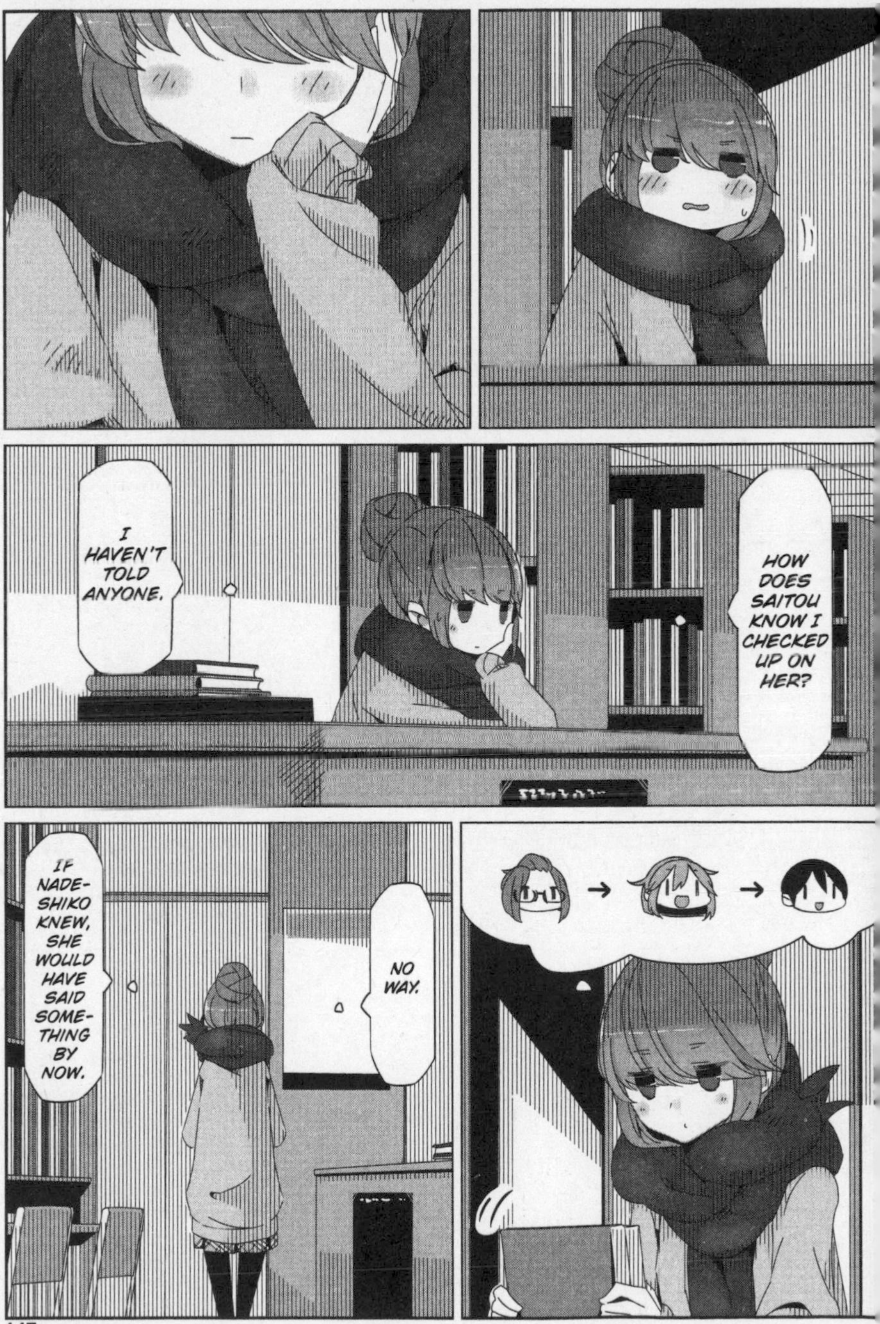
HOW DOES SAITOU KNOW I CHECKED UP ON HER?
I HAVEN'T TOLD ANYONE.
NO WAY.
IF NADESHIKO KNEW, SHE WOULD HAVE SAID SOMETHING BY NOW.

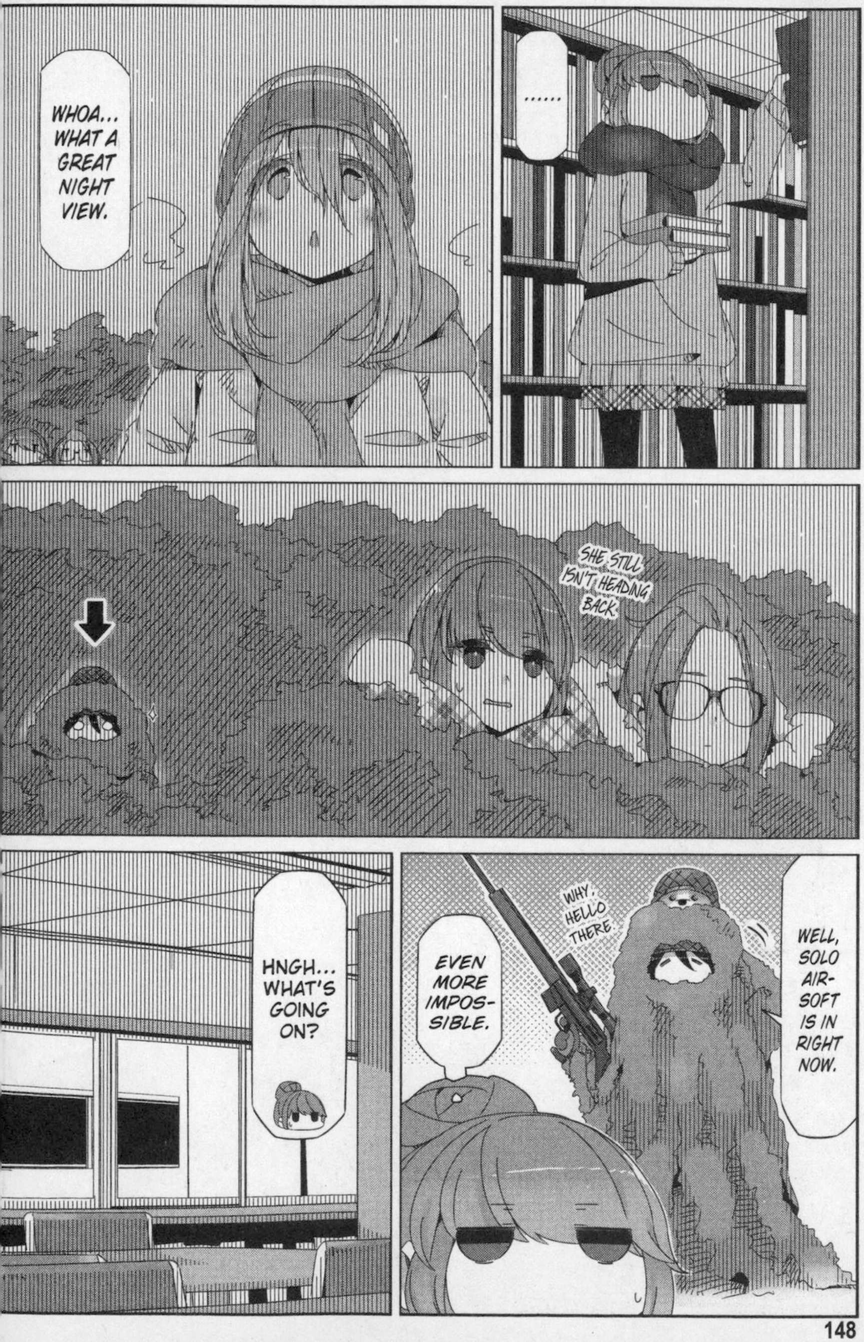
......
WHOA... WHAT A GREAT NIGHT VIEW.
SHE STILL ISN'T HEADING BACK.
WELL, SOLO AIR-SOFT IS IN RIGHT NOW.
WHY, HELLO THERE.
EVEN MORE IMPOS-SIBLE.
HNGH... WHAT'S GOING ON?

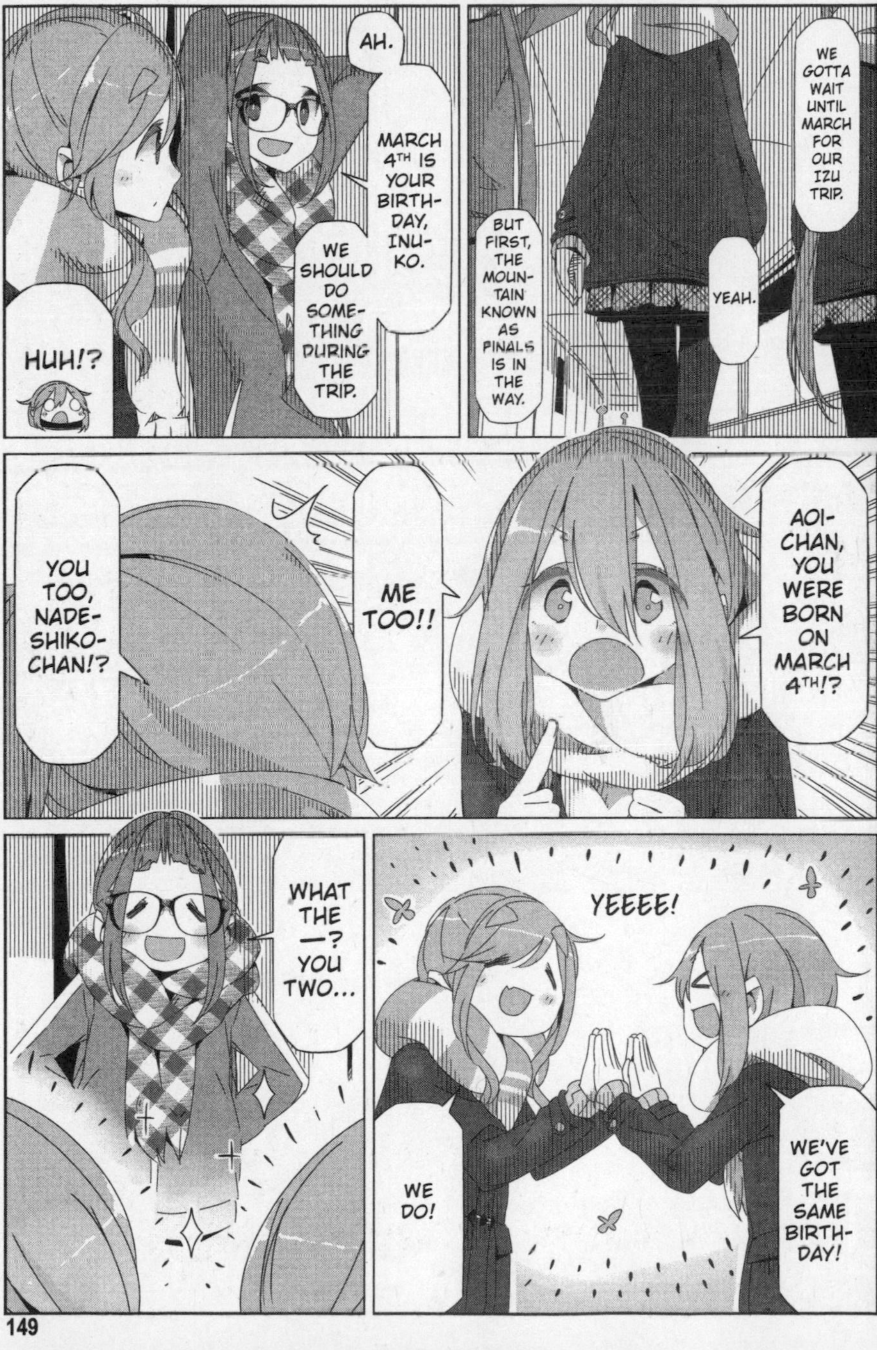
WE GOTTA WAIT UNTIL MARCH FOR OUR IZU TRIP.
YEAH.
BUT FIRST, THE MOUNTAIN KNOWN AS PINALS IS IN THE WAY.
AH.
MARCH 4TH IS YOUR BIRTHDAY, INUKO.
WE SHOULD DO SOMETHING DURING THE TRIP.
HUH!?
AOI-CHAN, YOU WERE BORN ON MARCH 4TH!?
ME TOO!!
YOU TOO, NADESHIKO-CHAN!?
YEEEE!
WE'VE GOT THE SAME BIRTHDAY!
WE DO!
WHAT THE—? YOU TWO...

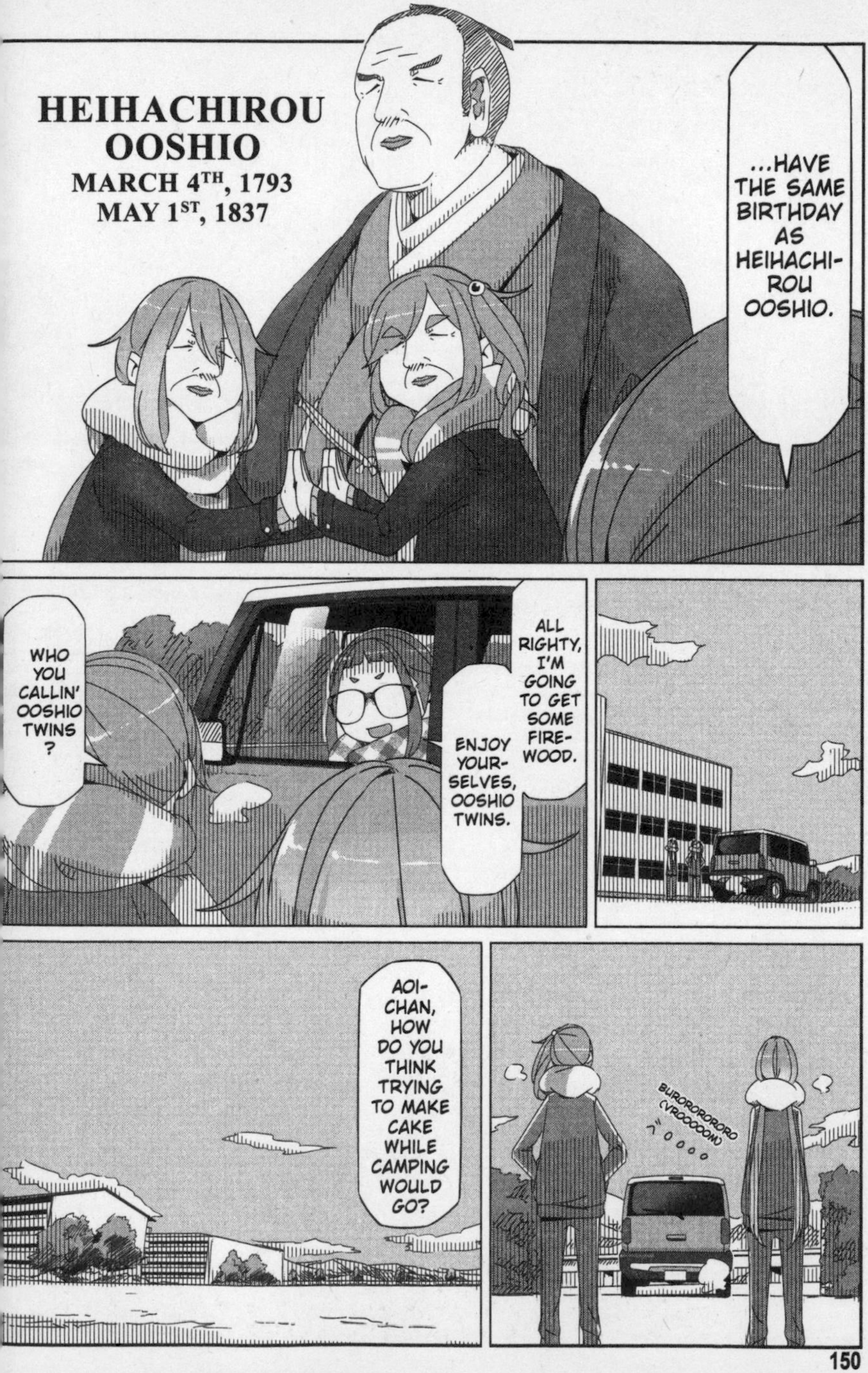
...HAVE THE SAME BIRTHDAY AS HEIHACHI-ROU OOSHIO.
HEIHACHIROU OOSHIO
MARCH 4TH, 1793
MAY 1ST, 1837
ALL RIGHTY, I'M GOING TO GET SOME FIRE-WOOD.
ENJOY YOUR-SELVES, OOSHIO TWINS.
WHO YOU CALLIN' OOSHIO TWINS?
BURORORORORO (VROOOOOM)
AOI-CHAN, HOW DO YOU THINK TRYING TO MAKE CAKE WHILE CAMPING WOULD GO?

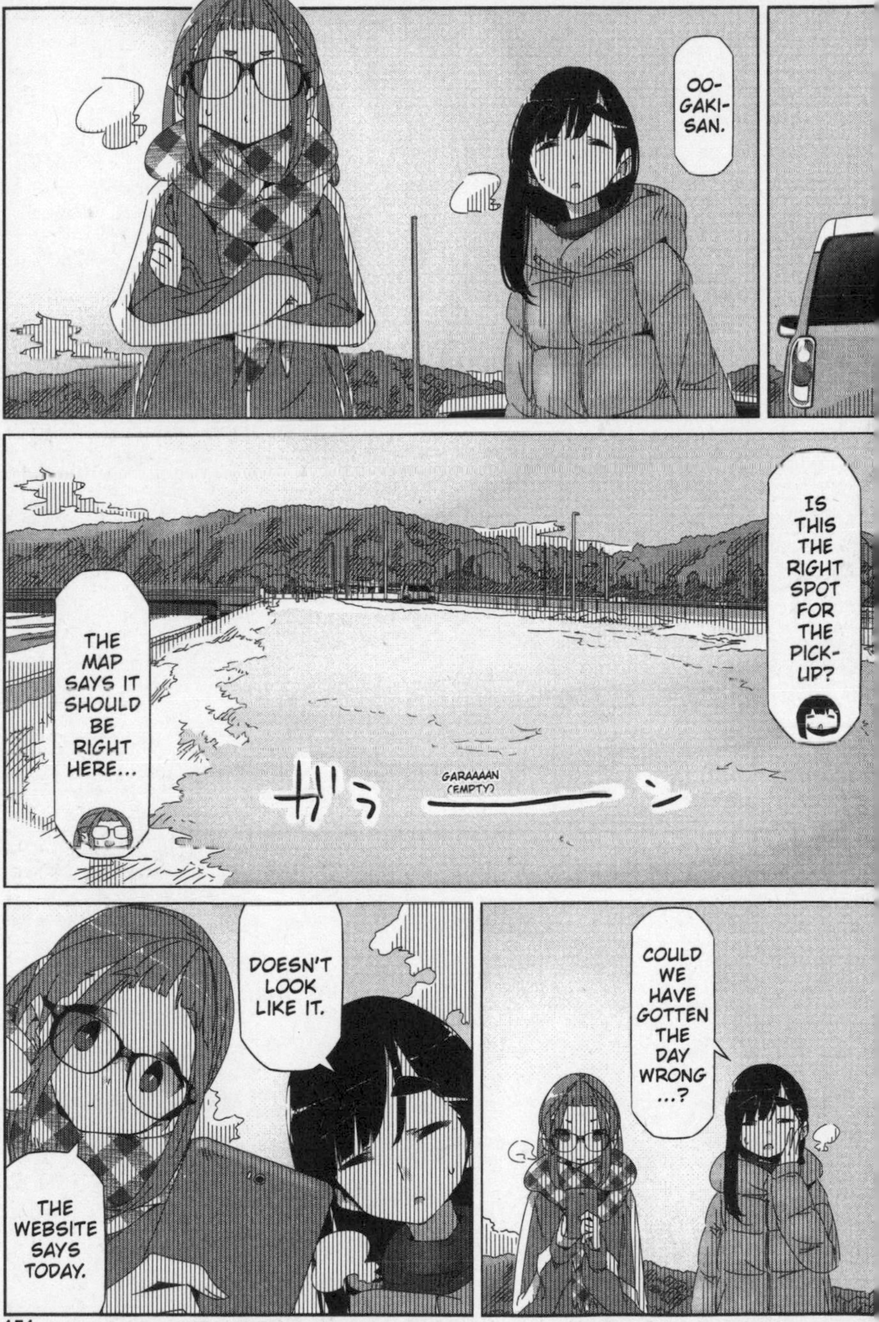
OO-GAKI-SAN.
IS THIS THE RIGHT SPOT FOR THE PICK-UP?
THE MAP SAYS IT SHOULD BE RIGHT HERE...
GARAAAAN (EMPTY)
COULD WE HAVE GOTTEN THE DAY WRONG ...?
DOESN'T LOOK LIKE IT.
THE WEBSITE SAYS TODAY.

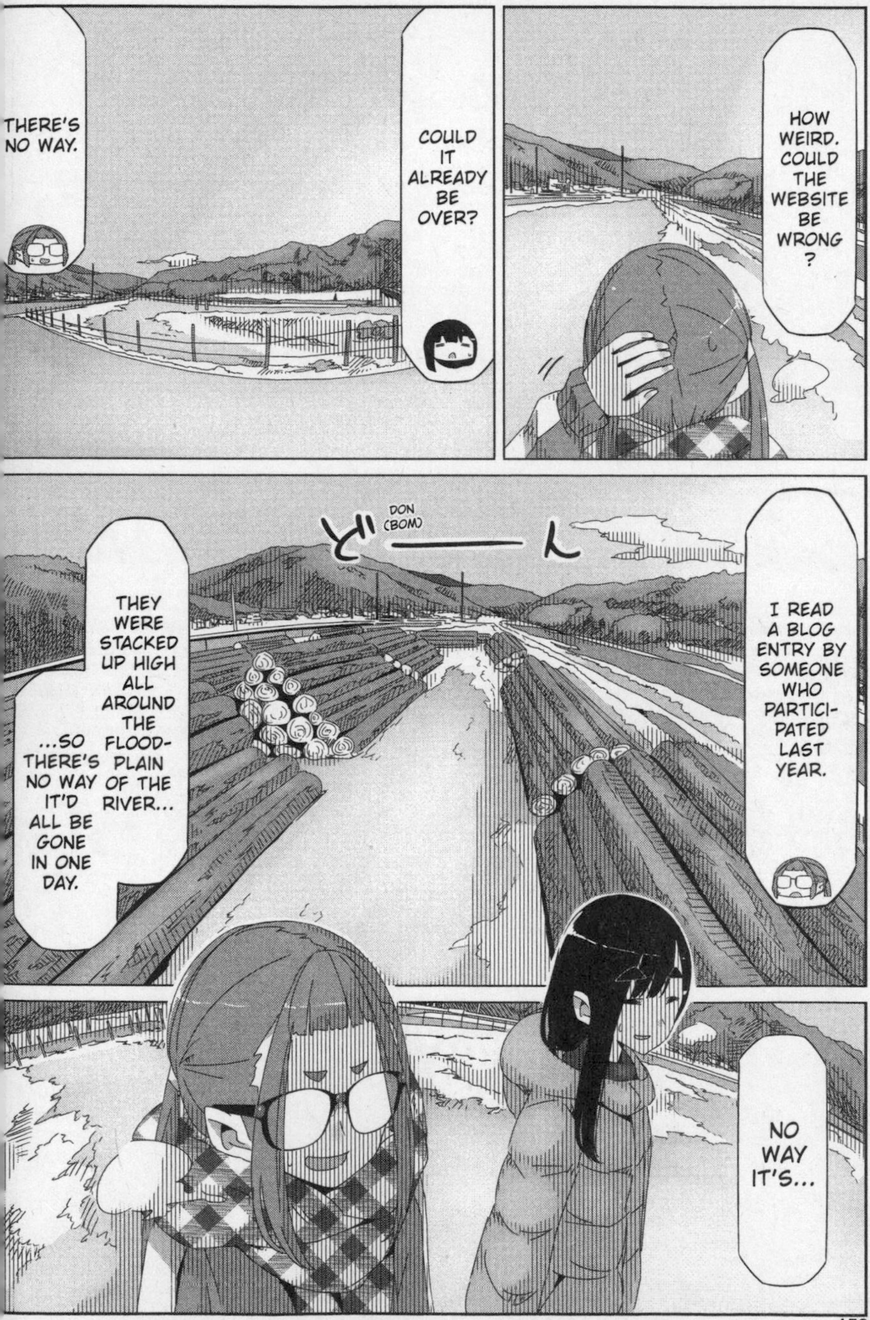
HOW WEIRD. COULD THE WEBSITE BE WRONG?
COULD IT ALREADY BE OVER?
THERE'S NO WAY.
DON (BOM)
どーーーん
I READ A BLOG ENTRY BY SOMEONE WHO PARTICIPATED LAST YEAR.
THEY WERE STACKED UP HIGH ALL AROUND THE FLOODPLAIN OF THE RIVER...
...SO THERE'S NO WAY IT'D ALL BE GONE IN ONE DAY.
NO WAY IT'S...

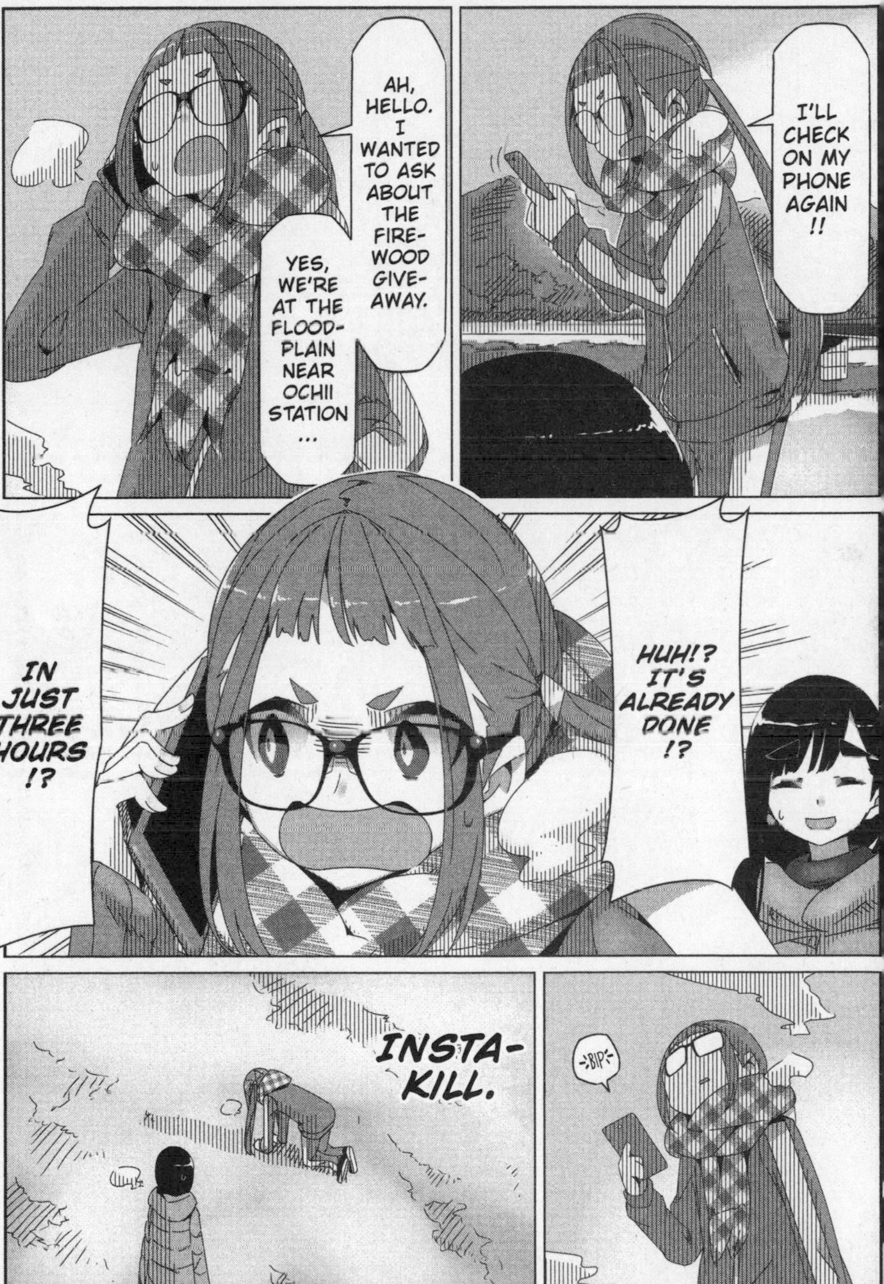
I'LL CHECK ON MY PHONE AGAIN!!
AH, HELLO. I WANTED TO ASK ABOUT THE FIRE-WOOD GIVE-AWAY.
YES, WE'RE AT THE FLOOD-PLAIN NEAR OCHII STATION...
HUH!? IT'S ALREADY DONE!?
IN JUST THREE HOURS!?
BIP
INSTA-KILL.

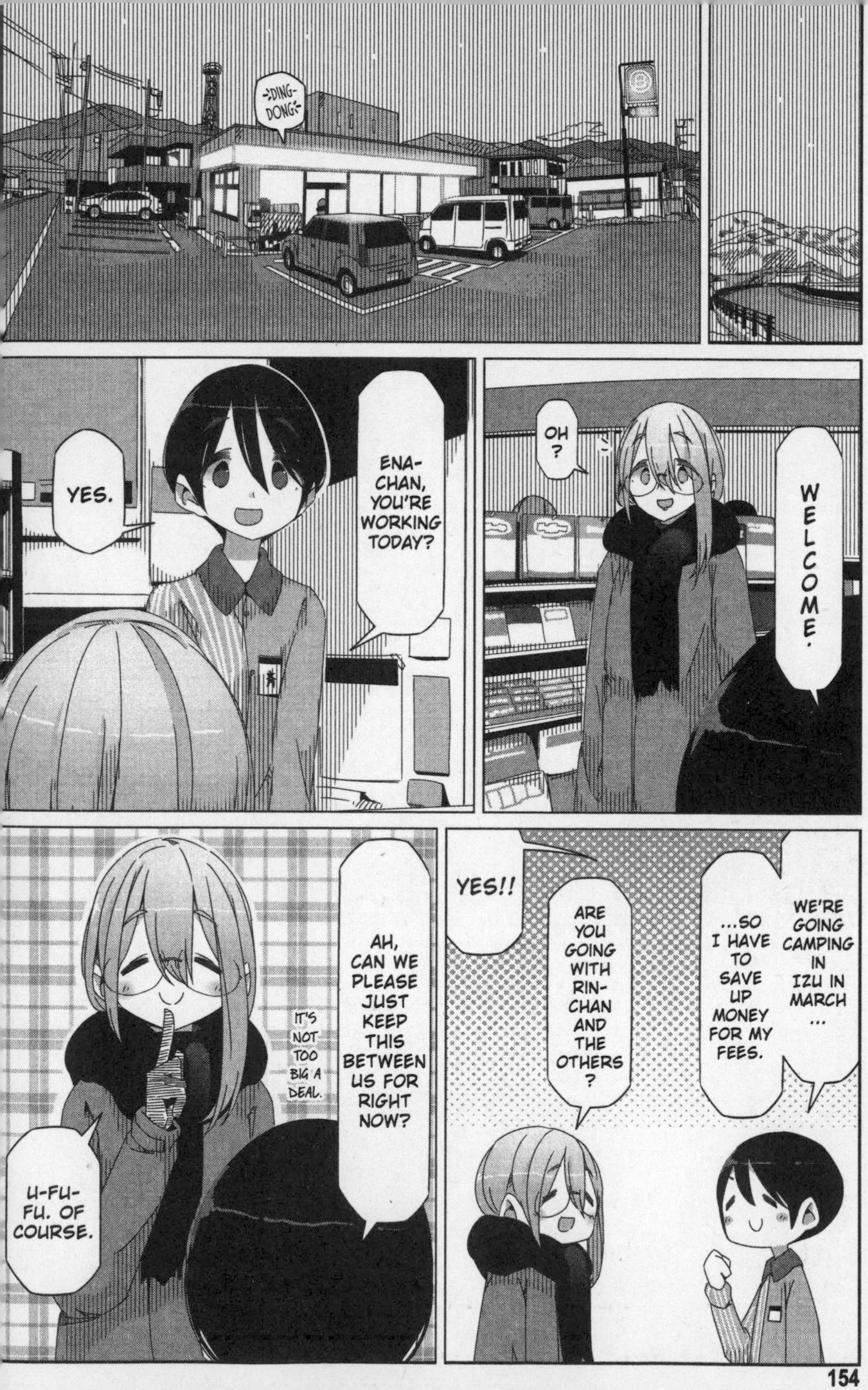
DING-DONG
WELCOME.
OH?
ENA-CHAN, YOU'RE WORKING TODAY?
YES.
WE'RE GOING CAMPING IN IZU IN MARCH...
...SO I HAVE TO SAVE UP MONEY FOR MY FEES.
ARE YOU GOING WITH RIN-CHAN AND THE OTHERS?
YES!!
AH, CAN WE PLEASE JUST KEEP THIS BETWEEN US FOR RIGHT NOW?
IT'S NOT TOO BIG A DEAL.
U-FU-FU. OF COURSE.

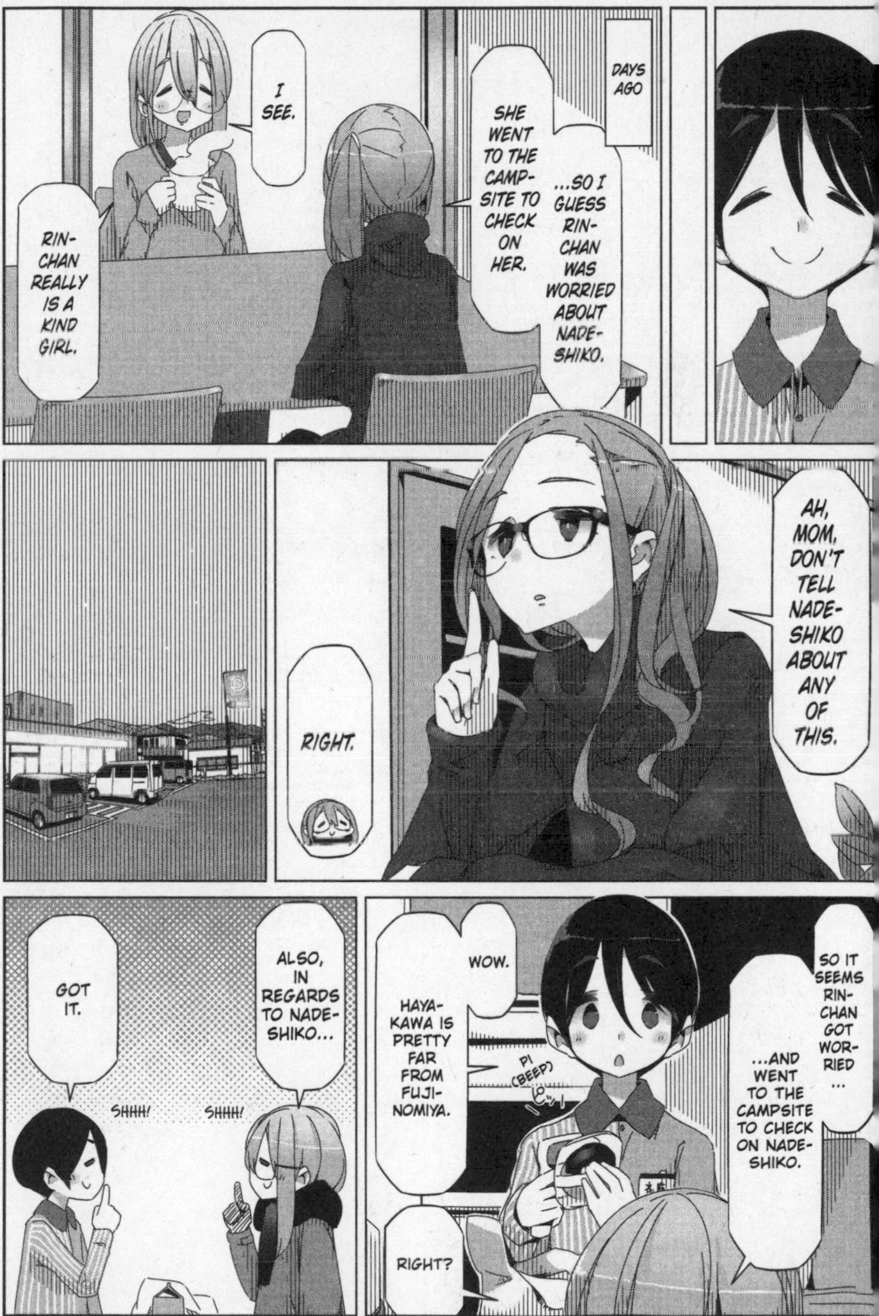
DAYS AGO
...SO I GUESS RIN-CHAN WAS WORRIED ABOUT NADESHIKO.
SHE WENT TO THE CAMPSITE TO CHECK ON HER.
I SEE.
RIN-CHAN REALLY IS A KIND GIRL.
AH, MOM, DON'T TELL NADESHIKO ABOUT ANY OF THIS.
RIGHT.
SO IT SEEMS RIN-CHAN GOT WORRIED...
...AND WENT TO THE CAMPSITE TO CHECK ON NADESHIKO.
WOW.
PI (BEEP)
HAYAKAWA IS PRETTY FAR FROM FUJINOMIYA.
RIGHT?
ALSO, IN REGARDS TO NADESHIKO...
SHHH!
GOT IT.
SHHH!

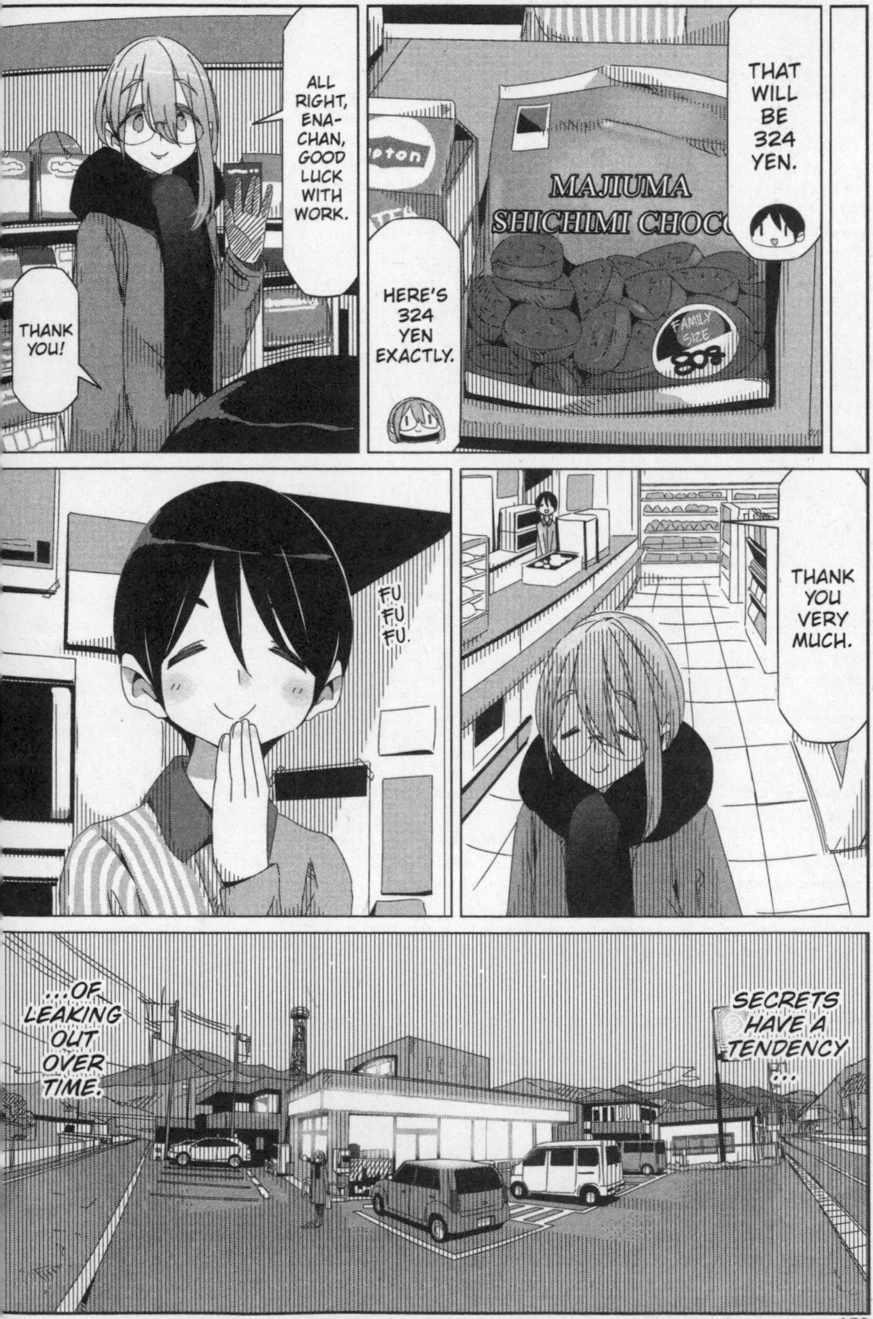
THAT WILL BE 324 YEN.
MAJIUMA SHICHIMI CHOC
FAMILY SIZE
HERE'S 324 YEN EXACTLY.
ALL RIGHT, ENA-CHAN, GOOD LUCK WITH WORK.
THANK YOU!
THANK YOU VERY MUCH.
FU FU FU.
SECRETS HAVE A TENDENCY...
...OF LEAKING OUT OVER TIME.

TRANSLATION NOTES

COMMON HONORIFICS

no honorific: Indicates familiarity or closeness; if used without permission or reason, addressing someone in this manner would constitute an insult.

-san: The Japanese equivalent of Mr./Mrs./Miss. If a situation calls for politeness, this is the fail-safe honorific.

-kun: Used most often when referring to boys, this indicates affection or familiarity. Occasionally used by older men among their peers, but it may also be used by anyone referring to a person of lower standing.

-chan: An affectionate honorific indicating familiarity used mostly in reference to girls; also used in reference to cute persons or animals of either gender.

-sensei: A respectful term for teachers, artists, or high-level professionals.

(o)nee: Japanese equivalent to "older sis."
(o)nii: Japanese equivalent to "older bro."

100 yen is approximately 1 USD.
1 centimeter is approximately 0.39 inches.

PAGE 3
Kiritanpo: Mashed rice used as dumplings in soups.

PAGE 8
Goggle Maps: In Japanese, this is called "Guruguru Maps." *Guruguru* refers to something spinning round and round.

PAGE 13
Rin-Rin-Rin-chan: In Japanese, this joke uses *ichirinsha* (unicycle), *rinkou*, and Rin-chan.

PAGE 36
Kappa: A river imp from Japanese folklore with a water dish on top of its head.

PAGE 37
Mame-mochi: Chewy, glutinous rice balls with a variety of whole beans mixed throughout.

Amazake: Literally "sweet *sake*," the drink actually usually contains little to no alcohol. It can be served hot or cold.

PAGE 38
***Nameko* mushrooms**: A popular mushroom in Japan often used in *miso* soups.

Hakuhou: Miso is a traditional Japanese fermented soybean paste. The *hakuhou* ("white phoenix") variation is a traditional Hayakawa specialty.

PAGE 39
Yabusame: A form of horseback archery with origins in twelfth century Japan as a way to train samurai.

TRANSLATION NOTES (continued)

PAGE 44
Corner Town: *Kadomachi* in Japanese, it's a spoof on an actual Japanese TV show called *Adomachi* about visiting various towns in Japan.

PAGE 48
Okonomiyaki: A grilled, savory pancake-like food consisting of flour, cabbage, egg, and a variety of other ingredients made to taste. "*Okonomiyaki*" literally means "grilled however you like."

PAGE 70
Fujikawa Healthy Green-Space Park: A reference to an actual campsite in the Fuji City area called Nodayama Healthy Green-Space Park (Nodayama *Kenkou Ryokuchi Kouen*).

PAGE 82
Wabi-sabi: A term with no direct English translation, it roughly means a general aesthetic traditional to Japan that emphasizes the beauty of imperfection and ephemerality. Cherry blossoms, which bloom brilliantly in the spring and die off quickly, are a quintessential example of *wabi-sabi*.

PAGE 137
"Fifty million yen": The figure depicted here is Yukichi Fukuzawa, the face on the Japanese ten-thousand yen note—in a sense, the Japanese equivalent of Benjamin Franklin as the face of the U.S. $100 bill.

PAGE 139
"I reckon": In Japanese, the characters say "*Zuraaa*," which is a dialect quirk found in Nagano Prefecture, Yamanashi Prefecture, and Shizuoka Prefecture. It's generally considered to sound rural or old-fashioned.

PAGE 141
Tarou Urashima: The Japanese fairy tale "Tarou Urashima" is about a man who rescues a sea turtle and is rewarded with a visit to the Dragon King's palace. There, he is entertained by the princess Otohime and receives a treasure box as a reward but is told to never open it. When he returns to the surface, he discovers one hundred years have passed, and when he defies instruction and opens the box, he turns into an old man.

PAGE 150
Heihachirou Ooshio: A neo-Confucian scholar famous for his leadership role in the rebellion against the Tokugawa shogunate.

PAGE 161
Mapo: A style of dish originating from Sichuan, China that is traditionally very spicy, most famously in the form of *mapo* tofu. Japanese versions tend to be much less spicy to match Japanese tastes.

Donburi: A dish where ingredients such as meat, vegetables, or fish are simmered together in sauce and served over rice.

INSIDE COVER
Three Oogakis: The city of Oogaki was originally a city in the south of Gifu Prefecture, Japan but in 2006 merged with two smaller, non-bordering towns in Gifu Prefecture called Kamiishizu and Sunomata. As a result, Oogaki City is now three disconnected areas under the same label—somewhat similar to how Alaska is separated from the continental United States by Canada.

◁ SIDE STORIES BEGIN ON THE NEXT PAGE ◁

AFTER-SCHOOL 52 OUTDOOR FOOD IS TASTY

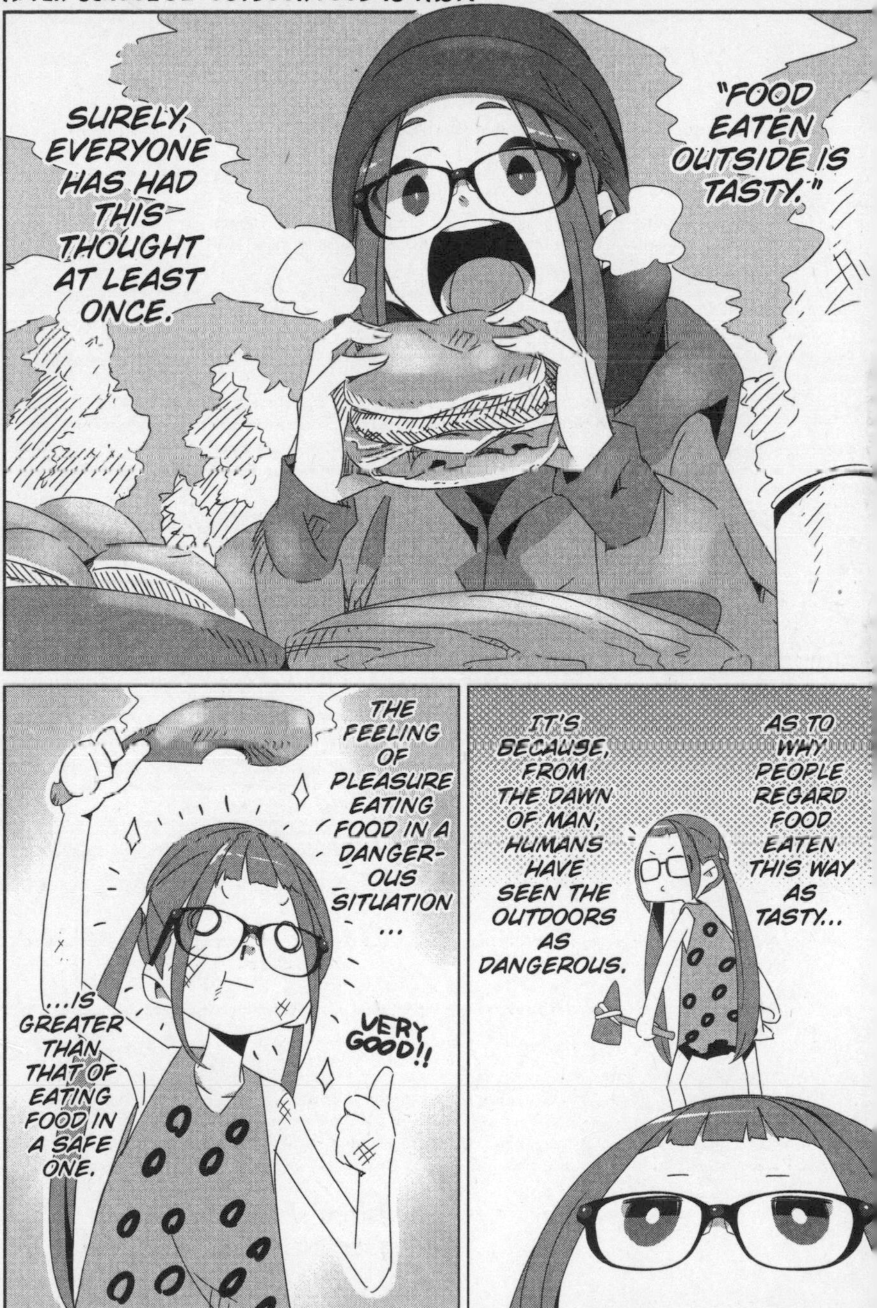
"FOOD EATEN OUTSIDE IS TASTY."
SURELY, EVERYONE HAS HAD THIS THOUGHT AT LEAST ONCE.
AS TO WHY PEOPLE REGARD FOOD EATEN THIS WAY AS TASTY...
IT'S BECAUSE, FROM THE DAWN OF MAN, HUMANS HAVE SEEN THE OUTDOORS AS DANGEROUS.
THE FEELING OF PLEASURE EATING FOOD IN A DANGEROUS SITUATION...
...IS GREATER THAN THAT OF EATING FOOD IN A SAFE ONE.
VERY GOOD!!

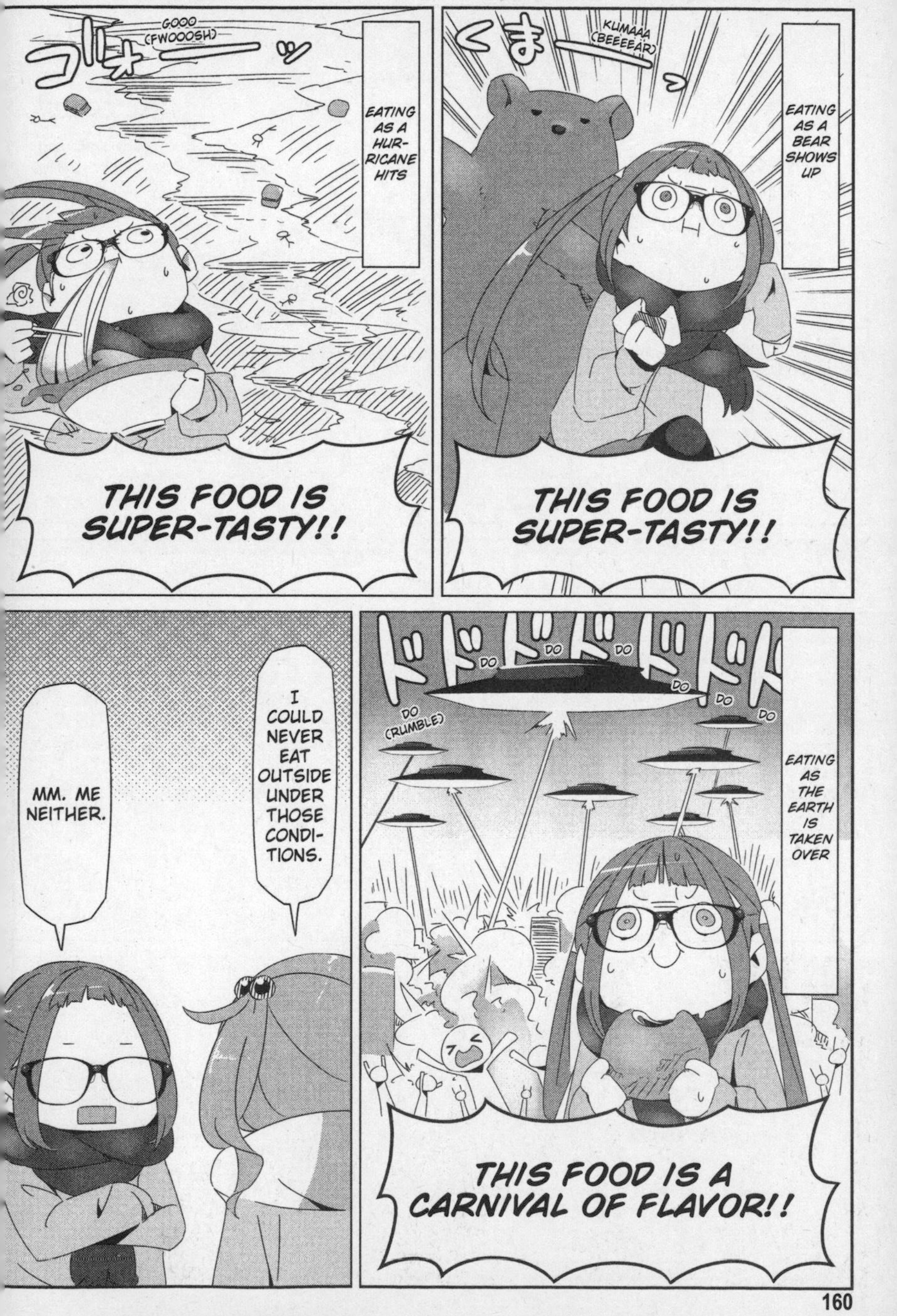
くまーーっ
KUMAAA (BEEEEAR)
EATING AS A BEAR SHOWS UP
THIS FOOD IS SUPER-TASTY!!
ゴォーーッ
GOOO (FWOOOSH)
EATING AS A HURRICANE HITS
THIS FOOD IS SUPER-TASTY!!
ドドドドドドド
DO DO DO DO DO DO DO (RUMBLE)
EATING AS THE EARTH IS TAKEN OVER
THIS FOOD IS A CARNIVAL OF FLAVOR!!
I COULD NEVER EAT OUTSIDE UNDER THOSE CONDITIONS.
MM. ME NEITHER.

AFTER-SCHOOL 53 JUST BY BOILING SOME WATER

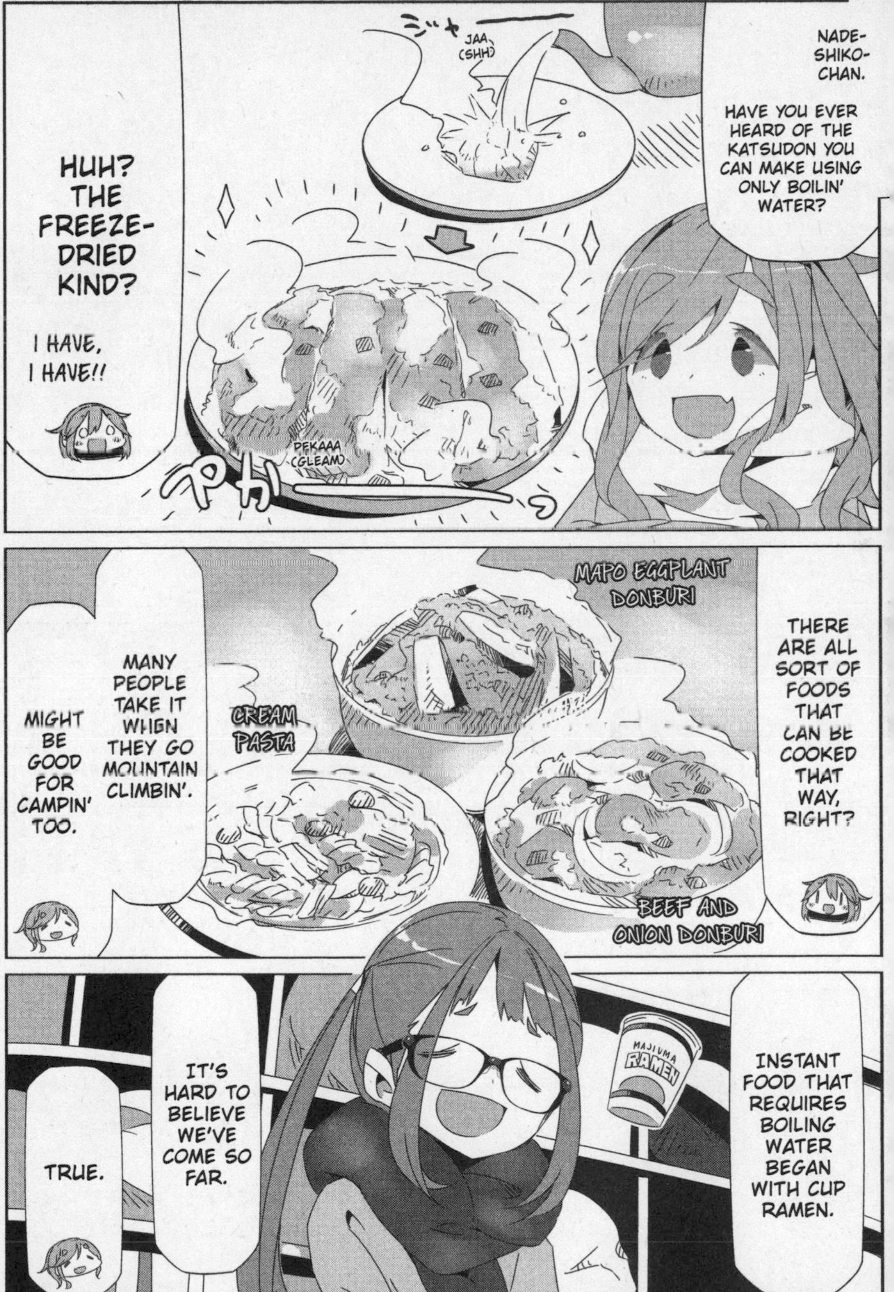
NADE-SHIKO-CHAN. HAVE YOU EVER HEARD OF THE KATSUDON YOU CAN MAKE USING ONLY BOILIN' WATER?
JAA (SHH)
HUH? THE FREEZE-DRIED KIND?
DEKAAA (GLEAM)
I HAVE, I HAVE!!
MAPO EGGPLANT DONBURI
THERE ARE ALL SORT OF FOODS THAT CAN BE COOKED THAT WAY, RIGHT?
BEEF AND ONION DONBURI
CREAM PASTA
MANY PEOPLE TAKE IT WHEN THEY GO MOUNTAIN CLIMBIN'.
MIGHT BE GOOD FOR CAMPIN' TOO.
INSTANT FOOD THAT REQUIRES BOILING WATER BEGAN WITH CUP RAMEN.
MAJIUMA RAMEN
IT'S HARD TO BELIEVE WE'VE COME SO FAR.
TRUE.

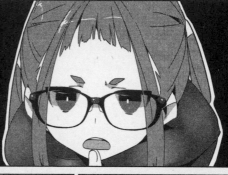

IN THAT TIME, IT HASN'T JUST BEEN FOOD.
I BELIEVE THE AGE OF USING BOILING WATER TO RETURN THINGS TO THEIR NATURAL SHAPE IS UPON US.
ジャーーッ
JAAA (SHH)
ホカ
HOKA
HOKA (WARM)
ホカ
DOWN JACKET
VIA BOILING WATER
ジャーーッ
JAAA
ホカ
HOKA
HOKA
ホカ
SLEEPING BAG
VIA BOILING WATER
YOU'D HAVE TO DRY IT BEFORE USING IT, OR IT'D BE GROSS.
NO WAY. IF YOU DRIED IT, IT'D RETURN TO NORMAL SIZE.

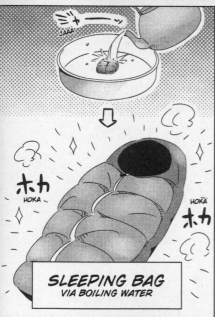

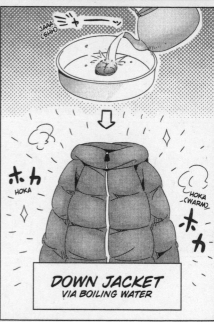

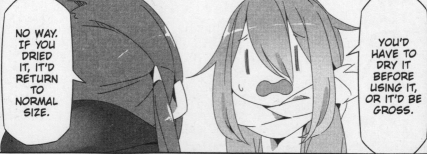

AFTER-SCHOOL 54 CONVENIENT OUTDOOR GOODS 2

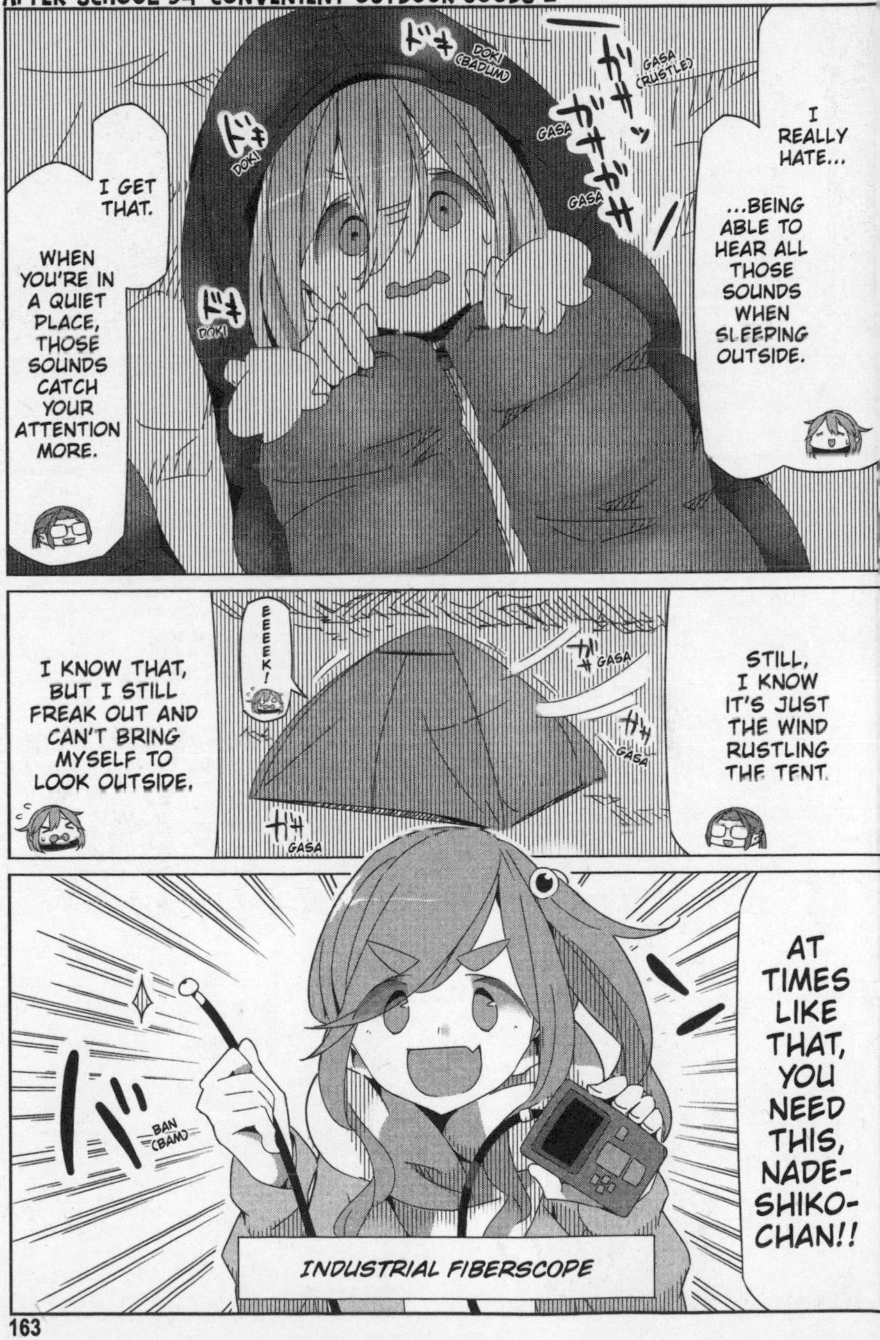

ドキ DOKI (BADUM)
ガサッ GASA (RUSTLE)
ガサ GASA
ガサ GASA
ドキ DOKI
ドキ DOKI
I REALLY HATE...
...BEING ABLE TO HEAR ALL THOSE SOUNDS WHEN SLEEPING OUTSIDE.
I GET THAT.
WHEN YOU'RE IN A QUIET PLACE, THOSE SOUNDS CATCH YOUR ATTENTION MORE.
STILL, I KNOW IT'S JUST THE WIND RUSTLING THE TENT.
ガサ GASA
ガサ GASA
EEEEK!
ガサ GASA
I KNOW THAT, BUT I STILL FREAK OUT AND CAN'T BRING MYSELF TO LOOK OUTSIDE.
AT TIMES LIKE THAT, YOU NEED THIS, NADE-SHIKO-CHAN!!
バ BAN (BAM)
INDUSTRIAL FIBERSCOPE

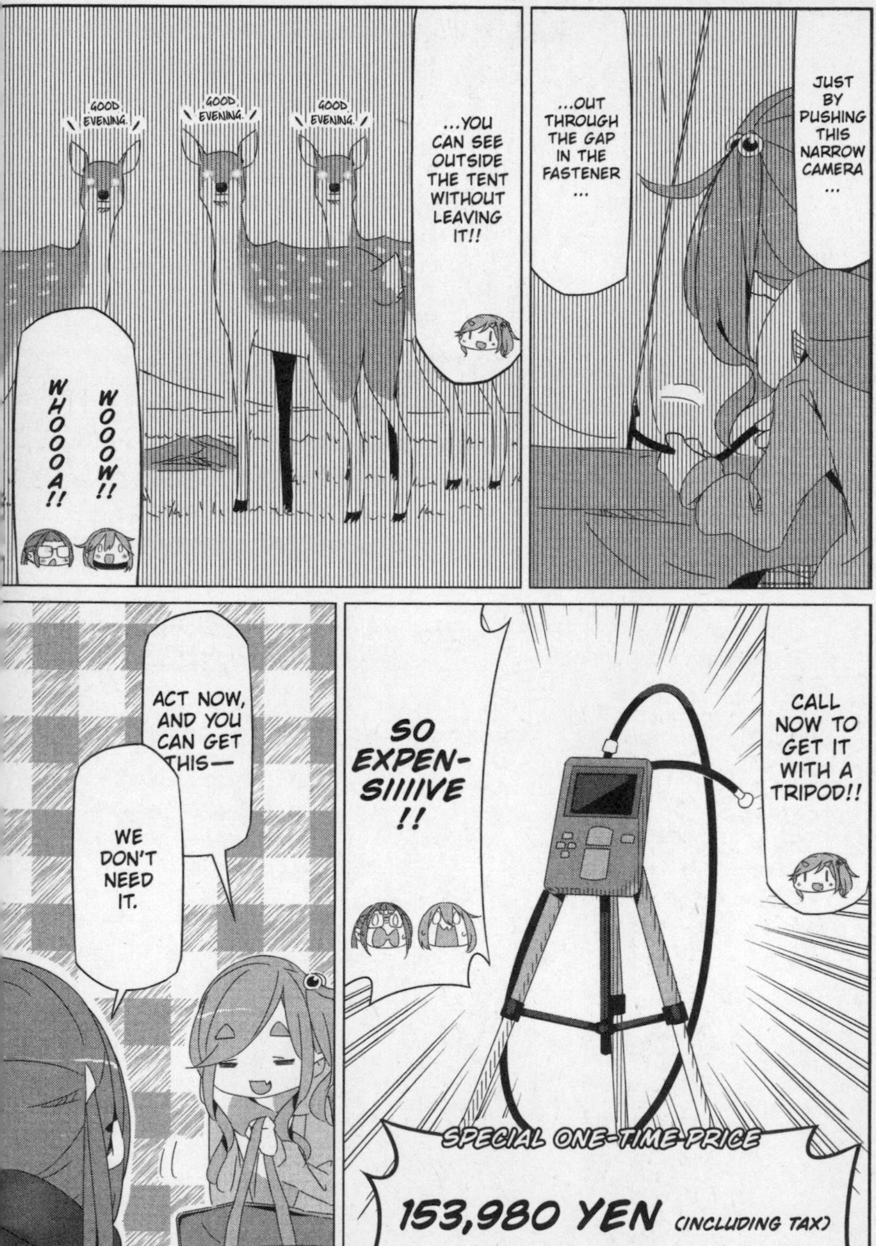

JUST BY PUSHING THIS NARROW CAMERA ...
...OUT THROUGH THE GAP IN THE FASTENER ...
...YOU CAN SEE OUTSIDE THE TENT WITHOUT LEAVING IT!!
GOOD EVENING.
GOOD EVENING.
GOOD EVENING.
WOOOOW!!
WHOOOOA!!
CALL NOW TO GET IT WITH A TRIPOD!!
SO EXPEN-SIIIIVE!!
SPECIAL ONE-TIME PRICE
153,980 YEN (INCLUDING TAX)
ACT NOW, AND YOU CAN GET THIS—
WE DON'T NEED IT.

AFTER-SCHOOL 55 SCAM WARNING

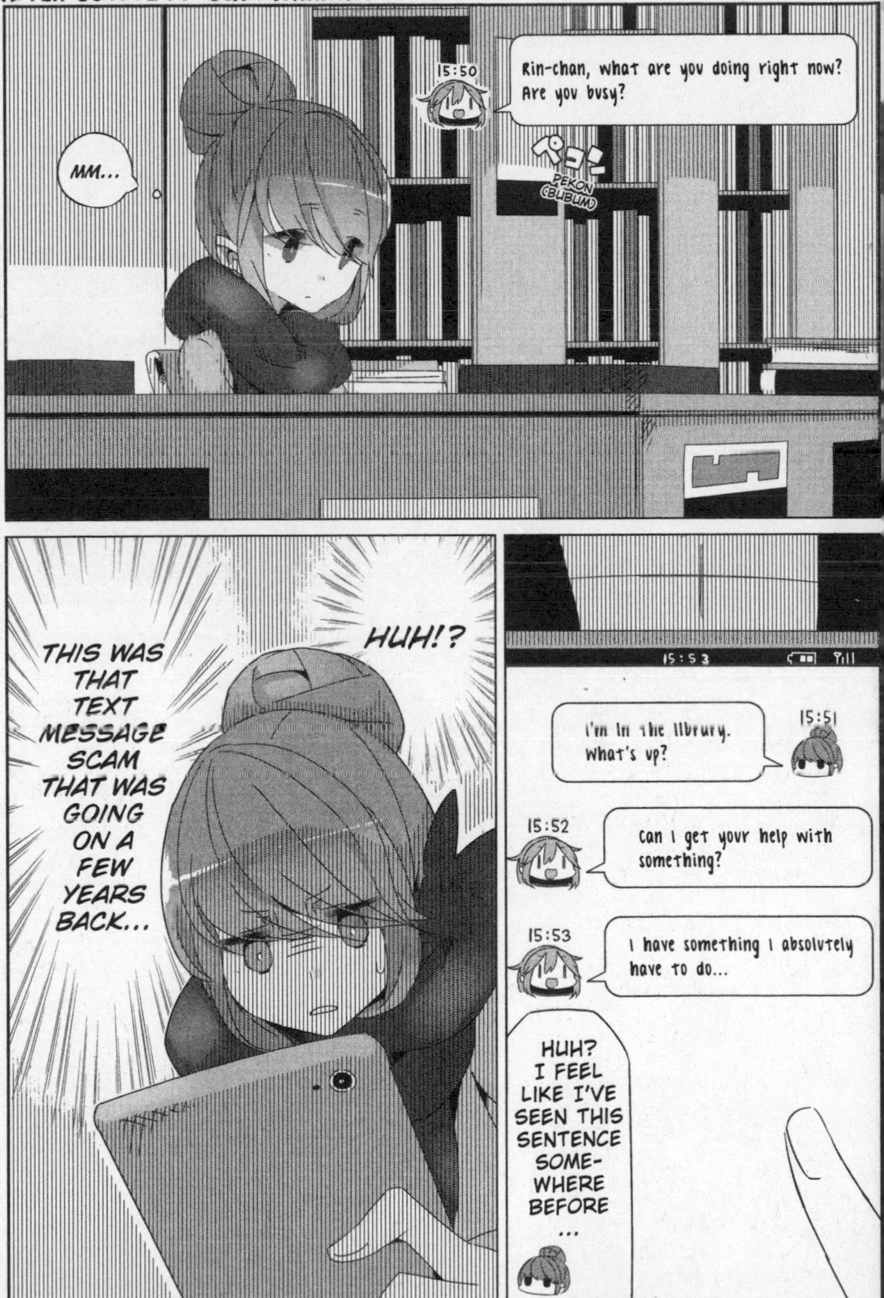
15:50
Rin-chan, what are you doing right now? Are you busy?
PEKON (BLING)
MM...
15:53
15:51
I'm in the library. What's up?
15:52
Can I get your help with something?
15:53
I have something I absolutely have to do...
HUH? I FEEL LIKE I'VE SEEN THIS SENTENCE SOME-WHERE BEFORE...
HUH!?
THIS WAS THAT TEXT MESSAGE SCAM THAT WAS GOING ON A FEW YEARS BACK...

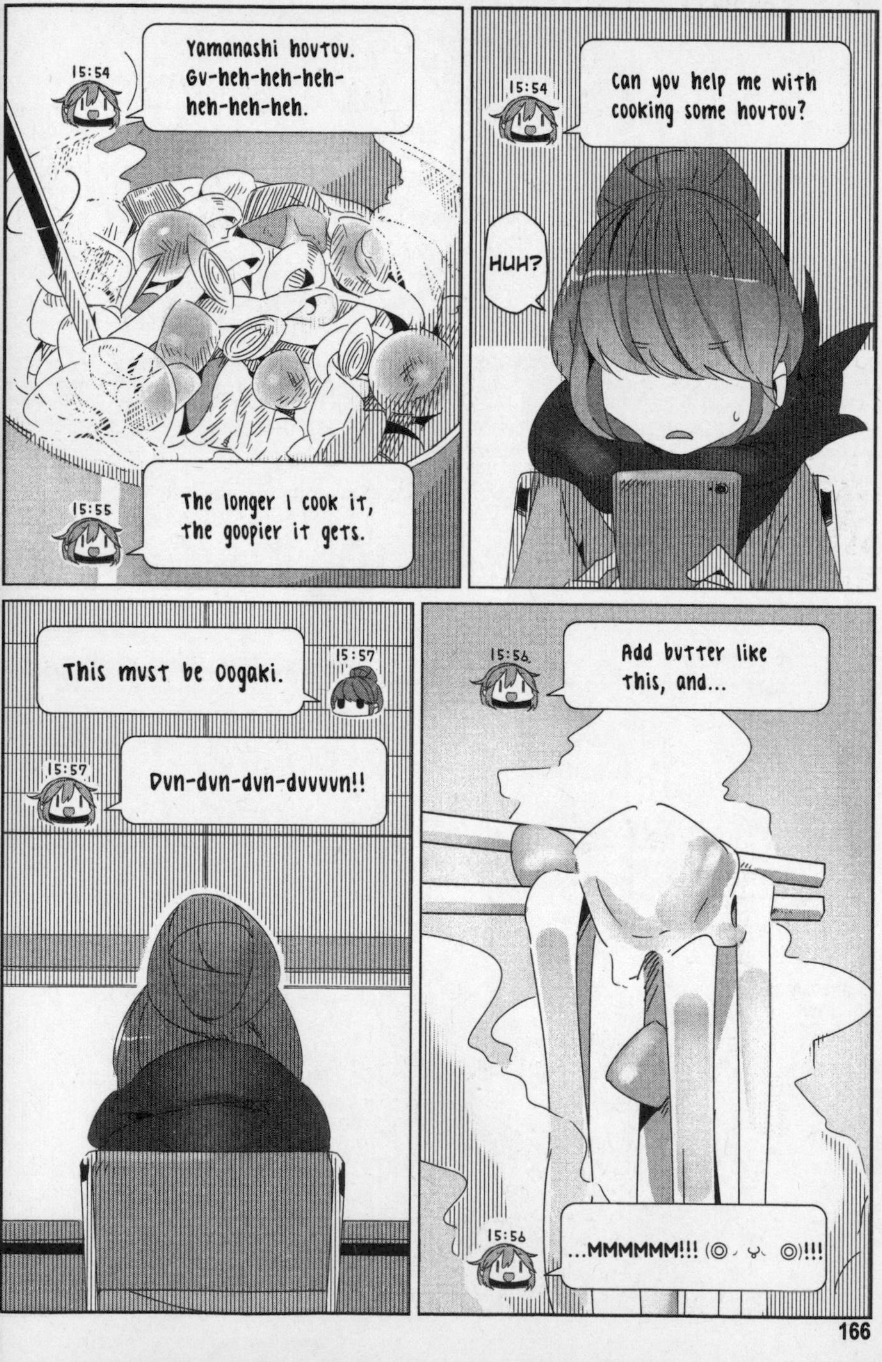
15:54
Can you help me with cooking some houtou?
HUH?
15:54
Yamanashi houtou. Gu-heh-heh-heh-heh-heh-heh.
15:55
The longer I cook it, the goopier it gets.
15:56
Add butter like this, and...
15:56
...MMMMMM!!! (◎◞౪◟◎)!!!
15:57
This must be Oogaki.
15:57
Dun-dun-dun-duuuun!!

AFTER-SCHOOL 56 THE WAFFLE MAKER TRAP

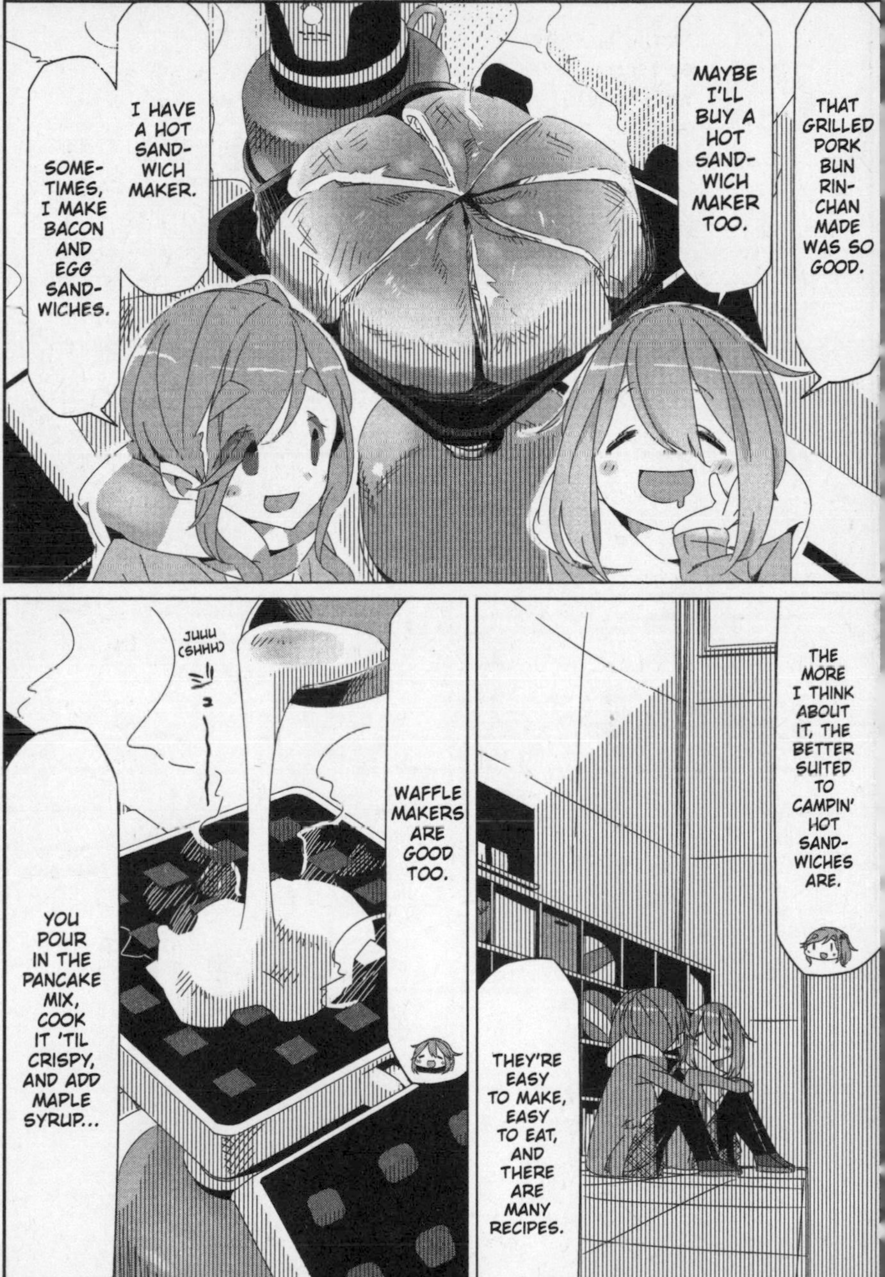
THAT GRILLED PORK BUN RIN-CHAN MADE WAS SO GOOD.
MAYBE I'LL BUY A HOT SANDWICH MAKER TOO.
I HAVE A HOT SANDWICH MAKER.
SOMETIMES, I MAKE BACON AND EGG SANDWICHES.
THE MORE I THINK ABOUT IT, THE BETTER SUITED TO CAMPIN' HOT SANDWICHES ARE.
THEY'RE EASY TO MAKE, EASY TO EAT, AND THERE ARE MANY RECIPES.
WAFFLE MAKERS ARE GOOD TOO.
JUUU (SHHH)
YOU POUR IN THE PANCAKE MIX, COOK IT 'TIL CRISPY, AND ADD MAPLE SYRUP...

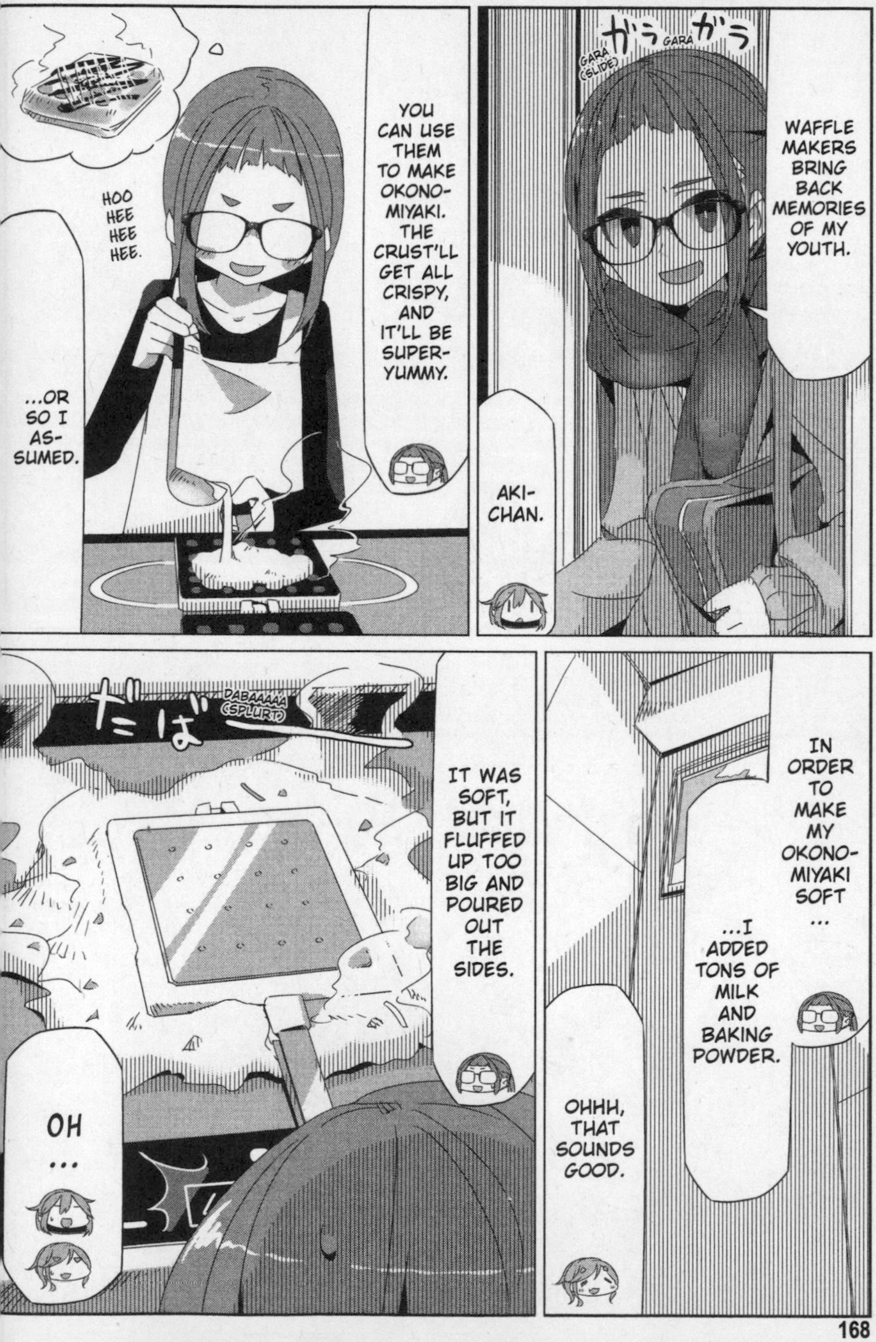
GARA GARA (SLIDE)
WAFFLE MAKERS BRING BACK MEMORIES OF MY YOUTH.
AKI-CHAN.
YOU CAN USE THEM TO MAKE OKONO-MIYAKI. THE CRUST'LL GET ALL CRISPY, AND IT'LL BE SUPER-YUMMY.
HOO HEE HEE HEE.
...OR SO I AS-SUMED.
IN ORDER TO MAKE MY OKONO-MIYAKI SOFT ...
...I ADDED TONS OF MILK AND BAKING POWDER.
OHHH, THAT SOUNDS GOOD.
DABAAAAAA (SPLURT)
IT WAS SOFT, BUT IT FLUFFED UP TOO BIG AND POURED OUT THE SIDES.
OH ...

AFTER-SCHOOL 57 TOYAMA AND MOUNT FUJI

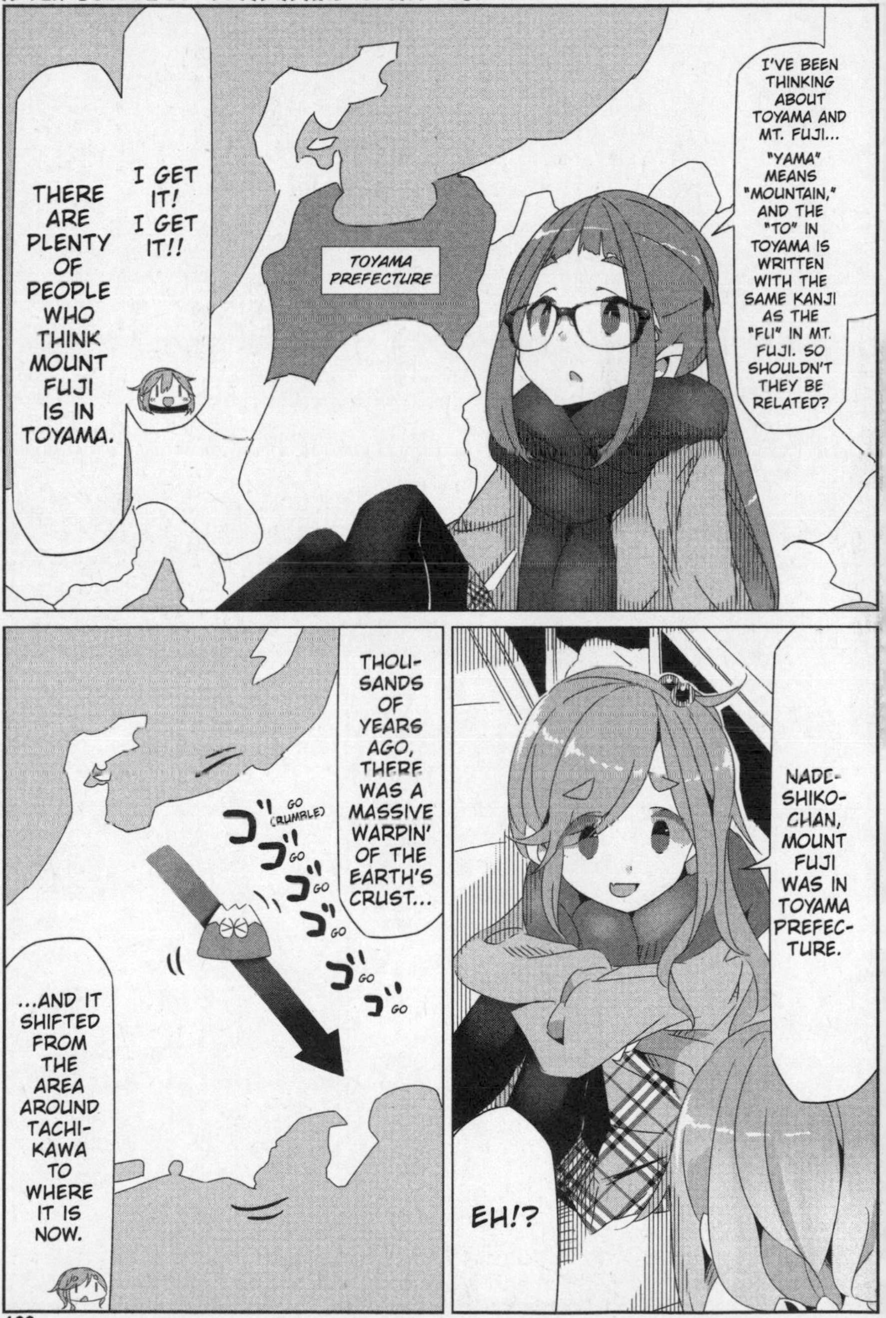
I'VE BEEN THINKING ABOUT TOYAMA AND MT. FUJI... "YAMA" MEANS "MOUNTAIN," AND THE "TO" IN TOYAMA IS WRITTEN WITH THE SAME KANJI AS THE "FU" IN MT. FUJI. SO SHOULDN'T THEY BE RELATED?
TOYAMA PREFECTURE
I GET IT! I GET IT!!
THERE ARE PLENTY OF PEOPLE WHO THINK MOUNT FUJI IS IN TOYAMA.
NADESHIKO-CHAN, MOUNT FUJI WAS IN TOYAMA PREFECTURE.
EH!?
THOUSANDS OF YEARS AGO, THERE WAS A MASSIVE WARPIN' OF THE EARTH'S CRUST...
GO (RUMBLE)
GO
GO
GO
GO
GO
...AND IT SHIFTED FROM THE AREA AROUND TACHIKAWA TO WHERE IT IS NOW.

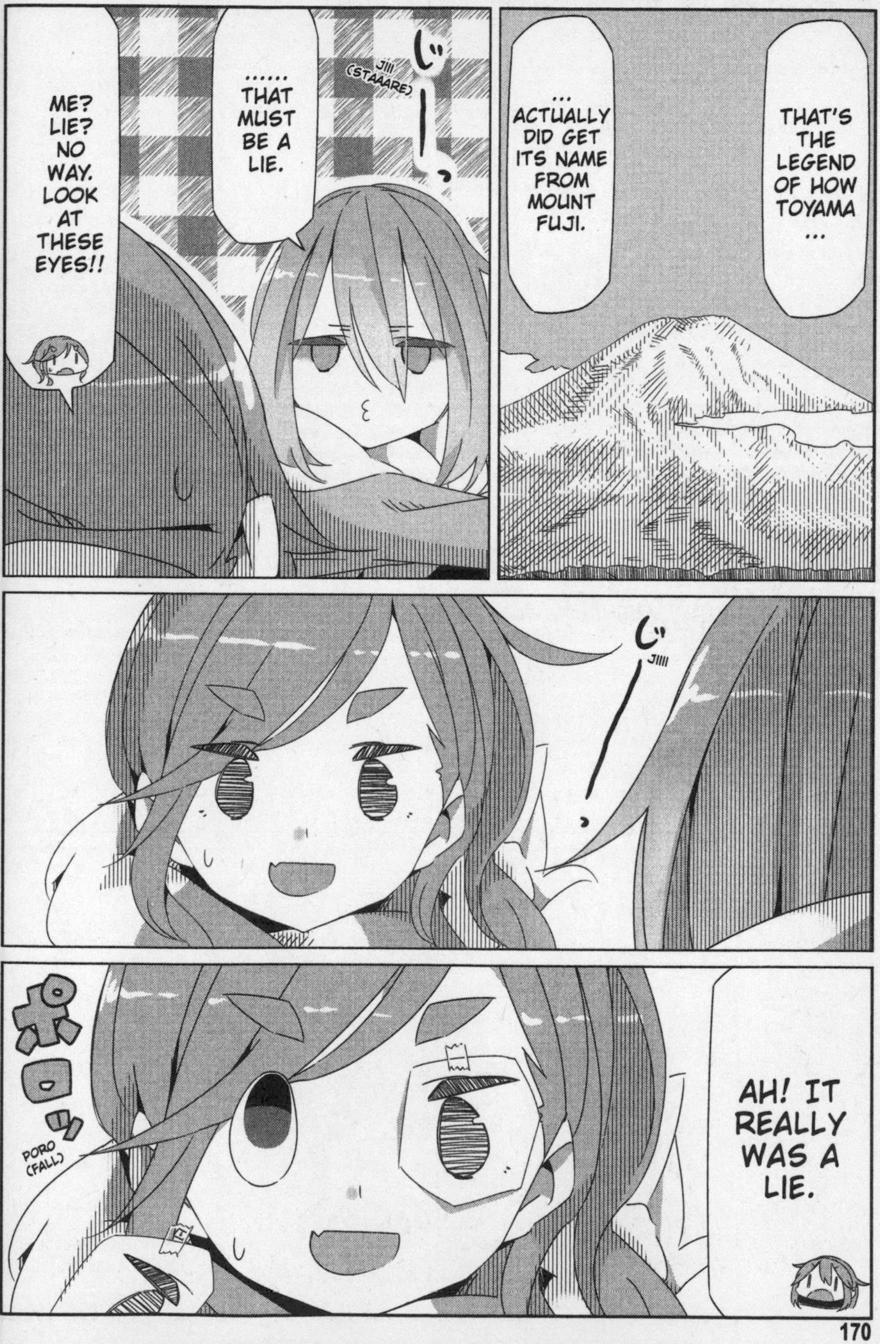
THAT'S THE LEGEND OF HOW TOYAMA ...
... ACTUALLY DID GET ITS NAME FROM MOUNT FUJI.
JIII (STAAARE)
...... THAT MUST BE A LIE.
ME? LIE? NO WAY. LOOK AT THESE EYES!!
JIIII
AH! IT REALLY WAS A LIE.
PORO (FALL)

AFTER-SCHOOL 58 WHAT'S TRUE OF MOST CAMPGROUNDS

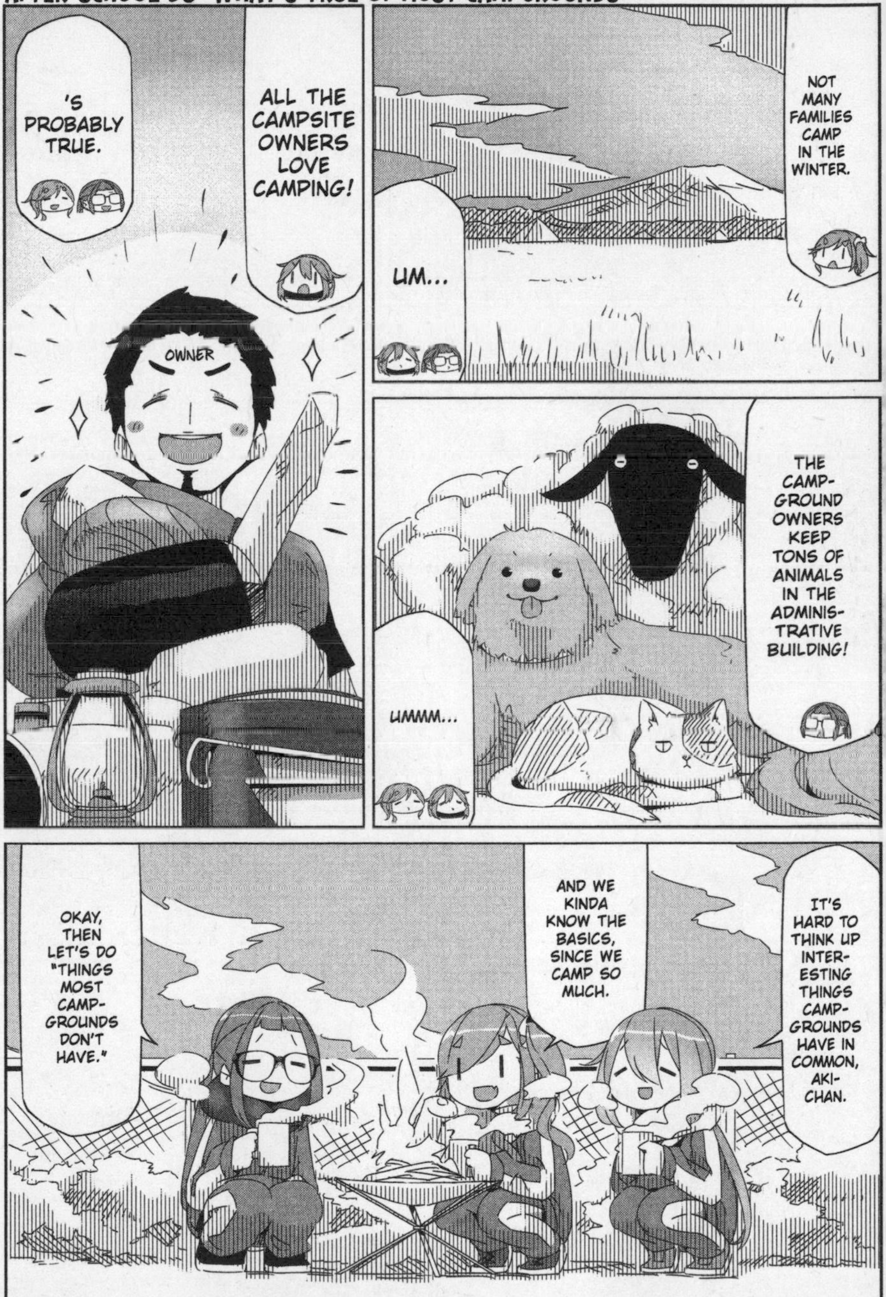

NOT MANY FAMILIES CAMP IN THE WINTER.
UM...
THE CAMPGROUND OWNERS KEEP TONS OF ANIMALS IN THE ADMINISTRATIVE BUILDING!
UMMM...
ALL THE CAMPSITE OWNERS LOVE CAMPING!
'S PROBABLY TRUE.
OWNER
IT'S HARD TO THINK UP INTERESTING THINGS CAMPGROUNDS HAVE IN COMMON, AKI-CHAN.
AND WE KINDA KNOW THE BASICS, SINCE WE CAMP SO MUCH.
OKAY, THEN LET'S DO "THINGS MOST CAMPGROUNDS DON'T HAVE."

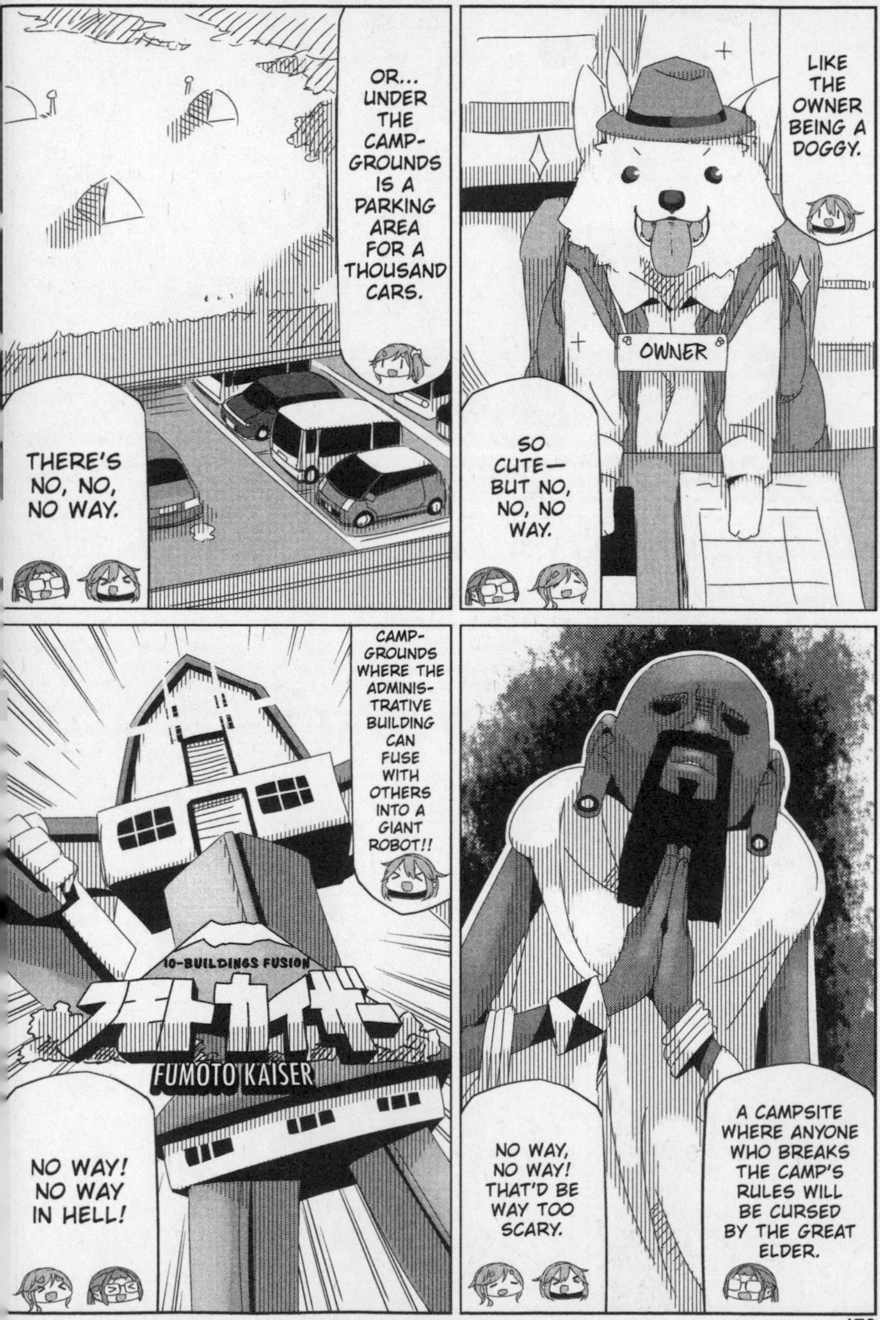
LIKE THE OWNER BEING A DOGGY.
OWNER
SO CUTE—BUT NO, NO, NO WAY.
OR... UNDER THE CAMP-GROUNDS IS A PARKING AREA FOR A THOUSAND CARS.
THERE'S NO, NO, NO WAY.
A CAMPSITE WHERE ANYONE WHO BREAKS THE CAMP'S RULES WILL BE CURSED BY THE GREAT ELDER.
NO WAY, NO WAY! THAT'D BE WAY TOO SCARY.
CAMP-GROUNDS WHERE THE ADMINIS-TRATIVE BUILDING CAN FUSE WITH OTHERS INTO A GIANT ROBOT!!
10-BUILDINGS FUSION
フモトカイザー
FUMOTO KAISER
NO WAY! NO WAY IN HELL!

AFTER-SCHOOL 59 THE CONVENIENT RENTAL TRUNK

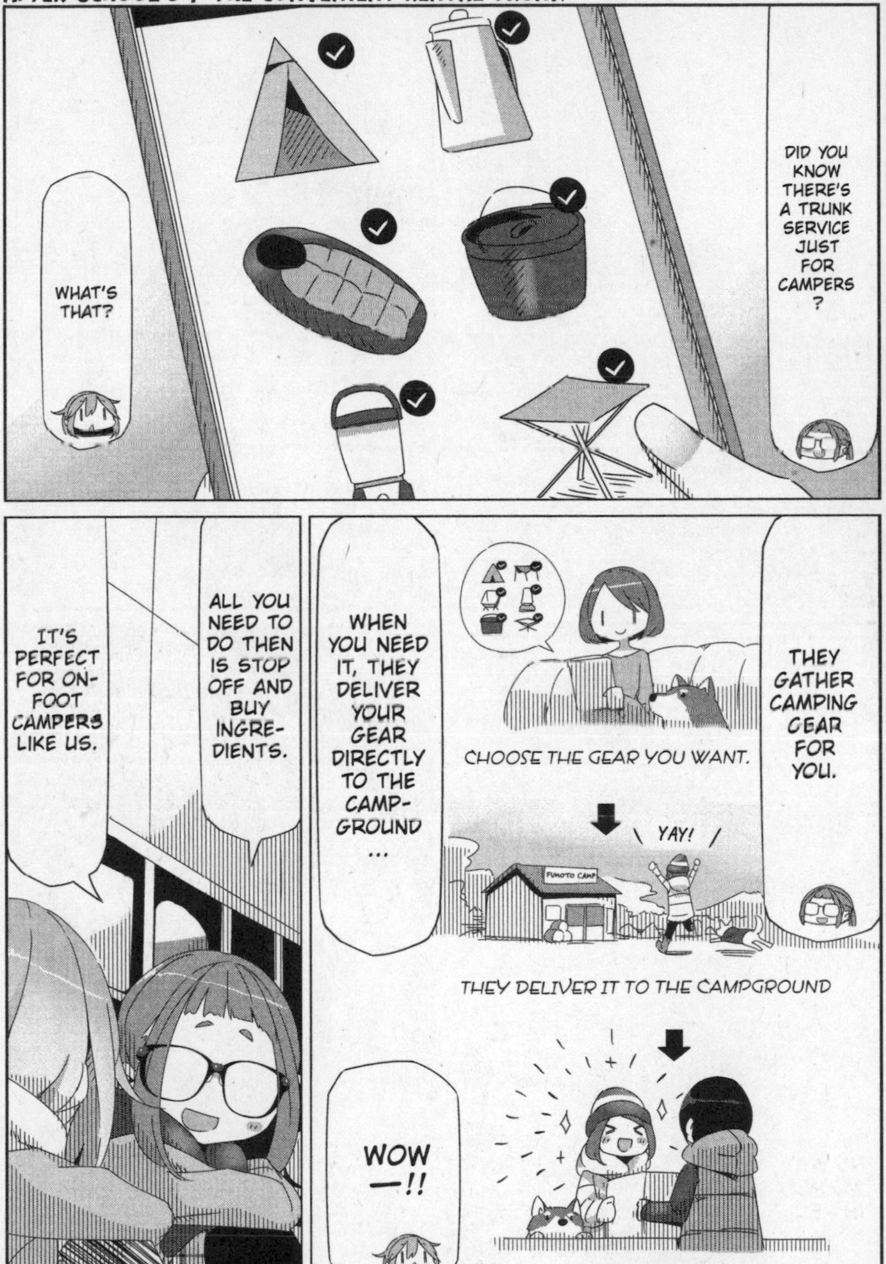
DID YOU KNOW THERE'S A TRUNK SERVICE JUST FOR CAMPERS?
WHAT'S THAT?
THEY GATHER CAMPING GEAR FOR YOU.
CHOOSE THE GEAR YOU WANT.
YAY!
FUMOTO CAMP
WHEN YOU NEED IT, THEY DELIVER YOUR GEAR DIRECTLY TO THE CAMPGROUND...
THEY DELIVER IT TO THE CAMPGROUND
PICK UP YOUR GEAR.
WOW—!!
ALL YOU NEED TO DO THEN IS STOP OFF AND BUY INGREDIENTS.
IT'S PERFECT FOR ON-FOOT CAMPERS LIKE US.

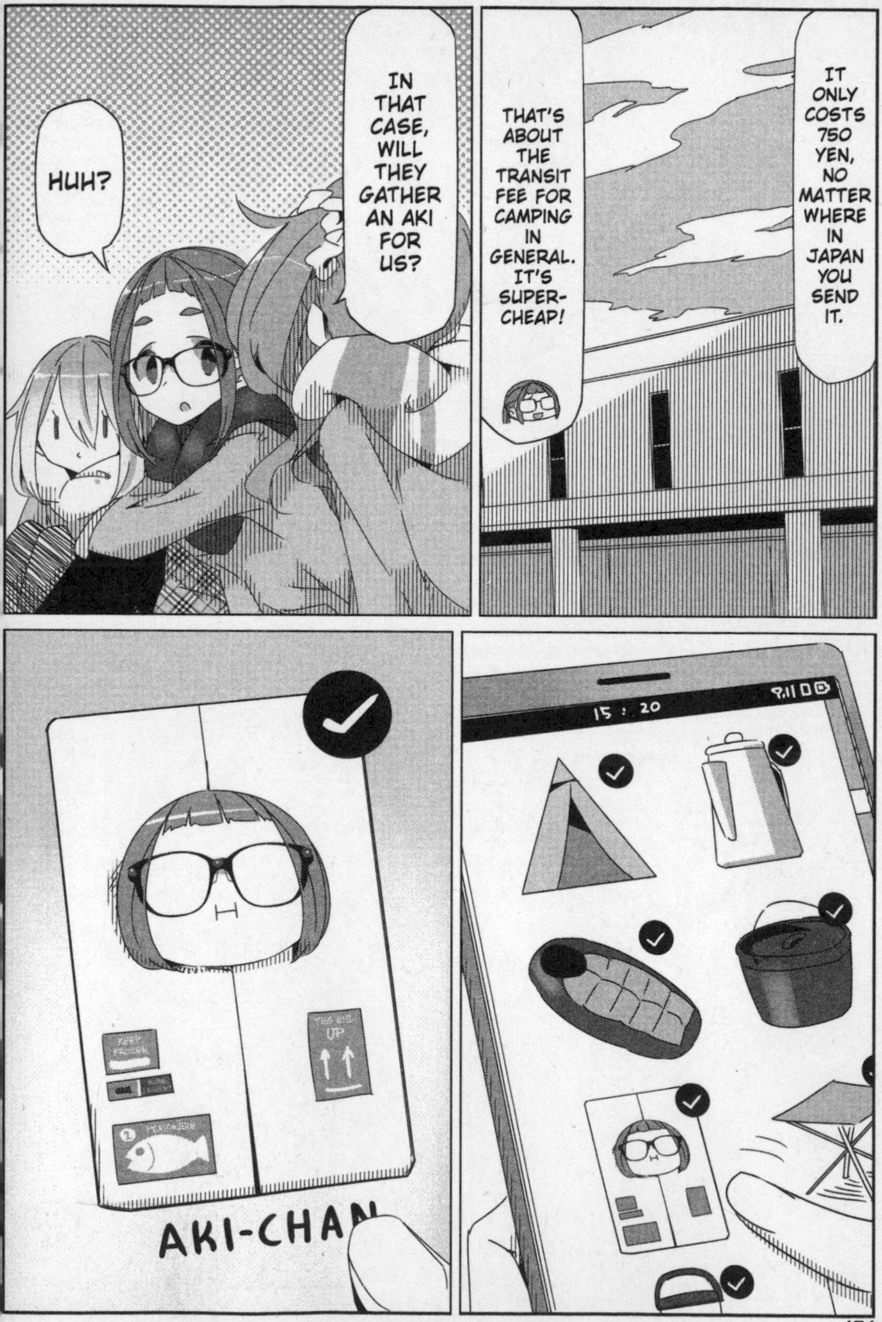
IT ONLY COSTS 750 YEN, NO MATTER WHERE IN JAPAN YOU SEND IT.
THAT'S ABOUT THE TRANSIT FEE FOR CAMPING IN GENERAL. IT'S SUPER-CHEAP!
IN THAT CASE, WILL THEY GATHER AN AKI FOR US?
HUH?
15 : 20
KEEP FROZEN
THIS END UP
AKI-CHAN

AFTER-SCHOOL 60 CAMP CLEANUP

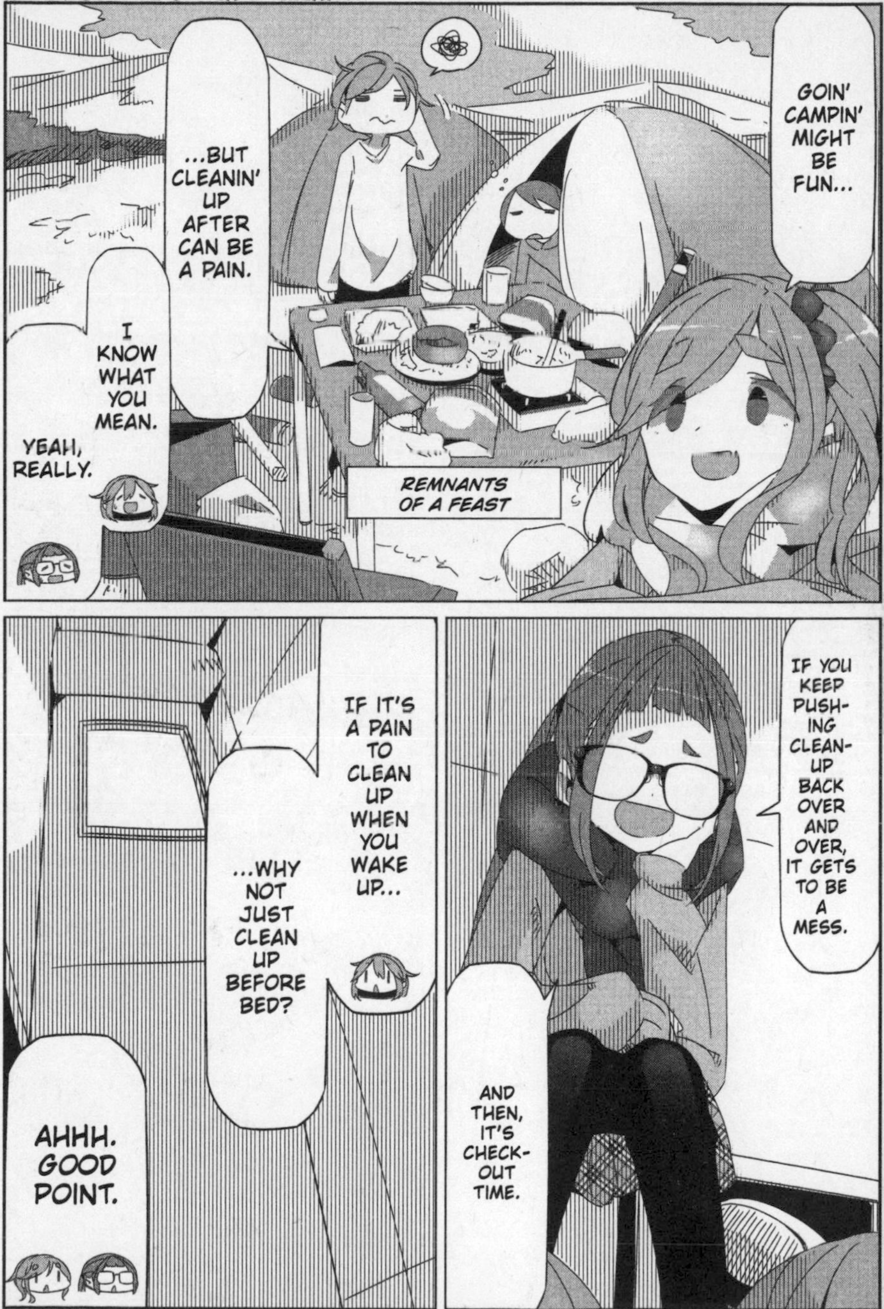
GOIN' CAMPIN' MIGHT BE FUN...
...BUT CLEANIN' UP AFTER CAN BE A PAIN.
REMNANTS OF A FEAST
I KNOW WHAT YOU MEAN.
YEAH, REALLY.
IF YOU KEEP PUSHING CLEAN-UP BACK OVER AND OVER, IT GETS TO BE A MESS.
AND THEN, IT'S CHECK-OUT TIME.
IF IT'S A PAIN TO CLEAN UP WHEN YOU WAKE UP...
...WHY NOT JUST CLEAN UP BEFORE BED?
AHHH. GOOD POINT.

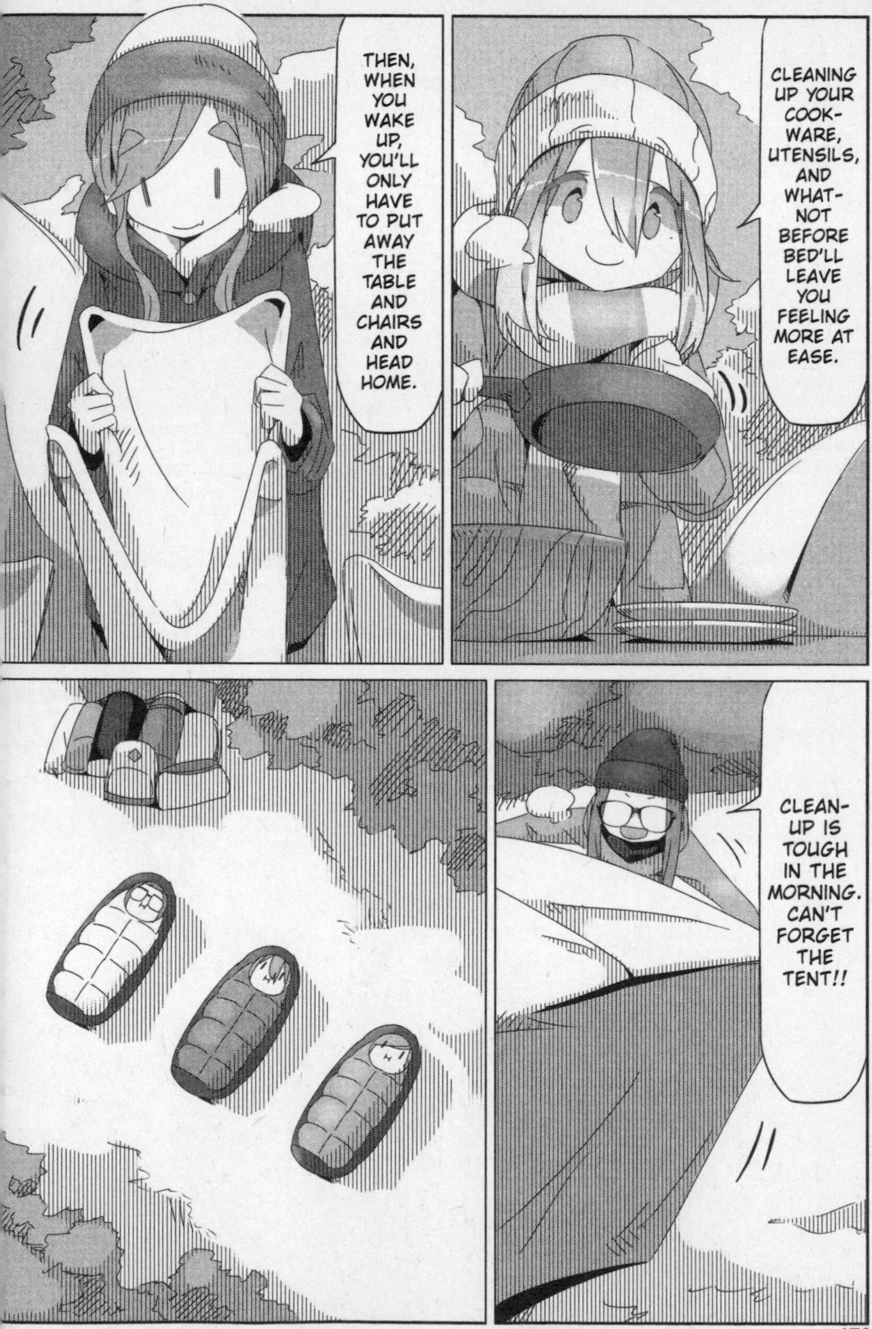
CLEANING UP YOUR COOKWARE, UTENSILS, AND WHATNOT BEFORE BED'LL LEAVE YOU FEELING MORE AT EASE.
THEN, WHEN YOU WAKE UP, YOU'LL ONLY HAVE TO PUT AWAY THE TABLE AND CHAIRS AND HEAD HOME.
CLEAN-UP IS TOUGH IN THE MORNING. CAN'T FORGET THE TENT!!

HOW DID YOU LIKE *LAID-BACK CAMP* VOLUME 7?
THIS TIME, WE HAVE STORIES SURROUNDING NADESHIKO'S SOLO CAMP, AS WELL AS FIREWOOD GATHERING AND MORE ROOM CAMP.

I'VE WRITTEN TO VOLUME 7, AND YET WE'RE STILL ONLY AT THE END OF JANUARY IN-UNIVERSE.
I THINK, FOR THE NEXT VOLUME, WE'LL SKIP AHEAD A BIT SO I CAN WRITE THE IZU CAMPING STORY.
I WANNA EAT THAT WASABI SOFT SERVE ICE CREAM...

THIS HAS BEEN AFRO.

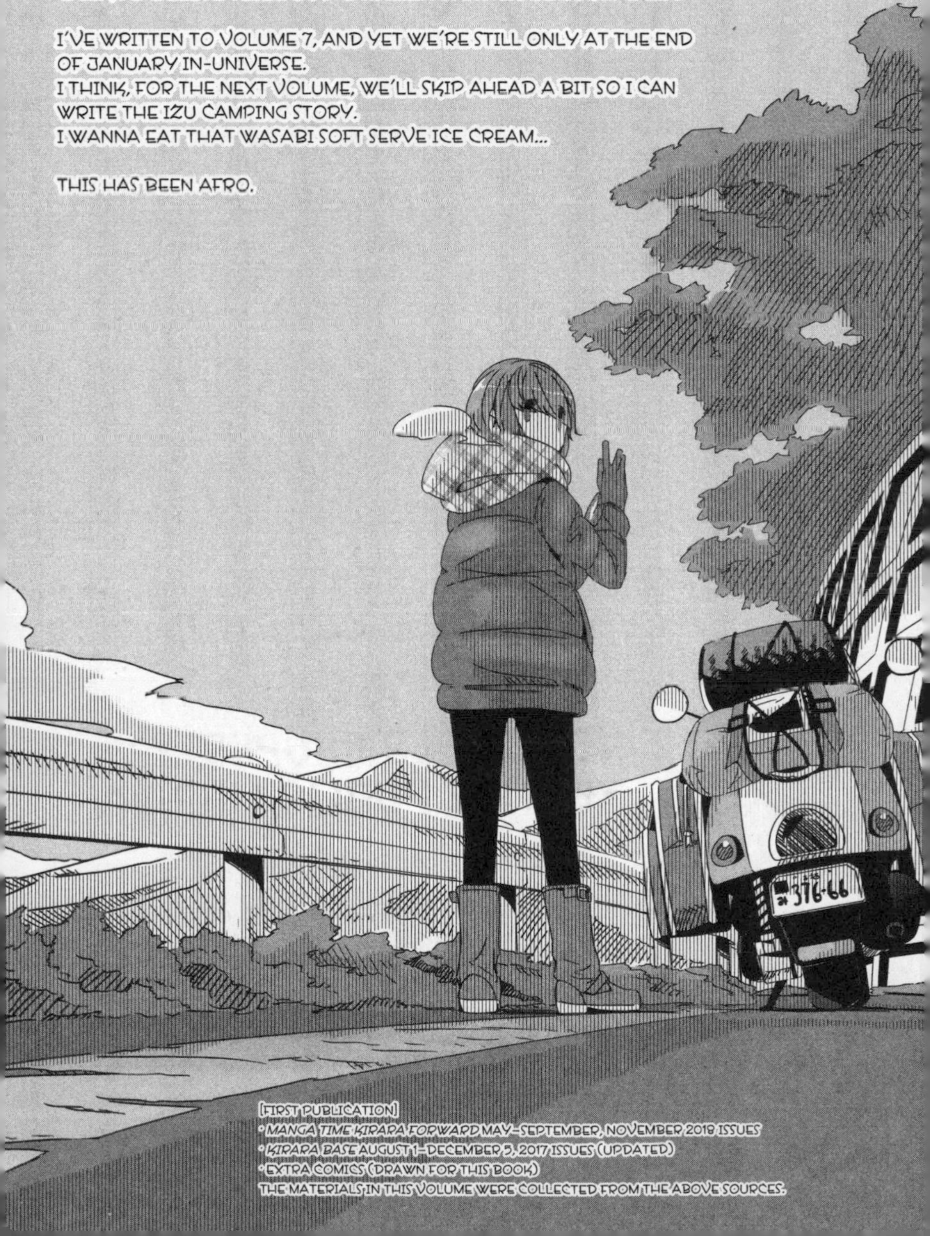

[FIRST PUBLICATION]
• *MANGA TIME KIRARA FORWARD* MAY–SEPTEMBER, NOVEMBER 2018 ISSUES
• *KIRARA BASE* AUGUST 1–DECEMBER 5, 2017 ISSUES (UPDATED)
• EXTRA COMICS (DRAWN FOR THIS BOOK)
THE MATERIALS IN THIS VOLUME WERE COLLECTED FROM THE ABOVE SOURCES.

LAID

Translation: **Amber Tamosaitis** ❉ Lettering: **DK**

YURUCAMP Vol. 7
© 2018 afro. All rights reserved. First published in Japan in 2018 by HOUBUNSHA CO., LTD., Tokyo. English translation rights in United States, Canada, and United Kingdom arranged with HOUBUNSHA CO., LTD. through Tuttle-Mori Agency, Inc., Tokyo.

English translation © 2019 by Yen Press, LLC

Yen Press
150 West 30th Street, 19th Floor
New York, NY 10001

Visit us at yenpress.com
facebook.com/yenpress
twitter.com/yenpress
yenpress.tumblr.com
instagram.com/yenpress

First Yen Press Edition: September 2019

Yen Press is an imprint of Yen Press, LLC.
The Yen Press name and logo are trademarks of Yen Press, LLC.

The publisher is not responsible for websites (or their content) that are not owned by the publisher.

Library of Congress Control Number: 2017959206

ISBNs: 978-1-9753-5812-9 (paperback)
        978-1-9753-0640-3 (ebook)

10 9 8 7 6 5 4 3 2 1

WOR

Printed in the United States of America